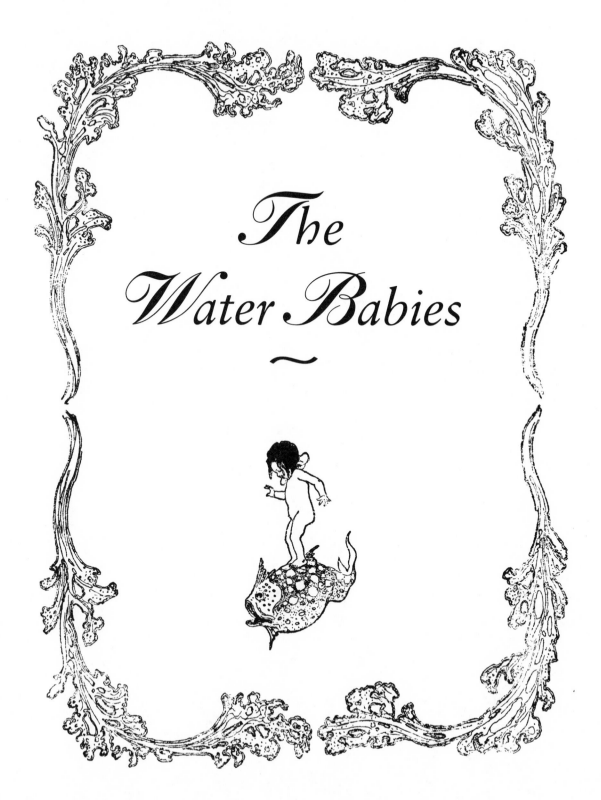

The Water Babies
~

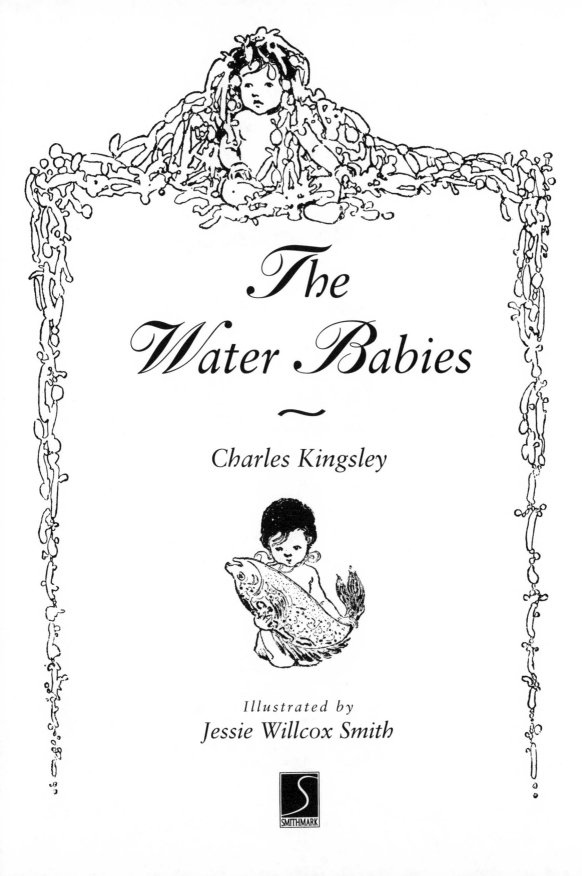

The Water Babies

~

Charles Kingsley

Illustrated by
Jessie Willcox Smith

SMITHMARK

This edition published in 1995
by SMITHMARK Publishers Inc.
16 East 32nd Street
New York
NY 10016
USA

SMITHMARK books are available for bulk
purchase for sales and promotion and premium
use. For details write or call the
manager of special sales,
SMITHMARK Publishers Inc.
16 East 32nd Street
New York
NY 10016
(212) 532-6600

Produced by
Anness Publishing Limited
Boundary Row Studios
1 Boundary Row
London SE1 8HP

ISBN 0-8317-1214-7

Editorial Director Joanna Lorenz
Project Editor Belinda Wilkinson

CONTENTS

TO

MY YOUNGEST SON

GRENVILLE ARTHUR

AND

TO ALL OTHER GOOD LITTLE BOYS

Come read me my riddle, each good little man;
If you cannot read it, no grown-up folk can.

Colour
Illustrations

He felt how comfortable it was to have nothing on him but himself. (Chapter 3)

"Oh, don't hurt me!" cried Tom. "I only want to look at you; you are so handsome". (Chapter 3)

He looked up at the broad yellow moon . . . and thought that she looked at him. (Chapter 4)

Tom reached and clawed down the hole after him. (Chapter 5)

They hugged and kissed each other for ever so long, they did not know why. (Chapter 5)

Mrs. Bedonebyasyoudid. (Chapter 6)

And there he saw the last of the Gairfowl, standing up on the Allalonestone, all alone. (Chapter 7)

Mrs. Doasyouwouldbedoneby. (Chapter 8)

CHAPTER ONE

I heard a thousand blended notes,
* While in a grove I sate reclined;*
In that sweet mood when pleasant thoughts
* Bring sad thoughts to the mind.*

To her fair works did Nature link
* The human soul that through me ran;*
And much it grieved my heart to think,
* What man has made of man.*
                              Wordsworth

Chapter One

~

Once upon a time there was a little chimney-sweep, and his name was Tom. That is a short name, and you have heard it before, so you will not have much trouble in remembering it. He lived in a great town in the North country, where there were plenty of chimneys to sweep and plenty of money for Tom to earn and his master to spend. He could not read nor write, and did not care to do either; and he never washed himself, for there was no water up the court where he lived. He had never been taught to say his prayers. He never had heard of God, or of Christ, except in words which you never have heard, and which it would have been well if he had never heard. He cried half his life, and laughed the other half. He cried when he had to climb the dark flues, rubbing his poor knees and elbows raw; and when the soot got into his eyes, which it did every day in the week; and when his master beat him, which he did every day in the week; and when he had not enough to eat, which happened every day in the week likewise. And he laughed the other half of the day, when he was tossing halfpennies with the other boys, or playing leap-frog over the posts, or bowling stones at the horses' legs as they trotted by, which last was excellent fun, when there was a wall at hand behind which to hide. As for chimney-sweeping, and being hungry, and being beaten, he took all that for the way of the world, like the rain and snow and thunder, and stood manfully with his back to it till it was over, as his old donkey did to a hailstorm; and then shook his ears and was as jolly as ever; and thought of the fine times coming, when he would be a man, and a master sweep, and sit in the public-house with a quart of beer and a long pipe, and play cards for silver money, and wear velveteens and ankle-jacks, and keep a white bulldog with one gray ear, and carry her puppies in his pocket, just like a man. And he would have apprentices, one, two, three, if he could. How he would bully them, and knock them about, just as his master did to him; and make them carry home the soot sacks, while he rode before them on his donkey, with a pipe in his mouth and a flower in his button-hole, like a king at the head of his army. Yes, there were good times coming; and, when his master let him have a pull at the leavings of his beer, Tom was the jolliest boy in the whole town.

One day a smart little groom rode into the court where Tom lived. Tom was just hiding behind a wall, to heave half a brick at his horse's legs, as is the custom of that country when they welcome strangers; but the groom saw him, and halloed to him to know where Mr. Grimes, the chimney-sweep, lived. Now, Mr. Grimes was Tom's own master, and Tom was a good man of business, and always civil to customers, so he put the half-brick down quietly behind the wall, and proceeded to take orders.

Mr. Grimes was to come up next morning to Sir John Harthover's, at the Place, for his old chimney-sweep was gone to prison, and the chimneys wanted sweeping. And so he rode away, not giving Tom time to ask what the sweep had gone to prison for, which was a matter of interest to Tom, as he had been in prison once or twice himself. Moreover, the groom looked so very neat and clean, with his drab gaiters, drab breeches, drab jacket, snow-white tie with a smart pin in it, and clean, round, ruddy face, that Tom was offended and disgusted at his appearance, and considered him a stuck-up fellow, who gave himself airs because he wore smart clothes, and other people paid for them; and went behind the wall to fetch the half- brick after all: but did not, remembering that he had come in the way of business, and was, as it were, under a flag of truce.

His master was so delighted at his new customer that he knocked Tom down out of hand, and drank more beer that night than he usually did in two, in order to be sure of getting up in time next morning; for the more a man's head aches when he wakes, the more glad he is to turn out, and have a breath of fresh air. And, when he did get up at four the next morning, he knocked Tom down again, in order to teach him (as young gentlemen used to be taught at public schools) that he must be an extra good boy that day, as they were going to a very great house, and might make a very good thing of it, if they could but give satisfaction.

And Tom thought so likewise, and, indeed, would have done and behaved his best, even without being knocked down. For, of all places upon earth, Harthover Place (which he had never seen) was the most wonderful; and, of all men on earth, Sir John (whom he had seen, having been sent to jail by him twice) was the most awful.

Harthover Place was really a grand place, even for the rich North country; with a house so large that in the frame-breaking riots, which Tom could just remember, the Duke of Wellington, with ten thousand soldiers and cannon to match, were easily housed therein: at least, so Tom believed; with a park full of deer, which Tom believed to be monsters who were in the habit of eating children; with miles of game preserves, in which Mr. Grimes and the collier-lads poached at times, on which occasions Tom saw pheasants, and wondered what they tasted like; with a noble salmon-river, in which Mr. Grimes and his friends would have liked to poach; but then they must have got into cold water, and that they did not like at all. In short, Harthover was a grand place, and Sir John was a grand old man, whom even Mr. Grimes respected, for not only could he send Mr. Grimes to prison when he deserved it, as he did once or twice a week; not only did he own all the land about for miles; not only was he a jolly, honest, sensible squire as ever kept a pack of hounds, who would do what he thought right by his neighbours, as well as get what he thought right for himself, but, what was more, he weighed full fifteen stone, was nobody knew how many inches round the chest, and could have thrashed Mr. Grimes himself in fair fight, which very few folk round there could do, and which, my dear little boy, would not have been right for him to do, as a great many things are not which one both can do, and would like very much to do. So Mr.

Grimes touched his hat to him when he rode through the town, and called him a "buirdly awd chap," and his young ladies "gradely lasses," which are two high compliments in the North country; and thought that that made up for his poaching Sir John's pheasants; whereby you may perceive that Mr. Grimes had not been to a properly-inspected Government National School.

Now, I dare say, you never got up at three o'clock on a midsummer morning. Some people get up then because they want to catch salmon; and some, because they want to climb Alps; and a great many more, because they must, like Tom. But, I assure you, that three o'clock on a midsummer morning is the pleasantest time of all the twenty-four hours, and all the three hundred and sixty-five days; and why every one does not get up then, I never could tell, save that they are all determined to spoil their nerves and their complexions, by doing all night what they might just as well do all day. But Tom, instead of going out to dinner at half-past eight at night, and to a ball at ten, and finishing off somewhere between twelve and four, went to bed at seven, when his master went to the public-house, and slept like a dead pig; for which reason he was as piert as a game-cock (who always gets up early to wake the maids) and just ready to get up when the fine gentlemen and ladies were just ready to go to bed.

So he and his master set out; Grimes rode the donkey in front, and Tom and the brushes walked behind; out of the court, and up the street, past the closed window-shutters, and the winking, weary policemen, and the roofs all shining gray in the gray dawn.

They passed through the pitmen's village, all shut up and silent now; and through the turnpike; and then they were out in the real country, and plodding along the black, dusty road, between back slag walls, with no sound but the groaning and thumping of the pit-engine in the next field. But soon the road grew white, and the walls likewise; and at the wall's foot grew long grass and gay flowers, all drenched with dew; and instead of the groaning of the pit-engine, they heard the skylark saying his matins high up in the air, and the pit-bird warbling in the sedges, as he had warbled all night long.

All else was silent. For old Mrs. Earth was still fast asleep; and like many pretty people, she looked still prettier asleep than awake. The great elm-trees in the gold-green meadows were fast asleep above, and the cows fast asleep beneath them; nay, the few clouds which were about were fast asleep likewise, and so tired that they had lain down on the earth to rest, in long white flakes and bars, among the stems of the elm-trees, and along the tops of the alders by the stream, waiting for the sun to bid them rise and go about their day's business in the clear blue overhead.

On they went; and Tom looked, and looked, for he never had been so far into the country before; and longed to get over a gate, and pick buttercups, and look for birds' nests in the hedge; but Mr. Grimes was a man of business, and would not have heard of that.

Soon they came up with a poor Irishwoman, trudging along with a bundle at her back. She had a gray shawl over her head, and a crimson madder petticoat; so you may be sure she came from Galway. She had neither shoes nor stockings, and limped along as if she were tired and footsore: but she was a very tall handsome woman, with bright gray eyes, and heavy black hair hanging about her cheeks. And she took Mr. Grimes's fancy so much, that when he came alongside he called out to her:

"This is a hard road for a gradely foot like that. Will ye up, lass, and ride behind me?"

But, perhaps, she did not admire Mr. Grimes's look and voice; for she answered quietly:

"No, thank you; I'd sooner walk with your little lad here."

"You may please yourself," growled Grimes, and went on smoking.

So she walked beside Tom, and talked to him, and asked him where he lived, and what he knew, and all about himself, till Tom thought he had never met such a pleasant-spoken woman. And she asked him, at last, whether he said his prayers; and seemed sad when he told he that he knew no prayers to say.

Then he asked her where she lived; and she said far away by the sea. And Tom asked her about the sea; and she told him how it rolled and roared over the rocks in winter nights, and lay still in the bright summer days for the children to bathe and play in it; and many a story more, till Tom longed to go and see the sea, and bathe in it likewise.

At last, at the bottom of a hill, they came to a spring: not such a spring as you see here, which soaks up out of a white gravel in the bog, among red fly-catchers, and pink bottle-heath, and sweet white orchis; nor such a one as you may see, too, here, which bubbles up under the warm sand-bank in the hollow lane, by the great tuft of lady-ferns, and makes the sand dance reels at the bottom, day and night, all the year round; not such a spring as either of those: but a real North country limestone fountain like one of those in Sicily or Greece, where the old heathen fancied the nymphs sat cooling themselves the hot summer's day, while the shepherds peeped at them from behind the bushes. Out of a low cave of rock, at the foot of a limestone crag, the great fountain rose, quelling and bubbling, and gurgling, so clear that you could not tell where the water ended and the air began; and ran away under the road, a stream large enough to turn a mill; among blue geranium, and golden globe-flower, and wild raspberry, and the bird-cherry with its tassels of snow.

And there Grimes stopped and looked; and Tom looked too. Tom was wondering whether anything lived in that dark cave, and came out at night to fly in the meadows. But Grimes was not wondering at all. Without a word, he got off his donkey, and clambered over the low road wall, and knelt down, and began dipping his ugly head into the spring – and very dirty he made it.

Tom was picking the flowers as fast as he could. The Irishwoman helped him, and showed him how to tie them up; and a very pretty nosegay they had made between them. But when he saw Grimes actually wash, he stopped, quite astonished; and when Grimes had finished, and began shaking his ears to dry them, he said:

"Why, master, I never saw you do that before."

"Nor will again, most likely. 'Twasn't for cleanliness I did it, but for coolness. I'd be ashamed to want washing every week or so, like any smutty collier-lad."

"I wish I might go and dip my head in," said poor little Tom. "It must be as good as putting it under the town-pump; and there is no beadle here to drive a chap away."

"Thou come along," said Grimes, "what dost want with washing thyself? Thou did not drink half a gallon of beer last night, like me."

"I don't care for you," said naughty Tom, and ran down to the stream, and began washing his face.

Grimes was very sulky, because the woman preferred Tom's company to his; so he dashed at him with horrid words, and tore him up from his knees, and began beating him. But Tom was accustomed to that, and got his head safe between Mr. Grimes's legs, and kicked his shins with all his might.

"Are you not ashamed of yourself, Thomas Grimes?" cried the Irishwoman over the wall.

Grimes looked up, startled at her knowing his name; but all he answered was, "No: nor never was yet;" and went on beating Tom.

"True for you. If you ever had been ashamed of yourself you would have gone over into Vendale long ago."

"What do you know about Vendale?" shouted Grimes; but he left off beating Tom.

"I know about Vendale, and about you, too. I know, for instance, what happened in Aldermire Copse, by night, two years ago come Martinmas."

"You do?" shouted Grimes; and leaving Tom, climbed up over the wall, and faced the woman. Tom thought he was going to strike her; but she looked him too full and fierce in the face for that.

"Yes; I was there," said the Irishwoman quietly.

"You are no Irishwoman, by your speech," said Grimes, after many bad words.

"Never mind who I am. I saw what I saw; and if you strike that boy again, I can tell what I know."

Grimes seemed quite cowed, and got on his donkey without another word.

"Stop!" said the Irishwoman. " I have one more word for you both; for you will both see me again, before all is over. Those that wish to be clean, clean they will be; and those that wish to be foul, foul they will be. Remember."

And she turned away, and through a gate into the meadow. Grimes stood still a moment, like a man who had been stunned. Then he rushed after her, shouting "You come back." But when he got into the meadow the woman was not there.

Had she hidden away? There was no place to hide in. But Grimes looked about, and Tom also, for he was as puzzled as Grimes himself, at her disappearing so suddenly; but look where they would, she was not there.

Grimes came back again, as silent as a post, for he was a little frightened; and getting on his donkey, filled a fresh pipe, and smoked away, leaving Tom in peace.

And now they had gone three miles and more, and came to Sir John's lodge-gates.

Very grand lodges they were, with very grand iron gates, and stone gate-posts, and on the top of each a most dreadful bogy, all teeth, horns, and tail, which was the crest which Sir John's ancestors wore in the Wars of the Roses; and very prudent men they were to wear it, for all their enemies must have run for their lives at the very first sight of them.

Grimes rang at the gate, and out came a keeper on the spot and opened.

"I was told to expect thee," he said. "Now, thou'lt be so good as to keep to the main avenue, and not let me find a hare or rabbit on thee when thou comest back. I shall look sharp for one, I tell thee."

"Not if it's in the bottom of the soot-bag," quoth Grimes, and at that he laughed; and the keeper laughed and said:

"If that's thy sort, I may as well walk up with thee to the hall."

"I think thou best had. It's thy business to see after thy game, man, and not mine."

So the keeper went with them; and to Tom's surprise, he and Grimes chatted together all the way quite pleasantly. He did not know that a keeper is only a poacher turned outside in, and a poacher a keeper turned inside out.

They walked up a great lime-avenue, a full mile long, and between their stems Tom peeped trembling at the horns of the sleeping deer, which stood up among the ferns. Tom had never seen such enormous trees, and as he looked up he fancied that the blue sky rested on their heads. But he was puzzled very much by a strange murmuring noise, which followed them all the way. So much puzzled, that at last he took courage to ask the keeper what it was.

He spoke very civilly, and caled him Sir, for he was horribly afraid of him, which pleased the keeper, and he told him that they were the bees about the lime-flowers.

"What are bees?" asked Tom.

"What make honey."

"What is honey?" asked Tom.

"Thou hold thy noise," said Grimes.

"Let the boy be," said the keeper. "He's a civil young chap now, and that's more than he'll be long, if he bides with thee."

Grimes laughed, for he took that for a compliment.

"I wish I were a keeper,' said Tom, "to live in such a beautiful place, and wear green velveteens, and have a real dog-whistle at my button, like you."

The keeper laughed; he was a kind-hearted fellow enough.

"Let well alone, lad, and ill too, at times. Thy life's safer than mine at all events, eh, Mr. Grimes?"

And Grimes laughed again, and then the two men began talking quite low. Tom could hear, though, that it was about some poaching fight – and at last Grimes said surlily:

"Hast thou anything against me?"

"Not now."

"Then don't ask me any questions till thou hast, for I am a man of honour."

And at that they both laughed again, and thought it a very good joke.

And by this time they were come up to the great iron gates in front of the house; and Tom stared through them at the rhododendrons and azaleas, which were all in flower; and then at the house itself, and wondered how many chimneys there were in it, and how long ago it was built, and what was the man's name that built it, and whether he got much money for his job?

These last were very difficult questions to answer. For Harthover had been built at ninety different times, and in nineteen different styles, and looked as if somebody had built a whole street of houses of every imaginable shape, and then stirred them together with a spoon.

For the attics were Anglo-Saxon.

The third-floor Norman.

The second Cinque-cento.

The first-floor Elizabethan.

The right wing Pure Doric.

The centre Early English, with a huge portico, copied from the Parthenon.

The left wing Pure Bœotian, which the country folk admired most of all, because it was just like the new barracks in the town, only three times as big.

The grand staircase was copied from the Catacombs at Rome.

The back staircase from the Tajmahal at Agra. This was built by Sir John's great-great-great-uncle, who won, in Lord Clive's Indian wars, plenty of money, plenty of wounds, and no more taste than his betters.

The cellars were copied from the caves of Elephanta.

The offices from the Pavilion at Brighton.

And the rest from nothing in heaven, or earth, or under the earth.

So that Harthover House was a great puzzle to antiquarians, and a thorough Naboth's vineyard to critics, and architects, and all persons who like meddling with other men's business, and spending other men's money. So they all were setting upon poor Sir John, year after year, and trying to talk him into spending a hundred thousand pounds or so, in building to please them and not himself. But he always put them off, like a canny North-countryman as he was. One wanted him to build a Gothic house, but he said he was no Goth; and another to build an Elizabethan, but he said he lived under good Queen Victoria, and not good Queen Bess; and another was bold enough to tell him that his house was ugly, but he said he lived inside it, and not outside; and another, that there was no unity in it; but he said that that was just why he liked the old place. For he liked to see how each Sir John, and Sir Hugh, and Sir Ralph, and Sir Randal, had left his mark upon the place, each after his own taste; and he had no more notion of disturbing his ancestors' work than of disturbing their graves. For now the house looked like a real live house, that had a history, and had grown and grown as the world grew; and that it was only an upstart fellow who did not know who his own grandfather was, who would change it for some spick and span new Gothic or Elizabethan thing, which looked as if it had been all spawned in a night, as mushrooms are. From which you may collect (if you have wit enough), that Sir John was a very sound-headed, sound-hearted squire, and just the man to keep the countryside in order, and show good sport with his hounds.

But Tom and his master did not go in through the great iron gates, as if they had been Dukes or Bishops, but round the back way, and a very long way round it was; and into a little back-door, where the ash-boy let them in, yawning horribly; and then in a passage the housekeeper met them, in such a flowered chintz dressing-gown, that Tom mistook her for My Lady herself, and she gave Grimes solemn orders about "You will take care of this, and take care of that," as if he was going up the chimneys, and not Tom. And Grimes listened, and said every now and then, under his voice, "You'll mind that, you little beggar?" and Tom did mind, all at least that he could. And then the housekeeper turned them into a grand room, all covered up in sheets of brown paper, and bade them begin, in a lofty and tremendous voice; and so after a whimper or two, and a kick from his master, into the grate Tom went, and up the chimney, while a housemaid stayed in the room to watch the furniture; to whom Mr. Grimes paid many playful and chivalrous compliments, but met with very slight encouragement in return.

How many chimneys he swept I cannot say: but he swept so many that he got quite tired, and puzzled too, for they were not like the town flues to which he was accustomed, but such as you would find – if you would only get up them and look, which perhaps you would not like to do – in old country- houses, large and crooked chimneys, which had been altered again and again, till they ran one into another, anastomosing (as Professor Owen would say) considerably. So Tom fairly lost his way in them; not that he cared much for that, though he was in pitchy darkness, for he was as much at home in a chimney as a mole is underground; but at last, coming down as he thought the right chimney, he came down the wrong one, and found himsellf standing on the hearthrug in a room the like of which he had never seen before.

Tom had never seen the like. He had never been in gentlefolks' rooms but when the carpets were all up, and the curtains down, and the furniture huddled together under a cloth, and the pictures covered with aprons and dusters; and he had often enough wondered what the rooms were like when they were all ready for the quality to sit in. And now he saw, and he thought the sight very pretty.

The room was all dressed in white; white window curtains, white bed curtains, white furniture, and white walls, with just a few lines of pink here and there. The carpet was all over gay little flowers; and the walls were hung with pictures in gilt frames, which amused Tom very much. There were pictures of ladies and gentlemen, and pictures of horses and dogs. The horses he liked; but the dogs he did not care for much, for there were no bull-dogs among them, not even a terrier. But the two pictures which took his fancy most were, one a man in long garments, with little children and their mothers round him, who was laying his hand upon the children's heads. That was a very pretty picture, Tom thought, to hand in a lady's room. For he could see that it was a lady's room, by the dresses which lay about.

The other picture was that of a man nailed to a cross, which surprised Tom much. He fancied that he had seen something like it in a shop window. But why was it there? "Poor man," thought Tom, "and he looks so kind and quiet. But why should the lady have such a sad picture as that in her room? Perhaps it was some kinsman of hers, who had been murdered by the savages in foreign parts, and she kept it there for a remembrance." And Tom felt sad, and awed, and turned to look at something else.

The next thing he saw, and that too puzzled him, was a washing-stand, with ewers and basins, and soap and brushes, and towels; and a large bath, full of clean water — what a heap of things all for washing! "She must be a very dirty lady," thought Tom, "by my master's rule, to want as much scrubbing as all that. But she must be very cunning to put the dirt out of the way so well afterwards, for I don't see a speck about the room, not even on the very towels."

And then, looking toward the bed, he saw that dirty lady, and held his breath with astonishment.

Under the snow-white coverlet, upon the snow-white pillow, lay the most beautiful little girl that Tom had ever seen. Her cheeks were almost as white as the pillow, and her hair was like threads of gold spread all about over the bed. She might have been as old as Tom, or maybe a year or two older; but Tom did not think of that. He thought only of her delicate skin and golden hair, and wondered whether she were a real live person, or one of the wax dolls he had seen in the shops. But when he saw her breathe, he made up his mind that she was alive, and stood staring at her, as if she had been an angel out of heaven.

No. She cannot be dirty. She never could have been dirty, thought Tom to himself. And then he thought, "And are all people like that when they are washed?" And he looked at his own wrist, and tried to rub the soot off, and wondered whether it ever would come off. "Certainly I should look much prettier then, if I grew at all like her."

And looking round, he suddenly saw, standing close to him, a little ugly, black, ragged figure, with bleared eyes and grinning white teeth. He turned on it angrily. What did such a little black ape want in that sweet young lady's room? And behold, it was himself, reflected in a great mirror, the like of which Tom had never seen before.

And Tom, for the first time in his life, found out that he was dirty; and burst into tears with shame and anger; and turned to sneak up the chimney again and hide, and upset the fender, and threw the fire-irons down, with a noise as of ten thousand tin kettles tied to ten thousand mad dogs' tails.

Up jumped the little white lady in her bed, and seeing Tom, screamed as shrill as any peacock. In rushed a stout old nurse from the next room, and seeing Tom likewise, made up her mind that he had come to rob, plunder, destroy, and burn; and dashed at him, as he lay over the fender, so fast that she caught him by the jacket.

But she did not hold him. Tom had been in a policeman's hands many a time, and out of them too, what is more; and he would have been ashamed to face his friends for ever if he had been stupid enough to be caught by an old woman: so he doubled under the good lady's arm, across the room, and out of the window in a moment.

He did not need to drop out, though he would have done so bravely enough. Nor even to let himself down a spout, which would have been an old game to him; for once he got up by a spout to the church roof, he said to take jackdaws' eggs, but the policemen said to steal lead; and when he was seen on high, sat there till the sun got too hot, and came down by another spout, leaving the policemen to go back to the station-house and eat their dinners.

But all under the window spread a tree, with great leaves, and sweet white flowers, almost as big as his head. It was a magnolia, I suppose; but Tom knew nothing about that, and cared less; for down the tree he went, like a cat, and across the garden lawn, and over the iron railings, and up the park towards the wood, leaving the old nurse to scream murder and fire at the window.

The under gardener, mowing, saw Tom, and threw down his scythe; caught his leg in it, and cut his shin open, whereby he kept his bed for a week: but in his hurry he never knew it, and gave chase to poor Tom. The dairymaid heard the noise, got the churn between her knees, and tumbled over it, spilling all the cream; and yet she jumped up, and gave chase to Tom. A groom cleaning Sir John's hack at the stables let him go loose, whereby he kicked himself lame in five minutes; but he ran out, and gave chase to Tom. Grimes upset the soot-sack in the new-gravelled yard, and spoilt it all utterly; but he ran out and gave chase to Tom. The old steward opened the park gate in such a hurry, that he hung up his pony's chin upon the spikes, and for aught I know it hangs there still; but he jumped off, and gave chase to Tom. The ploughman left his horses at the headland, and one jumped over the fence, and pulled the other into the ditch, plough and all; but he ran on, and gave chase to Tom. The keeper, who was taking a stoat out of a trap, let the stoat go, and caught his own finger; but he jumped up and ran after Tom, and considering what he said, and how he looked, I should have been sorry for Tom if he had caught him. Sir John looked out of his study window (for he was an early old gentleman), and up at the nurse, and a martin dropt mud in his eye, so that he had at last to send for the doctor; and yet he ran out and gave chase to Tom. The Irishwoman, too, was walking up to the house to beg – she must have got round by some byway: but she threw away her bundle, and gave chase to Tom likewise. Only my lady did not give chase; for when she had put her head out of the window, her night-wig fell into the garden, and she had to ring up her lady's-maid, and send her down for it privately; which quite put her out of the running, so that she came in nowhere, and is consequently not placed.

In a word, never was there heard at Hall Place, not even when the fox was killed in the conservatory, among acres of broken glass, and tons of smashed flower-pots, such a noise, row, hubbub, babel, shindy, hullabaloo, stramash, charivari, and total contempt of dignity, repose, and order, as that day, when Grimes, gardener, the groom, the dairymaid, Sir John, the steward, the ploughman, the keeper, and the Irishwoman, all ran up the park, shouting "Stop thief," in the belief that Tom had at least a thousand pounds' worth of jewels in his empty pockets; and the very magpies and jays followed Tom up, screaking and screaming, as if he were a hunted fox, beginning to droop his brush.

And all the while poor Tom paddled up the park with his little bare feet, like a small back gorilla fleeing to the forest. Alas for him! there was no big father gorilla therein to take his part; to scratch out the gardener's inside with one paw, toss the dairymaid into a tree with another, and wrench off Sir John's head with a third, while he cracked the keeper's skull with his teeth, as easily as if it had been a cocoa-nut or a paving-stone.

However, Tom did not remember ever having a father; so he did not look for one, and expected to have to take care of himself; while as for running, he could keep up for a couple of miles with any stage-coach, if there was the chance of a copper or a cigar-end, and turn coach wheels on his hands and feet ten times following, which is more than you can do. Wherefore his pursuers found it very difficult to catch him; and we will hope that they did not catch him at all.

Tom, of course, made for the woods. He had never been in a wood in his life: but he was sharp enough to know that he might hide in a bush, or swarm up a tree, and, altogether, had more chance there than in the open. If he had not known that, he would have been foolisher than a mouse or a minnow.

But when he got into the wood, he found it a very different sort of place from what he had fancied. He pushed into a thick cover of rhododendrons, and found himself at once caught in a trap. The boughs laid hold of his legs and arms, poked him in his face and his stomach, made him shut his eyes tight (though that was no great loss, for he could not see at best a yard before his nose); and when he got through the rhododendrons, the hassock-grass and sedges tumbled him over, and cut his poor little fingers afterwards most spitefully; the birches birched him as soundly as if he had been a nobleman at Eton, and over the face too (which is not fair swishing, as all brave boys will agree); and the lawyers tripped him up, and tore his shins as if they had sharks' teeth – which lawyers are likely enough to have.

"I must get out of this," thought Tom, "or I shall stay here till somebody comes to help me – which is just what I don't want."

But how to get out was the difficult matter. And indeed I don't think he would ever have got out at all, but have stayed there till the cock-robins covered him with leaves, if he had not suddenly run his head against a wall.

Now, running your head against a wall is not pleasant, especially if it is a loose wall, with the stones all set on edge, and a sharp-cornered one hits you between the eyes, and makes you see all manner of beautiful stars. The stars are very beautiful, certainly: but unfortunately they go in the twenty-thousandth part of a split second, and the pain which comes after them does not. And so Tom hurt his head; but he was a brave boy, and did not mind that a penny. He guessed that over the wall the cover would end; and up it he went, and over like a squirrel.

And there he was, out on the great grouse-moors, which the country folk called Harthover Fell – heather and bog and rock, stretching away and up, up to the very sky.

Now, Tom was a cunning little fellow – as cunning as an old Exmoor stag. Why not? Though he was but ten years old, he had lived longer than most stags, and had more wits to start with into the bargain.

He knew as well as a stag, that if he backed he might throw the hounds out. So the first thing he did when he was over the wall, was to make the neatest double sharp to his right, and run along under the wall for nearly half a mile.

Whereby Sir John, and the keeper, and the steward, and the gardener, and the ploughman, and the dairymaid, and all the hue-and-cry together went on ahead half a mile in the very opposite direction, and inside the wall, leaving him a mile off on the outside, while Tom heard their shouts die away in the wood, and chuckled to himself merrily.

At last he came to a dip in the land, and went to the bottom of it, and then he turned bravely away from the wall, and up the moor; for he knew that he had put a hill between him and his enemies, and could go on without their seeing him.

But the Irishwoman, alone of them all, had seen which way Tom went. She had kept ahead of every one the whole time: and yet she neither walked nor ran. She went along quite smoothly and gracefully, while her feet twinkled past each other so fast, that you could not see which was foremost; till every one asked the other who the strange woman was? and all agreed, for want of anything better to say, that she must be in league with Tom.

But when she came to the plantation they lost sight of her; and they could do no less. For she went quietly over the wall after Tom, and followed him wherever he went. Sir John and the rest saw no more of her; and out of sight was out of mind.

And now Tom was right away into the heather, over just such a moor as those in which you have been bred, except that there were rocks and stones lying about everywhere; and that instead of the moor growing flat as he went upwards, it grew more and more broken and hilly: but not so rough but that little Tom could jog along well enough, and find time, too, to stare about at the strange place, which was like a new world to him.

He saw great spiders there, with crowns and crosses marked on their backs, who sat in the middle of their webs, and when they saw Tom coming, shook them so fast that they became invisible. Then he saw lizards, brown, and gray, and green, and thought they were snakes, and would sting him: but they were as much frightened as he, and shot away into the heath. And then, under a rock, he saw a pretty sight – a great brown sharp-nosed creature, with a white tag to her brush, and round her, four or five smutty little cubs, the funniest fellows Tom ever saw. She lay on her back, rolling about, and stretching out her legs, and head, and tail in the bright sunshine; and the cubs jumped over her, and ran round her, and nibbled her paws and lugged her about by the tail; and she seemed to enjoy it mightily. But one selfish little fellow stole away from the rest to a dead crow close by, and dragged it off to hide it, though it was nearly as big as he was. Whereat all his little brothers set off after him in full cry, and saw Tom; and then all ran back, and up jumped Mrs. Vixen, and caught one up in her mouth, and the rest toddled after her, and into a dark crack in the rocks; and there was an end of the show.

And next he had a fright; for as he scrambled up a sandy brow — whirr-poof-poof-cock-cock-kick — something went off in his face, with a most horrid noise. He thought the ground had blown up, and the end of the world come.

And when he opened his eyes (for he shut them very tight), it was only an old cock-grouse, who had been washing himself in sand, like an Arab, for want of water; and who, when Tom had all but trodden on him, jumped up, with a noise like the express train, leaving his wife and children to shift for themselves, like an old coward, and went off, screaming "Cur-ru-u-uck, cur-ru-u-uck — murder, thieves, fire — cur-u-uck-cock-kick — the end of the world is come — kick-kick-cock-kick." He was always fancying that the end of the world was come, when anything happened which was farther off than the end of his own nose. But the end of the world was not come, any more than the twelfth of August was; though the old grouse-cock was quite certain of it.

So the old grouse came back to his wife and family an hour afterwards, and said solemnly, "Cock-cock-kick; my dears, the end of the world is not quite come; but I assure you it is coming the day after tomorrow — cock." But his wife had heard that so often, that she knew all about it, and a little more. And, besides, she was the mother of a family, and had seven little poults to wash and feed every day; and that made her very practical, and a little sharp-tempered; so all she answered was: "Kick-kick-kick — go and catch spiders, go and catch spiders — kick."

So Tom went on, and on, he hardly knew why: but he liked the great, wide, strange place, and the cool, fresh, bracing air. But he went more and more slowly as he got higher up the hill; for now the ground grew very bad indeed. Instead of soft turf and springy heather, he met great patches of flat limestone rock, just like ill-made pavements, with deep cracks between the stones and ledges, filled with ferns: so he had to hop from stone to stone, and now and then he slipped in between, and hurt his little bare toes, though they were tolerably tough ones: but still he would go on and up, he could not tell why.

What would Tom have said, if he had seen, walking over the moor behind him, the very same Irishwoman who had taken his part upon the road? But whether it was that he looked too little behind him, or whether it was that she kept out of sight behind the rocks and knolls, he never saw her, though she saw him.

And now he began to get a little hungry, and very thirsty; for he had run a long way, and the sun had risen high in heaven, and the rock was as hot as an oven, and the air danced reels over it, as it does over a limekiln, till everything round seemed quivering and melting in the glare.

But he could see nothing to eat anywhere, and still less to drink.

The heath was full of bilberries and whimberries: but they were only in flower yet, for it was June. And as for water, who can find that on the top of a limestock rock? Now and then he passed by a deep, dark swallow-hole, going down into the earth, as if it was the chimney of some dwarf's house underground; and more than once, as he passed, he could hear water falling, trickling, tinkling, many many feet below. How he longed to get down to it, and cool his poor baked lips! But, brave little chimney-sweep as he was, he dared not climb down such chimneys as those.

So he went on, and on, till his head spun round with the heat, and he thought his heard church-bells ringing a long way off.

"Ah!" he thought, "where there is a church, there will be houses and people; and, perhaps, some one will give me a bit and a sup." So he set off again, to look for the church; for he was sure that he heard the bells quite plain.

And in a minute more, when he looked round, he stopped again, and said, "Why, what a big place the world is!"

And so it was; for, from the top of the mountain, he could see – what could he not see?

Behind him, far below, was Harthover, and the dark woods, and the shining salmon river; and on his left, far below, was the town, and the smoking chimneys of the collieries; and far, far away, the river widened to the shining sea; and little white specks, which were ships, lay on its bosom. Before him lay, spread out like a map, great plains, and farms, and villages, amid dark knots of trees. They all seemed at his very feet; but he had sense to see that they were long miles away.

And to his right rose moor after moor, hill after hill, till they faded away, blue into blue sky. But between him and those moors, and really at his very feet, lay something, to which, as soon as Tom saw it, he determined to go, for that was the place for him.

A deep, deep green and rocky valley, very narrow, and filled with wood: but through the wood, hundreds of feet below him, he could see a clear stream glance. Oh, if he could but get down to that stream! Then, by the stream he saw the roof of a little cottage, and a little garden, set out in squares and beds. And there was a tiny little red thing moving in the garden, no bigger than a fly. As Tom looked down, he saw that it was a woman in a red petticoat. Ah! perhaps she would give him something to eat. And there were the church-bells ringing again. Surely there must be a village down there. Well, nobody would know him, or what had happened at the Place. The news could not have got there yet, even if Sir John had set all the policemen in the county after him; and he could get down there in five minutes.

Tom was quite right about the hue-and-cry not having got thither; for he had come, without knowing it, the best part of ten miles from Harthover: but he was wrong about getting down in five minutes, for the cottage was more than a mile off, and a good thousand feet below.

However, down he went, like a brave little man as he was, though he was very footsore, and tired, and hungry, and thirsty; while the church-bells rang so loud, he began to think that they must be inside his own head, and the river chimed and tinkled far below; and this was the song which it sang:-

> *Clear and cool, clear and cool,*
> *By laughing shallow, and dreaming pool;*
> *Cool and clear, cool and clear,*
> *By shining shingle, and foaming wear;*
> *Under the crag where the ouzel sings,*
> *And the ivied wall wherte the church-bell rings,*

Undefiled, for the undefiled;
  Play by me, bathe in me, mother and child.

Dank and foul, dank and foul,
  By the smoky town in its murky cowl;
Foul and dank, foul and dank,
  By wharf and sewer and slimey bank;
Darker and darker the further I go,
  Baser and baser the richer I grow;
Who dare sport with the sin-defiled?
  Shrink from me, turn from me, mother and child.

Strong and free, strong and free,
  The floodgates are open, away to the sea.
Free and strong, free and strong,
  Cleansing my streams as I hurry along
To the golden sands, and the leaping bar,
  And the taintless tide that awaits me afar,
As I lose myself in the infinite main,
  Like a soul that has sinned and is pardoned again.
Undefiled, for the undefiled,
  Play by me, bathe in me, mother and child.

So Tom went down; and all the while he never saw the Irishwoman going down behind him.

CHAPTER TWO

And is there care in heaven? and is there love
 In heavenly spirits to these creatures base
That may compassion of their evils move?
 There is: — else much more wretched were the case
Of men than beasts: But oh! the exceeding grace
 Of Highest God that loves His creatures so,
And all His works with mercy doth embrace,
 That blessed Angels He sends to and fro,
To serve to wicked man, to serve His wicked foe!
Spenser

Chapter Two

~

A mile off, and a thousand feet down. So Tom found it; though it seemed as if he could have chucked a pebble on to the back of the woman in the red petticoat who was weeding in the garden, or even across the dale to the rocks beyond.

For the bottom of the valley was just one field broad, and on the other side ran the stream; and above it, gray crag, gray down, gray stair, gray moor, walled up to heaven.

A quiet, silent, rich, happy place; a narrow crack cut deep into the earth; so deep, and so out of the way, that the bad bogies can hardly find it out. The name of the place is Vendale; and if you want to see it for yourself, you must go up into the High Craven, and search from Bolland Forest north by Ingleborough, to the Nine Standards and Cross Fell; and if you have not found it, you must turn south, and search the Lake Mountains, down to Scaw Fell and the sea; and then if you have not found it, you must go northward again by merry Carlisle, and search the Cheviots all across, from Annan Water to Berwick Law; and then, whether you have found Vendale or not, you will have found such a country, and such a people, as ought to make you proud of being a British boy.

So Tom went to go down; and first he went down three hundred feet of steep heather, mixed up with loose brown gritstone, as rough as a file; which was not pleasant to his poor little heels as he came bump, stump, jump, down the steep. And still he thought he could throw a stone into the garden.

Then he went down three hundred feet of limestone terraces, one below the other, as straight as if Mr. George White had ruled them with his ruler and then cut them out with his chisel. There was no heath there, but -

First, a little grass slope, covered with the prettiest flowers, rockrose and saxifrage, and thyme and basil, and all sorts of sweet herbs.

Then bump down a two-foot step of limestone.

Then another bit of grass and flowers.

Then bump down a one-foot step.

Then another bit of grass and flowers for fifty yards, as steep as the house-roof, where he had to slide down on his dear little tail.

Then another step of stone, ten feet high; and there he had to stop himself, and crawl along the edge to find a crack; for if he had rolled over, he would have rolled right into the old woman's garden, and frightened her out of her wits.

Then, when he had found a dark, narrow crack, full of green-stalked fern, such as hangs in the basket in the drawing-room, and had crawled down through it, with knees and elbows, as he would down a chimney, there was another grass slope, and another step, and so on, till – oh, dear me! I wish it was all over; and so did he. And yet he thought he could throw a stone into the old woman's garden.

At last he came to a bank of beautiful shrubs; whitebeam with its great silver-backed leaves, and mountain-ash, and oak; and below them cliff and crag, cliff and crag, with great beds of crown-ferns and wood-sedge; while through the shrubs he could see the stream sparkling, and hear it murmur on the white pebbles. He did not know that it was three hundred feet below.

You would have been giddy, perhaps, at looking down: but Tom was not. He was a brave little chimney-sweep; and when he found himself on the top of a high cliff, instead of sitting down and crying for his baba (though he never had had any baba to cry for), he said – "Ah, this will just suit me!" though he was very tired; and down he went, by stock and stone, sedge and ledge, bush and rush, as if he had been born of a jolly little black ape, with four hands instead of two.

And all the while, he never saw the Irishwoman coming down behind him.

But he was getting terribly tired now. The burning sun on the fells had sucked him up; but the damp heat of the woody crag sucked him up still more; and the perspiration ran out of the ends of his fingers and toes, and washed him cleaner than he had been for a whole year. But, of course, he dirtied everything terribly as he went. There has been a great black smudge all down the crag ever since. And there have been more black beetles in Vendale since than ever were known before; all, of course, owing to Tom's having blacked the original pappa of them all, just as he was setting off to be married, with a sky-blue cat and scaret leggings, as smart as a gardener's dog with a polyanthus in his mouth.

At last he got to the bottom. But, behold, it was not the bottom – as people usually find when they are coming down a mountain. For at the foot of the crag were heaps and heaps of fallen limestone of every size from that of your head to that of a stage-wagon, with holes between them full of sweet heath-fern; and before Tom got through them, he was out in the bright sunshine again; and then he felt, once for all and suddenly, as people generally do, that he was b-e-a-t, beat.

You must expect to be beat a few times in your life, little man, if you live such a life as a man ought to live, let you be as strong and healthy as you may: and when you are, you will find it a very ugly feeling. I hope that that day you may have a stout staunch friend by you who is not beat; for if you have not, you had best lie where you are, and wait for better times, as poor Tom did.

He could not get on. The sun was burning, and yet he felt chill all over. He was quite empty, and yet he felt quite sick. There was but two hundred yards of smooth pasture between him and the cottage, and yet he could not walk down it. He could hear the stream murmuring only one field beyond it, and yet it seemed to him as if it was a hundred miles off.

He lay down on the grass till the beetles ran over him, and the flies settled on his nose. I don't know when he would have got up again, if the gnats and the midges had not taken compassion on him. But the gnats blew their trumpets so loud in his ear, and the midges nibbled so at his hands and face wherever they could find a place free from soot, that at last he woke up, and stumbled away, down over a low wall, and into a narrow road, and up to the cottage door.

And a neat pretty cottage it was, with clipt yew hedges all round the garden, and yews inside too, cut into peacocks and trumpets and teapots and all kinds of queer shapes. And out of the open door came a noise like that of the frogs on the Great-A when they know that it is going to be scorching hot to-morrow – and how they know that I don't know, and you don't know, and nobody knows.

He came slowly up to the open door, which was all hung round with clematis and roses; and then peeped in, half afraid.

And there sat by the empty fire-place, which was filled with a pot of sweet herbs, the nicest old woman that ever was seen, in her red petticoat, and short dimity bedgown, and clean white cap, with a black silk handkerchief over it, tied under her chin. At her feet sat the grandfather of all the cats; and opposite her sat, on two benches, twelve or fourteen neat, rosy, chubby little children, learning their Chris-cross-row; and gabble enough they made about it.

Such a pleasant cottage it was, with a shiny, clean, stone floor, and curious old prints on the walls, and an old black oak sideboard full of bright pewter and brass dishes, and a cuckoo clock in the corner, which began shouting as soon as Tom appeared: not that it was frightened at Tom, but that it was just eleven o'clock.

All the children started at Tom's dirty, black figure; the girls began to cry, and the boys began to laugh, and all pointed at him rudely enough: but Tom was too tired to care for that.

"What art thou, and what dost want?" cried the old dame. "A chimney sweep! Away with thee. I'll have no sweeps here."

"Water," said poor little Tom, quite faint.

"Water? There's plenty i' the beck," she said, quite sharply.

"But I can't get there; I'm most clemmed with hunger and drought."
And Tom sank down upon the door-step, and laid his head against the post.

And the old dame looked at him through her spectacles one minute, and two, and three; and then she said, "He's sick; and a bairn's a bairn, sweep or none."

"Water," said Tom.

"God forgive me!" and she put by her spectacles, and rose, and came to Tom. "Water's bad for thee; I'll give thee milk." And she toddled off into the next room, and brought a cup of milk and a bit of bread.

Tom drank the milk off at one draught, and then looked up, revived.

"Where didst come from?" said the dame.

"Over Fell, there," said Tom, and pointed up into the sky.

"Over Harthover? and down Lewthwaite Crag? Art sure thou art not lying?"

"Why should I?" said Tom, and leant his head against the post.

"And how got ye up there?"

"I came over from the Place," and Tom was so tired and desperate he had no heart or time to think of a story, so he told all the truth in a few words.

"Bless thy little heart! And thou hast not been stealing, then?"

"No."

"Bless thy little heart! and I'll warrant not. Why, God's guided the bairn, because he was innocent! Away from the Place, and over Harthover Fell, and down Lewthwaite Crag! Who ever heard the like, if God hadn't led him? Why dost not eat thy bread?"

"I can't."

"It's good enough, for I made it myself."

"I can't," said Tom, and he laid his head on his knees, and then asked:

"Is it Sunday?"

"No, then; why should it be?"

"Because I hear the church bells ringing so."

"Bless thy pretty heart! The bairn's sick. Come wi' me, and I'll hap thee up somewhere. If thou wert a bit cleaner I'd put thee in my own bed, for the Lord's sake. But come along here."

But when Tom tried to get up, he was so tired and giddy that she had to help him and lead him.

She put him in an outhouse upon soft sweet hay and an old rug, and bade him sleep off his walk, and she would come to him when school was over, in an hour's time.

And so she went in again, expecting Tom to fall fast asleep at once.

But Tom did not fall asleep.

Instead of it, he turned and tossed and kicked about in the strangest way, and felt so hot all over that he longed to get into the river and cool himself; and then he fell half asleep and dreamt that he heard the little white lady crying to him, "Oh, you're so dirty; go and be washed;" and then that he heard the Irishwoman saying, "Those that wish to be clean, clean they will be." And then he heard the church bells ring so loud, close to him, too, that he was sure it must be Sunday, in spite of what the old dame had said; and he would go to church, and see what a church was like inside, for he had never been in one, poor little fellow, in all his life. But the people would never let him come in all over soot and dirt like that. He must go to the river and wash first. And he said out loud again and again, though being half asleep he did not know it, "I must be clean, I must be clean."

And all of a sudden he found himself, not in the outhouse on the hay, but in the middle of a meadow, over the road, with the stream just before him, saying continually, "I must be clean, I must be clean." He had got there on his own legs, between sleep and awake, as children will often get out of bed, and go about the room, when they are not quite well. But he was not a bit surprised, and went on to the bank of the brook, and lay down on the grass, and looked into the clear, clear limestone water, with every pebble at the bottom bright and clean, while the little silver trout dashed about in fright at the sight of his black face; and he dipped his hand in and found it so cool, cool, cool; and he said, "I will be a fish; I will swim in the water; I must be clean, I must be clean."

So he pulled off all his clothes in such haste that he tore some of them, which was easy enough with such ragged old things. And he put his poor hot sore feet into the water; and then his legs; and the further he went in, the more the church bells rang in his head.

"Ah," said Tom, "I must be quick and wash myself; the bells are ringing quite loud now; and they will stop soon, and then the door will be shut, and I shall never be able to get in at all."

Tom was mistaken; for in England the church doors are left open all service time, for everybody who likes to come in, Churchman or Dissenter;

ay, even if he were a Turk or a Heathen; and if any man dared to turn him out, as long as he behaved quietly, the good old English law would punish that man, as he deserved, for ordering any peaceable person out of God's house, which belongs to all alike. But Tom did not know that, any more than he knew a great deal more which people ought to know.

And all the while he never saw the Irishwoman; not behind him this time, but before.

For just before he came to the river side, she had stept down into the cool clear water; and her shawl and her petticoat floated off her, and the green water-weeds floated round her sides, and the white water-lilies floated round her head, and the fairies of the stream came up from the bottom, and bore her away and down upon their arms; for she was the Queen of them all; and perhaps of more besides.

"Where have you been?" they asked her.

"I have been smoothing sick folk's pillows, and whispering sweet dreams into their ears; opening cottage casements, to let out the stifling air; coaxing little children away from gutters, and foul pools where fever breeds; turning women from the gin-shop door, and staying men's hands as they were going to strike their wives; doing all I can to help those who will not help themselves: and little enough that is, and weary work for me. But I have brought you a new little brother, and watched him safe all the way here."

Then all the fairies laughed for joy at the thought that they had a little brother coming.

"But mind, maidens, he must not see you, or know that you are here. He is but a savage now, and like the beasts which perish; and from the beasts which perish he must learn. So you must not play with him, or speak to him, or let him see you: but only keep him from being harmed."

Then the fairies were sad, because they could not play with their new brother, but they always did what they were told.

And their Queen floated away down the river; and whither she went, thither she came. But all this Tom, of course, never saw or heard; and perhaps if he had, it would have made little difference in the story: for he was so hot and thirsty, and longed so to be clean for once, that he tumbled himself as quick as he could into the clear cool stream.

And he had not been in it two minutes before he fell fast asleep, into the quietest, sunniest, cosiest sleep that ever he had in his life; and he dreamt about the green meadows by which he had walked that morning, and the tall elm-trees, and the sleeping cows; and after that he dreamt of nothing at all.

The reason of his falling into such a delightful sleep is very simple; and yet hardly any one has found it out. It was merely that the fairies took him.

Some people think that there are no fairies. Cousin Cramchild tells little folks so in his Conversations. Well, perhaps there are none – in Boston, U.S., where he was raised. There are only a clumsy lot of spirits there, who can't make people hear without thumping on the table: but they get their living thereby, and I suppose that is all they want. And Aunt Agitate, in her Arguments on political economy, says there are none. Well, perhaps there are none – in her political economy. But it is a wide world, my little man – and thank heaven for it, for else, between crinolines and theories, some of us would get squashed – and plenty of room in it for fairies, without people seeing them; unless, of course, they look in the right place. The most wonderful and the strongest things in the world, you know, are just the things which no one can see. There is life in you; and it is the life in you which makes you grow, and move, and think: and yet you can't see it. And there is steam in a steam-engine; and that is what makes it move: and yet you can't see it; and so there may be fairies in the world, and they may be just what makes the world go round to the old tune of

C'est l'amour, l'amour, l'amour
Qui fait la monde à la ronde:

42

and yet no one may be able to see them except those whose hearts are going round to that same tune. At all events, we will make believe that there are fairies in the world. It will not be the last time by many a one that we shall have to make believe. And yet, after all, there is no need for that. There must be fairies; for this is a fairy-tale: and how can one have a fairy-tale if there are no fairies?

You don't see the logic of that? Perhaps not. Then please not to see the logic of a great many arguments exactly like it, which you will hear before your beard is gray.

The kind old dame came back at twelve, when school was over, to look at Tom: but there was no Tom there. She looked about for his footprints; but the ground was so hard that there was no slot, as they say in dear old North Devon. And if you grow up to be a brave healthy man you may know some day what no slot means, and know, too, I hope, what a slot does mean – a broad slot, with blunt claws, which makes a man put out his cigar, and set his teeth, and tighten his girths, when he sees it; and what his rights mean, if he has them, brow, bay, tray, and points; and see something worth seeing between Haddon Wood and Countisbury Cliff, with good Mr. Palk Collyns to show you the way, and mend your bones as fast as you smash them. Only when that jolly day comes, please don't break your neck; stogged in a mire you never will be, I trust; for you are a heath-cropper bred and born.

So the old dame went in again quite sulky, thinking that little Tom had tricked her with a false story, and shammed ill and then run away again.

But she altered her mind the next day. For, when Sir John and the rest of them had run themselves out of breath, and lost Tom, they went back again, looking very foolish.

And they looked more foolish still when Sir John heard more of the story from the nurse; and more foolish still, again, when they heard the whole story from Miss Ellie, the little lady in white. All she had seen was a poor little black chimney-sweep, crying and sobbing, and going to get up the chimney again. Of course she was very much frightened: and no wonder. But that was all. The boy had taken nothing in the room; by the mark of his little sooty feet, they could see that he had never been off the hearthrug till the nurse caught hold of him. It was all a mistake.

So Sir John told Grimes to go home, and promised him five shillings if he would bring the boy quietly up to him, without beating him, that he might be sure of the truth. For he took for granted, and Grimes, too, that Tom had made his way home.

But no Tom came back to Mr. Grimes that evening; and he went to the police-office, to tell them to look out for the boy. But no Tom was heard of. As for his having gone over those great fells to Vendale, they no more dreamed of that than of his having gone to the moon.

So Mr. Grimes came up to Harthover next day with a very sour face; but when he got there, Sir John was over the hills and far away; and Mr. Grimes had to sit in the outer servants' hall all day, and drink strong ale to wash away his sorrows; and they were washed away, long before Sir John came back.

For good Sir John had slept very badly that night; and he said to his lady, "My dear, the boy must have got over into the grouse-moors, and lost himself; and he lies very heavily on my conscience, poor little lad. But I know what I will do."

So, at five the next morning up he got, and into his bath, and into his shooting-jacket and gaiters, and into the stable-yard, like a fine old English gentleman, with a face as red as a rose, and a hand as hard as a table, and a back as broad as a bullock's; and bade them bring his shooting pony, and the keeper to come on his pony, and the huntsman, and the first whip, and the second whip, and the under-keeper with the blood-hound in a leash – a great dog as tall as a calf, of the colour of a gravel walk, with mahogany ears and nose, and a throat like a church bell. They took him up to the place where Tom had gone into the wood; and there the hound lifted up his mighty voice, and told them all he knew.

Then he took them to the place where Tom had climbed the wall; and they shoved it down, and all got through.

And then the wise dog took them over the moor, and over the fells, step by step, very slowly; for the scent was a day old, you know, and very light from the heat and drought. But that was why cunning old Sir John started at five in the morning.

And at last he came to the top of Lewthwaite Crag, and there he bayed, and looked up in their faces, as much as to say, "I tell you he is gone down here!"

They could hardly believe that Tom would have gone so far; and when they looked at that awful cliff, they could never believe that he would have dared to face it. But if the dog said so, it must be true.

"Heaven forgive us!" said Sir John. "If we find him at all, we shall find him lying at the bottom." And he slapped his great hand upon his great thigh, and said:

"Who will go down over Lewthwaite Crag, and see if that boy is alive? Oh that I were twenty years younger, and I would go down myself!" And so he would have done, as well as any sweep in the country. Then he said:

"Twenty pounds to the man who brings me that boy alive!" and as was his way, what he said he meant.

Now among the lot was a little groom-boy, a very little groom indeed; and he was the same who had ridden up the court, and told Tom to come to the Hall; and he said:

"Twenty pounds or none, I will go down over Lewthwaite Crag, if it's only for the poor boy's sake. For he was as civil a spoken little chap as ever climbed a flue."

So down over Lewthwaite Crag he went: a very smart groom he was at the top, and a very shabby one at the bottom; for he tore his gaiters, and he tore his breeches, and he tore his jacket, and he burst his braces, and he burst his boots, and he lost his hat, and what was worst of all, he lost his shirt pin, which he prized very much, for it was gold, and he had won it in a raffle at Malton, and there was a figure at the top of it of t'ould mare, noble old Beeswing herself, as natural as life; so it was a really severe loss: but he never saw anything of Tom.

And all the while Sir John and the rest were riding round, full three miles to the right, and back again, to get into Vendale, and to the foot of the crag.

When they came to the old dame's school, all the children came out to see. And the old dame came out too; and when she saw Sir John she curtsied very low, for she was a tenant of his.

"Well, dame, and how are you?" said Sir John.

"Blessings on you as broad as your back, Harthover," says she – she didn't call him Sir John, but only Harthover, for that is the fashion in the North country – "and welcome into Vendale: but you're no hunting the fox this time of year?"

"I am hunting, and strange game too," said he.

"Blessings on your heart, and what makes you look so sad the morn?"

"I'm looking for a lost child, a chimney-sweep, that is run away."

"Oh, Harthover, Harthover," says she, "ye were always a just man and a merciful; and ye'll no harm the poor little lad if I give you tidings of him?"

"Not I, not I, dame. I'm afraid we hunted him out of the house all on a miserable mistake, and the hound has brought him to the top of Lewthwaite Crag, and – "

Whereat the old dame broke out crying, without letting him finish his story.

"So he told me the truth after all, poor little dear! Ah, first thoughts are best, and a body's heart'll guide them right, if they will but hearken to it." And then she told Sir John all.

"Bring the dog here, and lay him on," said Sir John, without another word, and he set his teeth very hard.

And the dog opened at once; and went away at the back of the cottage, over the road, and over the meadow, and through a bit of alder copse; and there, upon an alder stump, they saw Tom's clothes lying. And then they knew as much about it all as there was any need to know.

And Tom?

Ah, now comes the most wonderful part of this wonderful story. Tom, when he woke, for of course he woke – children always wake after they have slept exactly as long as is good for them – found himself swimming about in the stream, being about four inches, or – that I may be accurate - 3.87902 inches long, and having round the parotid region of his fauces a set of external gills (I hope you understand all the big words) just like those of a sucking eft, which he mistook for a lace frill, till he pulled at them, found he hurt himself, and made up his mind that they were part of himself, and best left alone.

In fact, the fairies had turned him into a water baby.

A water baby? You never heard of a water baby. Perhaps not. That is the very reason why this story was written. There are a great many things in the world which you never heard of; and a great many more which nobody ever heard of; and a great many things, too, which nobody will ever hear of, at least until the coming of the Cocqcigrues, when man shall be the measure of all things.

"But there are no such things as water babies."

How do you know that? Have you been there to see? And if you had been there to see, and had seen none, that would not prove that there were none. If Mr. Grimes does not find a fox in Eversley Wood — as folks sometimes fear he never will — that does not prove that there are no such things as foxes. And as is Eversley Wood to all the woods in England, so are the waters we know to all the waters in the world. And no one has a right to say that no water babies exist, till they have seen no water babies existing; which is quite a different thing, mind, from not seeing water babies; and a thing which nobody ever did, or perhaps ever will do.

"But surely if there were water babies, somebody would have caught one at least?"

Well. How do you know that somebody has not?

"But they would have put it into spirits, or into the *Illustrated News*, or perhaps cut it into two halves, poor dear little thing, and sent one to Professor Owen, and one to Professor Huxley, to see what they would each say about it."

Ah, my dear little man! that does not follow at all, as you will see before the end of the story.

"But a water baby is contrary to nature."

Well, but, my dear little man, you must learn to talk about such things, when you grow older, in a very different way from that. You must not talk about "ain't" and "can't" when you speak of this great wonderful world round you, of which the wisest man knows only the very smallest corner, and is, as the great Sir Isaac Newton said, only a child picking up pebbles on the shore of a boundless ocean.

You must not say that this cannot be, or that that is contrary to nature. You do not know what nature is, or what she can do; and nobody knows; not even Sir Roderick Murchison, or Professor Owen, or Professor Sedgwick, or Professor Huxley, or Mr. Darwin, or Professor Faraday, or Mr. Grove, or any other of the great men whom good boys are taught to respect. They are very wise men; and you must listen respectfully to all they say: but even if they should say, which I am sure they never would, "That cannot exist. That is contrary to nature," you must wait a little, and see; for perhaps even they may be wrong. It is only children who read Aunt Agitate's Arguments, or Cousin Cramchild's Conversations; or lads who go to popular lectures, and see a man pointing at a few big ugly pictures on the wall, or making nasty smells with bottles and squirts, for an hour or two, and calling that anatomy or chemistry – who talk about "cannot exist," and "contrary to nature." Wise men are afraid to say that there is anything contrary to nature, except what is contrary to mathematical truth; for two and two cannot make five, and two straight lines cannot join twice, and a part cannot be as great as the whole, and so on (at least, so it seems at present): but the wiser men are, the less they talk about "cannot." That is a very rash, dangerous word, that "cannot"; and if people use it too often, the Queen of all the Fairies, who makes the clouds thunder and the fleas bite, and takes just as much trouble about one as about the other, is apt to astonish them suddenly by showing them, that though they say she cannot, yet she can, and what is more, will, whether they approve or not.

And therefore it is, that there are dozens and hundreds of things in the world which we should certainly have said were contrary to nature, if we did not see them going on under our eyes all day long. If people had never seen little seeds grow into great plants and trees, of quite different shape from themselves, and these trees again produce fresh seeds, to grow into fresh trees, they would have said, "The thing cannot be; it is contrary to nature." And they would have been quite as right in saying so, as in saying that most other things cannot be.

Or suppose again, that you had come, like M. Du Chaillu, a traveller from unknown parts; and that no human being had ever seen or heard of an elephant. And suppose that you described him to people, and said, "This is the shape, and plan, and anatomy of the beast, and of his feet, and of his trunk and of his grinders, and of his tusks, though they are not tusks at all, but two fore teeth run mad; and this is the section of his skull, more like a mushroom than a reasonable skull of a reasonable or unreasonable beast; and so forth, and so forth; and though the beast (which I assure you I have seen and shot) is first cousin to the little hairy coney of Scripture, second cousin to a pig, and (I suspect) thirteenth or fourteenth cousin to a rabbit, yet he is the wisest of all beasts, and can do everything save read, write and cast accounts." People would surely have said, "Nonsense; your elephant is contrary to nature;" and have thought you were telling stories – as the French thought of Le Vaillant when he came back to Paris and said that he had shot a giraffe; and as the king of the Cannibal Islands thought of the

English sailor, when he said that in his country water turned to marble, and rain fell as feathers. They would tell you, the more they knew of science, "Your elephant is an impossible monster, contrary to the laws of comparative anatomy, as far as yet known." To which you would answer the less, the more you thought.

Did not learned men, too, hold, till within the last twenty-five years, that a flying dragon was an impossible monster? And do we not now know that there are hundreds of them found fossil up and down the world? People call them Pterodactyles: but that is only because they are ashamed to call them flying dragons, after denying so long that flying dragons could exist.

The truth is, that folks' fancy that such and such things cannot be, simply because they have not seen them, is worth no more than a savage's fancy that there cannot be such a thing as a locomotive, because he never saw one running wild in the forest. Wise men know that their business is to examine what is, and not to settle what is not. They know that there are elephants; they know that there have been flying dragons; and the wiser they are, the less inclined they will be to say positively that there are no water babies.

No water babies, indeed? Why, wise men of old said that everything on earth had its double in the water; and you may see that is, if not quite true, still quite as true as most other theories which you are likely to hear for many a day. There are land babies — then why not water babies? Are there not water-rats, water-flies, water-crickets, water-crabs, water-tortoises, water-scorpions, water-tigers, and water-hogs, water-cats and water-dogs, sea-lions and sea-bears, sea-horses and sea-elephants, sea-mice and sea-urchins, sea-razors and sea-pens, sea-combs and sea-fans; and of plants, are there not water-grass, and water-crowfoot, water-milfoil, and so on, without end?

"But all these things are only nicknames; the water things are not really akin to the land things."

That's not always true. They are, in millions of cases, not only of the same family, but actually the same individual creatures. Do not even you know that a green drake, and an alder-fly, and a dragon-fly, live under water till they change their skins, just as Tom changed his? And if a water animal can continually change into a land animal, why should not a land animal sometimes change into a water animal? Don't be put down by any of Cousin Cramchild's arguments, but stand up to him like a man, and answer him (quite respectfully, of course) thus:-

If Cousin Cramchild says, that if there are water babies, they must grow into water men, ask him how he knows that they do not? and then, how he knows that they must, any more than the Proteus of the Adelsberg caverns grows into a perfect newt?

If he says that it is too strange a transformation for a land baby to turn into a water baby, ask him if he ever heard of the transformation of Syllis, or the Distomas, or the common jelly-fish, of which M. Quatrefages says excellently well – "who would not exclaim that a miracle had come to pass, if he saw a reptile come out of the egg dropped by the hen in his poultry-yard, and the reptile give birth at once to an indefinite number of fishes and birds? Yet the history of the jelly-fish is quite as wonderful as that would be." Ask him if he knows about all this; and if he does not, tell him to go and look for himself; and advise him (very respectfully, of course) to settle no more what strange things cannot happen, till he has seen what strange things do happen every day.

If he says that things cannot degrade, that is, change downwards into lower forms, ask him, who told him that water babies were lower than land babies? But even if they were, does he know about the strange degradation of the common goose-barnacles, which one finds sticking on ships' bottoms; or the still stranger degradation of some cousins of theirs, of which one hardly likes to talk, so shocking and ugly it is?

And, lastly, if he says (as he most certainly will) that these transformations only take place in the lower animals, and not in the higher, say that that seems to little boys, and to some grown people, a very strange fancy. For if the changes of the lower animals are so wonderful and so difficult to discover, why should not there be changes in the higher animals far more wonderful, and far more difficult to discover? And may not man, the crown and flower of all things, undergo some change as much more wonderful than all the rest, as the Great Exhibition is more wonderful than a rabbit-burrow? Let him answer that. And if he says (as he will) that not having seen such a change in his experience, he is not bound to believe it, ask him respectfully where his microscope has been? Does not each of us, in coming into this world, go through a transformation just as wonderful as that of a sea-egg, or a butterfly? and does not reason and analogy, as well as Scripture, tell us that that transformation is not the last? and that, though what we shall be, we know not, yet we are here but as the crawling caterpillar, and shall be hereafter as the perfect fly. The old Greeks, heathens as they were, saw as much as that two thousand years ago; and I care very little for Cousin Cramchild if he sees even less than they. And so forth, and so forth, till he is quite cross. And then tell him that if there are no water babies, at least, there ought to be; and that, at least, he cannot answer.

And meanwhile, my dear little man, till you know a great deal more about nature than Professor Owen and Professor Huxley put together, don't tell me about what cannot be, or fancy that anything is too wonderful to be true. "We are fearfully and wonderfully made," said old David; and so we are; and so is every thing around us, down to the very deal table. Yes; much more fearfully and wonderfully made, already, is the table, as it stands now, nothing but a piece of dead deal wood, than if, as foxes say, and geese believe, spirits could make it dance, or talk to you by rapping on it.

Am I in earnest? Oh dear no. Don't you know that this is a fairy tale, and all fun and pretence; and that you are not to believe one word of it, even if it is true?

But at all events, so it happened to Tom. And, therefore, the keeper, and the groom, and Sir John, made a great mistake, and were very unhappy (Sir John, at least) without any reason, when they found a black thing in the water, and said it was Tom's body, and that he had been drowned. They were utterly mistaken. Tom was quite alive; and cleaner, and merrier, than he ever had been. The fairies had washed him, you see, in the swift river, so thoroughly, that not only his dirt, but his whole husk and shell had been washed quite off him, and the pretty little real Tom was washed out of the inside of it, and swam away, as a caddis does when its case of stones and silk is bored through, and away it goes on its back, paddling to the shore, there to split its skin, and fly away as a caperer, on four fawn-coloured wings, with long legs and horns. They are foolish fellows, the caperers, and fly into the the candle at night, if you leave the door open. We will hope Tom will be wiser, now he has got safe out of his sooty old shell.

But good Sir John did not understand all this, not being a fellow of the Linnaean Society; and he took it into his head that Tom was drowned. When they looked into the empty pockets of his shell, and found no jewels there, nor money — nothing but three marbles, and a brass button with a string to it — then Sir John did something as like crying as ever he did in his life, and blamed himself more bitterly than he need have done. So he cried, and the groom-boy cried, and the huntsman cried, and the dame cried, and the little girl cried, and the dairymaid cried, and the old nurse cried (for it was somewhat her fault), and my lady cried, for though people have wigs, that is no reason why they should not have hearts: but the keeper did not cry, though he had been so good-natured to Tom the morning before; for he was so dried up with running after poachers, that you could no more get tears out of him than milk out of leather: and Grimes did not cry, for Sir John gave him ten pounds, and he drank it all in a week. Sir John sent, far and wide, to find Tom's father and mother: but he might have looked till Doomsday for them, for one was dead, and the other was in Botany Bay. And the little girl would not play with her dolls for a whole week, and never forgot poor little Tom. And soon my lady put a pretty little tombstone over Tom's shell in the little churchyard in Vendale, where the old dalesmen all sleep side by side between the limestone crags. And the dame decked it with garlands every Sunday, till she grew so old that she could not stir abroad; then the little children decked it for her. And always she sung an old, old song, as she sat spinning what she called her wedding-dress. The children could not understand it, but they liked it none the less for that; for it was very sweet, and very sad; and that was enough for them. And these are the words of it:

When all the world is young, lad,
  And all the trees are green;
And every goose a swan, lad,
  And every lass a queen;
Then hey for boot and horse, lad,
  And round the world away:
Young blood must have its course, lad,
  And every dog his day.

When all the world is old, lad,
  And all the trees are brown;
And all the sport is stale, lad,
  And all the wheels run down;
Creep home, and take your place there,
  The spent and maimed among:
God grant you find one face there,
  You loved when all was young.

Those are the words: but they are only the body of it: the soul of the song was the dear old woman's sweet face, and the sweet voice, and the sweet old air to which she sang; and that, alas! one cannot put on paper. And at last she grew so stiff and lame, that the angels were forced to carry her; and they helped her on with her wedding-dress, and carried her up over Harthover Fells, and a long way beyond that too, and there was a new schoolmistress in Vendale, and we will hope that she was not certificated.

And all the while Tom was swimming about in the river, with a pretty little lace-collar of gills about his neck, as lively as a grig, and as clean as a fresh-run salmon.

Now if you don't like my story, then go the schoolroom and learn your multiplication-table, and see if you like that better. Some people, no doubt, would do so. So much the better for us, if not for them. It takes all sorts, they say, to make a world.

CHAPTER THREE

He prayeth well who loveth well,
*   Both men and bird and beast;*
He prayeth best who loveth best,
*   All things both great and small:*
For the dear God who loveth us,
*   He made and loveth all.*
Coleridge

CHAPTER THREE

~

Tom was now quite amphibious. You do not know what that means? You had better, then, ask the nearest Government pupil-teacher, who may possibly answer you smartly enough, thus:

"Amphibious. Adjective, derived from two Greek words, *amphi,* a fish, and bios, a beast. An animal supposed by our ignorant ancestors to be compounded of a fish and a beast; which therefore, like the hippopotamus, can't live on the land, and dies in the water."

However that may be, Tom was amphibious; and what is better still, he was clean. For the first time in his life, he felt how comfortable it was to have nothing on him but himself. But he only enjoyed it: he did not know it, or think about it; just as you enjoy life and health, and yet never think about being alive and healthy; and may it be long before you have to think about it!

He did not remember having ever been dirty. Indeed, he did not remember any of his old troubles, being tired, or hungry, or beaten, or sent up dark chimneys. Since that sweet sleep, he had forgotten all about his master, and Harthover Place, and the little white girl, and in a word, all that had happened to him when he lived before; and what was best of all, he had forgotten all the bad words which he had learnt from Grimes, and the rude boys with whom he used to play.

That is not strange: for you know, when you came into this world, and became a land baby, you remembered nothing. So why should he, when he became a water baby?

Then have you lived before?

My dear child, who can tell? One can only tell that, by remembering, something which happpened where we lived before; and as we remember nothing, we know nothing about it; and no book, and no man, can ever tell us certainly.

There was a wise man once, a very wise man, and a very good man, who wrote a poem about the feelings which some children have about having lived before; and this is what he said:

> *Our birth is but a sleep and a forgetting;*
> *The soul that rises with us, our life's star,*
> *Hath elsewhere had its setting*
> *And cometh from afar:*
> *Not in entire forgetfulness*
> *And not in utter nakedness,*
> *But trailing clouds of glory, do we come*
> *From God, who is our home.*

There, you can know no more than that. But if I were you, I would believe that. For then the great fairy Science, who is likely to be queen of all the fairies for many a year to come, can only do you good, and never do you harm; and instead of fancying, with some people, that your body makes your soul, as if a steam-engine could make its own coke; or, with some other people, that your soul has nothing to do with your body, but is only stuck into it like a pin into a pincushion, to fall out with the first shake; — you will believe the one true,

orthodox,	inductive,
rationmal,	deductive,
philosophical,	seductive,

logical,
irrefragable,
nominalistic,
realistic,

productive,
salutary,
comfortable,

and on-all-accounts-to-be-received
doctrine of this wonderful fairy tale; which is, that your soul makes your body, just as a snail makes his shell. For the rest, it is enough for us to be sure that whether or not we lived before, we shall live again; though not, I hope, as poor little heathen Tom did. For he went downward into the water; but we, I hope, shall go upward to a very different place.

But Tom was very happpy in the water. He had been sadly overworked in the land-world; and so now, to make up for that, he had nothing but holidays in the water-world for a long, long time to come. He had nothing to do now but enjoy himself, and look at all the pretty things, which are to be seen in the cool clear water-world, where the sun is never too hot, and the frost is never too cold.

And what did he live on? Water-cresses, perhaps; or perhaps water-gruel, and water-milk: too many land babies do so likewise. But we do not know what one-tenth of the water things eat; so we are not answerable for the water babies.

Sometimes he went along the smooth gravel water-ways, looking at the crickets which ran in and out among the stones, as rabbits do on land; or he climbed over the ledges of rock, and saw the sand-pipes hanging in thousands, with every one of them a pretty little head and legs peeping out; or he went into a still corner, and watched the caddises eating dead sticks as greedily as you would eat plum-pudding, and building their houses with silk and glue. Very fanciful ladies they were; none of them would keep to the same materials for a day. One would begin with some pebbles; then she would stick on a piece of green weed; then she found a shell, and stuck it on too; and the poor shell was alive, and did not like at all being taken to build houses with: but the caddis did not let him have any voice in the matter, being rude and selfish, as vain people are apt to be; then she stuck on a piece of rotten wood, then a very smart pink stone, and so on, till she was patched all over like an Irishman's coat. Then she found a long straw five times as long as herself, and said, "Hurrah! my sister has a tail, and I'll have one too;" and she stuck it on her back, and marched about with it quite proud, though it was very inconvenient indeed. And, at that, tails became all the fashion among the caddis-baits in that pool, as they were at the end of the Long Pond last May, and they all toddled about with long straws sticking out behind, getting between each other's legs, and tumbling over each other, and looking so ridiculous, that Tom laughed at them till he cried, as we did. But they were quite right, you know; for people must always follow the fashion, even if it be spoon-bonnets.

Then sometimes he came to a deep still reach; and there he saw the water-forests. They would have looked to you only little weeds: but Tom, you must remember, was so little that everything looked a hundred times as big to him as it does to you, just as things do to a minnow, who sees and catches the little water-creatures which you can only see in a microscope.

And in the water-forest he saw the water-monkeys and water-squirrels (they had all six legs, though; every thing almost has six legs in the water, except efts and water babies); and nimbly enough they ran among the branches. There were water-flowers there, too, in thousands; and Tom tried to pick them: but as soon as he touched them, they drew themselves in and turned into knots of jelly; and then Tom saw that they were all alive – bells, and stars, and wheels, and flowers, of all beautiful shapes and colours; and all alive and busy, just as Tom was. So now he found that there was a great deal more in the world than he had fancied at first sight.

There was one wonderful little fellow, too, who peeped out of the top of a house built of round bricks. He had two big wheels and one little one, all over teeth, spinning round and round like the wheels in a thrashing-machine; and Tom stood and stared at him, to see what he was going to make with his machinery. And what do you think he was doing? Brick-making. With his two big wheels he swept together all the mud which floated in the water: all that was nice in it he put into his stomach and ate; and all the mud he put into the little wheel on his breast, which really was a round hole set with teeth; and there he spun it into a neat hard round brick; and then he took it and stuck it on the top of his house-wall, and set to work to make another. Now was not he a clever little fellow?

Tom thought so: but when he wanted to talk to him, the brick-maker was much too busy and proud of his work to take notice of him.

Now you must know that all the things under the water talk: only not such a language as ours; but such as horses, and dogs, and cows, and birds talk to each other; and Tom soon learned to understand them and talk to them; so that he might have had very pleasant company if he had only been a good boy. But I am sorry to say, he was too like some other little boys, very fond of hunting and tormenting creatures for mere sport. Some people say that boys cannot help it; that it is nature, and only a proof that we are all originally descended from beasts of prey. But whether it is nature or not, little boys can help it, and must help it. For if they have naughty, low, mischievous tricks in their nature, as monkeys have, that is no reason why they should give way to those tricks like monkeys, who know no better. And therefore they must not torment dumb creatures; for if they do, a certain old lady who is coming will surely give them exactly what they deserve.

But Tom did not know that; and he pecked and howked the poor water things about sadly, till they were all afraid of him, and got out of his way, or crept into their shells; so he had no one to speak to or play with.

The water-fairies, of course, were very sorry to see him so unhappy, and longed to take him, and tell him how naughty he was, and teach him to be good, and to play and romp with him too: but they had been forbidden to do that. Tom had to learn his lesson for himself by sound and sharp experience, as many another foolish person has to do, though there may be many a kind heart yearning over them all the while, and longing to teach them what they can only teach themselves.

At last one day he found a caddis, and wanted it to peep out of its house: but its house-door was shut. He had never seen a caddis with a house door before: so what must he do, the meddlesome little fellow, but pull it open, to see what the poor lady was doing inside. What a shame! How should you like to have any one breaking your bedroom-door in, to see how you looked when you were in bed? So Tom broke to pieces the door, which was the prettiest little grating of silk, stuck all over with shining bits of crystal; and when he looked in, the caddis poked out her head, and it had turned into just the shape of a bird's. But when Tom spoke to her she could not answer; for her mouth and face were tight tied up in a new nightcap of neat pink skin. However, if she didn't answer, all the other caddises did; for they held up their hands and shrieked like the cats in Struwwelpeter: "Oh, you nasty horrid boy; there you are at it again! And she had just laid herself up for a fortnight's sleep, and then she would have come out with such beautiful wings, and flown about, and laid such lots of eggs: and now you have broken her door, and she can't mend it because her mouth is tied up for a fortnight, and she will die. Who sent you here to worry us out of our lives?"

So Tom swam away. He was very much ashamed of himself, and felt all the naughtier; as little boys do when they have done wrong, and won't say so.

Then he came to a pool full of little trout, and began tormenting them, and trying to catch them: but they slipt through his fingers, and jumped clean out of water in their fright. But as Tom chased them, he came close to a great dark hover under an alder root, and out floushed a huge old brown trout ten times as big as he was, and ran right against him, and knocked all the breath out of his body; and I don't know which was the more frightened of the two.

Then he went on sulky and lonely, as he deserved to be; and under a bank he saw a very ugly dirty creature sitting, about half as big as himself; which had six legs, and a big stomach, and a most ridiculous head with two great eyes and a face just like a donkey's.

"Oh," said Tom, "you are an ugly fellow to be sure!" and he began making faces at him; and put his nose close to him, and halloed at him, like a very rude boy.

When, hey presto! all the thing's donkey-face came off in a moment, and out popped a long arm with a pair of pincers at the end of it, and caught Tom by the nose. It did not hurt him much; but it held him quite tight.

"Yah, ah! Oh, let me go!" cried Tom.

"Then let me go," said the creature. "I want to be quiet. I want to split."

Tom promised to let him alone, and he let go. "Why do you want to split?" said Tom.

"Because my brothers and sisters have all split, and turned into beautiful creatures with wings; and I want to split too. Don't speak to me. I am sure I shall split. I will split!"

Tom stood still, and watched him. And he swelled himself, and puffed, and stretched himself out stiff, and at last – crack, puff, bang – he opened all down his back, and then up to the top of his head.

And out of his inside came the most slender, elegant, soft creature, as soft and smooth as Tom: but very pale and weak, like a little child who has been ill a long time in a dark room. It moved its legs very feebly; and looked about it half ashamed, like a girl when she goes for the first time into a ball-room; and then it began walking slowly up a grass stem to the top of the water.

Tom was so astonished that he never said a word: but he started with all his eyes. And he went up to the top of the water, too, and peeped out to see what would happen.

And as the creature sat in the warm bright sun, a wonderful change came over it. It grew strong and firm; the most lovely colours began to show on its body, blue and yellow and black, spots and bars and rings; out of its back rose four great wings of bright brown gauze; and its eyes grew so large that they filled all its head, and shone like ten thousand diamonds.

"Oh, you beautiful creature!" said Tom; and he put out his hand to catch it.

But the thing whirred up into the air, and hung poised on its wings a moment, and then settled down again by Tom quite fearless.

"No!" it said, "you cannot catch me. I am a dragon-fly now, the king of all the flies; and I shall dance in the sunshine, and hawk over the river, and catch gnats, and have a beautiful wife like myself. I know what I shall do. Hurrah!" And he flew away into the air, and began catching gnats.

"Oh! come back, come back," cried Tom, "you beautiful creature. I have no one to play with, and I am so lonely here. If you will but come back I will never try to catch you."

"I don't care whether you do or not," said the dragon-fly; "for you can't. But when I have had my dinner, and looked a little about this pretty place, I will come back; and have a little chat about all I have seen in my travels. Why, what a huge tree this is! and what huge leaves on it!"

It was only a big dock: but you know the dragon-fly had never seen any but little water-trees; starwort, and milfoil, and water-crowfoot, and such like; so it did look very big to him. Besides, he was very short-sighted, as all dragon-flies are; and never could see a yard before his nose; any more than a great many other folks, who are not half as handsome as he.

The dragon-fly did come back, and chatted away with Tom. He was a little conceited about his fine colours and his large wings; but you know, he had been a poor dirty ugly creature all his life before; so there were great excuses for him. He was very fond of talking about all the wonderful things he saw in the trees and the meadows; and Tom liked to listen to him, for he had forgotten all about them. So in a little while they became great friends.

And I am very glad to say, that Tom learnt such a lesson that day, that he did not torment creatures for a long time after. And then the caddises grew quite tame, and used to tell him strange stories about the way they built their houses, and changed their skins, and turned at last into winged flies; till Tom began to long to change his skin, and have wings like them some day.

And the trout and he made it up (for trout very soon forget, if they have been frightened and hurt). So Tom used to play with them at hare and hounds, and great fun they had; and he used to try to leap out of the water, head over heels, as they did before a shower came on; but somehow he never could manage it. He liked most, though, to see them rising at the flies, as they sailed round and round under the shadow of the great oak, where the beetles fell flop into the water, and the green caterpillars let themselves down from the boughs by silk ropes for no reason at all; and then changed their foolish minds for no reason at all either; and hauled themselves up again into the tree, rolling up the rope in a ball between their paws; which is a very clever rope-dancer's trick, and neither Blondin nor Leotard could do it: but why they should take so much trouble about it no one can tell; for they cannot get their living, as Blondin and Leotard do, by trying to break their necks on a string.

And very often Tom caught them just as they touched the water; and caught the alder flies, and the caperers, and the cock-tailed duns and spinners, yellow, and brown, and claret, and gray, and gave them to his

He felt how comfortable it was to have nothing on him but himself. (Chapter 3)

"Oh, don't hurt me!" cried Tom. "I only want to
look at you; you are so handsome".
(Chapter 3)

friends the trout. Perhaps he was not quite kind to the flies; but one must do a good turn to one's friends when one can.

And at last he gave up catching even the flies; for he made acquaintance with one by accident, and found him a very merry little fellow. And this was the way it happened; and it is all quite true.

He was basking at the top of the water one hot day in July, catching duns and feeding the trout, when he saw a new sort, a dark gray little fellow with a brown head. He was a very little fellow indeed: but he made the most of himself, as people ought to do. He cocked up his head, and he cocked up his wings, and he cocked up his tail, and he cocked up the two whisks at his tail-end, and, in short, he looked the cockiest little man of all little men. And so he proved to be; for instead of getting away, he hopped upon Tom's finger, and sat there as bold as nine tailors; and he cried out in the tiniest, shrillest, squeakiest little voice you ever heard:

"Much obliged to you, indeed; but I don't want it yet."

"Want what?" said Tom, quite taken aback by his impudence.

"Your leg, which you are kind enough to hold out for me to sit on. I must just go and see after my wife for a few minutes. Dear me! what a troublesome business a family is!" (though the idle little rogue did nothing at all, but left his poor wife to lay all the eggs by herself). "When I come back, I shall be glad of it, if you'll be so good as to keep it sticking out just so;" and off he flew.

Tom thought him a very cool sort of personage; and still more so, when in five minutes he came back, and said – "Ah, you were tired waiting? Well, your other leg will do as well."

And he popped himself down on Tom's knee, and began chatting away in his squeaking voice.

"So you live under the water? It's a low place. I lived there for some time; and was very shabby and dirty. But I didn't choose that that should last. So I turned respectable, and came up to the top, and put on this gray suit. It's a very business-like suit, you think, don't you?"

"Very neat and quiet indeed," said Tom.

"Yes, one must be quiet, and neat, and respectable, and all that sort of thing for a little, when one becomes a family man. But I'm tired of it, that's the truth. I've done quite enough business, I consider, in the last week, to last me my life. So I shall put on a ball-dress, and go out and be a smart man, and see the gay world, and have a dance or two. Why shouldn't one be jolly if one can?"

"And what will become of your wife?"

"Oh! she is a very plain stupid creature, and that's the truth; and thinks about nothing but eggs. If she chooses to come, why, she may; and if not, why, I go without her – and here I go."

And, as he spoke, he turned quite pale, and then quite white.

"Why, you're ill!" said Tom. But he did not answer.

"You're dead," said Tom, looking at him as he stood on his knee as white as a ghost.

"No, I ain't!" answered a little squeaking voice over his head. "This is me up here, in my ball-dress; and that's my skin. Ha, ha! you could not do such a trick as that!"

And no more Tom could, nor Houdin, nor Robin, nor Frikell, nor all the conjurers in the world. For the little rogue had jumped clean out of his own skin, and left it standing on Tom's knee, eyes, wings, legs, tail, exactly as if it had been alive.

"Ha, ha!" he said, and he jerked and skipped up and down, never stopping an instant, just as if he had St. Vitus's dance. "Ain't I a pretty fellow now?"

And so he was; for his body was white, and his tail orange, and his eyes all the colours of a peacock's tail. And what was the oddest of all, the whisks at the end of his tail had grown five times as long as they were before.

"Ah!" said he, "now I will see the gay world. My living won't cost me much, for I have no mouth, you see, and no inside; so I can never be hungry, nor have the stomach-ache neither."

No more he had. He had grown as dry and hard and empty as a quill, as such silly shallow-hearted fellows deserve to grow.

But, instead of being ashamed of his emptiness, he was quite proud of it, as a good many fine gentlemen are, and began flirting and flipping up and down, and singing:

> *"My wife shall dance, and I shall sing,*
> *So merrily pass the day;*
> *For I hold it one of the wisest things,*
> *To drive dull care away."*

And he danced up and down for three days and three nights, till he grew so tired, that he tumbled into the water, and floated down. But what became of him Tom never knew, and he himself never minded; for Tom heard him singing to the last, as he floated down:

"To drive full care away-ay-ay!"

And if he did not care, why, nobody else cared either.

But one day Tom had a new adventure. He was sitting on a water-lily leaf, he and his friend the dragon-fly, watching the gnats dance. The dragon-fly had eaten as many as he wanted, and was sitting quite still and sleepy, for it was very hot and bright. The gnats (who did not care the least for their poor brothers' death) danced a foot over his head quite happily, and a large black fly settled within an inch of his nose, and began washing his own face and combing his hair with his paws: but the dragon-fly never stirred, and kept on chatting to Tom about the times when he lived under the water.

Suddenly, Tom heard the strangest noise up the stream; cooing, and grunting, and whining, and squeaking, as if you had put into a bag two stock-doves, nine mice, three guinea-pigs, and a blind puppy, and left them there to settle themselves and make music.

He looked up the water, and there he saw a sight as strange as the noise; a great ball rolling over and over down the stream, seeming one moment of soft brown fur, and the next of shining glass: and yet it was not a ball; for sometimes it broke up and streamed away in pieces, and then it joined again; all the while the noise came out of it louder and louder.

Tom asked the dragon-fly what it could be: but, of course, with his short sight, he could not even see it, though it was not ten yards away. So he took the neatest little header into the water, and started off to see for himself; and, when he came near, the ball turned out to be four or five beautiful creatures, many times larger than Tom, who were swimming about, and rolling, and diving, and twisting, and wrestling, and cuddling, and kissing, and biting, and scratching, in the most charming fashion that ever was seen. And if you don't believe me, you may go to the Zoological Gardens (for I am afraid that you won't see it nearer, unless, perhaps, you get up at five in the morning, and go down to Cordery's Moor, and watch by the great withy pollard which hangs over the backwater, where the otters breed sometimes), and then say, if otters at play in the water are not the merriest, lithest, gracefullest creatures you ever saw.

But, when the biggest of them saw Tom, she darted out from the rest, and cried in the water-language sharply enough, "Quick, children, here is something to eat, indeed!" and came at poor Tom, showing such a wicked pair of eyes, and such a set of sharp teeth in a grinning mouth, that Tom, who had thought her very handsome, said to himself, "Handsome is that handsome does," and slipt in between the water-lily roots as fast as he could, and then turned round and made faces at her.

"Come out," said the wicked old otter, "or it will be worse for you."

But Tom looked at her from between two thicks roots, and shook them with all his might, making horrible faces all the while, just as he used to grin through the railings at the old women, when he lived before. It was not quite well-bred, no doubt; but you know, Tom had not finished his education yet.

"Come away, children," said the otter in disgust, "it is not worth eating, after all. It is only a nasty eft, which nothing eats, not even those vulgar pike in the pond."

"I am not an eft!" said Tom; "efts have tails."

"You are an eft," said the otter, very positively; "I see your two hands quite plain, and I know you have a tail."

"I tell you I have not," said Tom. "Look here!" and he turned his pretty little self quite round; and, sure enough, he had no more tail than you.

The otter might have got out of it by saying that Tom was a frog: but, like a great many other people, when she had once said a thing, she stood to it, right or wrong; so she answered:

"I say you are an eft, and therefore you are, and not fit food for gentlefolk like me and my children. You may stay there till the salmon eat you" (she knew the salmon would not, but she wanted to frighten poor Tom). "Ha! ha! they will eat you, and we will eat them;" and the otter laughed such a wicked cruel laugh – as you may hear them do sometimes; and the first time that you hear it you will probably think it is bogies.

"What are salmon?" asked Tom.

"Fish, you eft, great fish, nice fish to eat. They are the lords of the fish, and we are the lords of the salmon;" and she laughed again. "We hunt them up and down the pools, and drive them up into a corner, the silly things; they are so proud, and bully the little trout, and the minnows, till they see us coming, and then they are so meek all at once; and we catch them, but we disdain to eat them all; we just bite out their soft throats and suck their sweet juice – oh, so good!" – (and she licked her wicked lips) – "and then throw them away, and go and catch another. They are coming soon, children, coming soon; I can smell the rain coming up off the sea, and then hurrah for a fresh, and a salmon, and plenty of eating all day long."

And the otter grew so proud that she turned head over heels twice, and then stood upright half out of the water, grinning like a Cheshire cat.

"And where do they come from?" asked Tom, who kept himself very close, for he was considerably frightened.

"Out of the sea, eft, the great wide sea, where they might stay and be safe if they liked. But out of the sea the silly things come, into the great river down below, and we come up to watch for them; and when they go down again we go down and follow them. And there we fish for the bass and the pollock, and have jolly days along the shore, and toss and roll in the breakers, and sleep snug in the warm dry crags. Ah, that is a merry life too, children, if it were not for those horrid men."

"What are men?" asked Tom; but somehow he seemed to know before he asked.

"Two-legged things, eft: and, now I come to look at you, they are actually something like you, if you had not a tail" (she was determined that Tom should have a tail), "only a great deal bigger, worse luck for us; and they catch the fish with hooks and lines, which get into our feet sometimes, and set pots along the rocks to catch lobsters. They speared my poor dear husband as he went out to find something for me to eat. I was laid up among the crags then, and we were very low in the world, for the sea was so rough that no fish would come in shore. But they speared him, poor fellow, and I saw them carrying him away upon a pole. Ah, he lost his life for your sakes, my children, poor dear obedient creature that he was."

And the otter grew so sentimental (for otters can be very sentimental when they choose, like a good many people who are both cruel and greedy, and no good to anybody at all) that she sailed solemnly away down the burn, and Tom saw her no more for that time. And lucky it was for her that she did so; for no sooner was she gone, then down the bank came seven little rough terrier dogs, snuffing and yapping, and grubbing and splashing, in full cry after the otter. Tom hid among the water-lilies till they were gone; for he could not guess that they were the water-fairies come to help him.

But he could not help thinking of what the otter had said about the great river and the broad sea. And, as he thought, he longed to go and see them. He could not tell why; but the more he thought, the more he grew discontented with the narrow little stream in which he lived, and all his companions there; and wanted to get out into the wide wide world, and enjoy all the wonderful sights of which he was sure it was full.

And once he set off to go down the stream. But the stream was very low; and when he came to the shallows he could not keep under water, for there was no water left to keep under. So the sun burnt his back and made him sick; and he went back again and lay quiet in the pool for a whole week more.

And then, on the evening of a very hot day, he saw a sight.

He had been very stupid all day, and so had the trout; for they would not move an inch to take a fly, though there were thousands on the water, but lay dozing at the bottom under the shade of the stones; and Tom lay dozing too, and was glad to cuddle their smooth cool sides, for the water was quite warm and unpleasant.

But toward evening it grew suddenly dark, and Tom looked up and saw a blanket of black clouds lying right across the valley above his head, resting on the crags right and left. He felt not quite frightened, but very still; for everything was still. There was not a whisper of wind, nor a chirp of a bird to be heard; and next a few great drops of rain fell plop into the water, and one hit Tom on the nose and made him pop his head down quickly enough.

And then the thunder roared, and the lightning flashed, and leapt across Vendale and back again, from cloud to cloud, and cliff to cliff, till the very rocks in the stream seemed to shake; and Tom looked up at it through the water, and thought it the finest thing he ever saw in his life.

But out of the water he dared not put his head; for the rain came down by bucketsful, and the hail hammered like shot on the stream, and churned it into foam; and soon the stream rose, and rushed down, higher and higher, and fouler and fouler, full of beetles, and sticks, and straws, and worms, and addle-eggs, and wood-lice, and leeches, and odds and ends, and

70

omnium-gatherums, and this, that, and the other, enough to fill nine museums.

Tom could hardly stand against the stream, and hid behind a rock. But the trout did not; for out they rushed from among the stones, and began gobbling the beetles and leeches in the most greedy and quarrelsome way, and swimming about with great worms hanging out of their mouths, tugging and kicking to get them away from each other.

And now, by the flashes of the lightning, Tom saw a new sight – all the bottom of the stream alive with great eels, turning and twisting along, all down stream and away. They had been hiding for weeks past in the cracks of the rocks, and in burrows in the mud; and Tom had hardly ever seen them, except now and then at night: but now they were all out, and went hurrying past him so fiercely and wildly that he was quite frightened. And as they hurried past he could hear them say to each other, "We must run, we must run. What a jolly thunderstorm! Down to the sea, down to the sea!"

And then the otter came by with all her brood, twining and sweeping along as fast as the eels themselves; and she spied Tom as she came by, and said:

"Now is your time, eft, if you want to see the world. Come along, children, never mind those nasty eels: we shall breakfast on salmon tomorrow. Down to the sea, down to the sea!"

Then came a flash brighter than all the rest, and by the light of it – in the thousandth part of a second they were gone again – but he had seen them, he was certain of it – three beautiful little white girls, with their arms twined round each other's necks, floating down the torrent, as they sang, "Down to the sea, down to the sea."

"Oh, stay! Wait for me!" cried Tom; but they were gone: yet he could hear their voices clear and sweet through the roar of thunder and water and wind, singing as they died away, "Down to the sea!"

"Down to the sea?" said Tom; "everything is going to the sea, and I will go too. God-bye, trout." But the trout were so busy gobbling worms that they never turned to answer him; so that Tom was spared the pain of bidding them farewell.

And now, down the rushing stream, guided by the bright flashes of the storm; past tall birch-fringed rocks, which shone out one moment as clear as day, and the next were dark as night; past dark hovers under swirling banks, from which great trout rushed out on Tom, thinking him to be good to eat, and turned back sulkily, for the fairies sent them home again with a tremendous scolding, for daring to meddle with a water baby; on through narrow strids and roaring cataracts, where Tom was deafened and blinded for a moment by the rushing waters; along deep reaches, where the white water-lilies tossed and flapped beneath the wind and hail; past sleeping villages; under dark bridge-arches, and away and away to the sea. And Tom could not stop, and did not care to stop; he would see the great world below, and the salmon, and the breakers, and the wide, wide sea.

And when the daylight came, Tom found himself out in the salmon-river.

And what sort of a river was it? Was it like an Irish stream, winding through the brown bogs, where the wild ducks squatter up from among the white water-lilies, and the curlews flit to and fro, crying "Tullie-wheep, mind your sheep"; and Dennis tells you strange stories of the Peishtamore, the great bogy-snake which lies in the black peat pools, among the old pine stems, and puts his head out at night to snap at the cattle as they come down to drink? – But you must not believe all that Dennis tells you, mind; for if you ask him:

"Is there a salmon here, do you think, Dennis?"

"Is it salmon, thin, your honour manes? Salmon? Cartloads it is of thim, thin, an' ridgmens, shouldthering ache other out of water, av' ye'd but the luck to see thim."

Then you fish the pool all over, and never get a rise.

"But there can't be a salmon here, Dennis! and, if you'll but think, if one had come up last tide, he'd be gone to the higher pools by now."

"Shure thin, and your honour's the thrue fisherman, and understands it all like a book. Why, ye spake as if ye'd known the wather a thousand years! As I said, how could there be a fish here at all, just now?"

"But you said just now they were shouldering each other out of water?"

And then Dennis will look up at you with his handsome, sly, soft, sleepy, good-natured, untrustable, Irish gray eye, and answer with the prettiest smile:

"Shure, and didn't I think your honour would like a pleasant answer?"

So you must not trust Dennis, because he is in the habit of giving pleasant answers: but, instead of being angry with him, you must remember that he is a poor Paddy, and knows no better; so you must just burst out laughing; and then he will burst out laughing too, and slave for you, and trot about after you, and show you good sport if he can – for he is an affectionate fellow, and as fond of sport as you are – and if he can't, tell you fibs instead, a hundred an hour; and wonder all the while why poor ould Ireland does not prosper like England and Scotland, and some other places, where folk have taken up a ridiculous fancy that honesty is the best policy.

Or was it like a Welsh salmon river, which is remarkable chiefly (at least, till this last year) for containing no salmon, as they have been all poached out by the enlightened peasantry, to prevent the *Cythrawl Sassenach* (which means you, my little dear, your kith and kin, and signifies much the same as the Chinese *Fan Quei*) from coming bothering into Wales, with good tackle, and ready money, and civilisation, and common honesty, and other like things of which the Cymry stand in no need whatsoever?

Or was it such a salmon stream as I trust you will see among the Hampshire water-meadows before your hairs are gray, under the wise new fishing laws? – when Winchester apprentices shall covenant, as they did three hundred years ago, not to be made to eat salmon more than three days a week; and fresh-run fish shall be as plentiful under Salisbury spire as they are in Hollyhole at Christchurch; in the good time coming, when folks shall see that, of all Heaven's gifts of food, the one to be protected most carefully is that worthy gentleman salmon, who is generous enough to go down to the sea weighing five ounces, and to come back next year weighing five pounds, without having cost the soil or the state one farthing?

Or was it like a Scotch stream, such as Arthur Clough drew in his *Bothie*:-

> *Where over a ledge of granite*
> *Into a granite basin the amber torrent descended. . . .*
> *Beautiful there for the colour derived from green rocks under;*
> *Beautiful most of all, where beads of foam uprising*
> *Mingle their clouds of white with the delicate hue of the stillness...*
> *Cliff over cliff for its sides, with rowan and pendant birch boughs...*

Ah, my little man, when you are a big man, and fish such a stream as that, you will hardly care, I think, whether she be roaring down in full spate, like coffee covered with scald cream, while the fish are swirling at your fly as an oar-blade swirls in a boat-race, or flashing up the cataract like silver arrows, out of the fiercest of the foam; or whether the fall be dwindled to a single thread, and the shingle below be as white and dusty as a turnpike road, while the salmon huddle together in one dark cloud in the clear amber pool, sleeping away their time till the rain creeps back again off the sea. You will not care much, if you have eyes and brains; for you will lay down your rod contentedly, and drink in at your eyes the beauty of that glorious place; and listen to the water-ouzel piping on the stones, and watch the yellow roes come down to drink, and look up at you with their great soft trustful eyes, as much as to say, "You could not have the heart to shoot at us?" And then, if you have sense, you will turn and talk to the great giant of a gillie who lies basking on the stone beside you. He will tell you no fibs, my little man; for he is a Scotchman, and fears God, and not the priest; and, as you talk with him, you will be surprised more and more at his knowledge, his sense, his humour, his courtesy; and you will find out – unless you have found it out before – that a man may learn from his Bible to be a more thorough gentleman than if he had been brought up in all the drawing-rooms in London.

No. It was none of these, the salmon stream at Harthover. It was such a stream as you see in dear old Bewick; Bewick, who was born and bred upon them. A full hundred yards broad it was, sliding on from broad pool to broad shallow, and broad shallow to broad pool, over great fields of shingle, under oak and ash coverts, past low cliffs of sandstone, past green meadows, and fair parks, and a great house of gray stone, and brown moors above, and here and there against the sky the smoking chimney of a colliery. You must look at Bewick to see just what it was like, for he has drawn it a hundred times with the care and the love of a true north countryman; and, even if you do not care about the salmon river, you ought, like all good boys, to know your Bewick.

At least, so old Sir John used to say, and very sensibly he put it too, as he was wont to do:

"If they want to describe a finished young gentleman in France, I hear, they say of him, '*Il sait son Rabelais.*' But if I want to describe one in England, I say, 'He knows his Bewick.' And I think that is the higher compliment."

But Tom thought nothing about what the river was like. All his fancy was, to get down to the wide wide sea.

And after a while he came to a place where the river spread out into broad, still, shallow reaches, so wide that little Tom, as he put his head out of the water, could hardly see across.

And there he stopped. He got a little frightened. "This must be the sea," he thought. "What a wide place it is. If I go on into it I shall surely lose my way, or some strange thing will bite me. I will stop here and look out for the otter, or the eels, or some one to tell me where I shall go."

So he went back a little way, and crept into a crack of the rock, just where the river opened out into the wide shallows, and watched for some one to tell him his way: but the otter and the eels were gone on miles and miles down the stream.

There he waited, and slept too, for he was quite tired with his night's journey; and, when he woke, the stream was clearing to a beautiful amber hue, though it was still very high. And after a while he saw a sight which made him jump up; for he knew in a moment it was one of the things which he had come to look for.

Such a fish! ten times as big as the biggest trout, and a hundred times as big as Tom, sculling up the stream past him, as easily as Tom had sculled down.

Such a fish! shining silver from head to tail, and here and there a crimson dot; with a grand hooked nose, and grand curling lip, and a grand bright eye, looking round him as proudly as a king, and surveying the water right and left as if it all belonged to him. Surely he must be the salmon, the king of all the fish.

Tom was so frightened that he longed to creep into a hole; but he need not have been; for salmon are all true gentlemen, and, like true gentlemen, they look noble and proud enough, and yet, like true gentlemen, they never harm or quarrel with any one, but go about their own business, and leave rude fellows to themselves.

The salmon looked him full in the face, and then went on without minding him, with a swish or two of his tail which made the stream boil again. And in a few minutes came another, and then four or five, and so on; and all passed Tom, rushing and plunging up the cataract with strong strokes of their silver tails, now and then leaping clean out of water and up over a rock, shining gloriously, for a moment in the bright sun; while Tom was so delighted that he could have watched them all day long.

And at last one came up bigger than all the rest; but he came slowly, and stopped, and looked back, and seemed very anxious and busy. And Tom saw that he was helping another salmon, an especially handsome one, who had not a single spot upon it, but was clothed in pure silver from nose to tail.

"My dear," said the great fish to his companion, "you really look dreadfully tired, and you must not over-exert yourself at first. Do rest yourself behind this rock;" and he showed her gently with his nose, to the rock where Tom sat.

You must know that this was the salmon's wife. For salmon, like other true gentlemen, always choose their lady, and love her, and are true to her, and take care of her, and work for her, and fight for her, as every true gentleman ought; and are not like vulgar chub and roach and pike, who have no high feelings, and take no care of their wives.

Then he saw Tom, and looked at him very fiercely one moment, as if he were going to bite him.

"What do you want here?" he said, very fiercely.

"Oh, don't hurt me!" cried Tom. "I only want to look at you; you are so handsome."

"Ah?" said the salmon, very stately but very civilly. "I really beg your pardon; I see what you are, my little dear. I have met one or two creatures like you before, and found them very agreeable and well-behaved. Indeed, one of them showed me a great kindness lately, which I hope to be able to repay. I hope we shall not be in your way here. As soon as this lady is rested, we shall proceed on our journey."

What a well-bred old salmon he was!

"So you have seen things like me before?" asked Tom.

"Several times, my dear. Indeed, it was only last night that one at the river's mouth came and warned me and my wife of some new stake-nets which had got into the stream, I cannot tell how, since last winter, and showed us the way round them, in the most charmingly obliging way."

"So there are babies in the sea?" cried Tom, and clapped his little hands. "Then I shall have some one to play with there? How delightful!"

"Were there no babies up this stream?" asked the lady salmon.

"No; and I grew so lonely. I thought I saw three last night; but they were gone in an instant, down to the sea. So I went too; for I had nothing to play with but caddises and dragon-flies and trout."

"Ugh" cried the lady, "what low company!"

"My dear, if he has been in low company, he has certainly not learnt their low manners," said the salmon.

"No, indeed, poor little dear: but how sad for him to live among such people as caddises, who have actually six legs, the nasty things; and dragon-flies, too! why, they are not even good to eat; for I tried them once, and they are all hard and empty; and, as for trout, every one knows what they are." Whereon she curled up her lip, and looked dreadfully scornful, while her husband curled up his too, till he looked as proud as Alcibiades.

"Why do you dislike the trout so?" asked Tom.

"My dear, we do not even mention them, if we can help it; for I am sorry to say they are relations of ours who do us no credit. A great many years ago they were just like us: but they were so lazy, and cowardly, and greedy, that instead of going down to the sea every year to see the world and grow strong and fat, they chose to stay and poke about in the little streams and eat worms and grubs: and they are very properly punished for it; for they have grown ugly and brown and spotted and small; and are actually so degraded in their tastes, that they will eat our children."

"And then they pretend to scrape acquaintance with us again," said the lady. "Why, I have actually known one of them propose to a lady salmon, the little impudent little creature."

"I should hope," said the gentleman, "that there are very few ladies of our race who would degrade themselves by listening to such a creature for an instant. If I saw such a thing happen, I should consider it my duty to put them both to death upon the spot." So the old salmon said, like an old blue-blooded hidalgo of Spain; and what is more, he would have done it too. For you must know, no enemies are so bitter against each other as those who are of the same race; and a salmon looks on a trout, as some great folks look on some little folks, as something just too much like himself to be tolerated.

CHAPTER FOUR

Sweet is the lore which Nature brings;
  Our meddling intellect
Mis-shapes the beauteous forms of things
  We murder to dissect.
Enough of science and of art:
  Close up these barren leaves;
Come forth, and bring with you a heart
  That watches and receives.

Wordsworth

CHAPTER FOUR

~

So the salmon went up, after Tom had warned them of the wicked old otter; and Tom went down, but slowly and cautiously, coasting along the shore. He was many days about it, for it was many miles down to the sea; and perhaps he would never have found his way, if the fairies had not guided him, without his seeing their fair faces, or feeling their gentle hands.

And, as he went, he had a very strange adventure. It was a clear still September night, and the moon shone so brightly down through the water, that he could not sleep, though he shut his eyes as tight as possible. So at last he came up to the top, and sat upon a little point of rock, and looked up at the broad yellow moon, and wondered what she was, and thought that she looked at him. And he watched the moonlight on the rippling river, and the black heads of the firs, and the silver-frosted lawns, and listened to the owl's hoot, and the snipe's bleat, and the fox's bark, and the otter's laugh; and smelt the soft perfume of the birches, and the wafts of heather honey off the grouse-moor far above; and felt very happy, though he could not well tell why. You, of course, would have been very cold sitting there on a September night, without the least bit of clothes on your wet back; but Tom was a water baby, and therefore felt cold no more than a fish.

Suddenly, he saw a beautiful sight. A bright red light moved along the river side, and threw down into the water a long tap-root of flame. Tom, curious little rogue that he was, must needs go and see what it was; so he swam to the shore, and met the light as it stopped over a shallow run at the edge of a low rock.

And there, underneath the light, lay five or six great salmon, looking up at the flame with their great goggle eyes, and wagging their tails, as if they were very much pleased at it.

Tom came to the top, to look at this wonderful light nearer, and made a splash.

And he heard a voice say:

"There was a fish rose."

He did not know what the words meant: but he seemed to know the sound of them, and to know the voice which spoke them; and he saw on the bank three great two-legged creatures, one of whom held the light, flaring and sputtering, and another a long pole. And he knew that they were men, and was frightened, and crept into a hole in the rock, from which he could see what went on.

The man with the torch bent down over the water, and looked earnestly in; and then he said:

"Tak that muckle fellow, lad; he's ower fifteen pounds; and haud your hand steady."

Tom felt that there was some danger coming, and longed to warn the foolish salmon, who kept staring up at the light as if he were bewitched. But, before he could make up his mind, down came the pole through the water; there was a fearful splash and struggle, and Tom saw that the poor salmon was speared right through, and was lifted out of the water.

And then, from behind, there sprung on these three men three other men; and there were shouts, and blows, and words which Tom recollected to have heard before; and he shuddered and turned sick at them now, for he felt somehow that they were strange, and ugly, and wrong, and horrible.

And it all began to come back to him. They were men; and they were fighting; savage, desperate, up-and-down fighting, such as Tom had seen too many times before.

And he stopped his little ears, and longed to swim away; and was very glad that he was a water baby, and had nothing to do any more with horrid dirty men, with foul clothes on their backs and foul words on their lips: but he dared not stir out of his hole; while the rock shook over his head with the trampling and struggling of the keepers and the poachers.

All of a sudden there was a tremendous splash, and a frightful flash, and a hissing, and all was still.

For into the water, close to Tom, fell one of the men; he who held the light in his hand. Into the swift river he sank, and rolled over and over in the current. Tom heard the men above run along, seemingly looking for him: but he drifted down into the deep hole below, and there lay quite still, and they could not find him.

Tom waited a long time, till all was quiet; and then he peeped out, and saw the man lying. At last he screwed up his courage, and swam down to him. "Perhaps," he thought, "the water has made him fall asleep, as it did me."

Then he went nearer. He grew more and more curious, he could not tell why. He must go and look at him. He would go very quietly, of course; so he swam round and round him, closer and closer; and, as he did not stir, at last he came quite close and looked him in the face.

The moon shone so bright that Tom could see every feature; and, as he saw, he recollected, bit by bit. It was his old master, Grimes.

Tom turned tail, and swam away as fast as he could.

"Oh dear me!" he thought, "now he will turn into a water baby. What a nasty troublesome one he will be! And perhaps he will find me out, and beat me again."

So he went up the river again a little way, and lay there the rest of the night under an alder root; but, when morning came, he longed to go down again to the big pool, and see whether Mr. Grimes had turned into a water baby yet.

So he went very carefully, peeping round all the rocks, and hiding under all the roots. Mr. Grimes lay there still; he had not turned into a water baby. In the afternoon Tom went back again. He could not rest till he had found out what had become of Mr. Grimes. But this time Mr. Grimes was gone; and Tom made up his mind that he was turned into a water baby.

He might have made himself easy, poor little man; Mr. Grimes did not turn into a water baby, or anything like one at all. But he did not make himself easy; and a long time he was fearful lest he should meet Grimes suddenly in some deep pool. He could not know that the fairies had carried him away, and put him where they put everything which falls into the water, exactly where it ought to be. But, do you know? what had happened to Mr. Grimes had such an effect on him that he never poached salmon any more. And it is quite certain that, when a man becomes a confirmed poacher, the only way to cure him is to put him under water for twenty-four hours, like Grimes. So, when you grow to be a big man, do you behave as all honest fellows should; and never touch a fish or a head of game which belongs to another man without his express leave; and then people will call you a gentleman, and treat you like one; and perhaps give you good sport: instead of hitting you into the river, or calling you a poaching snob.

Then Tom went on down, for he was afraid of staying near Grimes; and as he went, all the vale looked sad. The red and yellow leaves showered down into the river; the flies and beetles were all dead and gone; the chill autumn fog lay low upon the hills, and sometimes spread itself so thickly on the river, that he could not see his way. But he felt his way instead, following the flow of the stream, day after day, past great bridges, past boats and barges, past the great town, with its wharfs, and mills, and tall smoking chimneys, and ships which rode at anchor in the stream; and now and then he ran against their hawsers, and wondered what they were, and peeped out, and saw the sailors lounging on board, smoking their pipes; and ducked under again, for he was terribly afraid of being caught by man and turned into a chimney-sweep once more. He did not know that the fairies were close to him always, shutting the sailors' eyes lest they should see him, and turning him aside from millraces, and sewer-mouths, and all foul and dangerous things. Poor little fellow, it was a dreary journey for him; and more than once he longed to be back in Vendale, playing with the trout in the bright summer sun. But it could not be. What has been once can never come over again. And people can be little babies, even water babies, only once in their lives.

Besides, people who make up their minds to go and see the world, as Tom did, must needs find it a weary journey. Lucky for them if they do not lose heart and stop half way, instead of going on bravely to the end as Tom did. For then they will remain neither boys nor men, neither fish, flesh, nor good red herring; having learnt a great deal too much, and yet not enough; and sown their wild oats, without having the advantage of reaping them.

But Tom was always a brave, determined little English bull-dog, who never knew when he was beaten; and on and on he held, till he saw a long way off the red buoy through the fog. And then he found, to his surprise, the stream turned round, and running up inland.

It was the tide, of course: but Tom knew nothing of the tide. He only knew that in a minute more the water, which had been fresh, turned salt all round him. And then there came a change over him. He felt as strong, and light, and fresh, as if his veins had run champagne; and gave, he did not know why, three skips out of the water, a yard high, and head over heels, just as the salmon do when they first touch the noble rich salt water, which, as some wise men tell us, is the mother of all living things.

He did not care now for the tide being against him. The red buoy was in sight, dancing in the open sea; and to the buoy he would go, and to it he went. He passed great shoals of bass and mullet, leaping and rushing in after the shrimps, but he never heeded them, or they him; and once he passed a great black shining seal who was coming in after the mullet. The seal put his head and shoulders out of water, and stared at him, looking exactly like a fat old greasy negro with a gray pate. And Tom, instead of being frightened, said, "How d'ye do, sir; what a beautiful place the sea is!" And the old seal, instead of trying to bite him, looked at him with his soft sleepy winking eyes, and said, "Good tide to you, my little man; are you looking for your brothers and sisters? I passed them all at play outside."

"Oh, then," said Tom, "I shall have playfellows at last!" and he swam on to the buoy, and got upon it (for he was quite out of breath) and sat there, and looked round for water babies: but there were none to be seen.

The sea-breeze came in freshly with the tide, and blew the fog away; and the little waves danced for joy around the buoy, and the old buoy danced with them. The shadows of the clouds ran races over the bright blue bay, and yet never caught each other up; and the breakers plunged merrily upon the wide white sands, and jumped up over the rocks, to see what the green fields inside were like, and tumbled down and broke themselves all to pieces, and never minded it a bit, but mended themselves and jumped up again. And the terns hovered over Tom like huge white dragon-flies with black heads, and the gulls laughed like girls at play, and the sea-pies, with their red bills and legs, flew to and fro from shore to shore, and whistled sweet and wild. And Tom looked and looked, and listened; and he would have been very happy, if he could only have seen the water babies. Then, when the tide turned, he left the buoy, and swam round and round in search of them: but in vain. Sometimes he thought he heard them laughing: but it was only the laughter of the ripples. And sometimes he thought he saw them at the bottom: but it was only white and pink shells. And once he was sure he had found one, for he saw two bright eyes peeping out of the sand. So he dived down, and began scraping the sand away, and cried, "Don't hide; I do want some one to play with so much!" And out jumped a great turbot, with his ugly eyes and mouth all awry, and flopped away along the bottom, knocking poor Tom over. And he sat down at the bottom of the sea, and cried salt tears from sheer disappointment.

To have come all this way, and faced so many dangers, and yet to find no water babies! How hard! Well, it did seem hard: but people, even little babies, cannot have all they want without waiting for it, and working for it too, my little man, as you will find out some day.

And Tom sat upon the buoy long days, long weeks, looking out to sea, and wondering when the water babies would come back; and yet they never came.

Then he began to ask all the strange things which came in out of the sea if they had seen any; and some said "Yes," and some said nothing at all.

He asked the bass and the pollock; but they were so greedy after the shrimps that they did not care to answer him a word.

Then there came in a whole fleet of purple sea-snails, floating along, each on a sponge full of foam, and Tom said, "Where do you come from, you pretty creatures? and have you seen the water babies?"

And the sea-snails answered, "Whence we come we know not; and whither we are going, who can tell? We float out our little life in the mid-ocean, with the warm sunshine above our heads, and the warm gulf stream below; and that is enough for us. Yes, perhaps we have seen the water babies. We have seen many strange things as we sailed along." And they floated away, the happy stupid things, and all went ashore upon the sands.

Then there came in a great lazy sunfish, as big as a fat pig cut in half; and he seemed to have been cut in half too, and squeezed in a clothes-press till he was flat; but to all his big body and big fins he had only a little rabbit's mouth, no bigger than Tom's; and, when Tom questioned him, he answered in a little squeaky, feeble voice:

"I'm sure I don't know, I've lost my way. I meant to go to the Chesapeake, and I'm afraid I've got wrong, somehow. Dear me! it was all by following that pleasant warm water. I'm sure I've lost my way."

And, when Tom asked him again, he could only answer, "I've lost my way. Don't talk to me, I want to think."

But, like a good many other people, the more he tried to think the less he could think; and Tom saw him blundering about all day, till the coast-guardsmen saw his big fin above the water, and rowed out, and struck a boat-hook into him, and took him away. They took him up to the town and showed him for a penny a head, and made a good day's work of it. But of course Tom did not know that.

Then there came by a shoal of porpoises, rolling as they went — papas, and mammas, and little children — and all quite smooth and shiny, because the fairies French-polish them every morning; and they sighed so softly as they came by, that Tom took courage to speak to them: but all they answered was, "Hush, hush, hush"; for that was all they had learnt to say.

And then there came a shoal of basking sharks, some of them as long as a boat, and Tom was frightened at them. But they were very lazy, good-natured fellows, not greedy tyrants, like white sharks and blue sharks and ground sharks and hammerheads, who eat men, or saw-fish and threshers and ice-sharks, who hunt the poor old whales. They came and rubbed their great sides against the buoy, and lay basking in the sun with their backfins out of water; and winked at Tom: but he never could get them to speak. They had eaten so many herrings that they were quite stupid; and Tom was glad when a collier brig came by, and frightened them all away; for they did smell most horribly, certainly, and he had to hold his nose tight as long as they were there.

And then there came by a beautiful creature, like a ribbon of pure silver with a sharp head and very long teeth: but it seemed very sick and sad. Sometimes it rolled helpless on its side; and then it dashed away glittering like white fire; and then it lay sick again and motionless.

"Where do you come from?" asked Tom. "And why are you so sick and sad?"

"I come from the warm Carolinas, and the sandbanks fringed with pines; where the great owl-rays leap and flap, like giant bats, upon the tide. But I wandered north and north, upon the treacherous warm gulf stream, till I met with the cold icebergs, afloat in the mid-ocean. So I got tangled among the icebergs, and chilled with their frozen breath. But the water babies helped me from among them, and set me free again. And now I am mending every day; but I am very sick and sad; and perhaps I shall never get home again to play with the owl-rays any more."

"Oh!" cried Tom. "And you have seen water babies? Have you seen any near here?"

"Yes; they helped me again last night, or I should have been eaten by a great black porpoise."

How vexatious! The water babies close to him, and yet he could not find one.

And then he left the buoy, and used to go along the sands and round the rocks, and come out in the night – like the forsaken Merman in Mr. Arnold's beautiful, beautiful poem, which you must learn by heart some day - and sit upon a point of rock, among the shining sea-weeds, in the low October tides, and cry and call for the water babies: but he never heard a voice call in return. And, at last, with his fretting and crying, he grew quite lean and thin.

But one day among the rocks he found a playfellow. It was not a water baby, alas! but it was a lobster; and a very distinguished lobster he was; for he had live barnacles on his claws, which is a great mark of distinction in lobsterdom, and no more to be bought for money than a good conscience or the Victoria Cross.

Tom had never seen a lobster before; and he was mightily taken with this one; for he thought him the most curious, odd, ridiculous creature he had ever seen; and there he was not far wrong; for all the ingenious men, and all the scientific men, and all the fanciful men, in the world, with all the old German bogy-painters into the bargain, could never invent, if all their wits were boiled into one, anything so curious, and so ridiculous, as a lobster.

He had one claw knobbed and the other jagged; and Tom delighted in watching him hold on to the seaweed with his knobbed claw, while he cut up salads with his jagged one, and then put them into his mouth, after smelling at them, like a monkey. And always the little barnacles threw out their casting nets and swept the water, and came in for their share of whatever there was for dinner.

But Tom was most astonished to see how he fired himself off – snap! like the leap-frogs which you make out of a goose's breast-bone. Certainly he took the most wonderful shots, and backwards, too. For, if he wanted to go into a narrow crack ten yards off, what do you think he did? If he had gone in head foremost, of course he could not have turned round. So he used to turn his tail to it, and lay his long horns, which carry his sixth sense in their tips (and nobody knows what that sixth sense is), straight down his back to guide him, and twist his eyes back till they almost came out of their sockets, and then made ready, present, fire, snap! – and away he went, pop into the hole; and peeped out and twiddled his whiskers, as much as to say, "You couldn't do that."

Tom asked him about water babies. "Yes," he said. He had seen them often. But he did not think much of them. They were meddlesome little creatures, that went about helping fish and shells which got into scrapes. Well, for his part, he should be ashamed to be helped by little soft creatures that had not even a shell on their backs. He had lived quite long enough in the world to take care of himself.

He was a conceited fellow, the old lobster, and not very civil to Tom; and you will hear how he had to alter his mind before he was done, as conceited people generally have. But he was so funny, and Tom so lonely, that he could not quarrel with him; and they used to sit in holes in the rocks, and chat for hours.

And about this time there happened to Tom a very strange and important adventure – so important, indeed, that he was very near never finding the water babies at all; and I am sure you would have been sorry for that.

I hope that you have not forgotten the little white lady all this while. At least, here she comes, looking like a clean white good little darling, as she always was, and always will be. For it befel in the pleasant short December days, when the wind always blows from the south-west, till Old Father Christmas comes and spreads the great white table-cloth, ready for little boys and girls to give the birds their Christmas dinner of crumbs – it befel (to go on) in the pleasant December days, that Sir John was so busy hunting that nobody at home could get a word out of him. Four days a week he hunted, and very good sport he had; and the other two he went to the bench and the board of guardians, and very good justice he did; and, when he got home in time, he dined at five; for he hated this absurd new fashion of dining at eight in the hunting season which forces a man to make interest with the footman for cold beef and beer as soon as he comes in, and so spoil his appetite, and then sleep in an arm-chair in his bed-room, all stiff and tired, for two or three hours before he can get his dinner like a gentleman. And do you be like Sir John, my dear little man, when you are your own master; and, if you want either to read hard or ride hard, stick to the good old Cambridge hours of breakfast at eight and dinner at five, by which you may get two days' work out of one. But, of course, if you find a fox at three in the afternoon and run him till dark, and leave off twenty miles from home, why, you must wait for your dinner till you can get it, as better men than you have done. Only see that, if you go hungry, your horse does not: but give him his warm gruel and beer, and take him gently home, remembering that good horses don't grow on the hedge like blackberries.

It befel (to go on a second time) that Sir John, hunting all day and dining at five, fell asleep every evening, and snored so terribly that all the windows in Harthover shook, and the soot fell down the chimneys. Whereon my Lady, being no more able to get conversation out of him than a song out of a dead nightingale, determined to go off and leave him, and the doctor, and Captain Swinger the agent, to snore in concert every evening to their hearts' content. So she started for the sea-side with all the children, in order to put herself and them into condition by mild applications of iodine. She might as well have stayed at home and used Parry's liquid horse-blister, for there was plenty of it in the stables; and then she would have saved her money, and saved the chance, also, of making all the children ill instead of well (as hundreds are made), by taking them to some nasty smelling undrained lodging, and then wondering how they caught scarlatina and diphtheria: but people won't be wise enough to understand that till they are all dead of bad smells, and then it will be too late: besides, you see, Sir John did certainly snore very loud.

But where she went to nobody must know, for fear young ladies should begin to fancy that there are water babies there; and so hunt and howk after them (besides raising the price of lodgings), and keep them in aquariums, as the ladies at Pompeii (as you may see by the paintings) used to keep Cupids in cages. But nobody ever heard that they starved the Cupids, or let them die of dirt and neglect, as English young ladies do by the poor sea-beasts. So nobody must know where my Lady went. Letting water babies die is as bad as taking singing-birds' eggs; for, though there are thousands, ay, millions, of both of them in the world, yet there is not one too many.

Now it befel that, on the very shore, and over the very rocks, where Tom was sitting with his friend the lobster, there walked one day the little white lady, Ellie herself, and with her a very wise man indeed – Professor Ptthmllnsprts.

His mother was a Dutchwoman, and therefore he was born at Curaçao (of course you have learnt your geography, and therefore know why); and his father a Pole, and therefore he was brought up at Petropaulowski (of course you have learnt your modern politics, and therefore know why): but for all that he was as thorough an Englishman as ever coveted his neighbour's goods. And his name, as I said, was Professor Ptthmllnsprts, which is a very ancient and noble Polish name.

He was, as I said, a very great naturalist, and chief professor of Necrobioneopalaeonthydrochthonanthropopithekology in the new university which the King of the Cannibal Islands had founded; and, being a member of the Acclimatisation Society, he had come here to collect all the nasty things which he could find on the coast of England, and turn them loose round the Cannibal Islands, because they had not nasty things enough there to eat what they left.

But he was a very worthy kind good-natured little old gentleman; and very fond of children (for he was not the least a cannibal himself); and very good to all the world as long as it was good to him. Only one fault he had, which cock-robins have likewise, as you will see if you look out of the nursery window – that, when any one else found a curious worm, he would hop round them, and peck them, and set up his tail, and bristle up his feathers, just as a cock-robin would; and declare that he found the worm first; and that it was his worm: and, if not, that then it was not a worm at all.

He had met Sir John at Scarborough, or Fleetwood, or somewhere or other (if you don't care where, nobody else does), and had made acquaintance with him, and become very fond of his children. Now, Sir John knew nothing about sea-cockyolybirds, and cared less, provided the fishmonger sent him good fish for dinner; and my Lady knew as little: but she thought it proper that the children should know something. For in the stupid old times, you must understand, children were taught to know one thing, and to know it well: but in these enlightened new times they are taught to know a little about everything, and to know it all ill; which is a great deal pleasanter and easier, and therefore quite right.

So Ellie and he were walking on the rocks, and he was showing her about one in ten thousand of all the beautiful and curious things which are to be seen there. But little Ellie was not satisfied with them at all. She liked much better to play with live children, or even with dolls, which she could pretend were alive; and at last she said honestly, "I don't care about all these things, because they can't play with me, or talk to me. If there were little children now in the water, as there used to be, and I could see them, I should like that."

"Children in the water, you strange little duck?" said the professor.

"Yes," said Ellie. "I know there used to be children in the water, and mermaids too, and mermen. I saw them all in a picture at home, of a beautiful lady sailing in a car drawn by dolphins, and babies flying round her, and one sitting in her lap; and the mermaids swimming and playing, and the mermen trumpeting on conch-shells; and it is called 'The Triumph of Galatea'; and there is a burning mountain in the picture behind. It hangs on the great staircase, and I have looked at it every since I was a baby, and dreamt about it a hundred times; and it is so beautiful that it must be true."

Ah, you dear little Ellie, fresh out of heaven! when will people understand that one of the deepest and wisest speeches which can come out of a human mouth is that – "It is so beautiful that it must be true."

Not till they give up believing that Mr. John Locke (good man and honest though he was) was the wisest man that ever lived on earth: and recollect that a wiser man than he lived long before him; and that his name was Plato the son of Ariston.

But the professor was not in the least of that opinion. He held very strange theories about a good many things. He had even got up once at the British Association, and declared that apes had hippopotamus majors in their brains just as men have. Which was a shocking thing to say; for, if it were so, what would become of the faith, hope, and charity of immortal millions? You may think that there are other more important differences between you and an ape, such as being able to speak, and make machines, and know right from wrong, and say your prayers, and other little matters of that kind: but that is a child's fancy, my dear. Nothing is to be depended on but the great hippopotamus test. If you have a hippopotamus major in your brain, you are no ape, though you had four hands, no feet, and were more apish than the apes of all aperies. But if a hippopotamus major is ever discovered in one single ape's brain, nothing will save your great-great-great-great-great-great-great-great-great-great - great - greater - greatest - grandmother from having been an ape too. No, my dear little man; always remember that the one true, certain, final, and all-important difference between you and an ape is, that you have a hippopotamus major in your brain, and it has none; and that, therefore, to discover one in its brain will be a very wrong and dangerous thing, at which every one will be very much shocked, as you may suppose they were at the professor. – Though really, after all, it don't much matter: because – as Lord Dundreary and others would put it – nobody but men have hippopotamuses in their brains; so, if a hippopotamus was discovered in an ape's brain, why, it would not be one, you know, but something else.

But the professor had gone, I am sorry to say, even further than that; for he had read at the British Association at Melbourne, Australia, in the year 1999, a paper, which assured every one who found himself the better or wiser for the news, that there were not, never had been, and could not be, any rational or half-rational beings except men, anywhere, anywhen, or anyhow; that nymphs, satyrs, fauns, inui, dwarfs, trolls, elves, gnomes, fairies, brownies, nixes, wilis, kobolds, leprechaunes, cluricaunes, banshees, will-o'-the-wisps, follets, lutins, magots, goblins, afrits, marids, jinns, ghouls, peris, deevs, angels, archangels, imps, bogies, or worse, were nothing at all, and pure bosh and wind. And he had to get up very early in the morning to prove that, and to eat his breakfast overnight; but he did it, at least to his own satisfaction. Whereon a certain great divine, and a very clear divine was he, called him a regular Sadducee; and probably he was quite right. Whereon the professor, in return, called him a regular Pharisee; and probably he was quite right too. But they did not quarrel in the least; for, when men are men of the world, hard words run off them like water off a duck's back. So the professor and the divine met at dinner that evening, and sat together on the sofa afterwards for an hour, and talked over the state of female labour on the antarctic continent (for nobody talks shop after his claret), and each vowed that the other was the best company he ever met in his life. What an advantage it is to be men of the world!

From all which you may guess that the professor was not the least of little Ellie's opinion. So he gave her a succinct compendium of his famous paper at the British Association, in a form suited for the youthful mind. But, as we have gone over his arguments against water babies once already, which is once too often, we will not repeat them here.

Now little Ellie was, I suppose, a stupid little girl; for, instead of being convinced by Professor Ptthmllnsprts' arguments, she only asked the same questions over again.

"But why are there not water babies?"

I trust and hope that it was because the professor trod at that moment on the edge of a very sharp mussel, and hurt one of his corns sadly, that he answered quite sharply, forgetting that he was a scientific man, and therefore ought to have known that he couldn't know; and that he was a logician, and therefore ought to have known that he could not prove an universal negative – I say, I trust and hope it was because the mussel hurt his corn, that the professor answered quite sharply –

"Because there ain't."

Which was not even good English, my dear little boy; for, as you must know from Aunt Agitate's Arguments, the professor ought to have said, if he was so angry as to say anything of the kind – Because there are not: or are none: or are none of them; or (if he had been reading Aunt Agitate too), because they do not exist.

And he groped with his net under the weeds so violently, that, as it befel, he caught poor little Tom.

He felt the net very heavy; and lifted it out quickly, with Tom all entangled in the meshes.

"Dear me!" he cried. "What a large pink Holothurian; with hands, too! It must be connected with Synapta."

And he took him out.

"It has actually eyes!" he cried. "Why, it must be a Cephalopod! This is most extraordinary!"

"No, I ain't!" cried Tom, as loud as he could; for he did not like to be called bad names.

"It is a water baby!" cried Ellie; and of course it was.

"Water-fiddlesticks, my dear!" said the professor; and he turned away sharply.

There was no denying it. It was a water baby: and he had said a moment ago that there were none. What was he to do?

He would have liked, of course, to have taken Tom home in a bucket. He would not have put him in spirits. Of course not. He would have kept him alive, and petted him (for he was a very kind old gentleman), and written a book about him, and given him two long names, of which the first would have said a little about Tom, and the second all about himself;

for of course he would have called him Hydrotecnon Ptthmllnsprtsianum, or some other long name like that; for they are forced to call everything by long names now, because they have used up all the short ones, ever since they took to making nine species out of one. But – what would all the learned men say to him after his speech at the British Association? And what would Ellie say, after what he had just told her?

There was a wise old heathen once, who said, "Maxima debetur pueris reverentia" – The greatest reverence is due to children; that is, that grown people should never say or do anything wrong before children, lest they should set them a bad example. – Cousin Cramchild says it means, "The greatest respectfulness is expected from little boys." But he was raised in a country where little boys are not expected to be respectful, because all of them are as good as the President. Well, every one knows his own concerns best; so perhaps they are. But poor Cousin Cramchild, to do him justice, not being of that opinion, and having a moral mission, and being no scholar to speak of, and hard up for an authority – why, it was a very great temptation for him. But some people, and I am afraid the professor was one of them, interpret that in a more strange, curious, one-sided, left-handed, topsy-turvy, inside-out, behind-before fashion, than even Cousin Cramchild; for they make it mean, that you must show your respect for children, by never confessing yourself in the wrong to them, even if you know that you are so, lest they should lose confidence in their elders.

Now, if the professor had said to Ellie, "Yes, my darling, it is a water baby, and a very wonderful thing it is; and it shows how little I know of the wonders of Nature, in spite of forty years' honest labour. I was just telling you that there could be no such creatures: and, behold! here is one come to confound my conceit, and show me that Nature can do, and has done, beyond all that man's poor fancy can imagine. So, let us thank the Maker, and Inspirer, and Lord of Nature for all His wonderful and glorious works, and try and find out something about this one": – I think that, if the professor had said that, little Ellie would have believed him more firmly, and respected him more deeply, and loved him better, than ever she had done before. But he was of a different opinion. He hesitated a moment. He longed to keep Tom, and yet he half wished he never had caught him; and, at last, he quite longed to get rid of him. So he turned away, and poked Tom with his finger, for want of anything better to do; and said carelessly, "My

*He looked up at the broad yellow moon . . . and
thought that she looked at him.*
(Chapter 4)

Tom reached and clawed down the hole after him.
(Chapter 5)

dear little maid, you must have dreamt of water babies last night, your head is so full of them."

Now Tom had been in the most horrible and unspeakable fright all the while; and had kept as quiet as he could, though he was called a Holothurian and a Cephalopod; for it was fixed in his little head that if a man with clothes on caught him, he might put clothes on him too, and make a dirty black chimney-sweep of him again. But when the professor poked him, it was more than he could bear; and, between fright and rage, he turned to bay as valiantly as a mouse in a corner and bit the professor's finger till it bled.

"Oh! ah! yah!" cried he; and glad of an excuse to be rid of Tom, dropped him on to the sea-weed, and thence he dived into the water and was gone in a moment.

"But it was a water baby, and I heard it speak!" cried Ellie. "Ah, it is gone!" And she jumped down off the rock to try and catch Tom before he slipt into the sea.

Too late! and what was worse, as she sprang down, she slipped, and fell some six feet, with her head on a sharp rock, and lay quite still.

The professor picked her up, and tried to waken her, and called to her, and cried over her, for he loved her very much: but she would not awaken at all. So he took her up in his arms, and carried her to her governess, and they all went home; and little Ellie was put to bed, and lay there quite still; only now and then she woke up, and called out about the water baby: but no one knew what she meant, and the professor did not tell, for he was ashamed to tell.

And, after a week, one moonlight night, the fairies came flying in at the window, and brought her such a pretty pair of wings, that she could not help putting them on; and she flew with them out of the window, and over the land, and over the sea, and up through the clouds, and nobody heard or saw anything of her for a very long while.

And this is why they say that no one has ever yet seen a water baby. For my part, I believe that the naturalists get dozens of them when they are out dredging: but they say nothing about them, and throw them overboard again, for fear of spoiling their theories. But, you see the professor was found out, as every one is in due time. A very terrible old fairy found the professor out; she felt his bumps, and cast his nativity, and took the lunars of him carefully inside and out; and so she knew what he would do as well as if she had seen it in a print book, as they say in the dear old west country; and he did it; and so he was found out beforehand, as everybody always is; and the old fairy will find out the naturalists some day, and put them in *The Times*; and then on whose side will the laugh be?

So the old fairy took him in hand very severely there and then. But she says she is always most severe with the best people, because there is most chance of curing them, and therefore they are the patients who pay her best; for she has to work on the same salary as the Emperor of China's physicians (it is a pity that all do not), no cure, no pay.

So she took the poor professor in hand: and because he was not content with things as they are, she filled his head with things as they are not, to try if he would like them better; and because he did not choose to believe in a water baby when he saw it, she made him believe in worse things than water babies – in unicorns, fire-drakes, manticoras, basilisks, amphisboenas, griffins, phoenixes, rocs, orcs, dog-headed men, three-headed dogs, three-bodied geryons, and other pleasant creatures, which folks think never existed yet, and which folks hope never will exist, though they know nothing about the matter, and never will; and these creatures so upset, terrified, flustered, aggravated, confused, astounded, horrified, and totally flabbergasted the poor professor, that the doctors said that he was out of his wits for three months; and, perhaps, they were right, as they are now and then.

So all the doctors in the county were called in, to make a report on his case; and of course every one of them flatly contradicted the other: else what use is there in being men of science? But at last the majority agreed on a report, in the true medical language, one half bad Latin, the other half worse Greek, and the rest what might have been English, if they had only learnt to write it. And this is the beginning thereof –

"The subanhypaposupernal anastomoses of peritomic diacellurite in the encephalo digital region of the distinguished individual of whose symptomatic phaenomena we had the melancholy honour (subsequently to a preliminary diagnostic inspection) of making an inspectorial diagnosis, presenting the interexclusively quadrilateral and antinomian diathesis known as Bumpsterhausen's blue follicles, we proceeded – "

But what they proceeded to do my lady never knew; for she was so frightened at the long words that she ran for her life, and locked herself into her bedroom, for fear of being squashed by the words and strangled by the sentence. A boa constrictor, she said, was bad company enough: but what was a boa constrictor made of paving-stones?

"It was quite shocking! What can they think is the matter with him?" said she to the old nurse.

"That his wit's just addled; may be wi' unbelief and heathenery," quoth she.

"Then why can't they say so?"

And the heaven, and the sea, and the rocks, and the vales re-echoed – "Why indeed?" But the doctors never heard them.

So she made Sir John write to *The Times* to command the Chancellor of the Exchequer for the time being to put a tax on long words;-

A light tax on words over three syllables, which are necessary evils, like rats: but like them, must be kept down judiciously.

A heavy tax on words over four syllables, as heterodoxy, spontaneity, spiritualism, spuriosity, etc.

And on words over five syllables (of which I hope no one will wish to see any examples), a totally prohibitory tax.

And a similar prohibitory tax on words derived from three or more languages at once; words derived from two languages having become so common, that there was no more hope of rooting out them than of rooting out peth-winds.

The Chancellor of the Exchequer, being a scholar and a man of sense, jumped at the notion; for he saw in it the one and only plan for abolishing Schedule D: but when he brought in his bill, most of the Irish members, and (I am sorry to say) some of the Scotch likewise, opposed it most strongly, on the ground that in a free country no man was bound either to understand himself or to let others understand him. So the bill fell through on the first reading; and the Chancellor, being a philosopher, comforted himself with the thought, that it was not the first time that a woman had hit off a grand idea, and the men turned up their stupid noses thereat.

Now the doctors had it all their own way; and to work they went in earnest, and they gave the poor professor divers and sundry medicines, as prescribed by the ancients and moderns, from Hippocrates to Feuchtersleben, as below, viz.:-

1. Hellebore, to wit –

Hellebore of Aeta.

Hellebore of Galatia.

Hellebore of Sicily.

And all other Hellebores, after the method of the Helleborising Helleborists of the Helleboric era. But that would not do. Bumpsterhausen's blue follicles would not stir an inch out of his encephalo digital region.

2. Trying to find out what was the matter with him; after the method of -

Hippocrates.

Aretaeus.

Celsus.

Coelius Aurelianus,

And Galen: but they found that a great deal too much trouble, as most people have since; and so had recourse to –

3. Borage.

Cauteries.

Boring a hole in his head to let out fumes, which (says Gordonius) "will, without doubt, do much good." But it didn't.

Bezoar stone.

Diamargaritum.

A ram's brain boiled in spice.

Oil of wormwood.

Water of Nile.

Capers.

Good wine (but there was none to be got).

The water of a smith's forge.

Hops.

Ambergris.

Mandrake pillows.

Dormouse fat.

Hares' ears.

Starvation.

Camphor.

Salts and Senna.

Musk.

Opium.

Strait-waistcoats.

Bullyings.

Bumpings.

Blisterings.

Bleedings.

Bucketings with cold water.

Knockings down.

Kneeling on his chest till they broke it in, etc., etc.; after the mediaeval or monkish method: but that would not do. Bumpsterhausen's blue follicles stuck there still.

Then –

4. Coaxing.

Kissing.

Champagne and turtle.

Red herrings and soda water.

Good advice.

Gardening.

Croquet.

Musical soirées.

Aunt Sally.

Mild tobacco.

The Saturday Review.

A carriage with outriders, etc., etc., after the modern method. But that would not do.

And if he had but been a convict lunatic, and had shot at the Queen, killed all his creditors to avoid paying them, or indulged in any other little amiable eccentricity of that kind, they would have given him in addition –

The healthiest situation in England, on Easthampstead Plain.

Free run of Windsor Forest.

The Times every morning.

A double-barrelled gun and pointers, and leave to shoot three Wellington College boys a week (not more) in case black game were scarce.

But as he was neither mad enough nor bad enough to be allowed
such luxuries, they grew desperate, and fell into bad ways, viz.:-

5. Suffumigations of sulphur.

Heerwiggius his "Incomparable drink for madmen": only they
could not find out what it was.

Suffumigation of the liver of the fish * * * only they had forgotten
its name, so Dr. Gray could not well procure them a specimen.

Metallic tractors.

Holloway's Ointment.

Electro-biology.

Valentine Greatrakes his Stroking Cure.

Spirit-rapping.

Holloway's Pills.

Table-turning.

Morrison's Pills.

Homoeopathy.

Parr's Life Pills.

Mesmerism.

Pure Bosh.

Exorcisms, for which they read Malleus Maleficarum, Nideri
Formicarium, Delrio, Wierus, etc., but could not get one that
mentioned water babies.

Hydropathy.

Madame Rachel's Elixir of Youth.

The Poughkeepsie Seer his Prophecies.

The distilled liquor of addle eggs.

Pyropathy, as successfully employed by the old inquisitors, to cure the malady of thought, and now by the Persian Mollahs to cure that of rheumatism.

Geopathy, or burying him.

Atmopathy, or steaming him.

Sympathy, after the method of Basil Valentine his Triumph of Antimony, and Kenelm Digby his Weapon-salve, which some call a hair of the dog that bit him.

Hermopathy, or pouring mercury down his throat, to move the animal spirits.

Meteoropathy, or going up to the moon to look for his lost wits, as Ruggiero did for Orland Furioso's: only, having no hippogriff, they were forced to use a balloon; and, falling into the North Sea, were picked up by a Yarmouth herring-boat, and came home much the wiser, and all over scales.

Antipathy, or using him like "a man and a brother."

Apathy, or doing nothing at all.

With all other ipathies and opathies which Noodle has invented, and Foodle tried, since black-fellows chipped flints at Abbeville – which is a considerable time ago, to judge by the Great Exhibition.

But nothing would do; for he screamed and cried all day for a water baby, to come and drive away the monsters; and of course they did not try to find one, because they did not believe in them, and were thinking of nothing but Bumpsterhausen's blue follicles; having, as usual, set the cart before the horse, and taken the effect for the cause.

So they were forced at last to let the poor professor ease his mind by writing a great book, exactly contrary to all his old opinions; in which he proved that the moon was made of green cheese, and that all the mites in it (which you may see sometimes quite plain through a telescope, if you will only keep the lens dirty enough, as Mr. Weekes kept his voltaic battery) are nothing in the world but little babies, who are hatching and swarming up there in millions, ready to come down into this world whenever children want a new little brother or sister.

Which must be a mistake, for this one reason: that, there being no atmosphere round the moon (though some one or other says there is, at least on the other side, and that he has been round at the back of it to see, and found that the moon was just the shape of a Bath bun, and so wet that the man in the moon went about on Midsummer-day in Macintoshes and Cording's boots, spearing eels and sneezing); that therefore, I say, there being no atmosphere, there can be no evaporation; and, therefore, the dew-point can never fall below 71.5 below zero of Fahrenheit; and, therefore, it cannot be cold enough there about four 4 o'clock in the morning to condense the babies' mesenteric apophthegms into their left ventricles; and, therefore, they can never catch the hooping-cough; and if they did not have hooping-cough, they cannot be babies at all; and, therefore, there are no babies in the moon. – Q.E.D.

Which may seem a round-about reason; and so, perhaps, it is: but you will have heard worse ones in your time, and from better men than you are.

But one thing is certain; that, when the good old doctor got his book written, he felt considerably relieved from Bumpsterhausen's blue follicles, and a few things infinitely worse; to wit, from pride and vain-glory, and from blindness and hardness of heart; which are the true causes of Bumpsterhausen's blue follicles, and of a good many other ugly things beside. Whereon the foul flood-water in his brains ran down, and cleared to a fine coffee colour, such as fish like to rise in, till very fine clean fresh-run fish did begin to rise in his brains; and he caught two or three of them (which is exceedingly fine sport, for brain rivers), and anatomised them carefully, and never mentioned what he found out from them, except to little children; and became ever after a sadder and a wiser man; which is a very good thing to become, my dear little boy, even though one has to pay a heavy price for the blessing.

CHAPTER FIVE

Stern Lawgiver! yet thou dost wear
The Godhead's most benignant grace;
Nor know we anything so fair
As is the smile upon the face:
Flowers laugh before thee on their beds;
And fragrance in thy footing treads;
Thou dost preserve the stars from wrong;
And the most ancient Heavens, through Thee are fresh and strong.

Wordsworth – *Ode to Duty*

Chapter Five

~

$\mathcal{B}$ut what became of little Tom?

He slipt away off the rocks into the water, as I said before. But he could not help thinking of little Ellie. He did not remember who she was; but he knew that she was a little girl, though she was a hundred times as big as he. That is not surprising: size has nothing to do with kindred. A tiny weed may be first cousin to a great tree; and a little dog like Vick knows that Lioness is a dog too, though she is twenty times larger than herself. So Tom knew that Ellie was a little girl, and thought about her all that day, and longed to have had her to play with; but he had very soon to think of something else. And here is the account of what happened to him, as it was published next morning in the *Waterproof Gazette,* on the finest watered paper, for the use of the great fairy, Mrs. Bedonebyasyoudid, who reads the news very carefully every morning, and especially the police cases, as you will hear very soon.

He was going along the rocks in three-fathom water, watching the pollock catch prawns, and the wrasses nibble barnacles off the rocks, shells and all, when he saw a round cage of green withes; and inside it, looking very much ashamed of himself, sat his friend the lobster, twiddling his horns, instead of thumbs.

"What, have you been naughty, and have they put you in the lock-up?" asked Tom.

The lobster felt a little indignant at such a notion, but he was too much depressed in spirits to argue; so he only said, "I can't get out."

"Why did you get in?"

"After that nasty piece of dead fish." He had thought it looked and smelt very nice when he was outside, and so it did, for a lobster: but now he turned round and abused it because he was angry with himself.

"Where did you get in?"

"Through that round hole at the top."

"Then why don't you get out through it?"

"Because I can't"; and the lobster twiddled his horns more fiercely than ever, but he was forced to confess.

"I have jumped upwards, downwards, backwards, and sideways, at least four thousand times; and I can't get out: I always get up underneath there, and can't find the hole."

Tom looked at the trap, and having more wit than the lobster, he saw plainly enough what was the matter; as you may if you will look at a lobster-pot.

"Stop a bit," said Tom. "Turn your tail up to me, and I'll pull you through hind-foremost, and then you won't stick in the spikes."

But the lobster was so stupid and clumsy that he couldn't hit the hole. Like a great many fox-hunters, he was very sharp as long as he was in his own country; but as soon as they get out of it they lose their heads; and so the lobster, so to speak, lost his tail.

Tom reached and clawed down the hole after him, till he caught hold of him; and then, as was to be expected, the clumsy lobster pulled him in head foremost.

"Hullo! here is a pretty business," said Tom. "Now take your great claws, and break the points off those spikes, and then we shall both get out easily."

"Dear me, I never thought of that," said the lobster; "and after all the experiences of life that I have had!"

You see, experience is of very little good unless a man, or a lobster, has wit enough to make use of it. For a good many people, like old Polonius, have seen all the world, and yet remain little better than children after all.

But they had not got half the spikes away, when they saw a great dark cloud over them; and lo and behold, it was the otter.

How she did grin and grin when she saw Tom. "Yar!" said she, "you little meddlesome wretch, I have you now! I will serve you out for telling the salmon where I was!" And she crawled all over the pot to get in.

Tom was horribly frightened, and still more frightened when she found the hole in the top, and squeezed herself right down through it, all eyes and teeth. But no sooner was her head inside than valiant Mr. Lobster caught her by the nose, and held on.

And there they were all three in the pot, rolling over and over, and very tight packing it was. And the lobster tore at the otter, and the otter tore at the lobster, and both squeezed and thumped poor Tom till he had no breath left in his body; and I don't know what would have happened to him if he had not at last got on the otter's back, and safe out of the hole.

He was right glad when he got out: but he would not desert his friend who had saved him; and the first time he saw his tail uppermost he caught hold of it, and pulled with all his might.

But the lobster would not let go.

"Come along," said Tom; "don't you see she is dead?" And so she was, quite drowned and dead.

And that was the end of the wicked otter.

But the lobster would not let go.

"Come along, you stupid old stick-in-the-mud," cried Tom, "or the fisherman will catch you!" And that was true, for Tom felt some one above beginning to haul up the pot.

But the lobster would not let go.

Tom saw the fisherman haul him up to the boatside, and thought it was all up with him. But when Mr. Lobster saw the fisherman, he gave such a furious and tremendous snap, that he snapped out of his hand, and out of the pot, and safe into the sea. But he left his knobbed claw behind him; for it never came into his stupid head to let go after all, so he just shook his claw off as the easier method. It was something of a bull, that; but you must know the lobster was an Irish lobster, and was hatched off Island Magee at the mouth of Belfast Lough.

Tom asked the lobster why he never thought of letting go. He said very determinedly that it was a point of honour among lobsters. And so it is, as the Mayor of Plymouth found out once to his cost – eight or nine hundred years ago, of course; for if it had happened lately it would be personal to mention it.

For one day he was so tired with sitting on a hard chair, in a grand furred gown, with a gold chain round his neck, hearing one policeman after another come in and sing, "What shall we do with the drunken sailor, so early in the morning?" and answering them each exactly alike:

"Put him in the round house till he gets sober, so early in the morning – "

That, when it was over, he jumped up, and played leap-frog with the town-clerk till he burst his buttons, and then had his luncheon, and burst some more buttons, and then he said: "It is a low spring tide; I shall go out this afternoon and cut my capers."

Now he did not mean to cut such capers as you eat with boiled mutton. It was the commandant of artillery at Valetta who used to amuse himself with cutting them, and who stuck upon one of the bastions a notice, "No one allowed to cut capers here but me," which greatly edified the midshipmen in port, and the Maltese on the Nix Mangiare stairs. But all that the mayor meant was that he would go and have an afternoon's fun, like any school-boy, and catch lobsters with an iron hook.

So to the Mewstone he went, and for lobsters he looked. And, when he came to a certain crack in the rocks, he was so excited, that, instead of putting in his hook, he put in his hand; and Mr. Lobster was at home, and caught him by the finger; and held on.

"Yah!" said the mayor, and pulled as hard as he dared: but the more he pulled the more the lobster pinched, till he was forced to be quiet.

Then he tried to get his hook in with the other hand; but the hole was too narrow.

Then he pulled again; but he could not stand the pain.

Then he shouted and bawled for help; but there was no one nearer him than the men-of-war inside the breakwater.

Then he began to turn a little pale; for the tide flowed, and still the lobster held on.

Then he turned quite white; for the tide was up to his knees, and still the lobster held on.

Then he thought of cutting off his finger; but he wanted two things to do it with – courage and a knife; and he had got neither.

Then he turned quite yellow; for the tide was up to his waist, and still the lobster held on.

Then he thought over all the naughty things he ever had done; all the sand which he had put in the sugar, and the sloe-leaves in the tea, and the water in the treacle, and the salt in the tobacco (because his brother was a brewer, and a man must help his own kin).

Then he turned quite blue; for the tide was up to his breast, and still the lobster held on.

Then, I have no doubt, he repented fully of all the said naughty things which he had done, and promised to mend his life, as too many do when they think they have no life to mend. Whereby, as they fancy, they make a very cheap bargain. But the old fairy with the birch rod soon undeceives them.

And then he grew all colours at once, and turned up his eyes like a duck in thunder; for the water was up to his chin, and still the lobster held on.

And then came a man-of-war's boat round the Mewstone, and saw his head sticking up out of the water. One said it was a keg of brandy, and another that it was a cocoanut, and another that it was a buoy loose, and another that it was a black diver, and wanted to fire at it, which would not have been pleasant for the mayor: but just then such a yell came out of a great hole in the middle of it that the midshipman in charge guessed what it was, and bade pull up to it as fast as they could. So somehow or other the Jack- tars got the lobster out, and set the mayor free, and put him ashore at the Barbican. He never went lobster-catching again; and we will hope he put no more salt in the tobacco, not even to sell his brother's beer.

And that is the story of the Mayor of Plymouth, which has two advantages – first, that of being quite true; and second, that of having (as folks say all good stories ought to have) no moral whatsoever: no more, indeed, has any part of this book, because it is a fairy tale, you know.

And now happened to Tom a most wonderful thing; for he had not left the lobster five minutes before he came upon a water baby.

A real live water baby, sitting on the white sand, very busy about a little point of rock. And when it saw Tom it looked up for a moment, and then cried, "Why, you are not one of us. You are a new baby! Oh, how delightful!"

And it ran to Tom, and Tom ran to it, and they hugged and kissed each other for ever so long, they did not know why. But they did not want any introductions there under the water.

At last Tom said, "Oh, where have you been all this while? I have been looking for you so long, and I have been so lonely."

"We have been here for days and days. There are hundreds of us about the rocks. How was it you did not see us, or hear us when we sing and romp every evening before we go home?"

Tom looked at the baby again, and then he said:

"Well, this is wonderful! I have seen things just like you again and again, but I thought you were shells, or sea-creatures. I never took you for water babies like myself."

Now, was not that very odd? So odd, indeed, that you will, no doubt, want to know how it happened, and why Tom could never find a water baby till after he had got the lobster out of the pot. And, if you will read this story nine times over, and then think for yourself, you will find out why. It is not good for little boys to be told everything, and never to be forced to use their own wits. They would learn, then, no more than they do at Dr. Dulcimer's famous suburban establishment for the idler members of the youthful aristocracy, where the masters learn the lessons, and the boys hear them – which saves a great deal of trouble – for the time being.

"Now," said the baby, "come and help me, or I shall not have finished before my brothers and sisters come, and it is time to go home."

"What shall I help you at?"

"At this poor dear little rock; a great clumsy boulder came rolling by in the last storm, and knocked all its head off, and rubbed off all its flowers. And now I must plant it again with sea-weeds, and coral-line, and anemones, and I will make it the prettiest little rock-garden on all the shore."

So they worked away at the rock, and planted it, and smoothed the sand down round it, and capital fun they had till the tide began to turn. And then Tom heard all the other babies coming, laughing and singing and shouting and romping; and the noise they made was just like the noise of the ripple. So he knew that he had been hearing and seeing the water babies all along; only he did not know them, because his eyes and ears were not opened.

And in they came, dozens and dozens of them, some bigger than Tom and some smaller, all in the neatest little white bathing-dresses; and when they found that he was a new baby they hugged him and kissed him, and then put him in the middle and danced round him on the sand, and there was no one ever so happy as poor little Tom.

"Now, then," they cried all at once, "we must come away home, we must come away home, or the tide will leave us dry. We have mended all the broken seaweed, and put all the rock pools in order, and planted all the shells again in the sand, and nobody will see where the ugly storm swept in last week."

And this is the reason why the rock pools are always so neat and clean; because the water babies come in shore after every storm, to sweep them out, and comb them down, and put them all to rights again.

Only where men are wasteful and dirty, and let sewers run into the sea, instead of putting the stuff upon the fields like thrifty reasonable souls; or throw herrings' heads, and dead dog-fish, or any other refuse, into the water; or in any way make a mess upon the clean shore, there the water babies will not come, sometimes not for hundreds of years (for they cannot abide anything smelly or foul): but leave the sea-anemones and the crabs to clear away everything till the good, tidy sea has covered up all the dirt in soft mud and clean sand, where the water babies can plant live cockles and whelks and razor shells and sea-cucumbers and golden-combs, and make a pretty live garden again, after man's dirt is cleared away. And that, I suppose, is the reason why there are no water-babies at any watering place which I have ever seen.

And where is the home of the water babies? In St. Brandan's fairy isle.

Did you never hear of the blessed St. Brandan, how he preached to the wild Irish, on the wild, wild Kerry coast; he and five other hermits, till they were weary, and longed to rest? For the wild Irish would not listen to them, or come to confession and to mass, but liked better to brew potheen, and dance the pater o'pee, and knock each other over the head with shillelaghs, and shoot each from behind turf-dykes, and steal each other's cattle, and burn each other's homes; till St. Brandan and his friends were weary of them, for they would not learn to be peaceable Christians at all.

So St. Brandan went out to the point of old Dunmore, and looked over the tideway roaring round the Blasquets, at the end of all the world, and away into the ocean, and sighed – "Ah, that I had wings as a dove!" And far away, before the setting sun, he saw a blue fairy sea, and golden fairy islands, and he said, "Those are the islands of the blest." Then he and his friends got into a hooker, and sailed away and away to the westward, and were never heard of more. But the people who would not hear him were changed into gorillas, and gorillas they are until this day.

And when St. Brandan and the hermits came to that fairy isle, they found it overgrown with cedars, and full of beautiful birds; and he sat down under the cedars, and preached to all the birds in the air. And they liked his sermons so well that they told the fishes in the sea; and they came, and St. Brandan preached to them; and the fishes told the water babies, who live in the caves under the isle; and they came up by hundreds every Sunday, and St. Brandan got quite a neat little Sunday school. And there he taught the water babies for a great many hundred years, till his eyes grew too dim to see, and his beard grew so long that he dared not walk for fear of treading on it, and then he might have tumbled down. And at last he and the five hermits fell fast asleep under the cedar shades, and there they sleep unto this day. But the fairies took to the water babies, and taught them their lessons themselves.

And some say that St. Brandan will awake, and begin to teach the babies once more: but some think that he will sleep on, for better for worse, till the coming of the Cocqcigrues. But, on still, clear summer evenings, when the sun sinks down into the sea, among golden cloud-capes and cloud-islands, and lochs and friths of azure sky, the sailors fancy that they see, away to westward, St. Brandan's fairy isle.

But whether men can see it or not, St. Brandan's Isle once actually stood there; a great land out in the ocean, which has sunk and sunk beneath the waves. Old Plato called it Atlantis, and told strange tales of the wise men who lived therein, and of the wars they fought in the old times. And from off that island came strange flowers, which linger still about this land: the Cornish heath, and Cornish moneywort, and the delicate Venus's hair, and the London-pride which covers the Kerry mountains, and the little pink butterwort of Devon, and the great blue butterwort of Ireland, and the Connemara heath, and the bristle-fern of the Turk waterfall, and many a strange plant more; all fairy tokens left for wise men and good children from off St. Brandan's Isle.

Now when Tom got there, he found that the isle stood all on pillars, and that its roots were full of caves. There will pillars of black basalt, like Staffa; and pillars of green and crimson serpentine, like Kynance; and pillars ribboned with red and white and yellow sandstone, like Livermead; and there were blue grottoes, like Capri; and white grottoes, like Adelsberg; all curtained and draped with sea-weeds, purple and crimson, green and brown; and strewn with soft white sand, on which the water babies sleep every night. But, to keep the place clean and sweet, the crabs picked up all the scraps off the floor, and ate them like so many monkeys; while the rocks were covered with ten thousand sea anemones, and corals and madrepores, who scavenged the water all day long, and kept it nice and pure. But, to make up to them for having to do such nasty work, they were not left black and dirty, as poor chimney-sweeps and dustmen are. No; the fairies are more considerate and just than that; and have dressed them all in the most beautiful colours and patterns, till they look like vast flower-beds of gay blossoms. If you think I am talking nonsense, I can only say that it is true; and that an old gentleman named Fourier used to say that we ought to do the same by chimney-sweeps and dustmen, and honour them instead of despising them; and he was a very clever old gentleman: but, unfortunately for him and the world, as mad as a March hare.

And, instead of watchmen and policemen to keep out nasty things at night, there were thousands and thousands of water-snakes, and most wonderful creatures they were. They were all named after the Nereids, the sea-fairies who took care of them, Eunice and Polynoe, Phyllodoce and Psamathe, and all the rest of the pretty darlings who swim round their Queen Amphitrite, and her car of cameo shell. They were dressed in green velvet, and black velvet, and purple velvet; and were all jointed in rings; and some of them had three hundred brains apiece, so that they must have been uncommonly shrewd detectives; and some had eyes in their tails; and some had eyes in every joint, so that they kept a very sharp lookout; and when they wanted a baby-snake, they just grew one at the end of their own tails, and when it was able to take care of itself it dropped off; so that they brought up their families very cheaply. But if any nasty thing came by, out they rushed upon it; and then out of each of their hundreds of feet there sprang a whole cutler's shop of

Scythes,	Javelins,
Billhooks,	Lances,
Pickaxes,	Halberts,
Forks,	Gisarines,
Penknives,	Poleaxes,
Rapiers,	Fishhooks,
Sabres,	Bradawls,
Yataghans,	Gimblets,
Cresses,	Corkscrews,
Ghoorka swords,	Pins,
Tucks,	Needles,

And so forth,

which stabbed, shot, poked, pricked, scratched, ripped, pinked, and crimped those naughty beasts so terribly, that they had to run for their lives, or else be chopped into small pieces and be eaten afterwards. And, if that is not all, every word, true, then there is no faith in microscopes, and all is over with the Linnaean Society.

And there were the water babies in thousands, more than Tom, or you either, could count. All the little children whom the good fairies take to, because their cruel mothers and fathers will not; all who are untaught and brought up heathens, and all who come to grief by ill-usage or ignorance or neglect; all the little children who are overlaid, or given gin when they are young, or are let to drink out of hot kettles, or to fall into the fire; all the little children in alleys and courts, and tumble-down cottages, who die by fever, and cholera, and measles, and scarlatina, and nasty complaints which no one has any business to have, and which no one will have some day, when folks have common sense; and all the little children who have been killed by cruel masters, and wicked soldiers; they were all there, except, of course, the babes of Bethlehem who were killed by wicked King Herod; for they were taken straight to heaven long ago, as everybody knows, and we call them the Holy Innocents.

But I wish Tom had given up all his naughty tricks, and left off tormenting dumb animals, now that he had plenty of play-fellows to amuse him. Instead of that, I am sorry to say, he would meddle with the creatures, all but the water-snakes, for they would stand no nonsense. So he tickled the madrepores, to make them shut up; and frightened the crabs, to make them hide in the sand and peep out at him with the tips of their eyes; and put stones into the anemones' mouths to make them fancy that their dinner was coming.

The other children warned him, and said, "Take care what you are at. Mrs. Bedonebyasyoudid is coming." But Tom never heeded them, being quite riotous with high spirits and good luck, till, one Friday morning early, Mrs. Bedonebyasyoudid came indeed.

A very tremendous lady she was; and when the children saw her, they all stood in a row, very upright indeed, and smoothed down their bathing-dresses, and put their hands behind them, just as if they were going to be examined by the inspector.

And she had on a black bonnet, and a black shawl, and no crinoline at all; and a pair of large green spectacles, and a great hooked nose, hooked so much that the bridge of it stood quite up above her eyebrows; and under her arm she carried a great birch-rod. Indeed, she was so ugly, that Tom was tempted to make faces at her: but did not; for he did not admire the look of the birch-rod under her arm.

And she looked at the children one by one, and seemed very much pleased with them, though she never asked them one question about how

they were behaving; and then began giving them all sorts of nice sea-things
– sea-cakes, sea-apples, sea-oranges, sea-bull'seyes, sea-toffee; and to the
very best of all she gave sea-ices, made out of sea-cows' cream, which never
melt under water.

And, if you don't quite believe me, then just think – What is more
cheap and plentiful than sea-rock? Then why should there not be sea-toffee
as well? And every one can find sea-lemons (ready quartered too) if they will
look for them at low tide; and sea-grapes too sometimes, hanging in
bunches; and, if you will go to Nice, you will find the fish-market full of
sea-fruit, which they call "frutta di mare"; though I suppose they call them
"fruits de mer" now, out of compliment to that most successful, and
therefore most immaculate, potentate who is seemingly desirous of
inheriting the blessing pronounced on those who remove their neighbours'
landmark. And, perhaps, that is the very reason why the place is called
Nice, because there are so many nice things in the sea there: at least, if it is
not, it ought to be.

Now little Tom watched all these sweet things given away, till his
mouth watered, and his eyes grew as round as an owl's. For he hoped that
his turn would come at last; and so it did. For the lady called him up, and
held out her fingers with something in them, and popped it into his mouth;
and, lo and behold! it was a nasty cold, hard pebble.

"You are a very cruel woman," said he, and began to whimper.

"And you are a very cruel boy; who puts pebbles into the sea-
anemones' mouths, to take them in, and make them fancy that they had
caught a good dinner. As you did to them, so I must do to you."

"Who told you that?" said Tom."

"You did yourself, this very minute."

Tom had never opened his lips; so he was very much taken aback
indeed.

"Yes; every one tells me exactly what they have done wrong; and that
without knowing it themselves. So there is no use trying to hide anything
from me. Now go, and be a good boy, and I will put no more pebbles in
your mouth, if you put none in other creatures."

"I did not know there was any harm in it," said Tom.

"Then you know now. People continually say that to me: but I tell
them, if you don't know that fire burns, that is no reason that it should not

burn you; and if you don't know that dirt breeds fever, that is no reason why the fevers should not kill you. The lobster did not know that there was any harm in getting into the lobster pot; but it caught him all the same."

"Dear me," thought Tom, "she knows everything!" And so she did, indeed.

"And so, if you do not know that things are wrong, that is no reason why you should not be punished for them; though not as much, not as much, my little man" (and the lady looked very kindly, after all), "as if you did know."

"Well, you are a little hard on a poor lad," said Tom.

"Not at all; I am the best friend you ever had in all your life. But I will tell you; I cannot help punishing people when they do wrong. I like it no more than they do; I am often very, very sorry for them, poor things: but I cannot help it. If I tried not to do it, I should do it all the same. For I work by machinery, just like an engine; and am full of wheels and springs inside; and am wound up very carefully, so that I cannot help going."

"Was it long ago since they would you up?" asked Tom. For he thought, the cunning little fellow, "She will run down some day: or they may forget to wind her up, as old Grimes used to forget to wind up his watch when he came in from the public-house; and then I shall be safe."

"I was wound up once and for all, so long ago that I forget all about it."

"Dear me," said Tom, "you must have been made a long time!"

"I never was made, my child; and I shall go for ever and ever; for I am as old as Eternity, and yet as young as Time."

And there came over the lady's face a very curious expression – very solemn, and very sad; and yet very, very sweet. And she looked up and away, as if she were gazing through the sea, and through the sky, at something far, far off; and as she did so, there came such a quiet, tender, patient, hopeful smile over her face, that Tom thought for the moment that she did not look ugly at all. And no more she did; for she was like a great many people who have not a pretty feature in their faces, and yet are lovely to behold, and draw little children's hearts to them at once; because, though the house is plain enough, yet from the windows a beautiful and good spirit is looking forth.

And Tom smiled in her face, she looked so pleasant for the moment. And the strange fairy smiled too, and said:

"Yes. You thought me very ugly just now, did you not?"

Tom hung down his head, and got very red about the ears.

"And I am very ugly. I am the ugliest fairy in the world; and I shall be, till people behave themselves as they ought to do. And then I shall grow as handsome as my sister, who is the loveliest fairy in the world; and her name is Mrs. Doasyouwouldbedoneby. So she begins where I end, and I begin where she ends; and those who will not listen to her must listen to me, as you will see. Now, all of you run away, except Tom; and he may stay and see what I am going to do. It will be a very good warning for him to begin with, before he goes to school.

"Now, Tom, every Friday I come down here and call up all who have ill-used little children, and serve them as they served the children."

And at that Tom was frightened, and crept under a stone; which made the two crabs who lived there very angry, and frightened their friend the butter-fish into flapping hysterics: but he would not move for them.

And first she called up all the doctors who give little children so much physic (they were most of them old ones; for the young ones have learned better, all but a few army surgeons, who still fancy that a baby's inside is much like a Scotch grenadier's), and she set them all in a row; and very rueful they looked; for they knew what was coming.

And first she pulled all their teeth out; and then she bled them all round; and then she dosed them with calomel, and jalap, and salts and senna, and brimstone and treacle; and horrible faces they made; and then she gave them a great emetic of mustard and water, and no basons; and began all over again; and that was the way she spent the morning.

And then she called up a whole troop of foolish ladies, who pinch up their children's waists and toes; and she laced them all up in tight stays, so that they were choked and sick, and their noses grew red, and their hands and feet swelled; and then she crammed their poor feet into the most dreadfully tight boots, and made them all dance, which they did most clumsily indeed; and then she asked them how they liked it; and when they said not at all, she let them go: because they had only done it out of foolish fashion, fancying it was for their children's good, as if wasps' waists and pigs' toes could be pretty, or wholesome, or of any use to anybody.

Then she called up all the careless nurserymaids, and stuck pins into them all over, and wheeled them about in perambulators with tight straps across their stomachs and their heads and arms hanging over the side, till they were quite sick and stupid, and would have had sun-strokes: but, being under the water, they could only have water-strokes; which, I assure you, are nearly as bad, as you will find if you try to sit under a mill wheel. And mind – when you hear a rumbling at the bottom of the sea, sailors will tell you that it is a ground-swell: but now you know better. It is the old lady wheeling the maids about in perambulators.

And by that time she was so tired, she had to go to luncheon.

And after luncheon she set to work again, and called up all the cruel schoolmasters – whole regiments and brigades of them; and, when she saw them, she frowned most terribly, and set to work in earnest, as if the best part of the day's work was to come. More than half of them were nasty, dirty, frowzy, grubby, smelly old monks, who, because they dare not hit a man of their own size, amused themselves with beating little children instead; as you may see in the picture of old Pope Gregory (good man and true though he was, when he meddled with things which he did understand), teaching children to sing their fa-fa-mi-fa with a cat-o'-nine tails under his chair: but, because they never had any children of their own, they took into their heads (as some folks do still) that they were the only people in the world who knew how to manage children; and they first brought into England, in the old Anglo-Saxon times, the fashion of treating free boys, and girls too, worse than you would treat a dog or a horse: but Mrs. Bedonebyasyoudid has caught them all long ago; and given them many a taste of their own rods; and much good may it do them.

And she boxed their ears, and thumped them over the head with rulers, and pandied their hands with canes, and told them that they told stories, and were this and that bad sort of people; and the more they were very indignant, and stood upon their honour, and declared they told the truth, the more she declared they were not, and that they were only telling lies; and at last she birched them all round soundly with her great birch-rod, and set them each an imposition of three hundred thousand lines of Hebrew to learn by heart before she came back next Friday. And at that they all cried and howled so, that their breaths came all up through the sea like bubbles out of soda-water; and that is one reason of the bubbles in the sea. There are others: but that is the one which principally concerns little boys. And by that time she was so tired that she was glad to stop; and, indeed, she had done a very good day's work.

Tom did not quite dislike the old lady: but he could not help thinking her a little spiteful – and no wonder if she was, poor old soul; for, if she has to wait to grow handsome till people do as they would be done by, she will have to wait a very long time.

Poor old Mrs. Bedonebyasyoudid! she has a great deal of hard work before her, and had better have been born a washerwoman, and stood over a tub all day; but, you see, people cannot always choose their own profession.

But Tom longed to ask her one question; and after all, whenever she looked at him, she did not look cross at all; and now and then there was a funny smile in her face, and she chuckled to herself in a way which gave Tom courage, and at last he said:

"Pray, ma'am, may I ask you a question?"

"Certainly, my little dear."

"Why don't you bring all the bad masters here, and serve them out too? The butties that knock about the poor collier-boys; and the nailers that file off their lads' noses and hammer their fingers; and all the master sweeps, like my master Grimes? I saw him fall into the water long ago; so I surely expected he would have been here. I'm sure he was bad enough to me."

Then the old lady looked so very stern that Tom was quite frightened, and sorry that he had been so bold. But she was not angry with him. She only answered, "I look after them all the week round; and they are in a very different place from this, because they knew that they were doing wrong."

She spoke very quietly; but there was something in her voice which made Tom tingle from head to foot, as if he had got into a shoal of sea-nettles.

"But these people," she went on, "did not know that they were doing wrong: they were only stupid and impatient; and therefore I only punish them till they become patient, and learn to use their common sense like reasonable beings. But as for chimney-sweeps, and collier-boys, and nailer lads, my sister has set good people to stop all that sort of thing; and very much obliged to her I am; for if she could only stop the cruel masters from ill-using poor children, I should grow handsome at least a thousand years sooner. And now do you be a good boy, and do as you would be done by, which they did not; and then, when my sister, Madame Doasyouwouldbedoneby, comes on Sunday, perhaps she will take notice of you, and teach you how to behave. She understands that better than I do." And so she went.

Tom was very glad to hear that there was no chance of meeting Grimes again, though he was a little sorry for him, considering that he used sometimes to give him the leavings of the beer: but he determined to be a very good boy all Saturday; and he was; for he never frightened one crab, nor tickled any live corals, nor put stones into the sea-anemones' mouths, to make then fancy they had got a dinner; and, when Sunday morning came, sure enough, Mrs. Doasyouwouldbedoneby came too. Whereat all the little children began dancing and clapping their hands, and Tom danced too with all his might.

And as for the pretty lady, I cannot tell you what the colour of her hair was, or of her eyes: no more could Tom; for, when any one looks at her, all they can think of is, that she has the sweetest, kindest, tenderest, funniest, merriest face they ever saw, or want to see. But Tom saw that she was a very tall woman, as tall as her sister: but instead of being gnarly, and horny, and scaly, and prickly, like her, she was the most nice, soft, fat, smooth, pussy, cuddly, delicious creature who ever nursed a baby; and she understood babies thoroughly, for she had plenty of her own, whole rows and regiments of them, and has to this day. And all her delight was, whenever she had a spare moment, to play with babies, in which she showed herself a woman of sense; for babies are the best company, and the pleasantest playfellows, in the world; at least, so all the wise people in the world think. And therefore when the children saw her, they naturally all caught hold of her, and pulled her till she sat down on a stone, and climbed into her lap, and clung round her neck, and caught hold of her hands; and then they all put their thumbs into their mouths, and began cuddling and purring like so many kittens, as they ought to have done. While those who could get nowhere else sat down on the sand, and cuddled her feet - for no one, you know, wears shoes in the water, except horrid old bathing women, who are afraid of the water babies pinching their horny toes. And Tom stood staring at them; for he could not understand what it was all about.

"And who are you, you little darling?" she said.

"Oh, that is the new baby!" they all cried, pulling their thumbs out of their mouths; "and he never had any mother," and they all put their thumbs back again, for they did not wish to lose any time.

"Then I will be his mother, and he shall have the very best place; so get out all of you, this moment."

And she took up two great armfuls of babies – nine hundred under one arm, and thirteen hundred under the other – and threw them away, right and left, into the water. But they minded it no more than the naughty boys in Struwwelpeter minded when St. Nicholas dipped them in his inkstand; and did not even take their thumbs out of their mouths, but came paddling and wriggling back to her like so many tadpoles, till you could see nothing of her from head to foot for the swarm of little babies.

But she took Tom in her arms, and laid him in the softest place of all, and kissed him, and patted him, and talked to him, tenderly and low, such things as he had never heard before in his life; and Tom looked up into her eyes, and loved her, and loved, till he fell fast asleep from pure love.

And when he woke, she was telling the children a story. And what story did she tell them? One story she told them which begins every Christmas Eve, and yet never ends at all for ever and ever; and, as she went on, the children took their thumbs out of their mouths, and listened quite seriously; but not sadly at all; for she never told them anything sad; and Tom listened too, and never grew tired of listening. And he listened so long that he fell fast asleep again, and, when he woke, the lady was nursing him still.

"Don't go away," said little Tom. "This is so nice. I never had any one to cuddle me before."

"Don't go away," said all the children; "you have not sung us one song."

"Well, I have time for only one. So what shall it be?"

"The doll you lost! The doll you lost!" cried all the babies at once.

So the strange fairy sang:-

> *I once had a sweet little doll, dears,*
>   *The prettiest doll in the world;*
> *Her cheeks were so red and so white, dears,*
>   *And her hair was so charmingly curled.*
> *But I lost my poor little doll, dears,*
>   *As I played in the heath one day;*
> *And I cried for her more than a week, dears;*
>   *But I never could find where she lay.*
>
> *I found my poor little doll, dears,*
>   *As I played in the heath one day:*
> *Folks say she is terribly changed, dears,*
>   *For her paint is all washed away,*
> *And her arm trodden off by the cows, dears,*
>   *And her hair not the least bit curled:*
> *Yet for old sakes' sake she is still, dears,*
>   *The prettiest doll in the world.*

What a silly song for a fairy to sing!

And what silly water babies to be quite delighted at it!

Well, but you see they have not the advantage of Aunt Agitate's Arguments in the sea-land down below.

"Now," said the fairy to Tom, "will you be a good boy for my sake, and torment no more sea-beasts, till I come back?"

"And you will cuddle me again?" said poor little Tom.

"Of course I will, you little duck. I should like to take you with me, and cuddle you all the way, only I must not"; and away she went.

So Tom really tried to be a good boy, and tormented no sea-beasts after that, as long as he lived; and he is quite alive, I assure you, still.

Oh, how good little boys ought to be, who have kind pussy mammas to cuddle them and tell them stories; and how afraid they ought to be of growing naughty, and bringing tears into their mammas' pretty eyes!

CHAPTER SIX

Thou little child, yet glorious in the might
*   Of heaven-born freedom on thy Being's height,*
Why with such earnest pains dost thou provoke
*   The Years to bring the inevitable yoke —*
Thus blindly with thy blessedness at strife?
*   Full soon thy soul shall have her earthly freight,*
And custom lie upon thee with a weight
*   Heavy as frost, and deep almost as life.*

Wordsworth

*They hugged and kissed each other for ever so long,
they did not know why. (Chapter 5)*

Mrs. Bedonebyasyoudid. (Chapter 6)

Chapter Six

~

Here I come to the very saddest part of all my story. I know some people will only laugh at it, and call it much ado about nothing. But I know one man who would not; and he was an officer with a pair of gray moustaches as long as your arm, who said once in company, that two of the most heart-rendering sights in the world, which moved him most to tears, which he would do anything to prevent or remedy, were a child over a broken toy, and a child stealing sweets.

The company did not laugh at him; his moustaches were too long and too gray for that: but, after he was gone, they called him sentimental and so forth, all but one dear little old quaker lady with a soul as white as her cap, who was not, of course, generally partial to soldiers; and she said very quietly, like a quaker:

"Friends, it is borne upon my mind that that is a truely brave man."

Now you may fancy that Tom was quite good, when he had everything that he could want or wish: but you would be very much

129

mistaken. Being quite comfortable is a very good thing; but it does not make people good. Indeed, it sometimes makes them naughty, as it has made the people in America; and as it made the people in the Bible, who waxed fat and kicked, like horses overfed and underworked. And I am very sorry to say that this happened to little Tom. For he grew so fond of the sea-bull'seyes and sea-lollipops, that his foolish little head could think of nothing else: and he was always longing for more, and wondering when the strange lady would come again and give him some, and what she would give him, and how much, and whether she would give him more than the others. And he thought of nothing but lollipops by day, and dreamt of nothing else by night – and what happened then?

That he began to watch the lady to see where she kept the sweet things; and began hiding, and sneaking, and following her about, and pretending to be looking the other way, or going after something else, till he found out that she kept them in a beautiful mother-of-pearl cabinet, away in a deep crack of the rocks.

And he longed to go the cabinet, and yet he was afraid; and then he longed again, and was less afraid; and at last, by continual thinking about it, he longed so violently, that he was not afraid at all. And one night, when all the other children were asleep, and he could not sleep for thinking of lollipops, he crept away among the rocks, and got to the cabinet, and behold! it was open.

But, when he saw all the nice things inside, instead of being delighted, he was quite frightened, and wished he had never come there. And then he would only touch them, and he did; and then he would only taste one, and he did; and then he would only eat one, and he did; and then he would only eat two, and then three, and so on; and then he was terrified lest she should come and catch him, and began gobbling them down so fast that he did not taste them, or have any pleasure in them; and then he felt sick, and would have only one more; and then only one more again; and so on till he had eaten them all up.

And all the while, close behind him, stood Mrs. Bedonebyasyoudid.

Some people may say, But why did she not keep her cupboard locked? Well, I know. It may seem a very strange thing, but she never does keep her cupboard locked; every one may go and taste for themselves, and fare accordingly. It is very odd, but so it is; and I am quite sure that she knows best. Perhaps she wishes people to keep their fingers out of the fire, by having them burned.

She took off her spectacles, because she did not like to see too much; and in her pity she arched up her eyebrows into her very hair, and her eyes grew so wide that they would have taken in all the sorrows of the world, and filled with great big tears, as they too often do.

But all she said was:

"Ah, you poor little dear! you are just like all the rest."

But she said it to herself, and Tom neither heard nor saw her. Now, you must not fancy that she was sentimental at all. If you do, and think that she is going to let off you, or me, or any human being when we do wrong, because she is too tender-hearted to punish us, then you will find yourself very much mistaken, as many a man does every year and every day.

But what did the strange fairy do when she saw all her lollipops eaten?

Did she fly at Tom, catch him by the scruff of the neck, hold him, howk him, hump him, hurry him, hit him, poke him, pull him, pinch him, pound him, put him in the corner, shake him, slap him, set him on a cold stone to reconsider himself, and so forth?

Not a bit. You may watch her at work, if you know where to find her. But you will never see her do that. For, if she had, she knew quite well Tom would have fought, and kicked, and bit, and said bad words, and turned again that moment into a naughty little heathen chimney-sweep, with his hand, like Ishmael's of old, against every man and every man's hand against him.

Did she question him, hurry him, frighten him, threaten him, to make him confess? Not a bit. You may see her, as I said, at her work often enough, if you know where to look for her; but you will never see her do that. For if she had, she would have tempted him to tell lies in his fright; and that would have been worse for him, if possible, than even becoming a heathen chimney-sweep again.

No. She leaves that for anxious parents and teachers (lazy ones, some call them), who, instead of giving children a fair trial, such as they would expect and demand for themselves, force them by fright to confess their own faults — which is so cruel and unfair, that no judge on the bench dare do it to the wickedest thief or murderer, for the good British law forbids it

— ay, and even punish them to make them confess, which is so detestable a crime, that it is never committed now, save by Inquisitors, and Kings of Naples, and a few other wretched people of whom the world is weary. And then they say, "We have trained up the child in the way he should go, and when he grew up he has departed from it. Why, then, did Solomon say that he would not depart from it?" But perhaps the way of beating, and hurrying, and frightening, and questioning, was not the way that the child should go; for it is not even the way in which a colt should go, if you want to break it in, and make it a quiet, serviceable horse.

Some folks may say, "Ah! but the fairy does not need to do that, if she knows everything already." True. But if she did not know, she would not surely behave worse than a British judge and jury; and no more should parents and teachers either.

So she said nothing at all about the matter, not even when Tom came next day with the rest for sweet things. He was horribly afraid of coming; but he was still more afraid of staying away, lest any one should suspect him. He was dreadfully afraid, to, lest there should be no sweets — as was to be expected, he having eaten them all — and lest then the fairy should inquire who had taken them. But, behold! she pulled out just as many as ever, which astonished Tom, and frightened him still more.

And, when the fairy looked him full in the face, he shook from head to foot: however, she gave him his share like the rest, and he thought within himself that she could not have found him out.

But, when he put the sweets into his mouth, he hated the taste of them; and they made him so sick, that he had to get away as fast as he could; and terribly sick he was, and very cross and unhappy, all the week after.

Then, when the next week came, he had his share again; and again the fairy looked him full in the face; but more sadly than she had ever looked. And he could not bear the sweets, but took them again in spite of himself.

And, when Mrs. Doasyouwouldbedoneby came, he wanted to be cuddled like the rest; but she said very seriously:

"I should like to cuddle you; but I cannot, you are so horny and prickly."

And Tom looked at himself: and he was all over prickles, just like a sea-egg.

Which was quite natural; for you must know and believe that people's souls make their bodies, just as a snail makes its shell (I am not joking, my little man; I am in serious, solemn earnest). And, therefore, when Tom's soul grew all prickly with naughty tempers, his body could not help growing prickly to, so that nobody would cuddle him, or play with him, or even like to look at him.

What could Tom do now, but go away and hide in a corner, and cry? For nobody would play with him, and he knew full well why.

And he was so miserable all that week that, when the ugly fairy came, and looked at him once more full in the face, more seriously and sadly than ever, he could stand it no longer, and thrust the sweetmeats away, saying, "No, I don't want any; I can't bear them now," and then burst out crying, poor little man, and told Mrs. Bedonebyasyoudid every word as it happened.

He was horribly frightened when he had done so; for he expected her to punish him very severely. But, instead, she only took him up and kissed him, which was not quite pleasant, for her chin was very bristly indeed; but he was so lonely-hearted, he thought that rough kissing was better than none.

"I will forgive you, little man," she said. "I always forgive every one the moment they tell me the truth of their own accord."

"Then you will take away all these nasty prickles?"

"That is a very different matter. You put them there yourself, and only you can take them away."

"But how can I do that?" asked Tom, crying afresh.

"Well, I think it is time for you to go to school; so I shall fetch you a schoolmistress, who will teach you how to get rid of your prickles." And so she went away.

Tom was frightened at the notion of a schoolmistress; for he thought she would certainly come with a birch-rod or a cane; but he comforted himself, at last, that she might be something like the old woman in Vendale - which she was not in the least; for, when the fairy brought her, she was the most beautiful little girl that ever was seen, with long curls floating behind her like a golden cloud, and long robes floating all round her like a silver one.

"There he is," said the fairy; "and you must teach him to be good, whether you like or not."

"I know," said the little girl; but she did not seem quite to like, for she put her finger in her mouth, and looked at Tom under her brows; and Tom put his finger in his mouth, and looked at her under his brows, for he was horribly ashamed of himself.

The little girl seemed hardly to know how to begin; and perhaps she would never have begun at all, if poor Tom had not burst out crying, and begged her to teach him to be good, and help him to cure his prickles; and at that she grew so tender-hearted, that she began teaching him as prettily as ever child was taught in the world.

And what did the little girl teach Tom? She taught him, first, what you have been taught ever since you said your first prayers at your mother's knees; but she taught him much more simply. For the lessons in that world, my child, have no such hard words in them as the lessons in this, and therefore the water babies like them better than you like your lessons, and long to learn them more and more; and grown men cannot puzzle nor quarrel over their meaning, as they do here on land; for those lessons all rise clear and pure, like the Test out of Overton Pool, out of the everlasting ground of all life and truth.

So she taught Tom every day in the week; only on Sundays she always went away home, and the kind fairy took her place. And, before she had taught Tom many Sundays, his prickles had vanished quite away, and his skin was smooth and clean again.

"Dear me!" said the little girl; "why, I know you now. You are the very same little chimney-sweep who came into my bedroom."

"Dear me!" cried Tom. "And I know you, too, now. You are the very little white lady whom I saw in bed." And he jumped at her, and longed to hug and kiss her; but did not, remembering that she was a lady born; so he only jumped round and round her, till he was quite tired.

And then they began telling each other all their story – how he had got into the water, and she had fallen over the rock; and how he had swam down to the sea, and how she had flown out of the window; and how this, that, and the other, till it was all talked out: and then they both began over again, and I can't say which of the two talked fastest.

And then they set to work at their lessons again, and both liked them so well, that they went on well till seven full years were past and gone.

You may fancy that Tom was quite content and happy all those seven years; but the truth is, he was not. He had always one thing on his mind, and that was – where little Ellie went, when she went home on Sundays.

To a very beautiful place, she said.

But what was the beautiful place like, and where was it.

Ah! that is just what she could not say. And it is strange, but true, that no one can say; and that those who have been oftenest in it, or even nearest to it, can say least about it, and make people understand least what it is like. There are a good many folks about the Other-end-of-Nowhere (where Tom went afterwards) who pretend to know it from north to south as well as if they had been penny postmen there; but, as they are safe at the Other-end-of-Nowhere, nine hundred and ninety-nine million miles away, what they say cannot concern us.

But the dear, sweet, loving, wise, good, self-sacrificing people, who really go there, can never tell you anything about it, save that it is the most beautiful place in all the world; and, if you ask them more, they grow modest, and hold their peace, for fear of being laughed at; and quite right they are.

So all that good little Ellie could say was, that it was worth all the rest of the world put together. And of course that only made Tom the more anxious to go likewise.

"Miss Ellie," he said, at last, "I will know why I cannot go with you when you go home, on Sundays, or I shall have no peace, and give you none either."

"You must ask the fairies that."

So when the fairy, Mrs. Bedonebyasyoudid, came next, Tom asked her.

"Little boys who are only fit to play with sea-beasts cannot go there," she said. "Those who go there must go first where they do not like, and do what they do not like, and help somebody they do not like."

"Why, did Ellie do that?"

"Ask her"

And Ellie blushed, and said, "Yes, Tom; I did not like coming here at first; I was so much happier at home, where it is always Sunday. And I was afraid of you, Tom, at first, because – because – "

"Because I was all over prickles? But I am not prickly now, am I, Miss Ellie?"

"No," said Ellie. "I like you very much now; and I like coming here, too."

"And perhaps," said the fairy, "you will learn to like going where you don't like, and helping some one that you don't like, as Ellie has."

But Tom put his finger in his mouth, and hung his head down; for he did not see that at all.

So when Mrs. Doasyouwouldbedoneby came, Tom asked her; for he thought in his little head, She is not so strict as her sister, and perhaps she may let me off more easily.

Ah, Tom, Tom, silly fellow! and yet I don't know why I should blame you, while so many grown people have got the very same notion in their heads.

But, when you try it, they get just the same answer as Tom did. For, when he asked the second fairy, she told him just what the first did, and in the very same words.

Tom was very unhappy at that. And, when Ellie went home on Sunday, he fretted and cried all day, and did not care to listen to the fairy's stories about good children, though they were prettier than ever. Indeed, the more he overheard of them, the less he liked to listen, because they were all about children who did what they did not like, and took trouble for other people, and worked to feed their little brothers and sisters, instead of caring only for their play. And, when she began to tell a story about a holy child in old times, who was martyred by the heathen because it would not worship idols, Tom could bear no more, and ran away and hid among the rocks.

And, when Ellie came back, he was shy with her, because he fancied she looked down on him, and thought him a coward. And then he grew quite cross with her, because she was superior to him, and did what he could not do. And poor Ellie was quite surprised and sad; and at last Tom burst out crying; but he would not tell her what was really in his mind.

And all the while he was eaten up with curiosity to know where Ellie went to; so that he began not to care for his playmates, or for the sea-palace, or anything else. But perhaps that made matters all the easier for him; for he grew so discontented with everything round him, that he did not care to stay, and did not care where he went.

"Well," he said, at last, "I am so miserable here, I'll go; if only you will go with me?"

"Ah!" said Ellie, "I wish I might; but the worst of it is, that the fairy says that you must go alone, if you go at all. Now don't poke that poor crab about, Tom" (for he was feeling very naughty and mischievous), "or the fairy will have to punish you."

Tom was very nearly saying, "I don't care if she does"; but he stopped himself in time.

"I know what she wants me to do," he said, whining most dolefully. "She wants me to go after that horrid old Grimes. I don't like him, that's certain. And if I find him, he will turn me into a chimney-sweep again, I know. That's what I have been afraid of all along."

"No, he won't – I know as much as that. Nobody can turn water babies into sweeps, or hurt them at all, as long as they are good."

"Ah," said naughty Tom, "I see what you want; you are persuading me all along to go, because you are tired of me, and want to get rid of me."

Little Ellie opened her eyes very wide at that, and they were all brimming over with tears.

"Oh, Tom, Tom!" she said, very mournfully; and then she cried, "Oh, Tom! where are you?"

And Tom cried, "Oh, Ellie, where are you?"

For neither of them could see each other – not the least. Little Ellie vanished quite away, and Tom heard her voice calling him, and growing smaller and smaller, and fainter and fainter, till all was silent.

Who was frightened then but Tom? He swam up and down among the rocks, into all the halls and chambers, faster than ever he swam before, but could not find her. He shouted after her, but she did not answer; he asked all the other children, but they had not seen her; and at last he went up to the top of the water and began crying and screaming for Mrs. Doasyouwouldbedoneby, but she did not come. Then he began crying and screaming for Mrs. Bedonebyasyoudid – which perhaps was the best thing to do - for she came in a moment.

"Oh!" said Tom. "Oh, dear, oh, dear! I have been naughty to Ellie, and I have killed her – I know I have killed her."

"Not quite that," said the fairy; "but I have sent her away home, and she will not come back again for I do not know how long."

And at that Tom cried so bitterly, that the salt sea was swelled with his tears, and the tide was .3,954,620,819 of an inch higher than it had been the day before: but perhaps that was owing to the waxing of the moon. It may have been so; but it is considered right in the new philosophy, you know, to give spiritual causes for physical phenomena – especially in parlour tables; and, of course, physical causes for spiritual ones, like thinking, and praying, and knowing right from wrong. And so they odds it till it comes even, as folks say down in Berkshire.

"How cruel of you to send Ellie away!" sobbed Tom. "However, I will find her again, if I go to the world's end to look for her."

The fairy did not slap Tom, and tell him to hold his tongue: but she took him on her lap very kindly, just as her sister would have done; and put him in mind how it was not her fault, because she was wound up inside, like watches, and could not help doing things whether she liked or not. And then she told him how he had been in the nursery long enough, and must go out now and see the world, if he intended ever to be a man; and how he must go all alone by himself, as every one else that ever was born has to go, and see with his own eyes, and smell with his own nose, and make his own bed and lie on it, and burn his own fingers if he put them into the fire. And then she told him how many fine things there were to be seen in the world, and what an odd, curious, pleasant, orderly, respectable, well-managed, and, on the whole, successful (as, indeed, might have been expected) sort of place it was, if people would only be tolerably brave and honest and good in it; and then she told him not to be afraid of anything he met, for nothing would harm him if he remembered all his lessons, and did what he knew was right. And at last she comforted poor little Tom so much, that he was quite eager to go, and wanted to set out that minute.

"Only," he said, "if I might see Ellie once before I went!"

"Why do you want that?"

"Because – because I should be so much happier if I thought she had forgiven me."

And in the twinkling of an eye there stood Ellie, smiling, and looking so happy that Tom longed to kiss her; but was still afraid it would not be respectful, because she was a lady born.

"I am going, Ellie!" said Tom. "I am going, if it is to the world's end. But I don't like going at all, and that's the truth."

"Pooh! pooh! pooh!" said the fairy. "You will like it very well indeed, you little rogue, and you know that at the bottom of your heart. But if you don't, I will make you like it. Come here, and see what happened to people who do only what is pleasant."

And she took out of one of her cupboards (she had all sorts of mysterious cupboards in the cracks of the rocks) the most wonderful waterproof book, full of such photographs as never were seen. For she had found out photography (and this is a fact) more than 13,598,000 years before anybody was born; and, what is more, her photographs did not merely represent light and shade, as ours do, but colour also, and all colours, as you may see if you look at a black cock's tail, or a butterfly's wing, or, indeed, most things that are or can be, so to speak. And, therefore, her photographs were very curious and famous, and the children looked with great delight for the opening of the book.

And on the title-page was written, "The History of the great and famous nation of the Doasyoulikes, who came away from the country of Hardwork, because they wanted to play on the Jews'-harp all day long."

In the first picture they saw these Doasyoulikes living in the land of Readymade, at the foot of the Happygolucky Mountains, where flapdoodle grows wild; and if you want to know what that is, you must read "Peter Simple."

They lived very much such a life as those jolly old Greeks in Sicily, whom you may see painted on the ancient vases; and really there seemed to be great excuses for them, for they had no need to work.

Instead of houses, they lived in the beautiful caves of tufa, and bathed in the warm springs three times a day; and, as for clothes, it was so warm there that the gentlemen walked about in little besides a cocked hat and a pair of straps, or some light summer tackle of that kind; and the ladies all gathered gossamer in autumn (when they were not too lazy) to make their winter dresses.

They were very fond of music, but it was too much trouble to learn the piano or the violin; and, as for dancing, that would have been too great an exertion. So they sat on ant-hills all day long, and played on the Jews'-harp; and, if the ants bit them, why, they just got up and went to the next ant-hill, till they were bitten there likewise.

And they sat under the flapdoodle-trees, and let the flapdoodle drop into their mouths; and under the vines, and squeezed the grape-juice down their throats; and, if any little pigs ran about ready roasted, crying, "Come and eat me," as was their fashion in that country, they waited till the pigs ran against their mouths, and then took a bite, and were content, just as so many oysters would have been.

They needed no weapons, for no enemies ever came near their land; and no tools, for everything was ready-made to their hand; and the stern old fairy Necessity never came near them to hunt them up, and make them use their wits, or die.

And so on, and so on, and so on, till there were never such comfortable, easy-going, happy-go-lucky people in the world.

"Well, that is a jolly life," said Tom.

"You think so?" said the fairy. "Do you see that great peaked mountain there behind," said the fairy, "with smoke coming out of its top?"

"Yes."

"And do you see all those ashes, and slag, and cinders, lying about?"

"Yes."

"Then turn over the next five hundred years, and you will see what happens next."

And behold the mountain had blown up like a barrel of gunpowder, and then boiled over like a kettle; whereby one-third of the Doasyoulikes were blown into the air; and another third were smothered in ashes; so that there was only one-third left.

"You see," said the fairy, "what comes of living on a burning mountain."

"Oh, why did you not warn them?" said little Ellie.

"I did warn them all that I could. I let the smoke come out of the mountain; and wherever there is smoke there is fire. And I laid the ashes and cinders all about; and wherever there are cinders, cinders may be again. But they did not like to face facts, my dears, as very few people do; and so they invented a cock-and-bull story, which, I am sure, I never told them, that the smoke was the breath of a giant, whom some gods or other had buried under the mountain; and that the cinders were what the dwarfs roasted the little pigs whole with; and other nonsense of that kind. And, when folks are in that humour, I cannot teach them, save by the good old birch-rod."

And then she turned over the next five hundred years: and there were the remnant of the Doasyoulikes, doing as they liked, as before. They were too lazy to move away from the mountain; so they said, If it has blown up once, that is all the more reason that it should not blow up again. And they were few in number: but they only said, The more the merrier, but the fewer the better fare. However, that was not quite true; for all the flapdoodle-trees were killed by the volcano, and they had eaten all the roast pigs, who, of course, could not be expected to have little ones. So they had to live very hard, on nuts and roots which they scratched out of the ground with sticks. Some of them talked of sowing corn, as their ancestors used to do, before they came into the land of Readymade; but they had forgotten how to make ploughs (they had forgotten even how to make Jews'-harps by this time), and had eaten all the seed-corn which they brought out of the land of Hardwork years since; and, of course, it was too much trouble to go away and find more. So they lived miserably on roots and nuts, and all the weakly little children had great stomachs, and then died.

"Why," said Tom, "they are growing no better than savages."

And look how ugly they are all getting," said Ellie.

"Yes; when people live on poor vegetables instead of roast-beef and plum-pudding, their jaws grow large, and their lips grow coarse, like the poor Paddies who eat potatoes."

And she turned over the next five hundred years. And there they were all living up in trees, and making nests to keep off the rain. And underneath the tree lions were prowling about.

"Why," said Ellie, "the lions seem to have eaten a good many of them, for there are very few left now."

"Yes," said the fairy; "you see it was only the strongest and most active ones who could climb the trees and so escape."

"But what great, hulking, broad-shouldered chaps they are," said Tom; "they are a rough lot as ever I saw."

"Yes, they are getting very strong now; for the ladies will not marry any but the very strongest and fiercest gentlemen, who can help them up the trees out of the lions' way."

And she turned over the next five hundred years. And in that they were fewer still, and stronger, and fiercer; but their feet had changed shape very oddly, for they laid hold of the branches with their great toes, as if they had been thumbs, just as a Hindoo tailor uses his toes to thread his needle.

The children were very much surprised, and asked the fairy whether that was her doing.

"Yes, and no," she said, smiling. "It was only those who could use their feet as well as their hands who could get a good living; or, indeed, get married; so that they got the best of everything, and starved out all the rest; and those who are left keep up a regular breed of toe-thumb-men, as a breed of short-horns, or Skye terriers, or fancy pigeons is kept up."

"But there is a hairy one among them," said Ellie.

"Ah!" said the fairy, "that will be a great man in his time, and chief of all the tribe."

And, when she turned over the next five hundred years, it was true.

For this hairy chief had had hairy children, and they hairier children still; and every one wished to marry hairy husbands, and have hairy children too; for the climate was growing so damp that none but the hairy ones could live: all the rest coughed and sneezed, and had sore throats, and went into consumption, before they could grow up to be men and women.

Then the fairy turned over the next five hundred years. And they were fewer still.

"Why, there is one on the ground picking up roots," said Ellie, "and he cannot walk upright."

No more he could; for in the same way that the shape of their feet had altered, the shape of their backs had altered also.

"Why," cried Tom, "I declare they are all apes."

"Something fearfully like it, poor foolish creatures," said the fairy. "They are grown so stupid now, that they can hardly think; for none of them have used their wits for many hundred years. They have almost forgotten, too, how to talk. For each stupid child forgot some of the words it heard from its stupid parents, and had not wits enough to make fresh words for itself. Besides, they are grown so fierce and suspicious and brutal that they keep out of each other's way, and mope and sulk in the dark forests, never hearing each other's voice, till they have forgotten almost what speech is like. I am afraid they will all be apes very soon, and all by doing only what they liked."

And in the next five hundred years they were all dead and gone, by bad food and wild beasts and hunters; all except one tremendous old fellow with jaws like a jack, who stood full seven feet high; and M. Du Chaillu came up to him, and shot him, as he stood roaring and thumping his breast. And he remembered that his ancestors had once been men, and tried to say, "Am I not a man and a brother?" but had forgotten how to use his tongue; and then he had tried to call for a doctor, but he had forgotten the word for one. So all he said was, "Ubboboo!" and died.

And that was the end of the great and jolly nation of the Doasyoulikes. And when Tom and Ellie came to the end of the book, they looked very sad and solemn; and they had good reason so to do, for they really fancied that the men were apes, and never thought, in their simplicity, of asking whether the creatures had hippopotamus majors in their brains or not; in which case, as you have been told already, they could not possibly have been apes, though they were more apish than the apes of all aperies.

"But could you not have saved them from becoming apes?" said little Ellie, at last.

"At first, my dear; if only they would have behaved like men, and set to work to do what they did not like. But the longer they waited, and behaved like the dumb beasts, who only do what they like, the stupider and clumsier they grew; till at last they were past all cure, for they had thrown their own wits away. It is such things as this that help to make me so ugly, that I know not when I shall grow fair."

"And where are they all now?" asked Ellie.

"Exactly where they ought to be, my dear."

"Yes!" said the fairy, solemnly, half to herself, as she closed the wonderful book. "Folks say now that I can make beasts into men, by circumstance, and selection, and competition, and so forth. Well, perhaps they are right; and perhaps, again, they are wrong. That is one of the seven things which I am forbidden to tell, till the coming of the Cocqcigrues; and, at all events, it is no concern of theirs. Whatever their ancestors were, men they are; and I advise them to behave as such, and act accordingly. But let them recollect this, that there are two sides to every question, and a downhill as well as an uphill road; and, if I can turn beasts into men, I can, by the same laws of circumstance, and selection, and competition, turn men into beasts. You were very near being turned into a beast once or twice, little Tom. Indeed, if you had not made up your mind to go on this journey, and see the world, like an Englishman, I am not sure but that you would have ended as an eft in a pond."

"Oh, dear me!" said Tom; "sooner than that, and be all over slime, I'll go this minute, if it is to the world's end."

CHAPTER SEVEN

And Nature, the old Nurse, took
    The child upon her knee,
Saying "Here is a story-book
    Thy father hath written for thee.

"Come wander with me," she said,
    "Into regions yet untrod,
And read what is still unread
    In the Manuscripts of God."

And he wandered away and away
    With Nature, the dear old Nurse,
Who sang to him night and day
    The rhymes of the universe.

Longfellow

Chapter Seven

~

"Now," said Tom, "I am ready to be off, if it's to the world's end."

"Ah!" said the fairy, "that is a brave, good boy. But you must go farther than the world's end, if you want to find Mr. Grimes; for he is at the Other-end-of-Nowhere. You must go to Shiny Wall, and through the white gate that never was opened; and then you will come to Peacepool, and Mother Carey's Haven, where the good whales go when they die. And there Mother Carey will tell you the way to the Other-end-of-Nowhere, and there you will find Mr. Grimes."

"Oh, dear!" said Tom. "But I do not know my way to Shiny Wall, or where it is at all."

"Little boys must take the trouble to find out things for themselves, or they will never grow to be men; so that you must ask all the beasts in the sea and the birds in the air, and if you have been good to them, some of them will tell you the way to Shiny Wall."

"Well," said Tom, "it will be a long journey, so I had better start at once. Good-bye, Miss Ellie; you know I am getting a big boy, and I must go out and see the world."

"I know you must," said Ellie; "but you will not forget me, Tom. I shall wait here till you come."

And she shook hands with him, and bade him good-bye. Tom longed very much again to kiss her; but he thought it would not be respectful, considering she was a lady born; so he promised not to forget her: but his little whirl-about of a head was so full of the notion of going out to see the world, that it forgot her in five minutes; however, though his head forgot her, I am glad to say his heart did not.

So he asked all the beasts in the sea, and all the birds in the air, but none of them knew the way to Shiny Wall. For why? He was still too far down south.

Then he met a ship, far larger than he had ever seen – a gallant ocean-steamer, with a long cloud of smoke trailing behind; and he wondered how she went on without sails, and swam up to her to see. A school of dolphins were running races round and round her, going three feet for her one, and Tom asked them the way to Shiny Wall; but they did not know. Then he tried to find out how she moved, and at last he saw her screw, and was so delighted with it that he played under her quarter all day, till he nearly had his nose knocked off by the fans, and thought it time to move. Then he watched the sailors upon deck, and the ladies, with their bonnets and parasols; but none of them could see him, because their eyes were not opened – as, indeed, most people's eyes are not.

At last there came out into the quarter-gallery a very pretty lady, in deep black widow's weeds, and in her arms a baby. She leaned over the quarter-gallery, and looked back and back toward England far away; and as she looked she sang:

I

Soft, soft wind, from out the sweet south sliding,
   Waft thy silver cloud-webs athwart the summer sea;
Thin, thin threads of mist on dewy fingers twining,
   Weave a veil of dappled gauze to shade my babe and me.

II

Deep, deep Love, within thine own abyss abiding,
Pour Thyself abroad, O Lord, on earth and air and sea

Worn weary hearts within Thy holy temple hiding,
Shield from sorrow, sin, and shame my helpless babe and me.

Her voice was so soft and low, and the music of the air so sweet, that Tom could have listened to it all day. But as she held the baby over the gallery-rail, to show it the dolphins leaping and the water gurgling in the ship's wake, lo! and behold, the baby saw Tom.

He was quite sure of that; for when their eyes met, the baby smiled and held out its hands; and Tom smiled and held out his hands too; and the baby kicked and leaped, as if it wanted to jump overboard to him.

"What do you see, my darling?" said the lady; and her eyes followed the baby's till she too caught sight of Tom, swimming about among the foam-beads below.

She gave a little shriek and start; and then she said, quite quietly, "Babies in the sea? Well, perhaps it is the happiest place for them," and waved her hand to Tom, and cried, "Wait a little, darling, only a little; and perhaps we shall go with you and be at rest."

And at that an old nurse, all in black, came out and talked to her, and drew her in. And Tom turned away northward, sad and wondering; and watched the great steamer slide away into the dusk, and the lights on board peep out one by one, and die out again, and the long bar of smoke fade away into the evening mist, till all was out of sight.

And he swam northward again, day after day, till at last he met the King of the Herrings, with a curry-comb growing out of his nose, and a sprat in his mouth for a cigar, and asked him the way to Shiny Wall; so he bolted his sprat head foremost, and said:

"If I were you, young gentleman, I should go to the Allalonestone, and ask the last of the Gairfowl. She is of a very ancient clan, very nearly as ancient as my own; and knows a good deal which these modern upstarts don't, as ladies of old houses are likely to do."

Tom asked his way to her, and the King of the Herrings told him very kindly; for he was a courteous old gentleman of the old school, though he was horribly ugly, and strangely bedizened too, like the old dandies who lounge in the club-house windows.

But just as Tom had thanked him and set off, he called after him: "Hi! I say, can you fly?"

"I never tried," says Tom. "Why?"

"Because, if you can, I should advise you to say nothing to the old lady about it. There; take a hint. Good-bye."

And away Tom went for seven days and seven nights due north-west, till he came to a great codbank, the like of which he never saw before. The great cod lay below in tens of thousands, and gobbled shell-fish all day long; and the blue sharks roved above in hundreds, and gobbled them when they came up. So they ate, and ate, and ate each other, as they had done since the making of the world; for no man had come here yet to catch them, and find out how rich old Mother Carey is.

And there he saw the last of the Gairfowl, standing up on the Allalonestone, all alone. And a very grand old lady she was, full three feet high, and bolt upright, like some old Highland chieftainess. She had on a black velvet gown, and a white pinner and apron, and a very high bridge to her nose (which is a sure mark of high breeding), and a large pair of white spectacles on it, which made her look rather odd: but it was the ancient fashion of her house.

And instead of wings, she had two little feathery arms, with which she fanned herself, and complained of the dreadful heat; and she kept on crooning an old song to herself, which she learned when she was a little baby-bird, long ago –

> *Two little birds, they sat on a stone,*
> *One swam away, and then there was one;*
> *With a fal-lal-la-lady.*
> *The other swam after, and then there was one,*
> *And so the poor stone was left all alone;*
> *With a fal-la-la-lady.*

It was "flew" away, properly, and not "swam" away; but, as she could not fly, she had a right to alter it. However, it was a very fit song for her to sing, because she was a lady herself.

Tom came up to her very humbly, and made his bow; and the first thing she said was:

"Have you wings? Can you fly?"

"Oh dear, no, ma'am; I should not think of such a thing," said cunning little Tom.

"Then I shall have great pleasure in talking to you, my dear. It is quite refreshing nowadays to see anything without wings. They must all have wings, forsooth, now, every new upstart sort of bird, and fly. What can they want with flying, and raising themselves above their proper station in life? In the days of my ancestors no birds ever thought of having wings, and did very well without; and now they all laugh at me because I keep to the good old fashion. Why, the very marrocks and dovekies have got wings, the vulgar creatures, and poor little ones enough they are; and my own cousins too, the razorbills, who are gentlefolk born, and ought to know better than to ape their inferiors."

And so she was running on, while Tom tried to get in a word edgeways; and at last he did, when the old lady got out of breath, and began fanning herself again; and then he asked if she knew the way to Shiny Wall.

"Shiny Wall? Who should know better than I? We all came from Shiny Wall, thousands of years ago, when it was decently cold, and the climate was fit for gentlefolk; but now, what with the heat, and what with these vulgar-winged things who fly up and down and eat everything, so that gentlepeople's hunting is all spoiled, and one really cannot get one's living, or hardly venture off the rock for fear of being flown against by some creature that would not have dared to come within a mile of one a thousand years ago – what was I saying? Why, we have quite gone down in the world, my dear, and have nothing left but our honour. And I am the last of my family. A friend of mine and I came and settled on this rock when we were young, to be out of the way of low people. Once we were a great nation, and spread over all the Northern Isles. But men shot us so, and knocked us on the head, and took our eggs – why, if you will believe it, they say that on the coast of Labrador the sailors used to lay a plank from the rock on board the thing they call their ship, and drive us along the plank by hundreds, till we tumbled down into the ship's waist in heaps; and then, I suppose, they ate us, the nasty fellows! Well – but – what was I saying? At last there were none of us left, except on the old Gairfowlskerry, just off the Iceland coast, up which no man could climb. Even there we had no peace; for one day, when I was quite a young girl, the land rocked, and the sea boiled, and the sky grew dark, and all the air was filled with smoke and dust, and down tumbled the old Gairfowlskerry into the sea. The dovekies and marrocks, of course, all flew away; but we were too proud to do that. Some of us were dashed to pieces, and some drowned; and those who were left got away to Eldey, and the dovekies tell me they are all dead now, and that another Gairfowlskerry has risen out of the sea close to the old one, but that it is such a poor flat piece that it is not safe to live on; and so here I am left alone."

This was the Gairfowl's story, and, strange as it may seem, it is every word of it true.

"If you only had had wings!" said Tom, "then you might all have flown away too."

"Yes, young gentleman; and if people are not gentlemen and ladies, and forget that *noblesse oblige*, they will find it as easy to get on in the world as other people who don't care what they do. Why, if I had not recollected that *noblesse oblige*, I should not have been all alone now." And the poor old lady sighed.

"How was that, ma'am?"

"Why, my dear, a gentleman came hither with me, and after we had been here some time, he wanted to marry – in fact, he actually proposed to me. Well, I can't blame him; I was young, and very handsome then, I don't deny; but you see, I could not hear of such a thing, because he was my deceased sister's husband, you see?"

"Of course not, ma'am," said Tom; though, of course, he knew nothing about it. "She was very much diseased, I suppose?"

"You do not understand me, my dear. I mean, that being a lady, and with right and honourable feelings, as our house always has had, I felt it my duty to snub him, and howk him, and peck him continually, to keep him at his proper distance; and, to tell the truth, I once pecked him a little too hard, poor fellow, and he tumbled backwards off the rock, and – really, it was very unfortunate, but it was not my fault – a shark coming by saw him flapping, and snapped him up. And since then I have lived all alone –

With a fal-la-la-lady.

And soon I shall be gone, my little dear, and nobody will miss me; and then the poor stone will be left all alone."

"But, please, which is the way to Shiny Wall?" said Tom.

"Oh, you must go, my little dear – you must go. Let me see – I am sure - that is — really, my poor old brains are getting quite puzzled. Do you know, my little dear, I am afraid, if you want to know, you must ask some of these vulgar birds about, for I have quite forgotten."

And the poor old Gairfowl began to cry tears of pure oil; and Tom was quite sorry for her; and for himself too, for he was at his wit's end whom to ask.

But by there came a flock of petrels, who are Mother Carey's own chickens; and Tom thought them much prettier than Lady Gairfowl, and so perhaps they were; for Mother Carey had had a great deal of fresh experience between the time that she invented the Gairfowl and the time that she invented them. They flitted along like a flock of black swallows, and hopped and skipped from wave to wave, lifting up their little feet behind them so daintily, and whistling to each other so tenderly, that Tom fell in love with them at once, and called them to know the way to Shiny Wall?

"Shiny Wall? Do you want Shiny Wall? Then come with us, and we will show you. We are Mother Carey's own chickens, and she sends us out over all the seas, to show the good birds the way home."

Tom was delighted, and swam off to them, after he had made his bow to the Gairfowl. But she would not return his bow; but held herself bolt upright, and wept tears of oil as she sang:

And so the poor stone was left all alone;
With a fal-la-la-lady.

But she was wrong there; for the stone was not left all alone; and the next time that Tom goes by it, he will see a sight worth seeing.

The old Gairfowl is gone already: but there are better things come in her place; and when Tom comes he will see the fishing-smacks anchored there in hundreds, from Scotland, and from Ireland, and from the Orkneys, and the Shetlands, and from all the Northern ports, full of the children of the old Norse Vikings, the masters of the sea. And the men will be hauling in the great cod by thousands, till their hands are sore from the lines; and they will be making cod-liver oil and guano, and salting down the fish; and there will be a man-of-war steamer there to protect them, and a lighthouse to show them the way; and you and I, perhaps, shall go some day to the Allalonestone to the great summer sea-fair, and dredge strange creatures

such as man never saw before; and we shall hear the sailors boast that it is
not the worst jewel in Queen Victoria's crown, for there are eighty miles of
codbank, and food for all the poor folk in the land. That is what Tom will
see, and perhaps you and I shall see it too. And then we shall not be sorry
because we cannot get a gairfowl to stuff, much less find gairfowl enough
to drive them into stone pens and slaughter them, as the old Norsemen did,
or drive them on board along a plank till the ship was victualled with them,
as the old English and French rovers used to do, of whom dear old Hakluyt
tells – but we shall remember what Mr. Tennyson says, how

> *The old order changeth, yielding place to new,*
> *And God fulfils Himself in many ways.*

And now Tom was all agog to start for Shiny Wall; but the petrels said
no. They must go first to Allfowlsness, and wait there for the great gathering
of all the seabirds, before they start for their summer breeding-places far away
in the Northern Isles; and there they would be sure to find some birds which
were going to Shiny Wall; but where Allfowlsness was, he must promise
never to tell, lest men should go there and shoot the birds, and stuff them,
and put them into stupid museums, instead of leaving them to play and
breed and work in Mother Carey's water-garden, where they ought to be.

So where Allfowlsness is nobody must know; and all that is to be said
about it is, that Tom waited there many days; and as he waited, he saw a very
curious sight. On the rabbit burrows on the shore there gathered hundreds and
hundreds of hoodie-crows, such as you see in Cambridgeshire. And they made
such a noise, that Tom came on shore and went up to see what was the matter.

And there he found them holding their great caucus, which they hold every year in the North; and all their stump-orators were speechifying; and for a tribune, the speaker stood on an old sheep's skull.

And they cawed and cawed, and boasted of all the clever things they had done; how many lambs' eyes they had picked out, and how many dead bullocks they had eaten, and how many young grouse they had swallowed whole, and how many grouse-eggs they had flown away with, stuck on the point of their bills, which is the hoodie-crow's particularly clever feat, of which he is as proud as a gipsy is of doing the hokany-baro; and what that is, I won't tell you.

And at last they brought out the prettiest, neatest young lady-crow that ever was seen, and set her in the middle, and all began abusing and vilifying, and rating, and bullyragging at her, because she had stolen no grouse-eggs, and had actually dared to say that she would not steal any. So she was to be tried publicly by their laws (for the hoodies always try some offenders in their great yearly parliament). And there she stood in the middle, in her black gown and gray hood, looking as meek and as neat as a quakeress, and they all bawled at her at once –

And it was in vain that she pleaded

That she did not like grouse-eggs;

That she could get her living very well without them;

That she was afraid to eat them, for fear of the gamekeepers;

That she had not the heart to eat them, because the grouse were such pretty, kind, jolly birds;

And a dozen reasons more.

For all the other scaul-crows set upon her, and pecked her to death there and then, before Tom could come to help her; and then flew away, very proud of what they had done.

Now, was not this a scandalous transaction?

But they are true republicans, these hoodies, who do every one just what he likes, and make other people do so too; so that, for any freedom of speech, thought, or action, which is allowed among them, they might as well be American citizens of the new school.

But the fairies took the good crow, and gave her nine new sets of feathers running, and turned her at last into the most beautiful bird of paradise with a green velvet suit and a long tail, and sent her to eat fruit in the Spice Islands, where cloves and nutmegs grow.

And Mrs. Bedonebyasyoudid settled her account with the wicked hoodies. For, as they flew away, what should they find but a nasty dead dog? — on which they all set to work, pecking and gobbling and cawing and quarrelling, to their hearts' content. But the moment afterwards, they all threw up their bills into the air, and gave one screech; and then turned head over heels backward, and fell down dead, one hundred and twenty-three of them at once. For why? The fairy had told the gamekeeper in a dream, to fill the dead dog full of strychnine; and so he did.

And after a while the birds began to gather at Allfowlsness, in thousands and tens of thousands, blackening all the air; swans and brant geese, harlequins and eiders, harelds and garganeys, smews and goosanders, divers and loons, grebes and dovekies, auks and razorbills, gannets and petrels, skuas and terns, with gulls beyond all naming or numbering; and they paddled and washed and splashed and combed and brushed themselves on the sand, till the shore was white with feathers; and they quacked and clucked and gabbled and chattered and screamed and whooped as they talked over matters with their friends, and settled where they were to go and breed that summer, till you might have heard them ten miles off; and lucky it was for them that there was no one to hear them but the old keeper, who lived all alone upon the Ness, in a turf hut thatched with heather and fringed round with great stones slung across the roof by bent-ropes, lest the winter gales should blow the hut right away. But he never minded the birds nor hurt them, because they were not in season; indeed, he minded but two things in the whole world, and those were, his Bible and his grouse; for he was as good an old Scotchman as ever knit stockings on a winter's night — only, when all the birds were going, he toddled out, and took off his cap to them, and wished them a merry journey and a safe return; and then gathered up all the feathers which they had left, and cleaned them to sell down south, and make feather-beds for stuffy people to lie on.

Then the petrels asked this bird and that whether they would take Tom to Shiny Wall; but one set was going to Sutherland, and one to the Shetlands, and one to Norway, and one to Spitzbergen, and one to Iceland, and one to Greenland; and none would go to Shiny Wall. So the good-natured petrels said that they would show him part of the way themselves, but they were only going as far as Jan Mayen's Land; and after that he must shift for himself.

And then all the birds rose up, and streamed away in long black lines, north, and north-east, and north-west, across the bright blue summer sky; and their cry was like ten thousand packs of hounds, and ten thousand peals of bells. Only the puffins stayed behind, and killed the young rabbits, and laid their eggs in the rabbit-burrows; which was rough practice, certainly; but a man must see to his own family.

And, as Tom and the petrels went north-eastward, it began to blow right hard; for the old gentleman in the gray great-coat, who looks after the big copper boiler in the Gulf of Mexico, had got behind-hand with his work; so Mother Carey had sent an electric message to him for more steam; and now the steam was coming, as much in an hour as ought to have come in a week, puffing and roaring and swishing and swirling, till you could not see where the sky ended and the sea began. But Tom and the petrels never cared, for the gale was right abaft, and away they went over the crests of the billows, as merry as so many flying-fish.

And at last they saw an ugly sight – the black side of a great ship, water-logged in the trough of the sea. Her funnel and her masts were overboard, and swayed and surged under her lee; her decks were swept as clean as a barn floor, and there was no living soul on board.

The petrels flew up to her, and wailed round her; for they were very sorry indeed, and also they expected to find some salt pork; and Tom scrambled on board of her and looked round, frightened and sad.

And there, in a little cot, lashed tight under the bulwark, lay a baby fast asleep; the very same baby, Tom saw at once, which he had seen in the singing lady's arms.

He went up to it, and wanted to wake it; but behold, from under the cot out jumped a little black and tan terrier dog, and began barking and snapping at Tom, and would not let him touch the cot.

Tom knew the dog's teeth could not hurt him; but at least it could shove him away, and did; and he and the dog fought and struggled, for he wanted to help the baby, and did not want to throw the poor dog overboard; but, as they were struggling, there came a tall green sea, and walked in over the weather side of the ship, and swept them all into the waves.

"Oh, the baby, the baby!" screamed Tom; but the next moment he did not scream at all; for he saw the cot settling down through the green water, with the baby smiling in it, fast asleep; and he saw the fairies come up from below, and carry baby and cradle gently down in their soft arms; and then he knew it was all right, and that there would be a new water baby in St. Brandan's Isle.

And the poor little dog?

Why, after he had kicked and coughed a little, he sneezed so hard, that he sneezed himself clean out of his skin, and turned into a water-dog, and jumped and danced round Tom, and ran over the crests of the waves, and snapped at the jelly-fish and the mackerel, and followed Tom the whole way to the Other-end-of-Nowhere.

Then they went on again, till they began to see the peak of Jan Mayen's Land, standing up like a white sugar-loaf, two miles above the clouds.

And there they fell in with a whole flock of molly-mocks, who were feeding on a dead whale.

"These are the fellows to show you the way," said Mother Carey's chickens; "we cannot help you further north. We don't like to get among the ice park, for fear it should nip our toes; but the mollys dare fly anywhere."

So the petrels called to the mollys; but they were so busy and greedy, gobbling and pecking and spluttering and fighting over the blubber, that they did not take the least notice.

"Come, come," said the petrels, "you lazy greedy lubbers, this young gentleman is going to Mother Carey, and if you don't attend on him, you won't earn your discharge from her, you know."

"Greedy we are," says a great fat old molly, "but lazy we ain't; and, as for lubbers, we're no more lubbers than you. Let's have a look at the lad."

And he flapped right into Tom's face, and stared at him in the most impudent way (for the mollys are audacious fellows, as all whalers know), and then asked him where he hailed from, and what land he sighted last.

And, when Tom told him, he seemed pleased, and said he was a good plucked one to have got so far.

"Come along, lads," he said to the rest, "and give this little chap a cast over the pack, for Mother Carey's sake. We've eaten blubber enough for to-day, and we'll e'en work out a bit of our time by helping the lad."

So the mollys took Tom up on their backs, and flew off with him, laughing and joking – and oh, how they did smell of train oil!

"Who are you, you jolly birds?" asked Tom.

"We are the spirits of the old Greenland skippers (as every sailor knows), who hunted here, right whales and horse-whales, full hundreds of years agone. But, because we were saucy and greedy, we were all turned into mollys, to eat whale's blubber all our days. But lubbers we are none, and could sail a ship now against any man in the North Seas, though we don't hold with this new-fangled steam. And it's a shame of those black imps of petrels to call us so; but because they're her Grace's pets, they think they may say anything they like."

"And who are you?" asked Tom of him, for he saw that he was the king of all the birds.

"My name is Hendrick Hudson, and a right good skipper was I; and my name will last to the world's end, in spite of all the wrong I did. For I discovered Hudson River, and I named Hudson's Bay; and many have come in my wake that dared not have shown me the way. But I was a hard man in my time, that's truth, and stole the poor Indians off the coast of Maine, and sold them for slaves down in Virginia; and at last I was so cruel to my sailors, here in these very seas, that they set me adrift in an open boat, and I never was heard of more. So now I'm the king of all the mollys, till I've worked out my time."

And now they came to the edge of the pack, and beyond it they could see Shiny Wall looming, through mist, and snow, and storm. But the pack rolled horribly upon the swell, and the ice giants fought and roared, and leapt upon each other's backs, and ground each other to powder, so that Tom was afraid to venture among them, lest he should be ground to powder too. And he was the more afraid, when he saw lying among the ice pack the wrecks of many a gallant ship; some with masts and yards all standing, some with the seamen frozen fast on board. Alas, alas, for them! They were all true English hearts; and they came to their end like good knights-errant, in searching for the white gate that never was opened yet.

But the good molleys took Tom and his dog up, and flew with them safe over the pack and the roaring ice giants, and set them down at the foot of Shiny Wall.

"And where is the gate?" asked Tom.

"There is no gate," said the mollys.

"No gate?" cried Tom aghast.

"None; never a crack of one, and that's the whole of the secret, as better fellows, lad, than you have found to their cost; and if there had been, they'd have killed by now every right whale that swims the sea."

"What am I to do, then?"

"Dive under the floe, to be sure, if you have pluck."

"I've not come so far to turn now," said Tom; "so here goes for a header."

"A lucky voyage to you, lad," said the mollys; "we knew you were one of the right sort. So good-bye."

"Why don't you come to?" asked Tom.

But the mollys only wailed sadly. "We can't go yet, we can't go yet," and flew away over the pack.

So Tom dived under the great white gate which never was opened yet, and went on in black darkness, at the bottom of the sea, for seven days and seven nights. And yet he was not a bit frightened. Why should he be? He was a brave English lad, whose business is to go out and see all the world.

And at last he saw the light, and clear clear water overhead; and up he came a thousand fathoms, among clouds of sea-moths, which fluttered round his head. There were moths with pink heads and wings and opal bodies, that flapped about slowly; moths with brown wings that flapped about quickly; yellow shrimps that hopped and skipped most quickly of all; and jellies of all the colours in the world, that neither hopped nor skipped, but only dawdled and yawned, and would not get out of his way. The dog snapped at them till his jaws were tired; but Tom hardly minded them at all, he was so eager to get to the top of the water, and see the pool where the good whales go.

And a very large pool it was, miles and miles across, though the air was so clear that the ice cliffs on the opposite side looked as if they were close at hand. All round it the ice cliffs rose, in walls and spires and battlements, and caves and bridges, and stories and galleries, in which the ice-fairies live, and drive away the storms and clouds, that Mother Carey's pool may lie calm from year's end to year's end. And the sun acted

And there he saw the last of the Gairfowl,
standing up on the Allalonestone, all alone.
(Chapter 7)

Mrs. Doasyouwouldbedoneby.
(Chapter 8)

policeman, and walked round outside every day, peeping just over the top of the ice wall, to see that all went right; and now and then he played conjuring tricks, or had an exhibition of fireworks, to amuse the ice-fairies. For he would make himself into four or five suns at once, or paint the sky with rings and crosses and crescents of white fire, and stick himself in the middle of them, and wink at the fairies; and I dare say they were very much amused, for anything's fun in the country.

And there the good whales lay, the happy sleepy beasts, upon the still oily sea. They were all right whales, you must know, and finners, and razor-backs, and bottle-noses, and spotted sea-unicorns with long ivory horns. But the sperm whales are such raging, ramping, roaring, rumbustious fellows, that, if Mother Carey let them in, there would be no more peace in Peacepool. So she packs them away in a great pond by themselves at the South Pole, two hundred and sixty-three miles south-south-east of Mount Erebus, the great volcano in the ice; and there they butt each other with their ugly noses, day and night from year's end to year's end. And if they think that sport – why, so do their American cousins.

But here there were only good quiet beasts, lying about like the black hulls of sloops, and blowing every now and then jets of white steam, or sculling round with their huge mouths open, for the sea-moths to swim down their throats. There were no threshers there to thresh their poor old backs, or sword-fish to stab their stomachs, or saw-fish to rip them up, or ice-sharks to bite lumps out of their sides, or whalers to harpoon and lance them. They were quite safe and happy there; and all they had to do was to wait quietly in Peacepool, till Mother Carey sent for them to make them out of old beasts into new.

Tom swam up to the nearest whale, and asked the way to Mother Carey.

"There she sits in the middle," said the whale.

Tom looked; but he could see nothing in the middle of the pool, but one peaked iceberg; and he said so.

"That's Mother Carey," said the whale, "as you will find when you get to her. There she sits making old beasts into new all the year round."

"How does she do that?"

"That's her concern, not mine," said the old whale; and yawned so wide (for he was very large) that there swam into his mouth 943 sea-moths, 13,846 jelly-fish no bigger than pins' heads, a string of salpae nine yards long, and forty-three little ice-crabs, who gave each other a parting pinch all round, tucked their legs under their stomachs, and determined to die decently, like Julius Caesar.

"I suppose," said Tom, "she cuts up a great whale like you into a whole shoal of porpoises?"

At which the old whale laughed so violently that he coughed up all the creatures; who swam away again very thankful at having escaped out of that terrible whalebone net of his, from which bourne no traveller returns; and Tom went on to the iceberg, wondering.

And, when he came near it, it took the form of the grandest old lady he had ever seen – a white marble lady, sitting on a white marble throne. And from the foot of the throne there swam away, out and out into the sea, millions of new-born creatures, of more shapes and colours than man ever dreamed. And they were Mother Carey's children, whom she makes out of the sea-water all day long.

He expected, of course – like some grown people who ought to know better – to find her snipping, piecing, fitting, stitching, cobbling, basting, filing, planing, hammering, turning, polishing, moulding, measuring, chiselling, clipping, and so forth, as men do when they go to work to make anything.

But, instead of that, she sat quite still with her chin upon her hand, looking down into the sea with two great grand blue eyes, as blue as the sea itself. Her hair was as white as the snow – for she was very very old – in fact, as old as any thing which you are likely to come across, except the difference between right and wrong.

And, when she saw Tom, she looked at him kindly.

"What do you want, my little man? It is long since I have seen a water baby here."

Tom told her his errand, and asked the way to the Other-end-of-Nowhere.

"You ought to know yourself, for you have been there already."

"Have I, ma'am? I'm sure I forget all about it."

"Then look at me."

And, as Tom looked into her great blue eyes, he recollected the way perfectly.

Now, was not that strange?

"Thank you, ma'am," said Tom. "Then I won't trouble your ladyship any more; I hear you are very busy."

"I am never more busy than I am now," she said, without stirring a finger.

"I heard, ma'am, that you were always making new beasts out of old."

"So people fancy. But I am not going to trouble myself to make things, my little dear. I sit here and make them make themselves."

"You are a clever fairy, indeed," thought Tom. And he was quite right.

That is a grand trick of good old Mother Carey's, and a grand answer, which she has had occasion to make several times to impertinent people.

There was once, for instance, a fairy who was so clever that she found out how to make butterflies. I don't mean sham ones; no, but real live ones, which would fly, and eat, and lay eggs, and do everything that they ought; and she was so proud of her skill that she went flying straight off to the North Pole, to boast to Mother Carey how she could make butterflies.

But Mother Carey laughed.

"Know, silly child," she said, "that any one can make things, if they will take time and trouble enough; but it is not every one who, like me, can make things make themselves."

But people do not yet believe that Mother Carey is as clever as all that comes to; and they will not till they, too, go the journey to the Other-end-of-Nowhere.

"And now, my pretty little man," said Mother Carey, "you are sure you know the way to the Other-end-of-Nowhere?"

Tom thought; and behold, he had forgotten it utterly.

"That is because you took your eyes off me."

Tom looked at her again, and recollected; and then looked away, and forgot in an instant.

"But what am I to do, ma'am? For I can't keep looking at you when I am somewhere else."

"You must do without me, as most people have to do, for nine hundred and ninety-nine thousandths of their lives; and look at the dog instead; for he knows the way well enough, and will not forget it. Besides, you may meet some very queer-tempered people there, who will not let you pass without this passport of mine, which you must hang round your neck and take care of; and, of course, as the dog will always go behind you, you must go the whole way backward."

"Backward!" cried Tom. "Then I shall not be able to see my way."

"On the contrary, if you look forward, you will not see a step before you, and be certain to go wrong; but, if you look behind you, and watch carefully whatever you have passed, and especially keep your eye on the dog, who goes by instinct, and therefore can't go wrong, then you will know what is coming next as plainly as if you saw it in a looking-glass."

Tom was very much astonished; but he obeyed her, for he had learnt always to believe what the fairies told him.

"So it is, my dear child," said Mother Carey; "and I will tell you a story, which will show you that I am perfectly right, as it is my custom to be."

"Once on a time, there were two brothers. One was called Prometheus, because he always looked before him, and boasted that he was wise beforehand. The other was called Epimetheus, because he always looked behind him, and did not boast at all; but said humbly, like the Irishman, that he had sooner prophesy after the event.

"Well, Prometheus was a very clever fellow, of course, and invented all sorts of wonderful things. But, unfortunately, when they were set to work, to work was just what they would not do; wherefore very little has come of them, and very little is left of them; and now nobody knows what they were, save a few archaeological old gentlemen who scratch in queer corners, and find little there save Ptinum Furem, Blaptem Mortisagam, Acarum Horridum, and Tineam Laciniarum.

"But Epimetheus was a very slow fellow, certainly, and went among men for a clod, and a muff, and a milksop, and a slow-coach, and a bloke, and a boodle, and so forth. And very little he did, for many years; but what he did, he never had to do over again.

"And what happened at last? There came to the two brothers the most beautiful creature that ever was seen, Pandora by name; which means, All the gifts of the Gods. But because she had a strange box in her hand, this fanciful, forecasting, suspicious, prudential, theoretical, deductive, prophesying Prometheus, who was always settling what was going to happen, would have nothing to do with pretty Pandora and her box.

"But Epimetheus took her and it, as he took everything that came; and married her for better for worse, as every man ought, whenever he has even the chance of a good wife. And they opened the box between them, of course, to see what was inside; for, else, of what possible use could it have been to them?

"And out flew all the ills which flesh is heir to; all the children of the four great bogies, Self-will, Ignorance, Fear, and Dirt – for instance:

Measles,	Famines,
Monks,	Quacks,
Scarlatina,	Unpaid bills,
Idols,	Tight stays,
Whooping-coughs,	Potatoes,
Popes,	Bad wine,
Wars,	Despots,
Peacemongers,	Demagogues,

And, worst of all, Naughty Boys and Girls:

But one thing remained at the bottom of the box, and that was, Hope.

"So Epimetheus got a great deal of trouble, as most men do in this world; but he got the three best things in the world into the bargain – a good wife, and experience, and hope; while Prometheus had just as much trouble, and a great deal more (as you will hear), of his own making; with nothing beside, save fancies spun out of his own brain, as a spider spins her web out of her stomach.

"And Prometheus kept on looking before him so far ahead, that as he was running about with a box of lucifers (which were the only useful things he ever invented, and do as much harm as good), he trod on his own nose, and tumbled down (as most deductive philosophers do), whereby he set the Thames on fire; and they have hardly put it out again yet. So he had to be chained to the top of a mountain, with a vulture by him to give him a peck whenever he stirred, lest he should turn the whole world upside down with his prophecies and his theories.

"But stupid old Epimetheus went working and grubbing on, with the help of his wife Pandora, always looking behind him to see what had happened, till he really learnt to know now and then what would happen next; and understood so well which side his bread was buttered, and which way the cat jumped, that he began to make things which would work, and go on working, too; to till and drain the ground, and to make looms, and ships, and railroads, and steam ploughs, and electric telegraphs, and all the things which you see in the Great Exhibition; and to foretell famine, and bad weather, and the price of stocks, and the end of President Lincoln's policy; till at last he grew as rich as a Jew, and as fat as a farmer; and people thought twice before they meddled with him, but only once before they asked him to help them; for, because he earned his money well, he could afford to spend it well likewise.

"And his children are the men of science, who get good lasting work done in the world; but the children of Prometheus are the fanatics, and the theorists, and the bigots, and the bores, and the noisy, windy people, who go telling silly folk what will happen, instead of looking to see what has happened already."

Now, was not Mother Carey's a wonderful story? And, I am happy to say, Tom believed it every word.

For so it happened to Tom likewise. He was very sorely tried; for though, by keeping the dog to heels (or rather to toes, for he had to walk backward), he could see pretty well which way the dog was hunting, yet it was much slower work to go backwards than to go forwards. But, what was more trying still, no sooner had he got out of Peacepool, than there came running to him all the conjurers, fortune-tellers, astrologers, prophesiers, projectors, prestigiators, as many as were in those parts (and there are too many of them everywhere), Old Mother Shipton on her broomstick, with

Merlin, Thomas the Rhymer, Gerbertus, Rabanus Maurus, Nostradamus, Zadkiel, Raphael Moore, Old Nixon, and a good many in black coats and white ties who might have known better, considering in what century they were born, all bawling and screaming at him, "Look a-head, only look a-head; and we will show you what man never saw before, and right away to the end of the world!"

But I am proud to say that, though Tom had not been at Cambridge – for, if he had, he would have certainly been senior wrangler – he was such a little dogged, hard, gnarly, foursquare brick of an English boy, that he never turned his head round once all the way from Peacepool to the Other-end-of-Nowhere; but kept his eye on the dog, and let him pick out the scent, hot or cold, straight or crooked, wet or dry, up hill or down dale; by which means he never made a single mistake and saw all the wonderful and hitherto by-no-mortal-man-imagined things, which it is my duty to relate to you in the next chapter.

CHAPTER EIGHT

Come to me, O ye children!
  For I hear you at your play;
And the questions that perplexed me
  Have vanished quite away.

Ye open the Eastern windows,
  That look towards the sun,
Where thoughts are singing swallows,
  And the brooks of morning run.

For what are all our contrivings
  And the wisdom of our books
When compared with your caresses,
  And the gladness of your looks?

Ye are better than all the ballads
  That ever were sung or said;
For ye are living poems,
  And all the rest are dead.

Longfellow

Chapter Eight and Last

~

Here begins the never-to-be-too-much-studied account of the nine-hundred-and-ninety-ninth part of the wonderful things which Tom saw, on his journey to the Other-end-of-Nowhere; which all good little children are requested to read; that, if ever they get to the Other-end-of-Nowhere, as they may very probably do, they may not burst out laughing, or try to run away, or do any other silly vulgar thing which may offend Mrs. Bedonebyasyoudid.

Now, as soon as Tom had left Peacepool, he came to the white lap of the great sea-mother, ten thousand fathoms deep; where she makes world-pap all day long, for the steam-giants to knead, and the fire-giants to bake, till it has risen and hardened into mountain loaves and island-cakes.

And there Tom was very near being kneaded up in the world-pap, and turned into a fossil water baby; which would have astonished the Geological Society of New Zealand some hundreds of thousands of years hence.

For, as he walked along in the silence of the sea twilight, on the soft white ocean floor, he was aware of a hissing, and a roaring, and a thumping, and a pumping, as of all the steam-engines in the world at once. And, when he came near, the water grew boiling hot; not that that hurt him in the least; but it also grew as foul as gruel; and every moment he stumbled over dead shells, and fish, and sharks, and seals, and whales, which had been killed by the hot water.

And at last he came to the great sea-serpent himself, lying dead at the bottom; and, as he was too thick to scramble over, Tom had to walk round him three-quarters of a mile and more which put him out of his path sadly; and, when he had got round, he came to the place called Stop. And there he stopped, and just in time.

For he was on the edge of a vast hole in the bottom of the sea, up which was rushing and roaring clear steam enough to work all the engines in the world at once; so clear, indeed, that it was quite light at moments; and Tom could see almost up to the top of the water above, and down below into the pit for nobody knows how far.

But, as soon as he bent his head over the edge, he got such a rap on the nose from pebbles, that he jumped back again; for the steam, as it rushed up, rasped away the sides of the hole, and hurled it up into the sea in a shower of mud and gravel and ashes; and then it spread all round, and sank again, and covered in the dead fish so fast, that before Tom had stood there five minutes he was buried in silt up to his ankles, and began to be afraid that he should have been buried alive.

And perhaps he would have been, but that while he was thinking, the whole piece of ground on which he stood was torn off and blown upwards, and away flew Tom a mile up through the sea, wondering what was coming next.

At last he stopped – thump! and found himself tight in the legs of the most wonderful bogy which he had ever seen.

It had I don't know how many wings, as big as the sails of a windmill, and spread out in a ring like them; and with them it hovered over the steam which rushed up, as a ball hovers over the top of a fountain. And for every wing above it had a leg below, with a claw like a comb at the tip, and a nostril at the root; and in the middle it had no stomach and one eye; and as for its mouth, that was all on one side, as the madreporiform tubercle in a star-fish is. Well, it was a very strange beast; but no stranger than some dozens which you may see.

"What do you want here," it cried quite peevishly, "getting in my way?" and it tried to drop Tom: but he held on tight to its claws, thinking himself safer where he was.

So Tom told him who he was, and what his errand was. And the thing winked its one eye, and sneered –

"I am too old to be taken in that way. You are come after gold – I know you are."

"Gold! What is gold?" And really Tom did not know; but the suspicious old bogy would not believe him.

But after a while Tom began to understand a little. For, as the vapours came up out of the hole, the bogy smelt them with his nostrils, and combed them and sorted them with his combs; and then, when they steamed up through them against his wings, they were changed into showers and streams of metal. From one wing fell gold-dust, and from another silver, and from another copper, and from another tin, and from another lead, and so on, and sank into the soft mud, into veins and cracks, and hardened there. Whereby it comes to pass that the rocks are full of metal.

But, all of a sudden, somebody shut off the steam below, and the hole was left empty in an instant; and then down rushed the water into the hole, in such a whirlpool that the bogy spun round and round as fast as a tee-totum. But that was all in his day's work, like a fair fall with the hounds; so all he did was to say to Tom –

"Now is your time, youngster, to get down, if you are in earnest, which I don't believe."

"You'll soon see," said Tom; and away he went, as bold as Baron Munchausen, and shot down the rushing cataract like a salmon at Ballisodare.

And, when he got to the bttom, he swam till he was washed on shore safe upon the Other-end-of-Nowhere; and he found it, to his surprise, as most other people do, much more like This-end-of-Somewhere than he had been in the habit of expecting.

And first he went through Waste-paper-land, where all the stupid books lie in heaps, up hill and down dale, like leaves in a winter wood; and there he saw people digging and grubbing among them, to make worse books out of bad ones, and threshing chaff to save the dust of it; and a very good trade they drove thereby, especially among children.

Then he went by the sea of slops, to the mountain of messes, and the territory of tuck, where the ground was very sticky, for it was all made of bad toffee (not Everton toffee, of course), and full of deep cracks and holes choked with wind-fallen fruit, and green gooseberries, and sloes, and crabs, and whinberris, and hips and haws, and all the nasty things which little children will eat if they can get them. But the fairies hide them out of the way in that country as fast as they can, and very hard work they have, and of very little use it is. For as fast as they hide away the old trash, foolish and wicked people make fresh trash full of lime and poisonous paints, and actually go and steal receipts out of old Madame Science's big book to invent poisons for little children, and sell them at wakes and fairs and tuckshops. Very well. Let them go on. Dr. Letheby and Dr. Hassall cannot catch them, though they are setting traps for them all day long. But the Fairy with the birch-rod will catch them all in time, and make them begin at one corner of their shops, and eat their way out at the other; by which time they will have got such stomach-aches as will cure them of poisoning little children.

Next he saw all the little people in the world, writing all the little books in the world, about all the other little people in the world; probably because they had no great people to write about; and if the names of the books were not Squeeky, nor the Pumplighter, nor the Narrow Narrow World, nor the Hills of the Chatttermuch, nor the Children's Twaddeday, why then they were something else. And all the rest of the little people in the world read the books, and thought themselves each as good as the President; and perhaps they were right, for every one knows his own business best. But Tom thought he would sooner have a jolly good fairy tale, about Jack the Giant-killer or Beauty and the Beast, which taught him something that he didn't know already.

And next he came to the centre of Creation (the hub, they call it there), which lies in latitude 42.21 south, and longitude 108.56 east.

And there he found all the wise people instructing mankind in the science of spirit-rapping, while their house was burning over their heads; and when Tom told them of the fire, they held an indignation meeting forthwith, and unanimously determined to hang Tom's dog for coming into their country with gunpowder in his mouth. Tom couldn't help saying that though they did fancy they had carried all the wit away with them out of Lincolnshire two hundred years ago, yet if they had had one such Lincolnshire nobleman among them as good old Lord Yarborough, he would have called for the fire-engines before he hanged other people's dogs. But it was of no use, and the dog was hanged; and Tom couldn't even have his carcase; for they had abolished the have-his-carcase act in that country, for fear lest when rogues fell out, honest men should come by their own. And so they would have succeeded perfectly, as they always do, only that (as they also always do) they failed in one little particular, viz., that the dog would not die, being a water-dog, but bit their fingers so abominably that they were forced to let him go, and Tom likewise, as British subjects. Whereon they recommenced rapping for the spirits of their fathers; and very much astonished the poor old spirits were when they came, and saw how, according to the laws of Mrs. Bedonebyasyoudid, their descendants had weakened their constitution by hard living.

Then came Tom to the Island of Polupragmosyne, which some call Rogues' Harbour (but they are wrong; for that is in the middle of Bramshill Bushes, and the county police have cleared it out long ago). There every one knows his neighbour's business better than his own; and a very noisy place it is, as might be expected, considering that all the inhabitants are *ex-officio* on the wrong side of the house in the "Parliament of Man, and the Federation of the World"; and are always making wry mouths, and crying that the fairies' grapes were sour.

There Tom saw ploughs drawing horses, nails driving hammers, birds' nests taking boys, books making authors, bulls keeping china-shops, monkeys shaving cats, dead dogs drilling live lions, blind brigadiers shelfed as principals of colleges, play-actors not in the least shelfed as popular preachers; and, in short, every one set to do something which he had not learnt, because in what he had learnt, or pretended to learn, he had failed.

There stands the Pantheon of the Great Unsuccessful, from the builders of the Tower of Babel to those of the Trafalgar Fountains; in which politicians lecture on the constitutions which ought to have marched, conspirators on the revolutions which ought to have made every one's fortune, projectors on the discoveries which ought to have set the Thames on fire; and (in due time) presidents on the union which ought to have reunited, and secretaries of state on the greenbacks which ought to have done just as well as hard money. There cobblers lecture on orthopedy (whatsoever that may be) because they cannot sell their shoes; and poets on Aesthetics (whatsoever that may be) because they cannot sell their poetry. There philosophers demonstrate that England would be the freest and richest country in the world, if she would only turn Papist again; penny-a-liners abuse *The Times*, because they have not wit enough to get on its staff; and young ladies walk about with lockets of Charles the First's hair (or of somebody else's, when the Jews' genuine stock is used up), inscribed with the neat and appropriate legend – which indeed is popular through all that land, and which, I hope, you will learn to translate in due time and to perpend likewise:-

Victrix causa diis placuit, sed victa puellis.

When he got into the middle of the town, they all set on him at once, to show him his way; or rather, to show him that he did not know his way; for as for asking him what way he wanted to go, no one ever thought of that.

But one pulled him hither, and another poked him thither, and a third cried –

"You mustn't go west, I tell you; it is destruction to go west."

"But I am not going west, as you may see," said Tom.

And another, "The east lies here, my dear; I assure you this is the east."

"But I don't want to go east," said Tom.

"Well then, at all events, whichever way you are going, you are going wrong," cried they all with one voice – which was the only thing which they ever agreed about; and all pointed at once to all the thirty-and-two points of the compass, till Tom thought all the sign-posts in England had got together, and fallen fighting.

And whether he would have ever escaped out of the town, it is hard to say, if the dog had not taken it into his head that they were going to pull his master to pieces, and tackled them so sharply about the gastrocnemius muscle, that he gave them some business of their own to think of at last; and while they were rubbing their bitten calves, Tom and the dog got safe away.

On the borders of that island he found Gotham, where the wise men live; the same who dragged the pond because the moon had fallen into it, and planted a hedge round the cuckoo, to keep spring all the year. And he found them bricking up the town gate, because it was so wide that little folks could not get through. And, when he asked why, they told him they were expanding their liturgy. So he went on; for it was no business of his; only he could not help saying that in his country, if the kitten could not get in at the same hole as the cat, she might stay outside and mew.

But he saw the end of such fellows, when he came to the island of the Golden Asses, where nothing but thistles grow. For there they were all turned into mokes with ears a yard long, for meddling with matters which they did not understand, as Lucius did in the story. And like him, mokes they must remain, till, by the laws of development, the thistles develop into roses. Till then, they must comfort themselves with the thought, that the longer their ears are, the thicker their hides; and so a good beating don't hurt them.

Then came Tom to the great land of Hearsay, in which are no less than thirty and odd kings, beside half a dozen Republics, and perhaps more by next mail.

And there he fell in with a deep, dark, deadly, and destructive war, waged by the princes and potentates of those parts, both spiritual and temporal, against what do you think? One thing I am sure of. That unless I told you, you would never know; nor how they waged that war either; for all their strategy and art military consisted in the safe and easy process of stopping their ears and screaming, "Oh, don't tell us!" and then running away.

So when Tom came into that land, he found them all, high and low, man, woman, and child, running for their lives day and night continually, and entreating not to be told they didn't know what; only the land being an island, and they having a dislike to the water (being a musty lot for the most part) they ran round and round the shore for ever, which (as the island was exactly of the same circumference as the planet on which we have the honour of living) was hard work, especially to those who had business to look after. But before them, as bandmaster and fugleman, ran a gentleman shearing a pig; the melodious strains of which animal led them for ever, if not to conquest, still to flight; and kept up their spirits mightily with the thought that they would at least have the pig's wool for their pains.

And running after them, day and night, came such a poor, lean, seedy, hard-worked old giant, as ought to have been cockered up, and had a good dinner given him, and a good wife found him, and been set to play with little children; and then he would have been a very presentable old fellow after all; for he had a heart, though it was considerably overgrown with brains.

He was made up principally of fish bones and parchment, put together with wire and Canada balsam; and smelt strongly of spirits, though he never drank anything but water; but spirits he used somehow, there was no denying. He had a great pair of spectacles on his nose, and a butterfly-net in one hand, and a geological hammer in the other; and was hung all over with pockets, full of collecting boxes, bottles, microscopes, telescopes, barometers, ordnance maps, scalpels, forceps, photographic apparatus, and all other tackle for finding out everything about everything, and a little more too. And, most strange of all, he was running not forwards but backwards, as fast as he could.

Away all the good folks ran from him, except Tom, who stood his ground and dodged between his legs; and the giant, when he had passed him, looked down, and cried, as if he was quite pleased and comforted –

"What? who are you? And you actually don't run away, like all the rest?" But he had to take his spectacles off, Tom remarked, in order to see him plainly.

Tom told him who he was; and the giant pulled out a bottle and a cork instantly, to collect him with.

But Tom was too sharp for that, and dodged between his legs and in front of him; and then the giant could not see him at all.

"No, no, no!" said Tom, "I've not been round the world, and through the world, and up to Mother Carey's Haven, beside being caught in a net and called a Holothurian and a Cephalopod, to be bottled up by any old giant like you."

And when the giant understood what a great traveller Tom had been, he made a truce with him at once, and would have kept him there to this day to pick his brains, so delighted was he at finding any one to tell him what he did not know before.

"Ah, you lucky little dog!" said he at last, quite simply – for he was the simplest, pleasantest, honestest, kindliest old Dominie Sampson of a giant that even turned the world upside down without intending it – "Ah, you lucky little dog! If I had only been where you have been, to see what you have seen!"

"Well," said Tom, "if you want to do that, you had best put your head under water for a few hours, as I did, and turn into a water baby, or some other baby, and then you might have a chance."

"Turn into a baby, eh? If I could do that, and know what was happening to me for but one hour, I should know everything then, and be at rest. But I can't; I can't be a little child again; and I suppose if I could, it would be no use, because then I should know nothing about what was happening to me. Ah, you lucky little dog!" said the poor old giant.

"But why do you run after all these poor people?" said Tom, who liked the giant very much.

"My dear, it's they that have been running after me, father and son, for hundreds and hundreds of years, throwing stones at me till they have knocked off my spectacles fifty times, and calling me a malignant and a turbaned Turk, who beat a Venetian and traduced the state – goodness only knows what they mean, for I never read poetry – and hunting me round and round – though catch me they can't, for every time I go over the same ground, I go the faster, and grow the bigger. While all I want is to be friends with them, and to tell them something to their advantage, like Mr. Joseph Ady; only somehow they are so strangely afraid of hearing it. But, I suppose, I am not a man of the world, and have no tact."

"But why don't you turn round and tell them so?"

"Because I can't. You see, I am one of the sons of Epimetheus, and must go backwards, if I am to go at all."

"But why don't you stop, and let them come up to you?"

"Why, my dear, only think. If I did, all the butterflies and cockyolybirds would fly past me, and then I could catch no more new species, and should grow rusty and mouldy, and die. And I don't intend to do that, my dear; for I have a destiny before me, they say; though what it is I don't know, and don't care."

"Don't care?" said Tom.

"No. Do the duty which lies nearest you, and catch the first beetle you come across, is my motto; and I have thriven by it for some hundred years. Now I must go on. Dear me, while I have been talking to you, at least nine new species have escaped me."

And on went the giant, behind before, like a bull in a china shop, till he ran into the steeple of the great idol temple (for they are all idolaters in those parts, of course, else they would never be afraid of giants), and knocked the upper half clean off, hurting himself horribly about the small of the back.

But little he cared; for as soon as the ruins of the steeple were well between his legs, he poked and peered among the falling stones, and shifted his spectacles, and pulled out his pocket-magnifier, and cried –

"An entirely new Oniscus, and three obscure Podurellae! Beside a moth which M. le Roi des Papillons (though he, like all Frenchmen, is given to hasty inductions) says is confined to the limits of the Glacial Drift. This is most important!"

And down he sat on the nave of the temple (not being a man of the world) to examine his Podurellae. Whereon (as was to be expected) the roof caved in bodily, smashing the idols, and sending the priests flying out of doors and windows, like rabbits out of a burrow when a ferret goes in.

But he never heeded; for out of the dust flew a bat, and the giant had him in a moment.

"Dear me! This is even more important! Here is a cognate species to that which Macgilliwaukie Brown insists is confined to the Buddhist

Temples of Little Thibet; and now when I look at it, it may be only a variety produced by difference of climate?"

And having bagged his bat, up he got, and on he went; while all the people ran, being in none the better humour for having their temple smashed for the sake of three obscure species of Podurella, and a Buddhist bat.

"Well," thought Tom; "this is a very pretty quarrel, with a good deal to be said on both sides. But it is no business of mine."

And no more it was; because he was a water baby, and had the original sow by the right ear; which you will never have unless you be a baby, whether of the water, the land, or the air, matters not, provided you can only keep on continually being a baby.

So the giant ran round after the people, and the people ran round after the giant, and they are running unto this day for aught I know, or do not know; and will run till either he, or they, or both, turn into little children. And then, as Shakespeare says (and therefore it must be true) –

Jack shall have Gill
Nought shall go ill
The man shall have his mare again, and all go well.

Then Tom came to a very famous island, which was called, in the days of the great traveller Captain Gulliver, the Isle of Laputa. But Mrs. Bedonebyasyoudid has named it over again, the Isle of Tomtoddies, all heads and no bodies.

And when Tom came near it, he heard such a grumbling and grunting and growling and wailing and weeping and whining that he thought people must be ringing little pigs, or cropping puppies' ears, or drowning kittens; but when he came nearer still, he began to hear words among the noise; which was the Tomtoddies' song which they sing morning and evening, and all night too, to their great idol Examination –

I can't learn my lesson: the examiner's coming!

And that was the only song which they knew.

And when Tom got on shore the first thing he saw was a great pillar, on one side of which was inscribed, "Playthings not allowed here"; at which he was so shocked that he would not stay to see what was written on the other side. Then he looked round for the people of the island; but instead of men, women, and children, he found nothing but turnips and radishes, beet and mangoldwurzel, without a single green leaf among them, and half of them burst and decayed, with toadstools growing out of them. Those which were left began crying to Tom, in half a dozen different languages at once, and all of them badly spoken, "I can't learn my lesson; do come and help me!" And one cried, "Can you show me how to extract this square-root?"

And another, "Can you tell me the distance between a Lyrae and a β Camelopardalis?"

And another, "What is the latitude and longitude of Snooksville, in Noman's County, Oregon, U.S.?"

And another, "What was the name of Mutius Scaevola's thirteenth cousin's grandmother's maid's cat?"

And another, "How long would it take a school-inspector of average activity to tumble head over heels from London to York?"

And another, "Can you tell me the name of a place that nobody ever heard of, where nothing ever happened, in a country which has not been discovered yet?"

And another, "Can you show me how to correct this hopelessly corrupt passage of Graidiocolosyrtus Tabenniticus, on the cause why crocodiles have no tongues?"

And so on, and so on, and so on, till one would have thought they were all trying for tide-waiters' places, or cornetcies in the heavy dragoons.

"And what good on earth will it do you if I did tell you?" quoth Tom.

Well, they didn't know that; all they knew was the examiner was coming.

Then Tom stumbled on the hugest and softest nimblecomequick turnip you ever saw filling a hole in a crop of swedes, and it cried to him, "Can you tell me anything at all about anything you like?"

"About what?" says Tom.

"About anything you like; for as fast as I learn things I forget them again. So my mamma says that my intellect is not adapted for methodic science, and says that I must go in for general information."

Tom told him that he did not know general information, nor any officers in the army; only he had a friend once that went for a drummer – but he could tell him a great many strange things which he had seen in his travels.

So he told him prettily enough, while the poor turnip listened very carefully; and the more he listened, the more he forgot, and the more water ran out of him.

Tom thought he was crying; but it was only his poor brains running away, from being worked so hard; and as Tom talked, the unhappy turnip streamed down all over with juice, and split and shrank till nothing was left of him but rind and water; whereat Tom ran away in a fright, for he thought he might be taken up for killing the turnip.

But, on the contrary, the turnip's parents were highly delighted, and considered him a saint and a martyr, and put up a long inscription over his tomb about his wonderful talents, early development, and unparalleled precocity. Were they not a foolish couple? But there was a still more foolish couple next to them, who were beating a wretched little radish, no bigger than my thumb, for sullenness and obstinacy and wilful stupidity, and never knew that the reason why it couldn't learn or hardly even speak was, that there was a great worm inside it eating out all its brains. But even they are no foolisher than some hundred score of papas and mammas, who fetch the rod when they ought to fetch a new toy, and send to the dark cupboard instead of to the doctor.

Tom was so puzzled and frightened with all he saw, that he was longing to ask the meaning of it; and at last he stumbled over a respectable old stick lying half covered with earth. But a very stout and worthy stick it was, for it belonged to good Roger Ascham in old time, and had carved on its head King Edward the Sixth, with the Bible in his hand.

"You see," said the stick, "there were as pretty little children once as you could wish to see, and might have been so still if they had been only left to grow up like human beings, and then handed over to me; but their foolish fathers and mothers, instead of letting them pick flowers, and make dirt-pies, and get birds' nests, and dance round the gooseberry bush, as little children should, kept them always at lessons, working, working, working, learning week-day lessons all week-days, and Sunday lessons all Sunday, and weekly examinations every Saturday, and monthly examinations every month, and yearly examinations every year, everything seven times over, as if once was not enough, and enough as good as a feast – till their brains grew big, and their bodies grew small, and they were all changed into turnips, with little but water inside; and still their foolish parents actually pick the leaves off them as fast as they grow, lest they should have anything green about them."

"Ah!" said Tom, "if dear Mrs. Doasyouwouldbedoneby knew of it she would send them a top of tops, and balls, and marbles, and ninepins, and make them all as jolly as sand-boys."

"It would be no use," said the stick. "They can't play now, if they tried. Don't you see how their legs have turned to roots and grown into the ground, by never taking any exercise, but sapping and moping always in the same place? But here comes the Examiner-of-all-Examiners. So you had better get away, I warn you, or he will examine you and your dog into the bargain, and set him to examine all the other dogs, and you to examine all the other water babies. There is no escaping out of his hands, for his nose is nine thousand miles long, and can go down chimneys and through keyholes, upstairs, downstairs, in my lady's chamber, examining all little boys, and the little boys' tutors likewise. But when he is thrashed – so Mrs. Bedonebyasyoudid has promised me – I shall have the thrashing of him; and if I don't lay it on with a will it's a pity."

Tom went off: but rather slowly and surlily; for he was somewhat minded to face this same Examiner-of-all-Examiners, who came striding among the poor turnips, binding heavy burdens and grievous to be borne, and laying them on little children's shoulders, like the Scribes and Pharisees of old, and not touching the same with one of his fingers; for he had plenty of money, and a fine house to live in, and so forth; which was more than the poor little turnips had.

But when he got near, he looked so big and burly and dictatorial, and shouted so loud to Tom to come and be examined, that Tom ran for his life, and the dog too. And really it was time; for the poor turnips, in their hurry and fright, crammed themselves so fast to be ready for the Examiner, that they burst and popped by dozens all round him, till the place sounded like Aldershot on a field-day, and Tom thought he should be blown into the air, dog and all.

As he went down to the shore he passed the poor turnip's new tomb. But Mrs. Bedonebyasyoudid had taken away the epitaph about talents and precocity and development, and put up one of her own instead which Tom thought much more sensible:

Instruction sore long time I bore,
  And cramming was in vain;
Till Heaven did please my woes to ease,
  By water on the brain.
So Tom jumped into the sea, and swam on his way, singing:
  Farewell, Tomtoddies all; I thank my stars
That nought I know save those three royal r's:
  Reading and riting sure, with rithmetick,
Will help a lad of sense through thin and thick.

Whereby you may see that Tom was no poet; but no more was John Bunyan, though he was as wise a man as you will meet in a month of Sundays.

And next he came to Oldwivesfabledom, where the folks were all heathens, and worshipped a howling ape.

And there he found a little boy sitting in the middle of the road, and crying bitterly.

"What are you crying for?" said Tom.

"Because I am not as frightened as I could wish to be."

"Not frightened? You are a queer little chap; but, if you want to be frightened, here goes – Boo!"

"Ah," said the little boy, "that is very kind of you; but I don't feel that it has made any impression."

Tom offered to upset him, punch him, stamp on him, fettle him over the head with a brick, or anything else whatsoever which would give him the slightest comfort.

But he only thanked Tom very civilly, in fine long words which he had heard other folk use, and which, therefore, he thought were fit and proper to use himself; and cried on till his papa and mamma came, and sent off for the Powwow man immediately. And a very good-natured gentleman and lady they were, though they were heathens; and taked quite pleasantly to Tom about his travels, till the Powwow man arrived, with his thunderbox under his arm.

And a well-fed, ill-favoured gentleman he was, as ever served her Majesty at Portland. Tom was a little frightened at first; for he thought it was Grimes. But he soon saw his mistake; for Grimes always looked a man in the face; and this fellow never did. And when he spoke, it was fire and smoke; and when he sneezed, it was squibs and crackers; and when he cried (which he did whenever it paid him), it was boiling pitch; and some of it was sure to stick.

"Here we are again!" cried he, like the clown in a pantomime. "So you can't feel frightened, my little dear – eh? I'll do that for you. I'll make an impression on you! Yah! Boo! Whirroo! Hullabaloo!"

And he rattled, thumped, brandished his thunderbox, yelled, shouted, raved, roared, stamped, and danced corrobory like any black fellow; and then he touched a spring in the thunderbox, and out popped turnip-ghosts and magic-lanthorns and pasteboard bogies and spring-heeled Jacks and sallabalas, with such a horrid din, clatter, clank, roll, rattle, and roar, that the little boy turned up the whites of his eyes, and fainted right away.

And at that his poor heathen papa and mamma were as much delighted as if they had found a gold mine; and fell down upon their knees before the Powwow man, and gave him a palanquin with a pole of solid silver and curtains of cloth of gold; and carried him about in it on their own backs; but as soon as they had taken him up, the pole stuck to their shoulders, and they could not set him down any more, but carried him on willy-nilly, as Sinbad carried the old man of the sea; which was a pitiable sight to see; for the father was a very brave officer, and wore two swords and a blue button; and the mother was as pretty a lady as ever had pinched feet like a Chinese. But you see, they had chosen to do a foolish thing just once too often; so by the laws of Mrs. Bedonebyasyoudid, they had to go on doing it whether they chose or not, till the coming of the Cocqcigrues.

Ah! don't you wish that some one would go and convert those poor heathens, and teach them not to frighten their little children into fits?

"Now, then," said the Powwow man to Tom, "wouldn't you like to be frightened, my little dear? For I can see plainly that you are a very wicked, naughty, graceless, reprobate boy."

"You're another," quoth Tom, very sturdily. And when the man ran at him, and cried "Boo!" Tom ran at him in return, and cried 'Boo!" likewise, right in his face, and set the little dog upon him; and at his legs the dog went.

At which, if you will believe it, the fellow turned tail, thunderbox and all, with a "Woof!" like an old sow on the common; and ran for his life, screaming, "Help! thieves! murder! fire! He is going to kill me! I am a ruined man! He will murder me; and break, burn, and destroy my precious and invaluable thunderbox; and then you will have no more thunder showers in the land. Help! help! help!"

At which the papa and mamma and all the people of Oldwivesfabledom, flew at Tom, shouting, "Oh, the wicked, impudent, hard-hearted, graceless boy! Beat him, kick him, shoot him, drown him, hang him, burn him!" and so forth; but luckily they had nothing to shoot, hang, or burn him with, for the fairies had hid all the killing-tackle out of the way a little while before; so they could only pelt him with stones; and some of the stones went clean through him, and came out the other side. But he did not mind that a bit; for the holes closed up again as fast as they were made, because he was a water baby. However, he was very glad when he was safe out of the country, for the noise there made him all but deaf.

Then he came to a very quiet place, called Leaveheavenalone. And there the sun was drawing water out of the sea to make steam-threads, and the wind was twisting them up to make cloud-patterns, till they had worked between them the loveliest wedding veil of Chantilly lace, and hung it up in their own Crystal Palace for any one to buy who could afford it; while the good old sea never grudged, for she knew they would pay her back honestly. So the sun span, and the wind wove, and all went well with the great steam-loom; as is likely, considering – and considering – and considering –

And at last, after innumerable adventures, each more wonderful than the last, he saw before him a huge building, much bigger, and – what is most surprising – a little uglier than a certain new lunatic asylum, but not built quite of the same materials. None of it, at least – or, indeed, for aught that I ever saw, any part of any other building whatsoever – is cased with nine-inch brick inside and out, and filled up with rubble between the walls, in order that any gentleman who has been confined during her Majesty's pleasure may be unconfined during his own pleasure, and take a walk in the neighbouring park to improve his spirits, after an hour's light and wholesome labour with his dinner-fork or one of the legs of his iron bedstead. No. The walls of this building were built on an entirely different principle, which need not be described, as it has not yet been discovered.

Tom walked towards this great building, wondering what it was, and having a strange fancy that he might find Mr. Grimes inside it, till he saw running toward him, and shouting "Stop!" three or four people, who, when they came nearer, were nothing else than policemen's truncheons, running along without legs or arms.

Tom was not astonished. He was long past that. Besides, he had seen the naviculae in the water move nobody knows how, a hundred times, without arms, or legs, or anything to stand in their stead. Neither was he frightened; for he had been doing no harm.

So he stopped; and when the foremost trunchon came up and asked his business, he showed Mother Carey's pass; and the truncheon looked at it in the oddest fashion; for he had one eye in the middle of his upper end, so that when he looked at anything, being quite stiff, he had to slope himself, and poke himself, till it was a wonder why he did not tumble over; but, being quite full of the spirit of justice (as all policemen, and their truncheons, ought to be), he was always in a position of stable equilibrium, whichever way he put himself.

"All right – pass on," said he at last. And then he added: "I had better go with you, young man." And Tom had no objection, for such company was both respectable and safe; so the truncheon coiled its thong neatly round its handle, to prevent tripping itself up – for the thong had got loose in running – and marched on by Tom's side.

"Why have you no policeman to carry you?" asked Tom, after a while.

"Because we are not like those clumsy-made truncheons in the land-world, which cannot go without having a whole man to carry them about. We do our own work for ourselves; and do it very well, though I say it who should not."

"Then why have you a thong to your handle?" asked Tom.

"To hang ourselves up by, of course, when we are off duty."

Tom had got his answer, and had no more to say, till they came up to the great iron door of the prison. And there the truncheon knocked twice, with its own head.

A wicket in the door opened, and out looked a tremendous old brass blunderbuss charged up to the muzzle with slugs, who was the porter; and Tom started back a little at the sight of him.

"What case is this?" he asked in a deep voice, out of his broad bell-mouth.

"If you please, sir, it is no case; only a young gentleman from her ladyship, who wants to see Grimes the master-sweep."

"Grimes?" said the blunderbuss. And he pulled in his muzzle, perhaps to look over his prison-lists.

"Grimes is up chimney No. 345," he said from inside. "So the young gentleman had better go on to the roof."

Tom looked up at the enormous wall, which seemed at least ninety miles high, and wondered how he should ever get up; but, when he hinted that to the truncheon, it settled the matter in a moment. For it whisked round, and gave him such a shove behind as sent him up to the roof in no time, with his little dog under his arm.

And there he walked along the leads, till he met another truncheon, and told him his errand.

"Very good," it said. "Come along; but it will be of no use. He is the most unremorseful, hard-hearted, foul-mouthed fellow I have in charge; and thinks about nothing but beer and pipes, which are not allowed here, of course."

So they walked along over the leads, and very sooty they were, and Tom thought the chimneys must want sweeping very much. But he was surprised to see that the soot did not stick to his feet, or dirty them in the least. Neither did the live coals, which were lying about in plenty, burn him; for, being a water baby, his radical humours were of a moist and cold nature, as you may read at large in Lemnius, Cardan, Van Helmont, and other gentlemen, who knew as much as they could, and no man can know more.

And at last they came to chimney No. 345. Out of the top of it, his head and shoulders just showing, stuck poor Mr. Grimes; so sooty, and bleared, and ugly, that Tom could hardly bear to look at him. And in his mouth was a pipe; but it was not a-light, though he was pulling at it with all his might.

"Attention, Mr. Grimes," said the truncheon; "here is a gentleman come to see you."

But Mr. Grimes only said bad words; and kept grumbling, "My pipe won't draw. My pipe won't draw."

"Keep a civil tongue, and attend!" said the truncheon; and popped up just like Punch, hitting Grimes such a crack over the head with itself, that his brains rattled inside like a dried walnut in its shell. He tried to get his hands out, and rub the place; but he could not, for they were stuck fast in the chimney.

Now he was forced to attend.

"Hey!" he said, "why, it's Tom! I suppose you have come here to laugh at me, you spiteful little atomy?"

Tom assured him he had not, but only wanted to help him.

"I don't want anything except beer, and that I can't get; and a light to this bothering pipe, and that I can't either."

"I'll get you one," said Tom; and he took up a live coal (there were plenty lying about) and put it to Grimes's pipe; but it went out instantly.

"It's no use," said the truncheon, leaning itself up against the chimney, and looking on. "I tell you, it is no use. His heart is so cold that it freezes everything that comes near him. You will see that presently, plain enough."

"Oh, of course, it's my fault. Everything's always my fault," said Grimes. "Now don't go to hit me again" (for the truncheon started upright, and looked very wicked); "you know, if my arms were only free, you daren't hit me then."

The truncheon leant back against the chimney, and took no notice of the personal insult, like a well-trained policeman as it was, though he was ready enough to avenge any transgression against morality or order.

"But can't I help you in any other way? Can't I help you to get out of this chimney?" said Tom.

"No," interposed the truncheon; "he has come to the place where everybody must help themselves; and he will find it out, I hope, before he is done with me."

"Oh, yes," said Grimes, "of course it's me. Did I ask to be brought here into the prison? Did I ask to be set to sweep your foul chimneys? Did I ask to have lighted straw put under me to make me go up? Did I ask to stick fast in the very first chimney of all, because it was so shamefully clogged up with soot? Did I ask to stay here – I don't know how long – a hundred years, I do believe, and never get my pipe, nor my beer, nor nothing fit for a beast, let alone a man."

"No," answered a solemn voice behind. "No more did Tom, when you behaved to him in the very same way."

It was Mrs. Bedonebyasyoudid. And, when the truncheon saw her, it started bolt upright – Attention! – and made such a low bow, that if it had not been full of the spirit of justice, it must have tumbled on its end, and probably hurt its one eye. And Tom made his bow too.

"Oh, ma'am," he said, "don't think about me; that's all past and gone, and good times and bad times and all times pass over. But may not I help poor Mr. Grimes? Mayn't I try and get some of these bricks away, that he may move his arms?"

"You may try, of course," she said.

So Tom pulled and tugged at the bricks; but he could not move one. And then he tried to wipe Mr. Grimes's face: but the soot would not come off.

"Oh, dear!" he said, "I have come all this way, through all these terrible places, to help you, and now I am of no use after all."

"You had best leave me alone," said Grimes; "you are a good-natured forgiving little chap, and that's truth; but you'd best be off. The hail's coming on soon, and it will beat the eyes out of your little head."

"What hail?"

"Why, hail that falls every evening here; and, till it comes close to me, it's like so much warm rain; but then it turns to hail over my head, and knocks me about like small shot."

"That hail will never come any more," said the strange lady. "I have told you before what it was. It was your mother's tears, those which she shed when she prayed for you by her bedside; but your cold heart froze it into hail. But she is gone to heaven now, and will weep no more for her graceless son."

Then Grimes was silent a while; and then he looked very sad.

"So my old mother's gone, and I never there to speak to her! Ah! a good woman she was, and might have been a happy one, in her little school there in Vendale, if it hadn't been for me and my bad ways."

"Did she keep the school in Vendale?" asked Tom. And then he told Grimes all the story of his going to her house, and how she could not abide the sight of a chimney-sweep, and then how kind she was, and how he turned into a water baby.

"Ah!" said Grimes, "good reason she had to hate the sight of a chimney-sweep. I ran away from her and took up with the sweeps, and never let her know where I was, nor sent her a penny to help her, and now it's too late – too late!" said Mr. Grimes.

And he began crying and blubbering like a great baby, till his pipe dropped out of his mouth, and broke all to bits.

"Oh dear, if I was but a little chap in Vendale again, to see the clear beck, and the apple-orchard, and the yew-hedge, how different I would go on! But it's too late now. So you go along, you kind little chap, and don't stand to look at a man crying, that's old enough to be your father, and never feared the face of man, nor of worse neither. But I'm beat now, and beat I must be. I've made my bed, and I must lie on it. Foul I would be, and foul I am, as an Irishwoman said to me once; and little I heeded it. It's all my own fault – but it's too late." And he cried so bitterly that Tom began crying too.

"Never too late," said the fairy, in such a strange soft new voice that Tom looked up at her; and she was so beautiful for the moment, that Tom half fancied she was her sister.

No more was it too late. For, as poor Grimes cried and blubbered on, his own tears did what his mother's could not do, and Tom's could not do, and nobody's on earth could do for him; for they washed the soot off his face and off his clothes; and then they washed the mortar away from between the bricks; and the chimney crumbled down; and Grimes began to get out of it.

Up jumped the truncheon, and was going to hit him on the crown a tremendous thump, and drive him down again like a cork into a bottle. But the strange lady put it aside.

"Will you obey me if I give you a chance?"

"As you please, ma'am. You're stronger than me, that I know too well, and wiser than me, I know too well also. And, as for being my own master, I've fared ill enough with that as yet. So whatever your ladyship pleases to order me; for I'm beat, and that's the truth."

"Be it so then – you may come out. But remember, disobey me again, and into a worse place still you go."

"I beg pardon, ma'am, but I never disobeyed you that I know of. I never had the honour of setting eyes upon you till I came to these ugly quarters."

"Never saw me? Who said to you, Those that will be foul, foul they will be?"

Grimes looked up; and Tom looked up to; for the voice was that of the Irishwoman who met them the day that they went out together to Harthover. "I gave you your warning then; but you gave it yourself a thousand times before and since. Every bad word that you said – every cruel and mean thing that you did – every time that you got tipsy – every day that you went dirty – you were disobeying me, whether you knew it or not."

"If I'd only known, ma'am – "

"You knew well enough that you were disobeying something, though you did not know it was me. But come out and take your chance. Perhaps it may be your last."

So Grimes stept out of the chimney, and, really, if it had not been for the scars on his face, he looked as clean and respectable as a master-sweep need look.

"Take him away," said she to the truncheon, "and give him his ticket-of-leave."

"And what is he to do, ma'am?"

"Get him to sweep out the crater of Etna; he will find some very steady men working out their time there, who will teach him his business; but mind, if that crater gets choked again, and there is an earthquake in consequence, bring them all to me, and I shall investigate the case very severely."

So the truncheon marched off Mr. Grimes, looking as meek as a drowned worm.

And for aught I know, or do not know, he is sweeping the crater of Etna to this very day.

"And now," said the fairy to Tom, "your work here is done. You may as well go back again."

"I should be glad enough to go," said Tom, "but how am I to get up that great hole again, now the steam has stopped blowing?"

"I will take you up the backstairs; but I must bandage your eyes first; for I never allow anybody to see those backstairs of mine."

"I am sure I shall not tell anybody about them, ma'am, if you bid me not."

"Aha! So you think, my little man. But you would soon forget your promise if you got back into the land-world. For, if people only once found out that you had been up my backstairs, you would have all the fine ladies kneeling to you, and the rich men emptying their purses before you, and statesmen offering you place and power; and young and old, rich and poor, crying to you, 'Only tell us the great backstairs secret, and we will be your slaves; we will make you lord, king, emperor, bishop, archbishop, pope, if you like – only tell us the secret of the backstairs. For thousands of years we have been paying, and petting, and obeying, and worshipping quacks who told us they had the key of the backstairs, and could smuggle us up them; and in spite of all our disappointments, we will honour, and glorify, and adore, and beatify, and translate, and apotheotise you likewise, on the chance of your knowing something about the backstairs, that we may all go on pilgrimage to it; and, even if we cannot get up it, lie at the foot of it, and cry –

> 'Oh, backstairs,
>
> *precious backstairs,*   *aristocratic backstairs,*
> *invaluable backstairs,*   *respectable backstairs,*

requisite backstairs,
necessary backstairs,
good-natured backstairs,
cosmopolitan backstairs,
comprehensive backstairs,
accommodating backstairs,
well-bred backstairs,
comfortable backstairs,
humane backstairs,
reasonable backstairs,
long-sought backstairs,
coveted backstairs,

gentlemanlike backstairs,
ladylike backstairs,
commercial backstairs,
economical backstairs,
practical backstairs,
logical backstairs,
deductive backstairs,
orthodox backstairs,
probable backstairs,
credible backstairs,
demonstrable backstairs,
irrefragable backstairs,

potent backstairs,
all-but-omnipotent backstairs,
etc

Save us from the consequences of our own actions, and from the cruel fairy, Mrs. Bedonebyasyoudid!' Do not you think that you would be a little tempted then to tell what you know, laddie?"

Tom thought so certainly. "But why do they want so to know about the backstairs?" asked he, being a little frightened at the long words, and not understanding them the least; as, indeed, he was not meant to do, or you either.

"That I shall not tell you. I never put things into little folks' heads which are but too likely to come there of themselves. So come – now I must bandage your eyes." So she tied the bandage on his eyes with one hand, and with the other she took it off.

"Now," she said, "you are safe up the stairs." Tom opened his eyes very wide, and his mouth too; for he had not, as he thought, moved a single step. But, when he looked round him, there could be no doubt that he was safe up the backstairs, whatsoever they may be, which no man is going to tell you, for the plain reason that no man knows.

The first thing which Tom saw was the black cedars, high and sharp against the rosy dawn; and St. Brandan's Isle reflected double in the still broad silver sea. The wind sang softly in the cedars, and the water sang among the caves; the sea-birds sang as they streamed out into the ocean, and the land-birds as they built among the boughs; and the air was so full of song that it stirred St. Brandan and his hermits, as they slumbered in the shade; and they moved their good old lips, and sang their morning hymn amid their dreams. But among all the songs one came across the water more sweet and clear than all; for it was the song of a young girl's voice.

And what was the song which she sang? Ah, my little man, I am too old to sing that song, and you too young to understand it. But have patience, and keep your eye single, and your hands clean, and you will learn some day to sing it yourself, without needing any man to teach you.

And as Tom neared the island, there sat upon a rock the most graceful creature that ever was seen, looking down, with her chin upon her hand, and paddling with her feet in the water. And when they came to her she looked up, and behold it was Ellie.

"Oh, Miss Ellie," said he, "how you are grown!"

"Oh, Tom," said she, "how you are grown, too!"

And no wonder; they were both quite grown up — he into a tall man, and she into a beautiful woman.

"Perhaps I may be grown," she said. "I have had time enough; for I have been sitting here waiting for you many a hundred years, till I thought you were never coming."

"Many a hundred years?" thought Tom; but he had seen so much in his travels that he had quite given up being astonished; and, indeed, he could think of nothing but Ellie. So he stood and looked at Ellie, and Ellie looked at him; and they liked the employment so much that they stood and looked for seven years more, and neither spoke nor stirred.

At last they heard the fairy say: "Attention, children! Are you never going to look at me again?"

"We have been looking at you all this while," they said. And so they thought they had been.

"Then look at me once more," said she.

They looked — and both of them cried out at once, "Oh, who are you, after all?"

"You are our dear Mrs. Doasyouwouldbedoneby"

"No, you are good Mrs. Bedonebyasyoudid; but you are grown quite beautiful now!"

"To you," said the fairy. "But look again."

"You are Mother Carey," said Tom, in a very low, solemn voice; for he had found out something which made him very happy, and yet frightened him more than all that he had ever seen.

"But you are grown quite young again."

"To you," said the fairy. "Look again."

"You are the Irishwoman who met me the day I went to Harthover!"

And when they looked she was neither of them, and yet all of them at once.

"My name is written in my eyes, if you have eyes to see it there."

And they looked into her great, deep, soft eyes, and they changed again and again into every hue, as the light changes in a diamond.

"Now read my name," said she, at last.

And her eyes flashed, for one moment, clear, white, blazing light: but the children could not read her name; for they were dazzled, and hid their faces in their hands.

"Not yet, young things, not yet," said she, smiling; and then she turned to Ellie.

"You may take him home with you now on Sundays, Ellie. He has won his spurs in the great battle, and become fit to go with you, and be a man; because he has done the thing he did not like."

So Tom went home with Ellie on Sundays, and sometimes on week-days, too; and he is now a great man of science, and can plan railroads, and steam-engines, and electric telegraphs, and rifled guns, and so forth; and knows everything about everything, except why a hen's egg don't turn into a crocodile, and two or three other little things which no one will know till the coming of the Cocqcigrues. And all this from what he learnt when he was a water baby, underneath the sea.

"And of course Tom married Ellie?"

My dear child, what a silly notion! Don't you know that no one ever marries in a fairy tale, under the rank of a prince or a princess?

"And Tom's dog?"

Oh, you may see him any clear night in July; for the old dog-star was so worn out by the last three hot summers that there have been no dog-days since; so that they had to take him down and put Tom's dog up in his place. Therefore, as new brooms sweep clean, we may hope for some warm weather this year. And that is the end of my story.

MORAL

~

And now, my dear little man, what should we learn from this parable?

We should learn thirty-seven or thirty-nine things, I am not exactly sure which; but one thing, at least, we may learn, and that is this – when we see efts in the ponds, never to throw stones at them, or catch them with crooked pins, or put them into vivariums with sticklebacks, that the sticklebacks may prick them in their poor little stomachs, and make them jump out of the glass into somebody's workbox, and so come to a bad end. For these efts are nothing else but the water babies who are stupid and dirty, and will not learn their lessons and keep themselves clean; and, therefore (as comparative anatomists will tell you fifty years hence, though they are not learned enough to tell you now), their skulls grow flat, their jaws grow out, and their brains grow small, and their tails grow long, and they lose all their ribs (which I am sure you would not like to do), and their skins grow dirty and spotted, and they never get into the clear rivers, much less into the great wide sea, but hang about in dirty ponds, and live in the mud, and eat worms, as they deserve to do.

But that is no reason why you should ill-use them; but only why you should pity them, and be kind to them, and hope that some day they will wake up, and be ashamed of their nasty, dirty, lazy, stupid life, and try to amend, and become something better once more. For, perhaps, if they do so, then after 379,423 years, nine months, thirteen days, two hours, and twenty-one minutes (for aught that appears to the contrary), if they work very hard and wash very hard all that time, their brains may grow bigger, and their jaws grow smaller, and their ribs come back, and their tails wither off, and they will turn into water babies again, and, perhaps, after that into land babies; and after that, perhaps, into grown men.

You know they won't? Very well, I dare say you know best. But, you see, some folks have a great liking for those poor little efts. They never did anybody any harm, or could if they tried; and their only fault is, that they do no good – any more than some thousands of their betters. But what with ducks, and what with pike, and what with sticklebacks, and what with water-beetles, and what with naughty boys, they are "sae sair hadden doun," as the Scotsmen say, that it is a wonder how they live; and some folks can't help hoping, with good Bishop Butler, that they may have another chance, to make things fair and even, somewhere, somewhen, somehow.

Meanwhile, do you learn your lessons, and thank God that you have plenty of cold water to wash in; and wash in it too, like a true Englishman. And then, if my story is not true, something better is; and if I am not quite right, still you will be, as long as you stick to hard work and cold water.

But remember always, as I told you at first, that this is all a fairy tale, and only fun and pretence; and, therefore, you are not to believe a word of it, even if it is true.

Peter Pan

~

J. M. Barrie

Illustrated by
Mabel Lucie Attwell

Contents

COLOUR
ILLUSTRATIONS

CHAPTER ONE

PETER BREAKS THROUGH

~

All children, except one, grow up. They soon know that they will grow up, and the way Wendy knew was this. One day when she was two years old she was playing in a garden, and she plucked another flower and ran with it to her mother. I suppose she must have looked rather delightful, for Mrs Darling put her hand to her heart and cried, "Oh, why can't you remain like this for ever!" This was all that passed between them on the subject, but henceforth Wendy knew that she must grow up. You always know after you are two. Two is the beginning of the end.

Of course they lived at 14, and until Wendy came her mother was the chief one. She was a lovely lady, with a romantic mind and such a sweet mocking mouth. Her romantic mind was like the tiny boxes, one within the other, that come from the puzzling East, however many you discover there is always one more; and her sweet mocking mouth had one kiss on it that Wendy could never get, though there it was, perfectly conspicuous in the right-hand corner.

The way Mr Darling won her was this: the many gentlemen who had been boys when she was a girl discovered simultaneously that they loved her, and they all ran to her house to propose to her except Mr Darling, who took a cab and nipped in first, and so he got her. He got all of her, except the innermost box and the kiss. He never knew about the box, and in time he gave up trying for the kiss. Wendy thought Napoleon could have got it, but I can picture him trying, and then going off in a passion, slamming the door.

Mr Darling used to boast to Wendy that her mother not only loved him but respected him. He was one of those deep ones who knows about stocks and shares. Of course no one really knows, but he quite seemed to know, and he often said stocks were up and shares were down in a way that would have made any woman respect him.

Mrs Darling was married in white, and at first she kept the books perfectly, almost gleefully, as if it were a game, not so much as a brussels sprout was missing; but by and by whole cauliflowers dropped out, and instead of them there were pictures of babies without faces. She drew them when she should have been totting up. They were Mrs Darling's guesses.

Wendy came first, then John, then Michael.

For a week or two after Wendy came it was doubtful whether they would be able to keep her, as she was another mouth to feed. Mr Darling was frightfully proud of her, but he was very honourable, and he sat on the edge of Mrs Darling's bed, holding her hand and calculating the expenses, while she looked at him imploringly. She wanted to risk it, come what might, but that was not his way; his way was with a pencil and a piece of paper, and if she confused him with suggestions he had to begin at the beginning again.

"Now don't interrupt," he would beg of her. "I have one pound seventeen here, and two and six at the office; I can cut off my coffee at the office, say ten shillings, making two nine and six, with your eighteen and three makes three nine seven, with five naught naught in my cheque-book makes eight nine seven – who is that moving? – eight nine seven, dot and carry seven – don't speak, my own – and the pound you lent to that man who came to the door - quiet, child – dot and carry child – there, you've done it! – did I say nine nine seven? yes, I said nine nine seven; the question is, can we try it for a year on nine nine seven?"

"Of course we can, George," she cried. But she was prejudiced in Wendy's favour, and he was really the grander character of the two.

"Remember mumps," he warned her almost threateningly and off he went again. "Mumps one pound, that is what I have put down, but I dare say it will be more like thirty shillings – don't speak – measles one five, German measles half a guinea, makes two fifteen six – don't waggle your finger – whooping-cough, say fifteen shillings" – and so on it went, and it added up differently each time; but at last Wendy just got through, with mumps reduced to twelve six, and the two kinds of measles treated as one.

There was the same excitement over John, and Michael had even a narrower squeak; but both were kept, and soon you might have seen the three of them going in a row to Miss Fulsom's Kindergarten school, accompanied by their nurse.

Mrs Darling loved to have everything just so, and Mr Darling had a passion for being exactly like his neighbours; so, of course, they had a nurse. As they were poor, owing to the amount of milk the children drank, this nurse was a prim Newfoundland dog, called Nana, who had belonged to no one in particular until the Darlings engaged her. She had always thought children important, however, and the Darlings had become acquainted with her in Kensington Gardens, where she spent most of her spare time peeping into perambulators, and was much hated by careless nursemaids, whom she followed to their homes and complained of to their mistresses. She proved to be quite a treasure of a nurse. How thorough she was at bath-time; and up at any moment of the night if one of her charges made the slightest cry. Of course her kennel was in the nursery. She had a genius for knowing when a cough is a thing to have no patience with and when it needs stocking round your throat. she believed to her last day in old-fashioned remedies like rhubarb leaf, and made sounds of contempt over all this new-fangled talk about germs, and so on. It was a lesson in propriety to see her escorting the children to school, walking sedately by their side when they were well behaved, and butting them back into line if they strayed. On John's footer days she never once forgot his sweater, and she usually carried an umbrella in her mouth in case of rain. There is a room in the basement of Miss Fulsom's school where the nurses wait. They sat on forms, while Nana lay on the floor, but that was the only difference. They affected to ignore her as of an inferior social status to themselves, and she despised their light talk. She resented visits to the nursery from Mrs Darling's friends, but if they did come she first whipped off Michael's pinafore and put him into the one with blue braiding, and smoothed out Wendy and made a dash at John's hair.

No nursery could possibly have been conducted more correctly, and Mr Darling knew it, yet he sometimes wondered uneasily whether the neighbours talked.

He had his position in the city to consider.

Nana also troubled him in another way. He had sometimes a feeling that she did not admire him. "I know she admires you tremendously, George," Mrs Darling would assure him, and then she would sign to the children to be specially nice to father. Lovely dances followed, in which the only other servant, Liza, was sometimes allowed to join. Such a midget she looked in her long skirt and maid's cap, though she had sworn, when engaged, that she would never see ten again. The gaiety of those romps! And gayest of all was Mrs Darling, who would pirouette so wildly that all you could see of her was the kiss, and then if you had dashed at her you might have got it. There never was a simpler, happier family until the coming of Peter Pan.

Mrs Darling first heard of Peter when she was tidying up her children's minds. It is the nightly custom of every good mother after her children are asleep to rummage in their minds and put things straight for next morning, repacking into their proper places the many articles that have wandered during the day. If you could keep awake (but of course you can't) you would see your own mother doing this, and you would find it very interesting to watch her. It is quite like tidying up drawers. You would see her on her knees, I expect, lingering humorously over some of your contents, wondering where on earth you had picked this thing up, making discoveries sweet and not so sweet, pressing this to her cheek as if it were as nice as a kitten, and hurriedly stowing that out of sight. When you wake in the morning, the naughtiness and evil passions with which you went to bed have been folded up small and placed at the bottom of your mind; and on the top, beautifully aired, are spread out your prettier thoughts, ready for you to put on.

I don't know whether you have ever seen a map of a person's mind. Doctors sometimes draw maps of other parts of you, and your own map can become intensely interesting, but catch them trying to draw a map of a child's mind, which is not only confused, but keeps going round all the time. There are zigzag lines on it, just like your temperature on a card, and these are probably roads in the island; for the Neverland is always more or less an island, with astonishing splashes of colour here and there, and coral reefs and rakish-looking craft in the offing, and savages and lonely lairs, and gnomes who are mostly tailors, and caves through which a river runs, and princes with six elder brothers, and a hut fast going to decay, and one very small old lady with a hooked nose. It would be an easy map if that were all; but there is also first day at school, religion, fathers, the round pond, needlework, murders, hangings, verbs that take the dative, chocolate-pudding day, getting into braces, say ninety-nine, threepence for pulling out your tooth yourself, and so on; and either these are part of the island or they are another map showing through, and it is all rather confusing, especially as nothing will stand still.

Of course the Neverlands vary a good deal. John's, for instance, had a lagoon with flamingoes flying over it at which John was shooting, while Michael, who was very small, had a flamingo with lagoons flying over it. John lived in a boat turned upside down on the sands, Michael in a wigwam, Wendy in a house of leaves deftly sewn together. John had no friends, Michael had friends at night, Wendy had a pet wolf forsaken by its parents; but on the whole the Neverlands have a family resemblance, and if they stood still in a row you could say of them that they have each other's nose, and so forth. On these magic shores children at play are for ever beaching their coracles. We too have been there; we can still hear the sound of the surf, though we shall land no more.

Of all delectable islands the Neverland is the snuggest and most compact; not large and sprawly, you know, with tedious distances between one adventure and another, but nicely crammed. When you play at it by day with the chairs and table-cloth, it is not in the least alarming but in the two minutes before you go to sleep it becomes very nearly real. That is why there are night-lights.

Occasionally in her travels through her children's minds Mrs Darling found things she could not understand, and of these quite the most perplexing was the word Peter. She knew of no Peter, and yet he was here and there in John and Michael's minds, while Wendy's began to be scrawled all over with him. The name stood out in bolder letters than any of the other words, and as Mrs Darling gazed she felt that it had an oddly cocky appearance.

"Yes, he is rather cocky," Wendy admitted with regret. Her mother had been questioning her.

"But who is he, my pet?"

"He is Peter Pan, you know, mother."

At first Mrs Darling did not know, but after thinking back into her childhood she just remembered a Peter Pan who was said to live with the fairies. There were odd stories about him; as that when children died he went part of the way with them, so that they should not be frightened. She had believed in him at the time, but now that she was married and full of sense she quite doubted whether there was any such person.

"Besides," she said to Wendy, "he would be grown up by this time."

"Oh no, he isn't grown up," Wendy assured her confidently, "and he is just my size." She meant that he was her size in both mind and body; she didn't know how she knew it, she just knew it.

Mrs Darling consulted Mr Darling, but he smiled pooh-pooh. "Mark my words," he said, "it is some nonsense Nana has been putting into their heads; just the sort of idea a dog would have. Leave it alone, and it will blow over."

But it would not blow over; and soon the troublesome boy gave Mrs Darling quite a shock.

Children have the strangest adventures without being troubled by them. For instance, they may remember to mention, a week after the event happened, that when they were in the wood they met their dead father and had a game with him. It was in this casual way that Wendy one morning made a disquieting revelation. Some leaves of a tree had been found on the nursery floor, which certainly were not there when the children went to bed, and Mrs Darling was puzzling over them when Wendy said with a tolerant smile:

"I do believe it is that Peter again!"

"Whatever do you mean, Wendy?"

"It is so naughty of him not to wipe," Wendy said, sighing. She was a tidy child.

She explained in quite a matter-of-fact way that she thought Peter sometimes came to the nursery in the night and sat on the foot of her bed and played on his pipes to her. Unfortunately she never woke, so she didn't know how she knew, she just knew.

"What nonsense you talk, precious. No one can get into the house without knocking."

"I think he comes in by the window," she said.

"My love, it is three floors up."

"Were not the leaves at the foot of the window, mother?"

It was quite true; the leaves had been found very near the window.

Mrs Darling did not know what to think, for it all seemed so natural to Wendy that you could not dismiss it by saying she had been dreaming.

"My child," the mother cried, "why did you not tell me of this before?"

"I forgot," said Wendy lightly. She was in a hurry to get her breakfast.

Oh, surely she must have been dreaming.

Peter... sat on the foot of her bed and played on his
pipes to her.

But, on the other hand, there were the leaves. Mrs Darling examined them carefully; they were skeleton leaves, but she was sure they did not come from any tree that grew in England. She crawled about the floor, peering at it with a candle for marks of a strange foot. She rattled the poker up the chimney and tapped the walls. She let down a tape from the window to the pavement, and it was a sheer drop of thirty feet, without so much as a spout to climb up by.

Certainly Wendy had been dreaming.

But Wendy had not been dreaming, as the very next night showed, the night on which the extraordinary adventures of these children may be said to have begun.

On the night we speak of all the children were once more in bed. It happened to be Nana's evening off, and Mrs Darling had bathed and sung to them till one by one they had let go her hand and slid away into the land of sleep.

They were looking so safe and cosy that she smiled at her fears now and sat down tranquilly by the fire to sew.

It was something for Michael, who on his birthday was getting into shirts. The fire was warm, however, and the nursery dimly lit by three night-lights and presently the sewing lay on Mrs Darling's lap. Then her head nodded, oh, so gracefully. She was asleep. Look at the four of them, Wendy and Michael over there, John here, and Mrs Darling by the fire. There should have been a fourth night-light.

While she slept she had a dream. She dreamt that the Neverland had come too near and that a strange boy had broken through from it. He did not alarm her, for she thought she had seen him before in the faces of many women who have no children. Perhaps he is to be found in the faces of some mothers also. But in her dream he had rent the film that obscures the Neverland, and she saw Wendy and John and Michael peeping through the gap.

The dream by itself would have been a trifle, but while she was dreaming the window of the nursery blew open, and a boy did drop on the floor. He was accompanied by a strange light, no bigger than your fist, which darted about the room like a living thing; and I think it must have been this light that wakened Mrs Darling.

She started up with a cry, and saw the boy, and somehow she knew

He was a lovely boy, clad in skeleton leaves…

at once that he was Peter Pan. If you or I or Wendy had been there we should have seen that he was very like Mrs Darling's kiss. He was a lovely boy, clad in skeleton leaves and the juices that ooze out of trees; but the most entrancing thing about him was that he had all his first teeth. When he saw she was a grown-up, he gnashed the little pearls at her.

CHAPTER TWO

THE SHADOW

~

Mrs Darling screamed, and, as if in answer to a bell, the door opened, and Nana entered, returned from her evening out. She growled and sprang at the boy, who leapt lightly through the window. Again Mrs Darling screamed, this time in distress for him, for she thought he was killed, and she ran down into the street to look for his little body, but it was not there; and she looked up, and in the black night she could see nothing but what she thought was a shooting star.

She returned to the nursery, and found Nana with something in her mouth, which proved to be the boy's shadow. As he leapt at the window Nana had closed it quickly, too late to catch him, but his shadow had not time to get out; slam went the window and snapped it off.

You may be sure Mrs Darling examined the shadow carefully, but it was quite the ordinary kind.

Nana had no doubt of what was the best thing to do with this shadow. She hung it out at the window, meaning "He is sure to come back for it; let us put it where he can get it easily without disturbing the children."

But unfortunately Mrs Darling could not leave it hanging out at the window; it looked so like the washing and lowered the whole tone of the house. She thought of showing it to Mr Darling, but he was totting up winter great-coats for John and Michael, with a wet towel round his head to keep his brain clear, and it seemed a shame to trouble him; besides, she knew exactly what he would say: "It all comes of having a dog for a nurse."

She decided to roll the shadow up and put it away carefully in a drawer, until a fitting opportunity came for telling her husband. Ah me!

The opportunity came a week later, on that never-to-be-forgotten Friday. Of course it was a Friday.

"I ought to have been specially careful on a Friday," she used to say afterwards to her husband, while perhaps Nana was on the other side of her, holding her hand.

"No, no," Mr Darling always said, "I am responsible for it all. I, George Darling, did it. *Mea culpa, mea culpa.*" He had had a classical education.

They sat thus night after night recalling that fatal Friday, till every detail of it was stamped on their brains and came through on the other side like the faces on a bad coinage.

"If only I had not accepted that invitation to dine at 27," Mrs Darling said.

"If only I had not poured my medicine into Nana's bowl," said Mr Darling.

"If only I had pretended to like the medicine," was what Nana's wet eyes said.

"My liking for parties, George."

"My fatal gift of humour, dearest."

"My touchiness about trifles, dear master and mistress."

Then one or more of them would break down altogether; Nana at the thought, "It's true, it's true, they ought not to have had a dog for a nurse." Many a time it was Mr Darling who put the handkerchief to Nana's eyes.

"That fiend!" Mr Darling would cry, and Nana's bark was the echo of it, but Mrs Darling never upbraided Peter; there was something in the right-hand corner of her mouth that wanted her not to call Peter names.

They would sit there in the empty nursery, recalling fondly every smallest detail of that dreadful evening. It had begun so uneventfully, so precisely like a hundred other evenings, with Nana putting on the water for Michael's bath and carrying him to it on her back.

"I won't go to bed," he had shouted, like one who still believed that he had the last word on the subject. "I won't, I won't. Nana, it isn't six o'clock yet. Oh dear, oh dear, I shan't love you any more, Nana. I tell you I won't be bathed, I won't, I won't!"

Then Mrs Darling had come in, wearing her white evening-gown. She had dressed early because Wendy so loved to see her in her evening-gown, with the necklace George had given her. She was wearing Wendy's bracelet on her arm; she had asked for the loan of it. Wendy so loved to lend her bracelet to her mother.

"...Nana, I tell you I won't be bathed, I won't,
I won't."

She had found her two older children playing at being herself and father on the occasion of Wendy's birth, and John was saying:

"I am happy to inform you, Mrs Darling, that you are now a mother," in just such a tone as Mr Darling himself may have used on the real occasion.

Wendy had danced with joy, just as the real Mrs Darling must have done.

Then John was born, with the extra pomp that he conceived due to the birth of a male, and Michael came from his bath to ask to be born also, but John said brutally that they did not want any more.

Michael had nearly cried. "Nobody wants me," he said, and of course the lady in evening-dress could not stand that.

"I do," she said. "I so want a third child."

"Boy or girl?" asked Michael, not too hopefully.

"Boy."

Then he had leapt into her arms. Such a little thing for Mr and Mrs Darling and Nana to recall now, but not so little if that was to be Michael's last night in the nursery.

They go on with their recollections.

"It was then that I rushed in like a tornado, wasn't it?" Mr Darling would say, scorning himself; and indeed he had been like a tornado.

Perhaps there was some excuse for him. He, too, had been dressing for the party, and all had gone well with him until he came to his tie. It is an astounding thing to have to tell, but this man, though he knew about stocks and shares, had no real mastery of his tie. Sometimes the thing yielded to him without a contest, but there were occasions when it would have been better for the house if he had swallowed his pride and used a made-up tie!

This was such an occasion. He came rushing into the nursery with the crumpled little brute of a tie in his hand.

"Why, what is the matter, father, dear?"

"Matter!" he yelled; he really yelled. "This tie, it will not tie." He became dangerously sarcastic. "Not round my neck! Round the bedpost! Oh yes, twenty times have I made it up round the bedpost, but round my neck, no! Oh dear no! begs to be excused!"

He thought Mrs Darling was not sufficiently impressed, and he went on sternly, "I warn you of this, mother, that unless this tie is round my neck we don't go out to dinner tonight, and if I don't go out to dinner tonight, I never go to the office again, and if I don't go to the office again, you and I starve, and our children will be flung into the streets."

Even then Mrs Darling was placid. "Let me try, dear," she said, and indeed that was what he had come to ask her to do; and with her nice cool hands she tied his tie for him, while the children stood around to see their fate decided. Some men would have resented her being able to do it so easily, but Mr Darling was far too fine a nature for that; he thanked her carelessly, at once forgot his rage, and in another moment was dancing around the room with Michael on his back.

"How wildly we romped!" said Mrs Darling now, recalling it.

"Our last romp!" Mr Darling groaned.

"Oh George, do you remember Michael suddenly said to me, 'How did you get to know me, mother?'"

"I remember!"

"They were rather sweet, don't you think, George?"

"And they were ours, ours, and now they are gone."

The romp had ended with the appearance of Nana, and most unluckily Mr Darling collided against her, covering his trousers with hairs. They were not only new trousers but they were the first he had ever had with braid on them, and he had to bite his lip to prevent the tears coming. Of course Mrs Darling brushed him, but he began to talk again about its being a mistake to have a dog for a nurse.

"George, Nana is a treasure."

"No doubt, but I have an uneasy feeling at times that she looks upon the children as puppies."

"Oh no, dear one, I feel sure she knows they have souls."

"I wonder," Mr Darling said thoughtfully, "I wonder." It was an opportunity, his wife felt, for telling him about the boy. At first he pooh-poohed the story, but he became thoughtful when she showed him the shadow.

"It is nobody I know," he said, examining it carefully, "but he does look a scoundrel."

"We were still discussing it, you remember," says Mr Darling, "when Nana came in with Michael's medicine. You will never carry the bottle in your mouth again, Nana, and it is all my fault."

Strong man though he was, there is no doubt that he had behaved rather foolishly over the medicine. If he had a weakness, it was for thinking that all his life he had taken medicine boldly; and so now, when Michael dodged the spoon in Nana's mouth, he had said reprovingly, "Be a man, Michael."

"Won't; won't," Michael cried naughtily. Mrs Darling left the room to get a chocolate for him, and Mr Darling thought this showed want of firmness.

"Mother, don't pamper him," he called after her. "Michael, when I was your age I took medicine without a murmur. I said 'Thank you, kind parents, for giving me bottles to make me well.'"

He really thought this was true, and Wendy, who was now in her night-gown, believed it also, and she said, to encourage Michael, "That medicine you sometimes take, father, is much nastier, isn't it?"

"Ever so much nastier," Mr Darling said bravely, "and I would take it now as an example to you, Michael, if I hadn't lost the bottle."

He had not exactly lost it; he had climbed in the dead of night to the top of the wardrobe and hidden it there. What he did not know was that the faithful Liza had found it, and put it back on his wash-stand.

"I know where it is, father," Wendy cried, always glad to be of service. "I'll bring it," and she was off before he could stop her. Immediately his spirits sank in the strangest way.

"John," he said, shuddering, "It's most beastly stuff. It's that nasty, sticky, sweet kind."

"It will soon be over, father," John said cheerily, and then in rushed Wendy with the medicine in a glass.

"I have been as quick as I could," she panted.

"You have been wonderfully quick," her father retorted, with a vindictive politeness that was quite thrown away upon her. "Michael first," he said doggedly.

"Father first," said Michael, who was of a suspicious nature.

"I shall be sick, you know," Mr Darling said threateningly.

"Come on, father," said John.

"Hold your tongue, John," his father rapped out.

Wendy was quite puzzled. "I thought you took it quite easily, father."

They are the children who fall out of their
perambulators.

They don't want us to land.

"... and Michael took his medicine...."

"That is not the point," he retorted. "The point is, that there is more in my glass than in Michael's spoon." His proud heart was nearly bursting. "And it isn't fair; I would say it though it were with my last breath – it isn't fair."

"Father, I am waiting," said Michael coldly.

"It's all very well to say you are waiting; so am I waiting."

"Father's a cowardy custard."

"So are you a cowardy custard."

"I'm not frightened."

"Neither am I frightened."

"Well, then, take it."

"Well, then, you take it."

Wendy had a splendid idea. "Why not both take it at the same time?"

"Certainly," said Mr Darling. "Are you ready, Michael?"

Wendy gave the words, one, two, three, and Michael took his medicine, but Mr Darling slipped his behind his back.

There was a yell of rage from Michael and "O father!" Wendy exclaimed.

"What do you mean by 'O father'?" Mr Darling demanded. "Stop that row, Michael. I meant to take mine, but I – I missed it."

It was dreadful the way all the three were looking at him, just as if they did not admire him. "Look here, all of you," he said entreatingly, as soon as Nana had gone into the bathroom. "I have just thought of a splendid joke. I shall pour my medicine into Nana's bowl, and she will drink it, thinking it is milk!"

It was the colour of milk; but the children did not have their father's sense of humour, and they looked at him reproachfully as he poured the medicine into Nana's bowl. "What fun," he said doubtfully, and they did not dare expose him when Mrs Darling and Nana returned.

"Nana, good dog," he said, patting her, "I have put a little milk into your bowl, Nana."

Nana wagged her tail, ran to the medicine, and began lapping it. Then she gave Mr Darling such a look, not an angry look: she showed him the great red tear that makes us so sorry for noble dogs, and crept into her kennel.

Peter has a mischievous way of stealing up behind
them and trying to blow them out.

Mr Darling was frightfully ashamed of himself, but he would not give in. In a horrid silence Mrs Darling smelt the bowl. "O George," she said, "It's your medicine!"

"It was only a joke," he roared, while she comforted her boys, and Wendy hugged Nana. "Much good," he said bitterly, "my wearing myself to the bone trying to be funny in this house."

And still Wendy hugged Nana. "That's right," he shouted. "Coddle her! Nobody coddles me. Oh dear no! I am only the breadwinner, why should I be coddled, why, why, why!"

"George," Mrs Darling entreated him, "not so loud; the servants will hear you." Somehow they had got into the way of calling Liza the servants.

"Let them," he answered recklessly. "Bring in the whole world. But I refuse to allow that dog to lord it in my nursery for an hour longer."

The children wept, and Nana ran to him beseechingly, but he waved her back. He felt he was a strong man again. "In vain, in vain," he cried; "the proper place for you is the yard, and there you go to be tied up this instant."

"George, George," Mrs Darling whispered, "remember what I told you about that boy."

Alas, he would not listen. He was determined to show who was master in that house, and when commands would not draw Nana from the kennel, he lured her out of it with honeyed words, and seizing her roughly, dragged her from the nursery. He was ashamed of himself, and yet he did it. It was all owing to his too affectionate nature, which craved for admiration. When he had tied her up in the backyard, the wretched father went and sat in the passage, with his knuckles to his eyes.

In the meantime Mrs Darling had put the children to bed in unwonted silence and lit their night-lights. They could hear Nana barking, and John whimpered, "It is because he is chaining her up in the yard," but Wendy was wiser.

"That is not Nana's unhappy bark," she said, little guessing what was about to happen; "that is her bark when she smells danger."

Danger!

"Are you sure, Wendy?"

"Oh yes."

Mrs Darling quivered and went to the window. It was securely fastened. She looked out, and the night was peppered with stars. They were crowding round the house, as if curious to see what was to take place there, but she did not notice this, nor that one or two of the smaller ones winked at her. Yet a nameless fear clutched at her heart and made her cry, "Oh, how I wish that I wasn't going to a party tonight!"

Even Michael, already half asleep, knew that she was perturbed, and he asked, "Can anything harm us, mother, after the night-lights are lit?"

"Nothing, precious," she said; "they are the eyes a mother leaves behind to guard her children."

She went from bed to bed singing enchantments over them, and little Michael flung his arms round her. "Mother," he cried, "I'm glad of you." They were the last words she was to hear from him for a long time.

No. 27 was only a few yards distant, but there had been a slight fall of snow, and Father and Mother Darling picked their way over it deftly not to soil their shoes. They were already the only persons in the street, and all the stars were watching them. Stars are beautiful, but they may not take an active part in anything, they must just look on for ever. It is a punishment put on them for something they did so long ago that no star now knows what it was. So the older ones have become glassy-eyed and seldom speak (winking is the star language), but the little ones still wonder. They are not really friendly to Peter, who has a mischievous way of stealing up behind them and trying to blow them out; but they are so fond of fun that they were on his side tonight, and anxious to get the grown-ups out of the way. So as soon as the door of 27 closed on Mr and Mrs Darling there was a commotion in the firmament, and the smallest of all the stars in the Milky Way screamed out:

"Now, Peter!"

CHAPTER THREE

COME AWAY, COME AWAY!

~

For a moment after Mr and Mrs Darling left the house the night-lights by the beds of the three children continued to burn clearly. They were awfully nice little night-lights, and one cannot help wishing that they could have kept awake to see Peter; but Wendy's light blinked and gave such a yawn that the other two yawned also, and before they could close their mouths all the three went out.

There was another light in the room now, a thousand times brighter than the night-lights, and in the time we have taken to say this, it has been in all the drawers in the nursery, looking for Peter's shadow, rummaged in the wardrobe and turned every pocket inside out. It was not really a light; it made this light by flashing about so quickly, but when it came to rest for a second you saw it was a fairy, no longer than your hand, but still growing. It was a girl called Tinker Bell, exquisitely gowned in a skeleton leaf, cut low and square, through which her figure could be seen to the best advantage. She was slightly inclined to *embonpoint*.

A moment after the fairy's entrance the window was blown open by the breathing of the little stars, and Peter dropped in. He had carried Tinker Bell part of the way, and his hand was still messy with the fairy dust.

"Tinker Bell," he called softly, after making sure that the children were asleep. "Tink, where are you?" She was in a jug for the moment, and liked it extremely; she had never been in a jug before.

"Oh, do come out of that jug, and tell me, do you know where they put my shadow?"

The loveliest tinkle as of golden bells answered him. It is the fairy language. You ordinary children can never hear it, but if you were to hear it you would know that you had heard it once before.

Tink said that the shadow was in the big box. She meant the chest of drawers, and Peter jumped at the drawers, scattering their contents to the floor with both hands, as kings toss ha'pence to the crowd. In a moment he had recovered his shadow, and in his delight he forgot that he had shut Tinker Bell up in the drawer.

If he thought at all, but I don't believe he ever thought, it was that he and his shadow, when brought near each other, would join like drops of water; and when they did not he was appalled. He tried to stick it on with soap from the bathroom, but that also failed. A shudder passed through Peter, and he sat on the floor and cried.

His sobs woke Wendy, and she sat up in bed. She was not alarmed to see a stranger crying on the nursery floor; she was only pleasantly interested.

"Boy," she said courteously, "why are you crying?"

Peter could be exceedingly polite also, having learned the grand manner at fairy ceremonies, and he rose and bowed to her beautifully. She was much pleased, and bowed beautifully to him from the bed.

"What's your name?" he asked.

"Wendy Moira Angela Darling," she replied with some satisfaction. "What is your name?"

"Peter Pan."

She was already sure that he must be Peter, but it did seem a comparatively short name.

"Is that all?"

"Yes," he said rather sharply. He felt for the first time that it was a shortish name.

"I'm so sorry," said Wendy Moira Angela.

"It doesn't matter," Peter gulped.

She asked where he lived.

"Second to the right," said Peter, "and then straight on till morning."

"What a funny address!"

Peter had a sinking. For the first time he felt that perhaps it was a funny address.

"No, it isn't," he said.

"I mean," Wendy said nicely, remembering that she was hostess, "is that what they put on the letters?"

He wished she had not mentioned letters.

"Don't get any letters," he said contemptuously.

"But your mother gets letters?"

"Don't have a mother," he said. Not only had he no mother, but he had not the slightest desire to have one. He thought them very over-rated persons. Wendy, however, felt at once that she was in the presence of a tragedy.

"O Peter, no wonder you were crying," she said, and got out of bed and ran to him.

"I wasn't crying about mothers," he said rather indignantly. "I was crying because I can't get my shadow to stick on. Besides, I wasn't crying."

"It has come off?"

"Yes."

Then Wendy saw the shadow on the floor, looking so draggled, and she was frightfully sorry for Peter. "How awful!" she said, but she could not help smiling when she saw that he had been trying to stick it on with soap. How exactly like a boy!

Fortunately she knew at once what to do. "It must be sewn on," she said, just a little patronizingly.

"What's sewn?" he asked.

"You're dreadfully ignorant."

"No, I'm not."

But she was exulting in his ignorance. "I shall sew it on for you, my little man," she said, though he was as tall as herself; and she got out her housewife, and sewed the shadow on to Peter's foot.

He tried to stick it on with soap...

"I dare say it will hurt a little," she warned him.

"Oh, I shan't cry," said Peter, who was already of the opinion that he had never cried in his life. And he clenched his teeth and did not cry; and soon his shadow was behaving properly, though still a little creased.

"Perhaps I should have ironed it," Wendy said thoughtfully; but Peter, boylike, was indifferent to appearances, and he was now jumping about in the wildest glee. Alas, he had already forgotten that he owed his bliss to Wendy. He thought he had attached the shadow himself. "How clever I am," he crowed rapturously, "oh, the cleverness of me!"

It is humiliating to have to confess that this conceit of Peter was one of his most fascinating qualities. To put it with brutal frankness, there never was a cockier boy.

But for the moment Wendy was shocked. "Your conceit," she exclaimed with frightful sarcasm; "of course I did nothing!"

"You did a little," Peter said carelessly, and continued to dance.

"A little!" she replied with hauteur; "if I am no use I can at least withdraw;" and she sprang in the most dignified way into bed and covered her face with the blankets.

To induce her to look up he pretended to be going away, and when this failed he sat on the end of the bed and tapped her gently with his foot. "Wendy," he said, "don't withdraw. I can't help crowing, Wendy, when I'm pleased with myself." Still she would not look up, though she was listening eagerly. "Wendy," he continued in a voice that no woman has ever yet been able to resist, "Wendy, one girl is more use than twenty boys."

Now Wendy was every inch a woman, though there were not very many inches, and she peeped out of the bedclothes.

"Do you really think so, Peter?"

"Yes, I do."

"I think it's perfectly sweet of you," she declared, "and I'll get up again;" and she sat with him on the side of the bed. She also said she would give him a kiss if he liked, but Peter did not know what she meant, and he held out his hand expectantly.

"Surely you know what a kiss is?" she asked, aghast.

"I shall know when you give it to me," he replied stiffly; and not to hurt his feelings she gave him a thimble.

"Now," said he, "shall I give you a kiss?" and she replied with a slight primness, "If you please." She made herself rather cheap by inclining her face towards him, but he merely dropped an acorn button into her hand; so she slowly returned her face to where it had been before, and said nicely that she would wear his kiss on the chain round her neck. It was lucky that she did put it on that chain, for it was afterwards to save her life.

When people in our set are introduced, it is customary for them to ask each other's age, and so Wendy, who always liked to do the correct thing, asked Peter how old he was. It was not really a happy question to ask him; it was like an examination paper that asks grammar, when what you want to be asked is Kings of England.

"I don't know," he replied uneasily, "but I am quite young." He really knew nothing about it; he had merely suspicions, but he said at a venture, "Wendy, I ran away the day I was born."

Wendy was quite surprised, but interested; and she indicated in the charming drawing-room manner, by a touch on her night-gown, that he could sit nearer her.

"It was because I heard father and mother," he explained in a low voice, "talking about what I was to be when I became a man." He was extraordinarily agitated now. "I don't want ever to be a man," he said with passion. "I want always to be a little boy and to have fun. So I ran away to Kensington Gardens and lived a long long time among the fairies."

She gave him a look of the most intense admiration, and he thought it was because he had run away, but it was really because he knew fairies. Wendy had lived such a home life that to know fairies struck her as quite delightful. She poured out questions about them, to his surprise, for they were rather a nuisance to him, getting in his way and so on, and indeed he sometimes had to give them a hiding. Still, he liked them on the whole, and he told her about the beginnings of fairies.

"You see, Wendy, when the first baby laughed for the first time, its laugh broke into a thousand pieces, and they all went skipping about, and that was the beginning of fairies."

Tedious talk this, but being a stay-at-home she liked it.

"And so," he went on good-naturedly, "there ought to be one fairy for every boy and girl."

"Ought to be? Isn't there?"

*"So I ran away to Kensington Gardens and lived a
long long time among the fairies."*

"No. You see, children know such a lot now, they soon don't believe
in fairies, and every time a child says, 'I don't believe in fairies,' there is a
fairy somewhere that falls down dead."

Really, he thought they had now talked enough about fairies, and it
struck him that Tinker Bell was keeping very quiet. "I can't think where
she has gone to," he said, rising, and he called Tink by name. Wendy's heart
went flutter with a sudden thrill.

"Peter," she cried, clutching him, "you don't mean to tell me that
there is a fairy in this room!"

"She was here just now," he said a little impatiently. "You don't hear
her, do you?" and they both listened.

"The only sound I hear," said Wendy, "is like a tinkle of bells."

"Well, that's Tink, that's the fairy language. I think I hear her too."

The sound came from the chest of drawers, and Peter made a merry face. No one could ever look quite so merry as Peter, and the loveliest of gurgles was his laugh. He had his first laugh still.

"Wendy," he whispered gleefully, "I do believe I shut her up in the drawer!"

He let poor Tink out of the drawer, and she flew about the nursery screaming with fury. "You shouldn't say such things," Peter retorted. "Of course I'm very sorry, but how could I know you were in the drawer?"

Wendy was not listening to him. "O Peter," she cried, "if she would only stand still and let me see her!"

"They hardly ever stand still," he said, but for one moment Wendy saw the romantic figure come to rest on the cuckoo clock. "O the lovely!" she cried, though Tink's face was still distorted with passion.

"Tink," said Peter amiably, "this lady says she wishes you were her fairy."

Tinker Bell answered insolently.

"What does she say, Peter?"

He had to translate. "She is not very polite. She says you are a great ugly girl, and that she is my fairy."

He tried to argue with Tink. "You know you can't be my fairy, Tink, because I am a gentleman and you are a lady."

To think Tink replied in these words. "You silly ass," and disappeared into the bathroom. "She is quite a common fairy," Peter explained apologetically; "she is called Tinker Bell because she mends the pots and kettles."

They were together in the arm-chair by this time, and Wendy plied him with more questions.

"If you don't live in Kensington Gardens now – "

"Sometimes I do still."

"But where do you live mostly now?"

"With the lost boys."

"Who are they?"

"They are the children who fall out of their perambulators when the nurse is looking the other way. If they are not claimed in seven days they are sent far away to the Neverland to defray expenses. I'm captain."

"What fun it must be!"

"Yes," said cunning Peter, "but we are rather lonely. You see we have no female companionship."

"Are none of the others girls?"

"Oh no; girls, you know, are much too clever to fall out of their prams."

This flattered Wendy immensely. "I think," she said, "it is perfectly lovely the way you talk about girls; John there just despises us."

For reply Peter rose and kicked John out of bed, blankets and all; one kick. This seemed to Wendy rather forward for a first meeting, and she told him with spirit that he was not captain in her house. However, John continued to sleep so placidly on the floor that she allowed him to remain there. "And I know you meant to be kind," she said, relenting, "so you may give me a kiss."

For a moment she had forgotten his ignorance about kisses. "I thought you would want it back," he said a little bitterly, and offered to return her the thimble.

"Oh dear," said the nice Wendy, "I don't mean a kiss, I mean a thimble."

"What's that?"

"It's like this." She kissed him.

"Funny!" said Peter gravely. "Now shall I give you a thimble?"

"If you wish to," said Wendy, keeping her head erect this time.

Peter thimbled her, and almost immediately she screeched. "What is it, Wendy?"

"It was exactly as if someone were pulling my hair."

"That must have been Tink. I never knew her so naughty before."

And indeed Tink was darting about again, using offensive language.

"She says she will do that to you, Wendy, every time I give you a thimble."

"But why?"

"Why, Tink?"

Again Tink replied, "You silly ass." Peter could not understand why, but Wendy understood; and she was just slightly disappointed when he admitted that he came to the nursery window not to see her but to listen to stories.

"You see I don't know any stories. None of the lost boys know any stories."

"How perfectly awful," Wendy said.

"Do you know," Peter asked, "why swallows build in the eaves of houses? It is to listen to the stories. O Wendy, your mother was telling you such a lovely story."

"Which story was it?"

"About the prince who couldn't find the lady who wore the glass slipper."

"Peter," said Wendy excitedly, "that was Cinderella, and he found her, and they lived happy ever after."

Peter was so glad that he rose from the floor, where they had been sitting, and hurried to the window. "Where are you going?" she cried with misgiving.

"To tell the other boys."

"Don't go, Peter," she entreated, "I know such lots of stories."

Those were her precise words, so there can be no denying that it was she who first tempted him.

He came back, and there was a greedy look in his eyes which ought to have alarmed her, but did not.

"Oh, the stories I could tell to the boys!" she cried, and then Peter gripped her and began to draw her towards the window.

"Let me go!" she ordered him.

"Wendy, do come with me and tell the other boys."

Of course she was very pleased to be asked, but she said, "Oh dear, I can't. Think of mummy! Besides, I can't fly."

"I'll teach you."

"Oh, how lovely to fly."

"I'll teach you how to jump on the wind's back, and then away we go."

"Oo!" she exclaimed rapturously.

"Wendy, Wendy, when you are sleeping in your silly bed you might be flying about with me saying funny things to the stars."

"Oo!"

"And, Wendy, there are mermaids."

"Mermaids! With tails?"

"Such long tails."

"Oh," cried Wendy, "to see a mermaid!"

He had become frightfully cunning. "Wendy," he said, "how we should all respect you."

She was wriggling her body in distress. It was quite as if she were trying to remain on the nursery floor.

But he had no pity for her.

"Wendy," he said, the sly one, "you could tuck us in at night."

"Oo!"

"None of us has ever been tucked in at night."

"Oo," and her arms went out to him.

"And you could darn our clothes, and make pockets for us. None of us has any pockets."

How could she resist? "Of course it's awfully fascinating!" she cried. "Peter, would you teach John and Michael to fly too?"

"If you like," he said indifferently; and she ran to John and Michael and shook them. "Wake up," she cried, "Peter Pan has come and he is to teach us to fly."

John rubbed his eyes. "Then I shall get up," he said. Of course he was on the floor already. "Hallo," he said, "I am up!"

Michael was up by this time also, looking as sharp as a knife with six blades and a saw, but Peter suddenly signed silence. Their faces assumed the awful craftiness of children listening for sounds from the grown-up world. All was as still as salt. Then everything was right. No, stop! Everything was wrong. Nana, who had been barking distressfully all the evening, was quiet now. It was her silence they had heard.

"Out with the light! Hide! Quick!" cried John, taking command for the only time throughout the whole adventure. And thus when Liza entered, holding Nana, the nursery seemed quite its old self, very dark; and you could have sworn you heard its three wicked inmates breathing angelically as they slept. They were really doing it artfully from behind the window curtains.

Liza was in a bad temper, for she was mixing the Christmas puddings in the kitchen, and had been drawn away from them, with a raisin still on her cheek, by Nana's absurd suspicions. She thought the best way of getting a little quiet was to take Nana to the nursery for a moment, but in custody of course.

"There, you suspicious brute," she said, not sorry that Nana was in disgrace, "they are perfectly safe, aren't they? Every one of the little angels sound asleep in bed. Listen to their gentle breathing."

Here Michael, encouraged by his success, breathed so loudly that they were nearly detected. Nana knew that kind of breathing, and she tried to drag herself out of Liza's clutches.

But Liza was dense. "No more of it, Nana," she said sternly, pulling her out of the room. "I warn you if you bark again I shall go straight for master and missus and bring them home from the party, and then, oh, won't master whip you, just."

She tied the unhappy dog up again, but do you think Nana ceased to bark? Bring master and missus home from the party! Why, that was just what she wanted. Do you think she cared whether she was whipped so long as her charges were safe? Unfortunately Liza returned to her puddings, and Nana, seeing that no help would come from her, strained and strained at the chain until at last she broke it. In another moment she had burst into the dining room of 27 and flung up her paws to heaven, her most expressive

" No more of it, Nana," she said sternly, pulling her
out of the room.

way of making a communication. Mr and Mrs Darling knew at once that something terrible was happening in their nursery, and without a good-bye to their hostess they rushed into the street.

But it was now ten minutes since three scoundrels had been breathing behind the curtains; and Peter Pan can do a great deal in ten minutes.

We now return to the nursery.

"It's all right," John announced, emerging from his hiding-place. "I say, Peter, can you really fly?"

Instead of troubling to answer him Peter flew round the room, taking in the mantelpiece on the way.

"How topping!" said John and Michael.

"How sweet!" cried Wendy.

"Yes, I'm sweet, oh, I am sweet!" said Peter, forgetting his manners again.

It looked delightfully easy, and they tried it first from the floor and then from the beds, but they always went down instead of up.

"I say, how do you do it?" asked John, rubbing his knee. He was quite a practical boy.

"You just think lovely wonderful thoughts," Peter explained, "and they lift you up in the air."

He showed them again.

"You're so nippy at it," John said; "couldn't you do it very slowly once?"

Peter did it both slowly and quickly. "I've got it now, Wendy!" cried John, but soon he found he had not. Not one of them could fly an inch, though even Michael was in words of two syllables, and Peter did not know A from Z.

Of course Peter had been trifling with them, for no one can fly unless the fairy dust has been blown on him. Fortunately, as we have mentioned, one of his hands was messy with it, and he blew some on each of them, with the most superb results.

"Now just wriggle your shoulders this way," he said, "and let go."

They were all on their beds, and gallant Michael let go first. He did not quite mean to let go, but he did it, and immediately he was borne across the room.

"I flewed!" he screamed while still in mid-air.

John let go and met Wendy near the bathroom.

"Oh, lovely!"

"Oh, ripping!"

"Look at me!"

"Look at me!"

"Look at me!"

They were not nearly so elegant as Peter, they could not help kicking a little, but their heads were bobbing against the ceiling, and there is almost nothing so delicious as that. Peter gave Wendy a hand at first, but had to desist, Tink was so indignant.

Up and down they went, and round and round. Heavenly was Wendy's word.

"I say," cried John, "why shouldn't we all go out!"

Of course it was to this that Peter had been luring them.

Michael was ready: he wanted to see how long it took him to do a billion miles. But Wendy hesitated.

"Mermaids!" said Peter again.

"Oo!"

"And there are pirates."

"Pirates," cried John, seizing his Sunday hat, "let us go at once."

It was just at this moment that Mr and Mrs Darling hurried with Nana out of 27. They ran into the middle of the street to look up at the nursery window; and, yes, it was still shut, but the room was ablaze with light, and most heart-gripping sight of all, they could see in shadow on the curtain three little figures in night attire circling round and round, not on the floor but in the air.

Not three figures, four!

In a tremble they opened the street door. Mr Darling would have rushed upstairs, but Mrs Darling signed to him to go softly. She even tried to make her heart go softly.

Will they reach the nursery in time? If so, how delightful for them, and we shall all breathe a sigh of relief, but there will be no story. On the other hand, if they are not in time, I solemnly promise that it will all come right in the end.

They would have reached the nursery in time had it not been that the little stars were watching them. Once again the stars blew the window open, and that smallest star of all called out:

"Cave, Peter!"

Then Peter knew that there was not a moment to lose. "Come," he cried imperiously, and soared out at once into the night followed by John and Michael and Wendy.

Mr and Mrs Darling and Nana rushed into the nursery too late. The birds were flown.

CHAPTER FOUR

THE FLIGHT

~

"Second to the right, and straight on till morning."

That, Peter had told Wendy, was the way to the Neverland; but even birds, carrying maps and consulting them at windy corners, could not have sighted it with these instructions. Peter, you see, just said anything that came into his head.

At first his companions trusted him implicitly, and so great were the delights of flying that they wasted time circling round church spires or any other tall objects on the way that took their fancy.

John and Michael raced, Michael getting a start.

They recalled with contempt that not so long ago they had thought themselves fine fellows for being able to fly round a room.

Not so long ago. But how long ago? They were flying over the sea before this thought began to disturb Wendy seriously. John thought it was their second sea and their third night.

Sometimes it was dark and sometimes light, and now they were very cold and again too warm. Did they really feel hungry at times, or were they merely pretending because Peter had such a jolly new way of feeding them? His way was to pursue birds who had food in their mouths suitable for humans and snatch it from them; then the birds would follow and snatch it back; and they would all go chasing each other gaily for miles, parting at last with mutual expressions of good-will. But Wendy noticed with gentle concern that Peter did not seem to know that this was rather an odd way of getting your bread and butter, nor even that there are other ways.

Certainly they did not pretend to be sleepy, they were sleepy; and that was a danger, for the moment they popped off, down they fell. The awful thing was that Peter thought this funny.

"There he goes again!" he would cry gleefully, as Michael suddenly dropped like a stone.

"Save him, save him!" cried Wendy, looking with horror at the cruel sea far below. Eventually Peter would dive through the air, and catch Michael just before he could strike the sea, and it was lovely the way he did it; but he always waited till the last moment, and you felt it was his cleverness that interested him and not the saving of human life. Also he was fond of variety, and the sport that engrossed him one moment would suddenly cease to engage him, so there was always the possibility that the next time you fell he would let you go.

He could sleep in the air without falling, by merely lying on his back and floating, but this was, partly at least, because he was so light that if you got behind him and blew he went faster.

"Do be more polite to him," Wendy whispered to John, when they were playing "Follow my Leader".

"Then tell him to stop showing off," said John.

When playing Follow my Leader, Peter would fly close to the water and touch each shark's tail in passing, just as in the street you may run your finger along an iron railing. They could not follow him in this with much success, so perhaps it was rather like showing off, especially as he kept looking behind to see how many tails they missed.

"You must be nice to him," Wendy impressed on her brothers. "What would we do if he were to leave us?"

"We could go back," Michael said.

"How could we ever find our way back without him?"

"Well, then, we could go on," said John.

"That is the awful thing, John. We should have to go on, for we don't know how to stop."

This was true; Peter had forgotten to show them how to stop.

John said that if the worst came to the worst, all they had to do was to go straight on, for the world was round, and so in time they must come back to their own window.

"And who is to get food for us, John?"

"I nipped a bit out of that eagle's mouth pretty neatly, Wendy."

"After the twentieth try," Wendy reminded him. "And even though we became good at picking up food, see how we bump against clouds and things if he is not near to give us a hand."

Indeed they were constantly bumping. They could now fly strongly, though they still kicked far too much; but if they saw a cloud in front of them, the more they tried to avoid it, the more certainly did they bump into it. If Nana had been with them she would have had a bandage round Michael's forehead by this time.

Peter was not with them for the moment, and they felt rather lonely up there by themselves. He could go so much faster than they that he would suddenly shoot out of sight, to have some adventure in which they had no share. He would come down laughing over something fearfully funny he had been saying to a star, but he had already forgotten what it was, or he would come up with mermaid scales sticking to him, and yet not be able to say for certain what had been happening. It was really rather irritating to children who had never seen a mermaid.

"And if he forgets them so quickly," Wendy argued, "how can we expect that he will go on remembering us?"

Indeed, sometimes when he returned he did not remember them, at least not well. Wendy was sure of it. She saw recognition come into his eyes as he was about to pass them the time of day and go on; once even she had to tell him her name.

"I'm Wendy," she said agitatedly.

He was very sorry. "I say, Wendy," he whispered to her, "always if you see me forgetting you, just keep on saying 'I'm Wendy', and then I'll remember."

Of course this was rather unsatisfactory. However, to make amends he showed them how to lie out flat on a strong wind that was going their way, and this was such a pleasant change that they tried it several times and found they could sleep thus with security. Indeed they would have slept longer, but Peter tired quickly of sleeping, and soon he would cry in his captain voice, "We get off here." So with occasional tiffs, but on the whole rollicking, they drew near the Neverland; for after many moons they did reach it, and, what is more, they had been going pretty straight all the time, not perhaps so much owing to the guidance of Peter or Tink as because the island was out looking for them. It is only thus that anyone may sight those magic shores.

"There it is," said Peter calmly.

"Where, where?"

"Where all the arrows are pointing."

Indeed a million golden arrows were pointing out the island to the children, all directed by their friend the sun, who wanted them to be sure of their way before leaving them for the night.

Wendy and John and Michael stood on tiptoe in the air to get their first sight of the island. Strange to say, they all recognized it at once, and until fear fell upon them they hailed it, not as something long dreamt of and seen at last, but as a familiar friend to whom they were returning home for the holidays.

"John, there's the lagoon."

"Wendy, look at the turtles burying their eggs in the sand."

"I say, John, I see your flamingo with the broken leg."

"Look, Michael, there's your cave."

"John, what's that in the brushwood?"

"It's a wolf with her whelps. Wendy, I do believe that's your little whelp."

"There's my boat, John, with her sides stove in."

"No, it isn't. Why, we burned your boat."

"That's her, at any rate. I say, John, I see the smoke of the redskin camp."

"Where? Show me, and I'll tell you by the way the smoke curls whether they are on the warpath."

"There, just across the Mysterious River."

"I see now. Yes, they are on the war-path right enough."

Michael suddenly dropped like a stone.

Peter was a little annoyed with them for knowing so much; but if he wanted to lord it over them his triumph was at hand, for have I not told you that anon fear fell upon them?

It came as the arrows went, leaving the island in gloom.

In the old days at home the Neverland had always begun to look a little dark and threatening by bedtime. Then unexplored patches arose in it and spread; black shadows moved about in them; the roar of the beasts of prey was quite different now, and above all, you lost the certainty that you would win. You were quite glad that the night-lights were on. You even liked Nana to say that this was just the mantelpiece over here, and that the Neverland was all make-believe.

Of course the Neverland had been make-believe in those days; but it was real now, and there were no night-lights, and it was getting darker every moment, and where was Nana?

They had been flying apart, but they huddled close to Peter now. His careless manner had gone at last, his eyes were sparkling, a tingle went through them every time they touched his body. They were now over the fearsome island, flying so low that sometimes a tree grazed their face. Nothing horrid was visible in the air, yet their progress had become slow and laboured, exactly as if they were pushing their way through hostile forces. Sometimes they hung in the air until Peter had beaten on it with his fists.

"They don't want us to land," he explained.

"Who are they?" Wendy whispered, shuddering.

But he could not or would not say. Tinker Bell had been asleep on his shoulder, but now he wakened her and sent her on in front.

Sometimes he poised himself in the air, listening intently with his hand to his ear, and again he would stare down with eyes so bright that they seemed to bore two holes to earth. Having done these things, he went on again.

His courage was almost appalling. "Do you want an adventure now," he said casually to John, "or would you like to have your tea first?"

Wendy said "tea first" quickly, and Michael pressed her hand in gratitude, but the braver John hesitated.

"What kind of adventure?" he asked cautiously.

"There's a pirate asleep in the pampas just beneath us," Peter told him. "If you like, we'll go down and kill him."

"I don't see him," John said after a long pause.

"I do."

"Suppose," John said a little huskily, "he were to wake up."

Peter spoke indignantly. "You don't think I would kill him while he was sleeping! I would wake him first, and then kill him. That's the way I always do."

"I say! Do you kill many?"

"Tons."

John said "how ripping", but decided to have tea first. He asked if there were many pirates on the island just now, and Peter said he had never known so many.

"Who is captain now?"

"Hook," answered Peter; and his face became very stern as he said that hated word.

"Jas. Hook?"

"Aye."

Then indeed Michael began to cry, and even John could speak in gulps only, for they knew Hook's reputation.

"He was Blackbeard's bo'sun," John whispered huskily. "He is the worst of them all. He is the only man of whom Barbecue was afraid."

"That's him," said Peter.

"What is he like? Is he big?"

"He is not so big as he was."

"How do you mean?"

"I cut off a bit of him."

"You!"

"Yes, me," said Peter sharply.

"I wasn't meaning to be disrespectful."

"Oh, all right."

"But, I say, what bit?"

"His right hand."

"Then he can't fight now?"

"Oh, can't he just!"

"Left-hander?"

"He has an iron hook instead of a right hand, and he claws with it."

"Claws!"

"I say, John," said Peter.

"Yes."

"Say, 'Aye, aye, sir.'"

"Aye, aye, sir."

"There is one thing," Peter continued, "that every boy who serves under me had to promise, and so must you."

John paled.

"It is this, if we meet Hook in open fight, you must leave him to me."

"I promise," John said loyally.

For the moment they were feeling less eerie, because Tink was flying with them, and in her light they could distinguish each other. Unfortunately she could not fly so slowly as they, and so she had to go round and round them in a circle in which they moved as in a halo. Wendy quite liked it, until Peter pointed out the drawback.

"She tells me," he said, "that the pirates sighted us before the darkness came, and got Long Tom out."

"The big gun?"

"Yes. And of course they must see her light, and if they guess we are near it they are sure to let fly."

"Wendy!"

"John!"

"Michael!"

"Tell her to go away at once, Peter," the three cried simultaneously, but he refused.

"She thinks we have lost the way," he replied stiffly, "and she is rather frightened. You don't think I would send her away all by herself when she is frightened!"

For a moment the circle of light was broken, and something gave Peter a loving little pinch.

"Then tell her," Wendy begged, "to put out her light."

"She can't put it out. That is about the only thing fairies can't do. It just goes out of itself when she falls asleep, same as the stars."

"Then tell her to sleep at once," John almost ordered.

"She can't sleep except when she's sleepy. It is the only other thing fairies can't do."

"Seems to me," growled John, "these are the only two things worth doing."

Here he got a pinch, but not a loving one.

"If only one of us had a pocket," Peter said, "we could carry her in it." However, they had set off in such a hurry that there was not a pocket between the four of them.

He had a happy idea. John's hat!

Tink agreed to travel by hat if it was carried in the hand. John carried it, though she had hoped to be carried by Peter. Presently Wendy took the hat, because John said it struck against his knee as he flew; and this, as we shall see, led to mischief, for Tinker Bell hated to be under an obligation to Wendy.

In the black topper the light was completely hidden, and they flew on in silence. It was the stillest silence they had ever known, broken once by a distant lapping, which Peter explained was the wild beasts drinking at the ford, and again by a rasping sound that might have been the branches of trees rubbing together, but he said it was the redskins sharpening their knives.

Even these noises ceased. To Michael the loneliness was dreadful. "If only something would make a sound!" he cried.

As if in answer to his request, the air was rent by the most tremendous crash he had ever heard. The pirates had fired Long Tom at them.

The roar of it echoed through the mountains, and the echoes seemed to cry savagely, "Where are they, where are they, where are they?"

Thus sharply did the terrified three learn the difference between an island of make-believe and the same island come true.

When at last the heavens were steady again, John and Michael found themselves alone in the darkness. John was treading the air mechanically, and Michael without knowing how to float was floating.

"Are you shot?" John whispered tremulously.

"I haven't tried yet," Michael whispered back.

We know now that no one had been hit. Peter, however, had been carried by the wind of the shot far out to sea, while Wendy was blown upwards with no companion but Tinker Bell.

It would have been well for Wendy if at that moment she had

dropped the hat.

I don't know whether the idea came suddenly to Tink, or whether she had planned it on the way, but she at once popped out of the hat and began to lure Wendy to her destruction.

Tink was not all bad: or, rather, she was all bad just now, but, on the other hand, sometimes she was all good. Fairies have to be one thing or the other, because being so small they unfortunately have room for one feeling only at a time. They are, however, allowed to change, only it must be a complete change. At present she was full of jealousy of Wendy. What she said in her lovely tinkle Wendy could not of course understand, and I believe some of it was bad words, but it sounded kind, and she flew back and forward, plainly meaning "Follow me, and all will be well."

What else could poor Wendy do? She called to Peter and John and Michael, and got only mocking echoes in reply. She did not yet know that Tink hated her with the fierce hatred of a very woman. And so, bewildered, and now staggering in her flight, she followed Tink to her doom.

Starkey sighted Nibs disappearing through the woods.

Peter kept watch.

CHAPTER FIVE

THE ISLAND COME TRUE

~

eeling that Peter was on his way back, the Neverland had again woke into life. We ought to use the pluperfect and say wakened, but woke is better and was always used by Peter.

In his absence things are usually quiet on the island. The fairies take an hour longer in the morning, the beasts attend to their young, the redskins feed heavily for six days and nights, and when pirates and lost boys meet they merely bite their thumbs at each other. But with the coming of Peter, who hates lethargy, they are all under way again: if you put your ear to the ground now, you would hear the whole island seething with life.

On this evening the chief forces of the island were disposed as follows. The lost boys were out looking for Peter, the pirates were out looking for the lost boys, the redskins were out looking for the pirates, and the beasts were out looking for the redskins. They were going round and round the island, but they did not meet because all were going at the same rate.

All wanted blood except the boys, who liked it as a rule, but tonight were out to greet their captain. The boys on the island vary, of course, in numbers, according as they get killed and so on; and when they seem to be growing up, which is against the rules, Peter thins them out; but at this time there were six of them, counting the Twins as two. Let us pretend to lie here among the sugar-cane and watch them as they steal by in single file, each with his hand on his dagger.

They are forbidden by Peter to look in the least like him, and they wear the skins of bears slain by themselves, in which they are so round and furry that when they fall they roll. They have therefore become very sure-footed.

The first to pass is Tootles, not the least brave but the most unfortunate of all that gallant band. He had been in fewer adventures than any of them, because the big things constantly happened just when he had stepped round the corner; all would be quiet, he would take the opportunity of going off to gather a few sticks for firewood, and then when he returned the others would be sweeping up the blood. The ill luck had given a gentle melancholy to his countenance, but instead of souring his nature had sweetened it, so that he was quite the humblest of the boys. Poor kind Tootles, there is danger in the air for you tonight. Take care lest an adventure is now offered you, which, if accepted, will plunge you in deeper woe. Tootles, the fairy Tink, who is bent on mischief this night, is looking for a tool, and she thinks you the most easily tricked of the boys. 'Ware Tinker Bell.

Would that he could hear us, but we are not really on the island, and he passes by, biting his knuckles.

Next comes Nibs, the gay and debonair, followed by Slightly, who cuts whistles out of the trees and dances ecstatically to his own tunes. Slightly is the most conceited of the boys. He thinks he remembers the days before he was lost, with their manners and customs, and this has given his nose an offensive tilt. Curly is fourth; he is a pickle, and so often has he had to deliver up his person when Peter said sternly, "Stand forth the one who did this thing," that now at the command he stands forth automatically whether he has done it or not. Last come the Twins, who cannot be described because we should be sure to be describing the wrong one. Peter never quite knew what twins were, and his band were not allowed to know anything he did not know, so these two were always vague about themselves, and did their best to give satisfaction by keeping close together in an apologetic sort of way.

The boys vanish in the gloom, and after a pause, but not a long pause, for things go briskly on the island, come the pirates on their track. We hear them before they are seen, and it is always the same dreadful song:

> "Avast belay, yo ho, heave to,
> A-pirating we go,
> And if we're parted by a shot
> We're sure to meet below!"

A more villainous-looking lot never hung in a row on Execution dock. Here, a little in advance, ever and again with his head to the ground listening, his great arms bare, pieces of eight in his ears as ornaments, is the handsome Italian Cecco, who cut his name in letters of blood on the back of the governor of the prison at Goa. That gigantic black behind him has had many names since he dropped the one with which dusky mothers still terrify their children on the banks of the Guidjo-mo. Here is Bill Jukes, every inch of him tattooed, the same Bill Jukes who got six dozen on the *Walrus* from Flint before he would drop the bag of moidores; and Cookson, said to be Black Murphy's brother (but this was never proved); and Gentleman Starkey, once an usher in a public school and still dainty in his ways of killing; and Skylights (Morgan's Skylights); and the Irish bo'sun Smee, an oddly genial man who stabbed, so to speak, without offence, and was the only Nonconformist in Hook's crew; and Noodler, whose hands were fixed on backwards; and Robt. Mullins and Alf Mason and many another ruffian long known and feared on the Spanish Main.

In the midst of them, the blackest and largest jewel in that dark setting, reclined James Hook, or, as he wrote himself, Jas. Hook, of whom it is said he was the only man that the Sea-Cook feared. He lay at his ease in a rough chariot drawn and propelled by his men, and instead of a right hand he had the iron hook with which ever and anon he encouraged them to increase their pace. As dogs this terrible man treated and addressed them, and as dogs they obeyed him. In person he was cadaverous and blackavised, and his hair was dressed in long curls, which at a little distance looked like black candles, and gave a singularly threatening expression to his handsome countenance.

His eyes were of the blue of the forget-me-not, and of a profound melancholy, save when he was plunging his hook into you, at which time two red spots appeared in them and lit them up horribly. In manner, something of the grand seigneur still clung to him, so that he even ripped you up with an air, and I have been told that he was a *raconteur* of repute. He was never more sinister than when he was most polite, which is probably the truest test of breeding; and the elegance of his diction, even when he was swearing, no less than the distinction of his demeanour, showed him one of a different caste from his crew. A man of indomitable courage, it was said of him that the only thing he shied at was the sight of his own blood, which was thick and of an unusual colour. In dress he somewhat aped the attire associated with the name of Charles II, having heard it said in some earlier period of his career that he bore a strange resemblance to the ill-fated Stuarts; and in his mouth he had a holder of his own contrivance which enabled him to smoke two cigars at once. But undoubtedly the grimmest part of him was his iron claw.

Let us now kill a pirate, to show Hook's method. Skylights will do. As they pass, Skylights lurches clumsily against him, ruffling his lace collar; the hook shoots forth, there is a tearing sound and one screech, then the body is kicked aside, and the pirates pass on. He has not even taken the cigars from his mouth.

Such is the terrible man against whom Peter Pan is pitted. Which will win?

On the trail of the pirates, stealing noiselessly down the war-path, which is not visible to inexperienced eyes, come the redskins, every one of them with his eyes peeled. They carry tomahawks and knives, and their naked bodies gleam with paint and oil. Strung around them are scalps, of boys as well of pirates, for these are the Piccaninny tribe, and not to be confused with the softer-hearted Delawares or the Hurons. In the van, on all fours, is Great Big Little Panther, a brave of so many scalps that in his present position they somewhat impede his progress. Bringing up the rear, the place of greatest danger, comes Tiger Lily, proudly erect, a princess in her own right. She is the most beautiful of dusky Dianas and the belle of the Piccaninnies, coquettish, cold and amorous by turns; there is not a brave who would not have the wayward thing to wife, but she staves off the altar with a hatchet. Observe how they pass over fallen twigs without making the slightest noise. The only sound to be heard is their somewhat

... and when pirates and lost boys meet they merely bite
their thumbs at each other.

heavy breathing. The fact is that they are all a little fat just now after the heavy gorging, but in time they will work this off. For the moment, however, it constitutes their chief danger.

The redskins disappear as they have come, like shadows, and soon their place is taken by the beasts, a great and motley procession: lions, tigers, bears, and the innumerable smaller savage things that flee from them, for every kind of beast, and, more particularly, all the maneaters, live cheek by jowl on the favoured island. Their tongues are hanging out, they are hungry tonight.

When they have passed, comes the last figure of all, a gigantic crocodile. We shall see for whom she is looking presently.

The crocodile passes, but soon the boys appear again, for the procession must continue indefinitely until one of the parties stops or changes its pace. Then quickly they will be on top of each other.

All are keeping a sharp look out in front, but none suspects that the danger may be creeping up from behind. This shows how real the island was.

The first to fall out of the moving circle was the boys. They flung themselves down on the sward, close to their underground home.

"I do wish Peter would come back," every one of them said nervously, though in height and still more in breadth they were all larger than their captain.

"I am the only one who is not afraid of the pirates," Slightly said in a tone that prevented his being a general favourite; but perhaps some distant sound disturbed him, for he added hastily, "but I wish he would come back, and tell us whether he has heard anything more about Cinderella."

They talked of Cinderella, and Tootles was confident that his mother must have been very like her.

It was only in Peter's absence that they could speak of mothers, the subject being forbidden by him as silly.

"All I remember about my mother," Nibs told them, "is that she often said to father, 'Oh, how I wish I had a cheque-book of my own.' I don't know what a cheque-book is, but I should just love to give my mother one."

While they talked they heard a distant sound. You or I, not being wild things of the woods, would have heard nothing, but they heard it, and it was the grim song:

"Yo ho, yo ho, the pirate life,
The flag o' skull and bones,
A merry hour, a hempen rope,
And hey for Davy Jones."

At once the lost boys – but where are they? They are no longer there. Rabbits could not have disappeared more quickly.

I will tell you where they are. With the exception of Nibs, who has darted away to reconnoitre, they are already in their home under the ground, a very delightful residence of which we shall see a good deal presently. But how have they reached it? for there is no entrance to be seen, not so much as a pile of brushwood which, if removed, would disclose the mouth of a cave. Look closely, however, and you may note that there are here seven large trees, each having in its hollow trunk a hole as large as a boy. These are the seven entrances to the home under the ground, for which Hook has been searching in vain these many moons. Will he find it tonight?

As the pirates advanced, the quick eye of Starkey sighted Nibs disappearing through the wood, and at once his pistol flashed out. But an iron claw gripped his shoulder.

"Captain, let go," he cried, writhing.

Now for the first time we hear the voice of Hook. It was a black voice. "Put back that pistol first," it said threateningly.

"It was one of those boys you hate. I could have shot him dead."

"Aye, and the sound would have brought Tiger Lily's redskins upon us. Do you want to lose your scalp?"

"Shall I after him, captain," asked pathetic Smee, "and tickle him with Johnny Corkscrew?" Smee had pleasant names for everything, and his cutlass was Johnny Corkscrew, because he wriggled it in the wound. One could mention many lovable traits in Smee. For instance, after killing, it was his spectacles he wiped instead of his weapon.

"Johnny's a silent fellow," he reminded Hook.

"Not now, Smee," Hook said darkly. "He is only one, and I want to mischief all the seven. Scatter and look for them."

The pirates disappeared among the trees, and in a moment their captain and Smee were alone. Hook heaved a heavy sigh; and I know not why it was, perhaps it was because of the soft beauty of the evening, but there came over him a desire to confide to his faithful bo'sun the story of his life. He spoke long and earnestly, but what it was all about Smee, who was rather stupid, did not know in the least.

Anon he caught the word Peter.

"Most of all," Hook was saying passionately, "I want their captain, Peter Pan. 'Twas he cut off my arm." He brandished the hook threateningly. "I've waited long to shake his hand with this. Oh, I'll tear him."

"And yet," said Smee, "I have often heard you say that hook was worth a score of hands, for combing the hair and other homely uses."

"Aye," the captain answered, "if I was a mother I would pray to have my children born with this instead of that," and he cast a look of pride upon his iron hand and one of scorn upon the other. Then again he frowned.

...the wolves dropped their tails and fled.

"Peter flung my arm," he said, wincing, "to a crocodile that happened to be passing by."

"I have often," said Smee, "noticed your strange dread of crocodiles."

"Not of crocodiles," Hook corrected him, "but of that one crocodile." He lowered his voice. "It liked my arm so much, Smee, that it has followed me ever since, from sea to sea and from land to land, licking its lips for the rest of me."

"In a way," said Smee, "it's a sort of compliment."

"I want no such compliments," Hook barked petulantly. "I want Peter Pan, who first gave the brute its taste for me."

He sat down on a large mushroom, and now there was a quiver in his voice. "Smee," he said huskily, "that crocodile would have had me before this, but by a lucky chance it swallowed a clock which goes tick tick inside it, and so before it can reach me I hear the tick and bolt." He laughed, but in a hollow way.

"Some day," said Smee, "the clock will run down, and then he'll get you."

Hook wetted his dry lips. "Aye," he said, "that's the fear that haunts me."

Since sitting down he had felt curiously warm. "Smee," he said, "this seat is hot." He jumped up. "Odds bobs, hammer and tongs, I'm burning."

They examined the mushroom, which was of a size and solidity

264

As one boy they bent and looked through their legs.

unknown on the mainland; they tried to pull it up, and it came away at once in their hands, for it had no root. Stranger still, smoke began at once to ascend. The pirates looked at each other. "A chimney!" they both exclaimed.

They had indeed discovered the chimney of the home under the ground. It was the custom of the boys to stop it with a mushroom when enemies were in the neighbourhood.

Not only smoke came out of it. There came also children's voices, for so safe did the boys feel in their hiding-place that they were gaily chattering. The pirates listened grimly, and then replaced the mushroom. They looked around them and noted the holes in the seven trees.

"Did you hear them say Peter Pan's from home?" Smee whispered, fidgeting with Johnny Corkscrew.

Hook nodded. He stood for a long time lost in thought, and at last a curdling smile lit up his swarthy face. Smee had been waiting for it. "Unrip your plan, captain," he cried eagerly.

"To return to the ship," Hook replied slowly through his teeth, "and cook a large rich cake of a jolly thickness with green sugar on it. There can be but one room below, for there is but one chimney. The silly moles had not the sense to see that they did not need a door apiece. That shows they have no mother. We will leave the cake on the shore of the mermaids' lagoon. These boys are always swimming about there, playing with the mermaids. They will find the cake and they will gobble it up, because, having no mother, they don't know how dangerous 'tis to eat rich damp cake." He burst into laughter, not hollow laughter now, but honest laughter. "Aha, they will die."

Smee had listened with growing admiration.

"It's the wickedest, prettiest policy ever I heard of," he cried, and in their exultation they danced and sang:

"Avast, belay, when I appear,
By fear they're overtook;
Naught's left upon your bones when you
Have shaken claws with Hook."

They began the verse, but they never finished it, for another sound broke in and stilled them. It was at first such a tiny sound that a leaf might have fallen on it and smothered it, but as it came nearer it was more distinct.

Tick tick tick tick.

Hook stood shuddering, one foot in the air.

"The crocodile," he gasped, and bounded away, followed by his bo'sun.

It was indeed the crocodile. It had passed the redskins, who were now on the trail of the other pirates. It oozed on after Hook.

Once more the boys emerged into the open; but the dangers of the night were not yet over, for presently Nibs rushed breathless into their midst, pursued by a pack of wolves. The tongues of the pursuers were hanging out; the baying of them was horrible.

"Save me, save me!" cried Nibs, falling on the ground.

"But what can we do, what can we do?"

It was a high compliment to Peter that at that dire moment their thoughts turned to him.

"What would Peter do?" they cried simultaneously.

Almost in the same breath they added, "Peter would look at them through his legs."

And then, "Let us do what Peter would do."

It is quite the most successful way of defying wolves, and as one boy they bent and looked through their legs.

The next moment is the long one; but victory came quickly, for as the boys advanced upon them in this terrible attitude, the wolves dropped their tails and fled.

Now Nibs rose from the ground, and the others thought that his staring eyes still saw the wolves. But it was not wolves he saw.

"I have seen a wonderfuller thing," he cried as they gathered round him eagerly. "A great white bird. It is flying this way."

"What kind of a bird, do you think?"

"I don't know," Nibs said, awestruck, "but it looks so weary, and as it flies it moans, 'Poor Wendy'."

"Poor Wendy?"

"I remember," said Slightly instantly, "there are birds called Wendies."

"See, it comes," cried Curly, pointing to Wendy in the heavens.

Wendy was now almost overhead, and they could hear her plaintive cry. But more distinct came the shrill voice of Tinker Bell. The jealous fairy had now cast off all disguise of friendship, and was darting at her victim from every direction, pinching savagely each time she touched.

"Hallo, Tink," cried the wondering boys.

Tink's reply rang out: "Peter wants you to shoot the Wendy."

It was not in their nature to question when Peter ordered. "Let us do what Peter wishes," cried the simple boys. "Quick, bows and arrows."

All but Tootles popped down their trees. He had a bow and arrow with him, and Tink noted it, and rubbed her little hands.

"Quick, Tootles, quick," she screamed. "Peter will be so pleased."

Tootles excitedly fitted the arrow to his bow. "Out of the way, Tink," he shouted; and then he fired, and Wendy fluttered to the ground with an arrow in her breast.

THE LITTLE HOUSE

~

Foolish Tootles was standing like a conqueror over Wendy's body when the other boys sprang, armed, from their trees.

"You are too late," he cried proudly, "I have shot the Wendy, Peter will be so pleased with me."

Overhead Tinker Bell shouted "Silly ass!" and darted into hiding. The others did not hear her. They had crowded round Wendy, and as they looked a terrible silence fell upon the wood. If Wendy's heart had been beating they would all have heard it.

Slightly was the first to speak. "This is no bird," he said in a scared voice. "I think it must be a lady."

"A lady?" said Tootles, and fell a-trembling.

"And we have killed her," Nibs said hoarsely.

They all whipped off their caps.

"Now I see," Curly said; "Peter was bringing her to us." He threw himself sorrowfully on the ground.

"A lady to take care of us at last," said one of the twins, "and you have killed her."

They were sorry for him, but sorrier for themselves, and when he took a step nearer them they turned from him.

Tootles' face was very white, but there was a dignity about him that had never been there before.

"I did it," he said, reflecting. "When ladies used to come to me in dreams, I said, 'Pretty mother, pretty mother.' But when at last she really came, I shot her."

He moved slowly away.

"Don't go," they called in pity.

"I must," he answered, shaking; "I am so afraid of Peter."

It was at this tragic moment that they heard a sound which made the heart of every one of them rise to his mouth. They heard Peter crow.

"Peter!" they cried, for it was always thus that he signalled his return.

"Hide her," they whispered, and gathered hastily around Wendy. But Tootles stood aloof.

Again came that ringing crow, and Peter dropped in front of them. "Greetings, boys," he cried, and mechanically they saluted, and then again was silence.

He frowned.

"I am back," he said hotly, "why do you not cheer?"

They opened their mouths, but the cheers would not come. He overlooked it in his haste to tell the glorious tidings.

"Great news, boys," he cried. "I have brought at last a mother for you all."

Still no sound, except a little thud from Tootles as he dropped on his knees.

"Have you not seen her?" asked Peter, becoming troubled. "She flew this way."

"Ah me," one voice said, and another said, "Oh, mournful day."

Tootles rose. "Peter," he said quietly, "I will show her to you;" and when the others would still have hidden her he said, "Back, twins, let Peter see."

So they all stood back, and let him see, and after he had looked for a little time he did not know what to do next.

"She is dead," he said uncomfortably. "Perhaps she is frightened at being dead."

He thought of hopping off in a comic sort of way till he was out of sight of her, and then never going near the spot any more. They would all have been glad to follow if he had done this.

But there was the arrow. He took it from her heart and faced his band.

"Whose arrow?" he demanded sternly.

"Mine, Peter," said Tootles on his knees.

"Oh, dastard hand," Peter said, and he raised the arrow to use it as a dagger.

Tootles did not flinch. He bared his breast. "Strike, Peter," he said firmly, "strike true."

Twice did Peter raise the arrow, and twice did his hand fall. "I cannot strike," he said with awe, "there is something stays my hand."

All looked at him in wonder, save Nibs, who fortunately looked at Wendy.

"It is she," he cried, "the Wendy lady; see, her arm."

Wonderful to relate, Wendy had raised her arm. Nibs bent over her and listened reverently. "I think she said 'Poor Tootles'," he whispered.

"She lives," Peter said briefly.

Slightly cried instantly, "The Wendy lady lives."

Then Peter knelt beside her and found his button. You remember she had put it on a chain that she wore round her neck.

"See," he said, "the arrow struck against this. It is the kiss I gave her. It has saved her life."

"I remember kisses," Slightly interposed quickly, "let me see it. Aye, that's a kiss."

Peter did not hear him. He was begging Wendy to get better quickly, so that he could show her the mermaids. Of course she could not answer yet, being still in a frightful faint; but from overhead came a wailing note.

"Listen to Tink," said Curly, "she is crying because the Wendy lives."

Then they had to tell Peter of Tink's crime, and almost never had they seen him look so stern.

"Listen, Tinker Bell," he cried; "I am your friend no more. Begone from me for ever."

She flew on to his shoulder and pleaded, but he brushed her off. Not until Wendy again raised her arm did he relent sufficiently to say, "Well, not for ever, but for a whole week."

Do you think Tinker Bell was grateful to Wendy for raising her arm? Oh dear no, never wanted to pinch her so much. Fairies indeed are strange, and Peter, who understood them best, often cuffed them.

But what to do with Wendy in her present delicate state of health?

"Let us carry her down into the house," Curly suggested.

"Aye," said Slightly, "that is what one does with ladies."

"No, no," Peter said, "you must not touch her. It would not be sufficiently respectful."

"That," said Slightly, "is what I was thinking."

"But if she lies there," Tootles said, "she will die."

"Aye, she will die," Slightly admitted, "but there is no way out."

"Yes, there is," cried Peter. "Let us build a little house round her."

They were all delighted. "Quick," he ordered them, "bring me each of you the best of what we have. Gut our house. Be sharp."

In a moment they were as busy as tailors the night before a wedding. They skurried this way and that, down for bedding, up for firewood, and while they were at it, who should appear but John and Michael. As they dragged along the ground they fell asleep standing, stopped, woke up, moved another step and slept again.

"John, John," Michael would cry, "wake up. Where is Nana, John, and mother?"

And then John would rub his eyes and mutter, "It is true, we did fly."

You may be sure they were very relieved to find Peter.

"Hallo, Peter," they said.

"Hallo," replied Peter amicably, though he had quite forgotten them. He was very busy at the moment measuring Wendy with his feet to see how large a house she would need. Of course he meant to leave room for chairs and a table. John and Michael watched him.

"Is Wendy asleep?" they asked.

"Yes."

"John," Michael proposed, "let us wake her and get her to make

Tootles excitedly fitted the arrow to his bow...
then he fired.

supper for us;" but as he said it some of the other boys rushed on carrying branches for the building of the house. "Look at them!" he cried.

"Curly," said Peter in his most captainy voice, "see that these boys help in the building of the house."

"Aye, aye, sir."

"Build a house?" exclaimed John.

"For the Wendy," said Curly.

"For Wendy?" John said aghast. "Why, she is only a girl."

"That," explained Curly, "is why we are her servants."

"You? Wendy's servants!"

"Yes," said Peter, "and you also. Away with them."

The astounded brothers were dragged away to hack and hew and carry. "Chairs and a fender first," Peter ordered. "Then we shall build the house round them."

"Aye," said Slightly, "that is how a house is built; it all comes back to me."

Peter thought of everything. "Slightly," he ordered, "fetch a doctor."

"Aye, aye," said Slightly at once, and disappeared, scratching his head. But he knew Peter must be obeyed, and he returned in a moment, wearing John's hat and looking solemn.

"Please, sir," said Peter, going to him, "are you a doctor?"

The difference between him and the other boys at such a time was that they knew it was make-believe, while to him make-believe and true were exactly the same thing. This sometimes troubled them, as when they had to make-believe that they had had their dinners.

If they broke down in their make-believe he rapped them on the knuckles.

"Yes, my little man," anxiously replied Slightly, who had chapped knuckles.

"Please, sir," Peter explained, "a lady lies very ill."

She was lying at their feet, but Slightly had the sense not to see her.

"Tut, tut, tut," he said, "where does she lie?"

"In yonder glade."

"I will put a glass thing in her mouth," said Slightly; and he made-believe to do it, while Peter waited. It was an anxious moment when the glass thing was withdrawn.

"How is she?" inquired Peter.

"Tut, tut, tut," said Slightly, "this has cured her."

"I am glad," Peter cried.

"I will call again in the evening," Slightly said; "give her beef tea out of a cup with a spout to it;" but after he had returned the hat to John he blew big breaths, which was his habit on escaping from a difficulty.

In the meantime the wood had been alive with the sound of axes; almost everything needed for a cosy dwelling already lay at Wendy's feet.

"If only we knew," said one, "the kind of house she likes best."

"Peter," shouted another, "she is moving in her sleep."

"Her mouth opens," cried a third, looking respectfully into it. "Oh, lovely!"

"Perhaps she is going to sing in her sleep," said Peter. "Wendy, sing the kind of house you would like to have."

Immediately, without opening her eyes, Wendy began to sing:

"I wish I had a pretty house,
The littlest ever seen,
With funny little red walls
And roof of mossy green."

They gurgled with joy at this, for by the greatest good luck the branches they had brought were sticky with red sap, and all the ground was carpeted with moss. As they rattled up the little house they broke into song themselves:

"We've built the little walls and roof
And made a lovely door,
So tell us, mother Wendy,
What are you wanting more?"
To this she answered rather greedily:
"Oh, really, next I think I'll have
Gay windows all about,
With roses peeping in, you know,
And babies peeping out."

With a blow of their fists they made windows, and large yellow leaves were the blinds. But roses – ?

"Roses," cried Peter sternly.

Quickly they made-believe to grow the loveliest roses up the walls. Babies?

To prevent Peter ordering babies, they hurried into song again:

"We've made the roses peeping out,
The babies are at the door,
We cannot make ourselves, you know,
'Cos we've been made before."

Peter, seeing this to be a good idea, at once pretended that it was his own. The house was quite beautiful, and no doubt Wendy was very cosy within, though, of course, they could no longer see her. Peter strode up and down, ordering finishing touches. Nothing escaped his eagle eye. Just when it seemed absolutely finished:

"There's no knocker on the door," he said.

They were very ashamed, but Tootles gave the sole of his shoe, and it made an excellent knocker.

Absolutely finished now, they thought.

Not a bit of it. "There's no chimney," Peter said; "we must have a chimney."

"It certainly does need a chimney," said John importantly. This gave Peter an idea. He snatched the hat off John's head, knocked out the bottom, and put the hat on the roof. The little house was so pleased to have such a capital chimney that, as if to say thank you, smoke immediately began to come out of the hat.

Now really and truly it was finished. Nothing remained to do but to knock.

"All look your best," Peter warned them; "first impressions are awfully important."

He was glad no one asked him what first impressions are; they were all too busy looking their best.

He knocked politely; and now the wood was as still as the children, not a sound to be heard except from Tinker Bell, who was watching from a branch and openly sneering.

What the boys were wondering was, would anyone answer the

knock? If a lady, what would she be like?

The door opened and a lady came out. It was Wendy. They all whipped off their hats.

She looked properly surprised, and this was just how they had hoped she would look.

"Where am I?" she said.

Of course Slightly was the first to get his word in. "Wendy lady," he said rapidly, "for you we built this house."

"Oh, say you're pleased," cried Nibs.

"Lovely, darling house," Wendy said, and they were the very words they had hoped she would say.

"And we are your children," cried the twins.

Then all went on their knees, and holding out their arms cried, "O Wendy lady, be our mother."

"Ought I?" Wendy said, all shining. "Of course it's frightfully fascinating, but you see I am only a little girl. I have no real experience."

"That doesn't matter," said Peter, as if he were the only person present who knew all about it, though he was really the one who knew least. "What we need is just a nice motherly person."

"Oh dear!" Wendy said, "you see I feel that is exactly what I am."

"It is, it is" they all cried; "we saw it at once."

"Very well," she said, "I will do my best. Come inside at once, you naughty children; I am sure your feet are damp. And before I put you to bed I have just time to finish the story of Cinderella."

In they went; I don't know how there was room for them, but you can squeeze very tight in the Neverland. And that was the first of the many joyous evenings they had with Wendy. By and by she tucked them up in the great bed in the home under the trees, but she herself slept that night in the little house, and Peter kept watch outside with drawn sword, for the pirates could be heard carousing far away and the wolves were on the prowl. The little house looked so cosy and safe in the darkness with a bright light showing through its blinds, and the chimney smoking beautifully, and Peter standing on guard.

After a time he fell asleep, and some unsteady fairies had to climb over him on their way home from an orgy. And any of the other boys obstructing the fairy path at night they would have mischiefed, but they just tweaked Peter's nose and passed on.

CHAPTER SEVEN

THE HOME UNDER
THE GROUND
~

One of the first things Peter did next day was to measure Wendy and John and Michael for hollow trees. Hook, you remember, had sneered at the boys for thinking they needed a tree apiece, but this was ignorance, for unless your tree fitted you it was difficult to go up and down, and no two of the boys were quite the same size. Once you fitted, you drew in your breath at the top, and down you went at exactly the right speed, while to ascend you drew in and let out alternately, and so wriggled up. Of course, when you have mastered the action you are able to do these things without thinking of them, and then nothing can be more graceful.

But you simply must fit, and Peter measures you for your tree as carefully as for a suit of clothes: the only difference being that the clothes are made to fit you, while you have to be made to fit the tree. Usually it is done quite easily, as by your wearing too many garments or too few; but if you are bumpy in awkward places or the only available tree is an odd shape, Peter does some things to you, and after that you fit. Once you fit, great

279

care must be taken to go on fitting, and this, as Wendy was to discover to her delight, keeps a whole family in perfect condition.

Wendy and Michael fitted their trees at the first try, but John had to be altered a little.

After a few days' practice they could go up and down as gaily as buckets in a well. And how ardently they grew to love their home under the ground; especially Wendy. It consisted of one large room, as all houses should do, with a floor in which you could dig if you wanted to go fishing, and in this floor grew stout mushrooms of a charming colour, which were used as stools. A Never tree tried hard to grow in the centre of the room, but every morning they sawed the trunk through, level with the floor. By tea-time it was always about two feet high, and then they put a door on top of it, the whole thus becoming a table; as soon as they cleared away, they sawed off the trunk again, and thus there was more room to play. There was an enormous fire-place which was in almost any part of the room where you cared to light it, and across this Wendy stretched strings, made of fibre, from which she suspended her washing. The bed was tilted against the wall by day, and let down at 6.30, when it filled nearly half the room; and all the boys except Michael slept in it, lying like sardines in a tin. There was a strict rule against turning round until one gave the signal, when all turned at once. Michael should have used it also; but Wendy would have a baby, and he was the littlest, and you know what women are, and the short and the long of it is that he was hung up in a basket.

It was rough and simple, and not unlike what baby bears would have made of an underground house in the same circumstances. But there was one recess in the wall, no longer than a bird-cage, which was the private apartment of Tinker Bell. It could be shut off from the rest of the home by a tiny curtain, which Tink, who was most fastidious, always kept drawn when dressing or undressing. No woman, however large, could have had a more exquisite boudoir and bedchamber combined. The couch, as she always called it, was a genuine Queen Mab, with club legs; and she varied the bedspreads according to what fruit-blossom was in season. Her mirror was a Puss-in-boots, of which there are now only three, unchipped, known to the fairy dealers; the wash-stand was Pie-crust and reversible, the chest of drawers an authentic Charming the Sixth, and the carpet and rugs of the best (the early) period of Margery and Robin. There was a chandelier from

Tiddlywinks for the look of the thing, but of course she lit the residence herself. Tink was very contemptuous of the rest of the house, as indeed was perhaps inevitable; and her chamber, though beautiful, looked rather conceited, having the appearance of a nose permanently turned up.

I suppose it was all especially entrancing to Wendy, because those rampagious boys of hers gave her so much to do. Really there were whole weeks when, except perhaps with a stocking in the evening, she was never above ground. The cooking, I can tell you, kept her nose to the pot. Their chief food was roasted bread-fruit, yams, coconuts, baked pig, mammee-apples, tappa rolls and bananas, washed down with calabashes of poe-poe; but you never exactly knew whether there would be a real meal or just a make-believe, it all depended upon Peter's whim. He could eat, really eat, if it was part of a game, but he could not stodge just to feel stodgy, which is what most children like better than anything else; the next best thing being to talk about it. Make-believe was so real to him that during a meal of it you could see him getting rounder. Of course it was trying, but you simply had to follow his lead, and if you could prove to him that you were getting loose for your tree he let you stodge.

Wendy's favourite time for sewing and darning was after they had all gone to bed. Then, as she expressed it, she had a breathing time for herself; and she occupied it in making new things for them, and putting double pieces on the knees, for they were all most frightfully hard on their knees.

When she sat down to a basketful of their stockings, every heel with a hole in it, she would fling up her arms and exclaim, "Oh dear, I am sure I sometimes think spinsters are to be envied."

Her face beamed when she exclaimed this.

You remember about her pet wolf. Well, it very soon discovered that she had come to the island and it found her out, and they just ran into each other's arms. After that it followed her about everywhere.

As time wore on did she think much about the beloved parents she had left behind? This is a difficult question, because it is quite impossible to say how time does wear on in the Neverland, where it is calculated by moons and suns, and there are ever so many more of them than on the mainland. But I am afraid that Wendy did not really worry about her father and mother; she was absolutely confident that they would always keep the window open for her to fly back by, and this gave her complete ease of mind. What did disturb her at times was that John remembered his parents vaguely only, as people he had once known, while Michael was quite willing to believe that she was really his mother. These things scared her a little, and nobly anxious to do her duty, she tried to fix the old life in their minds by setting them examination papers on it, as like as possible to the ones she used to do at school. The other boys thought this awfully interesting and insisted on joining, and they made slates for themselves, and sat round the table, writing and thinking hard about the questions she had written on another slate and passed round. They were the most ordinary questions – "What was the colour of Mother's eyes? Which was taller, Father or Mother? Was Mother blonde or brunette? Answer all three questions if possible." "(A) Write an essay of not less than 40 words on How I spent my last Holidays, or The Characters of Father and Mother compared. Only one of these to be attempted." Or "(1) Describe Mother's laugh; (2) Describe Father's laugh; (3) Describe Mother's Party Dress; (4) Describe the Kennel and its Inmate."

They were just everyday questions like these, and when you could not answer them you were told to make a cross and it was really dreadful what a number of crosses even John made. Of course the only boy who replied to every question was Slightly, and no one could have been more hopeful of coming out first, but his answers were perfectly ridiculous, and he really came out last: a melancholy thing.

Peter did not compete. For one thing he despised all mothers except Wendy, and for another he was the only boy on the island who could neither write nor spell; not the smallest word. He was above all that sort of thing.

By the way, the questions were all written in the past tense. What was the colour of Mother's eyes, and so on. Wendy, you see, had been forgetting too.

Adventures, of course, as we shall see, were of daily occurrence; but about this time Peter invented, with Wendy's help, a new game that fascinated him enormously, until he suddenly had no more interest in it, which, as you have been told, was what always happened with his games. It consisted in pretending not to have adventures, in doing the sort of thing John and Michael had been doing all their lives: sitting on stools flinging balls in the air, pushing each other, going out for walks and coming back without having killed so much as a grizzly. To see Peter doing nothing on a stool was a great sight; he could not help looking solemn at such times, to sit still seemed to him such a comic thing to do. He boasted that he had gone a walk for the good of his health. For several suns these were the most novel of all adventures to him; and John and Michael had to pretend to be delighted also; otherwise he would have treated them severely.

He often went out alone, and when he came back you were never absolutely certain whether he had had an adventure or not. He might have forgotten it so completely that he said nothing about it; and then when you went out you found the body; and, on the other hand, he might say a great deal about it, and yet you could not find the body. Sometimes he came home with his head bandaged, and then Wendy cooed over him and bathed it in lukewarm water, while he told a dazzling tale. But she was never quite sure, you know. There were, however, many adventures which she knew to be true because she was in them herself, and there were still more that were at least partly true, for the others boys were in them and said they were wholly true. To describe them all would require a book as large as an English-Latin, Latin-English Dictionary, and the most we can do is to give one as a specimen of an average hour on the island. The difficulty is which one to choose. Should we take the brush with the redskins at Slightly Gulch? It was a sanguinary affair, and especially interesting as showing one of Peter's peculiarities, which was that in the middle of a fight he would suddenly change sides. At the Gulch, when victory was still in the balance, sometimes leaning this way and sometimes that, he called out, "I'm redskin today; what are you, Tootles?" And Tootles answered "Redskin; what are you, Nibs?" and Nibs said, "Redskin; what are you Twin?" and so on; and they were all redskin; and of course this would have ended the fight had not the real redskins, fascinated by Peter's methods, agreed to be lost boys for that once, and so at it they all went again, more fiercely than ever.

The extraordinary upshot of this adventure was — but we have not decided yet that this is the adventure we are to narrate. Perhaps a better one would be the night attack by the redskins on the house under the ground, when several of them stuck in the hollow trees and had to be pulled out like corks. Or we might tell how Peter saved Tiger Lily's life in the Mermaid's Lagoon, and so made her his ally.

Or we could tell of that cake the pirates cooked so that the boys might eat it and perish; and how they placed it in one cunning spot after another; but always Wendy snatched it from the hands of her children, so that in time it lost its succulence, and became as hard as a stone, and was used as a missile, and Hook fell over it in the dark.

Or suppose we tell of the birds that were Peter's friends, particularly of the Never bird that built in a tree overhanging the lagoon, and how the nest fell into the water, and still the bird sat on her eggs, and Peter gave orders that she was not to be disturbed. That is a pretty story, and the end shows how grateful a bird can be; but if we tell it we must also tell the whole adventure of the lagoon, which would of course be telling two adventures rather than just one. A shorter adventure, and quite as exciting, was Tinker Bell's attempt, with the help of some street fairies, to have the sleeping Wendy conveyed on a great floating leaf to the mainland. Fortunately the leaf gave way and Wendy woke, thinking it was bathtime, and swam back. Or again, we might choose Peter's defiance of the lions, when he drew a circle round him on the ground with an arrow and defied them to cross it; and though he waited for hours, with the other boys and Wendy looking on breathlessly from trees, not one of them dared to accept his challenge.

Which of these adventures shall we choose? The best way will be to toss for it.

I have tossed, and the lagoon has won. This almost makes one wish that the gulch or the cake or Tink's leaf had won. Of course I could do it again, and make it best out of three; however, perhaps fairest to stick to the lagoon.

CHAPTER EIGHT

THE MERMAIDS' LAGOON

~

If you shut your eyes and are a lucky one, you may see at times a shapeless pool of lovely pale colours suspended in the darkness; then if you squeeze your eyes tighter, the pool begins to take shape, and the colours become so vivid that with another squeeze they must go on fire. But just before they go on fire you see the lagoon. This is the nearest you ever get to it on the mainland, just one heavenly moment; if there could be two moments you might see the surf and hear the mermaids singing.

The children often spent long summer days on this lagoon, swimming or floating most of the time, playing the mermaid games in the water and so forth. You must not think from this that the mermaids were on friendly terms with them; on the contrary, it was among Wendy's lasting regrets that all the time she was on the island she never had a civil word from one of them. When she stole softly to the edge of the lagoon she might see them by the score, especially on the Marooners' Rock, where they loved to bask, combing out their hair in a lazy way that quite irritated her;

or she might even swim, on tiptoe as it were, to within a yard of them, but then they saw her and dived, probably splashing her with their tails, not by accident, but intentionally.

They treated all the boys in the same way, except of course Peter, who chatted with them on Marooners' Rock by the hour, and sat on their tails when they got cheeky. He gave Wendy one of their combs.

The most haunting time at which to see them is at the turn of the moon, when they utter strange wailing cries; but the lagoon is dangerous for mortals then, and until the evening of which we have now to tell, Wendy had never seen the lagoon by moonlight, less from fear, for of course Peter would have accompanied her, than because she had strict rules about every one being in bed by seven. She was often at the lagoon, however, on sunny days after rain, when the mermaids come up in extraordinary numbers to play with their bubbles. The bubbles of many colours made in rainbow water they treat as balls, hitting them gaily from one to another with their tails, and trying to keep them in the rainbow till they burst. The goals are at each end of the rainbow, and the keepers only are allowed to use their hands. Sometimes hundreds of mermaids will be playing in the lagoon at a time, and it is quite a pretty sight.

But the moment the children tried to join in they had to play by themselves, for the mermaids immediately disappeared. Nevertheless we have proof that they secretly watched the interlopers, and were not above taking an idea from them; for John introduced a new way of hitting the bubble, with the head instead of the hand, and the mermaid goal-keepers adopted it. This is the one mark that John has left on the Neverland.

It must also have been rather pretty to see the children resting on a rock for half an hour after their midday meal. Wendy insisted on their doing this, and it had to be a real rest even though the meal was make-believe. So they lay there in the sun, and their bodies glistened in it, while she sat beside them and looked important.

It was one such day, and they were all on Marooners' Rock. The rock was not much larger than their great bed, but of course they all knew how not to take up much room, and they were dozing, or at least lying with their eyes shut, and pinching occasionally when they thought Wendy was not looking. She was very busy, stitching.

While she stitched a change came to the lagoon. Little shivers ran over it, and the sun went away and shadows stole across the water, turning it cold. Wendy could no longer see to thread her needle, and when she looked up, the lagoon that had always hitherto been such a laughing place seemed formidable and unfriendly.

It was not, she knew, that night had come, but something as dark as night had come. No, worse than that. It had not come, but it had sent that shiver through the sea to say that it was coming. What was it?

There crowded upon her all the stories she had been told of Marooners' Rock, so called because evil captains put sailors on it and leave them there to drown. They drown when the tide rises, for then it is submerged.

Of course she should have roused the children at once; not merely because of the unknown that was stalking towards them, but because it was no longer good for them to sleep on a rock grown chilly. But she was a young mother and she did not know this; she thought you simply must stick to your rule about half an hour after the midday meal. So, though fear was upon her, and she longed to hear male voices, she would not waken them. Even when she heard the sound of muffled oars, though her heart was in her mouth, she did not waken them. She stood over them to let them have their sleep out. Was it not brave of Wendy?

It was well for those boys then that there was one among them who could sniff danger even in his sleep. Peter sprang erect, as wide awake at once as a dog, and with one warning cry he roused the others.

He stood motionless, one hand to his ear.

"Pirates!" he cried. The others came closer to him. A strange smile was playing about his face, and Wendy saw it and shuddered. While that smile was on his face no one dared address him; all they could do was to stand ready to obey. The order came sharply and incisive.

"Dive!"

There was a gleam of legs, and instantly the lagoon seemed deserted. Marooners' Rock stood alone in the forbidding waters, as if it were itself marooned.

The boat drew nearer. It was the pirate dinghy, with three figures in her, Smee and Starkey, and the third a captive, no other than Tiger Lily. Her hands and ankles were tied, and she knew what was to be her fate. She was to be left on the rock to perish, an end to one of her race more terrible than death by fire or torture, for is it not written in the book of the tribe that there is no path through water to the happy hunting-ground? Yet her face was impassive; she was the daughter of a chief, she must die as a chief's daughter, it is enough.

They had caught her boarding the pirate ship with a knife in her mouth. No watch was kept on the ship, it being Hook's boast that the wind of his name guarded the ship for a mile around. Now her fate would help to guard it also. One more wail would go the round in that wind by night.

In the gloom that they brought with them the two pirates did not see the rock till they crashed into it.

"Luff, you lubber," cried an Irish voice that was Smee's; "here's the rock. Now, then, what we have to do is to hoist the redskin on to it, and leave her there to drown."

It was the work of one brutal moment to land the beautiful girl on the rock; she was too proud to offer a vain resistance.

Quite near the rock, but out of sight, two heads were bobbing up and down, Peter's and Wendy's. Wendy was crying, for it was the first tragedy she had seen. Peter had seen many tragedies, but he had forgotten them all. He was less sorry than Wendy for Tiger Lily; it was two against one that angered him, and he meant to save her. An easy way would have been to wait until the pirates had gone, but he was never one to choose the easy way.

There was almost nothing he could not do, and he now imitated the voice of Hook.

"Ahoy there, you lubbers," he called. It was a marvellous imitation.

"The captain," said the pirates, staring at each other in surprise.

"He must be swimming out to us," Starkey said, when they had looked for him in vain.

"We are putting the redskin on the rock," Smee called out.

"Set her free," came the astonishing answer.

"Free!"

"Yes, cut her bonds and let her go."

"But, captain — "

"At once, d'ye hear," cried Peter, "or I'll plunge my hook in you."

"This is queer," Smee gasped.

"Better do what the captain orders," said Starkey nervously.

But the window was barred.

The house under the ground.

*... then they saw her and dived, probably splashing her
with their tails.*

"Aye, aye," Smee said, and he cut Tiger Lily's cords. At once like an eel she slid between Starkey's legs into the water.

Of course Wendy was very elated over Peter's cleverness; but she knew that he would be elated also and very likely crow and thus betray himself, so at once her hand went out to cover his mouth. But it stayed even in the act, for "Boat ahoy!" rang over the lagoon in Hook's voice, and this time it was not Peter who had spoken.

Peter may have been about to crow, but his face puckered in a whistle of surprise instead.

"Boat ahoy!" again came the cry.

Now Wendy understood. The real Hook was also in the water.

He was swimming to the boat, and as his men showed a light to guide him he had soon reached them. In the light of the lantern Wendy saw his hook grip the boat's side; she saw his evil swarthy face as he rose dripping from the water, and, quaking, she would have liked to swim away, but Peter would not budge. He was tingling with life and also top-heavy with conceit. "Am I not a wonder, oh, I am a wonder!" he whispered to her; and though she thought so also, she was really glad for the sake of his reputation that no one heard him except herself.

He signed to her to listen.

The two pirates were very curious to know what had brought their captain to them, but he sat with his head on his hook in a position of profound melancholy.

"Captain, is all well?" they asked timidly, but he answered with a hollow moan.

"He sighs," said Smee.

"He sighs again," said Starkey.

"And yet a third time he sighs," said Smee.

"What's up, captain?"

Then at last he spoke passionately.

"The game's up," he cried, "those boys have found a mother."

Affrighted though she was, Wendy swelled with pride.

"O evil day," cried Starkey.

"What's a mother?" asked the ignorant Smee.

Wendy was so shocked that she exclaimed, "He doesn't know!" and always after this she felt that if you could have a pet pirate Smee would be her one.

Peter pulled her beneath the water, for Hook had started up, crying, "What was that?"

"I heard nothing," said Starkey, raising the lantern over the waters, and as the pirates looked they saw a strange sight. It was the nest I have told you of, floating on the lagoon, and the Never bird was sitting on it.

"See," said Hook in answer to Smee's question, "that is a mother. What a lesson! The nest must have fallen into the water, but would the mother desert her eggs? No."

There was a break in his voice, as if for a moment he recalled innocent days when – but he brushed away his weakness with his hook.

Smee, much impressed, gazed at the bird as the nest was borne past, but the more suspicious Starkey said, "If she is a mother, perhaps she is hanging about here to help Peter."

Hook winced. "Aye," he said, "that is the fear that haunts me."

He was roused from his dejection by Smee's eager voice.

"Captain," said Smee, "could we not kidnap these boys' mother and make her our mother."

"It is a princely scheme," cried Hook, and at once it took practical shape in his great brain. "We will seize the children and carry them to the boat: the boys we will make walk the plank, and Wendy shall be our mother."

Again Wendy forgot herself.

"Never!" she cried, and bobbed.

"What was that?"

But they could see nothing. They thought it must have been but a leaf in the wind. "Do you agree, my bullies?" asked Hook.

"There is my hand on it," they both said.

"And there is my hook. Swear."

They all swore. By this time they were on the rock and suddenly Hook remembered Tiger Lily.

"Where is the redskin?" he demanded abruptly.

He had a playful humour at moments, and they thought this was one of the moments.

"That is all right, captain," Smee answered complacently, "we let her go."

"Let her go!" cried Hook.

"'Twas your own orders," the bo'sun faltered.

"You called over the water to us to let her go," said Starkey.

"Brimstone and gall," thundered Hook, "what cozening is here?" His face had gone black with rage, but he saw that they believed their words, and he was startled. "Lads," he said, shaking a little, "I gave no such order."

"It is passing queer," Smee said, and they all fidgeted uncomfortably. Hook raised his voice, but there was a quiver in it.

"Spirit that haunts this dark lagoon tonight," he cried, "dost hear me?"

Of course Peter should have kept quiet, but of course he did not. He immediately answered in Hook's voice:

"Odds, bobs, hammer and tongs, I hear you."

In that supreme moment Hook did not blanch, even at the gills, but Smee and Starkey clung to each other in terror.

"Who are you, stranger, speak?" Hook demanded.

"I am James Hook," replied the voice, "captain of the *Jolly Roger*."

"You are not; you are not," Hook cried hoarsely.

"Brimstone and gall," the voice retorted, "say that again, and I'll cast anchor in you."

Hook tried a more ingratiating manner. "If you are Hook," he said almost humbly, "come, tell me, who am I?"

"A codfish," replied the voice, "only a codfish."

"A codfish!" Hook echoed blankly; and it was then, but not till then, that his proud spirit broke. He saw his men draw back from him.

"Have we been captained all this time by a codfish?" they muttered. "It is lowering to our pride."

They were his dogs snapping at him, but, tragic figure though he had become, he scarcely heeded them. Against such fearful evidence it was not their belief in him that he needed, it was his own. He felt his ego slipping from him. "Don't desert me, bully," he whispered hoarsely to it.

In the dark nature there was a touch of the feminine, as in all the great pirates, and it sometimes gave him intuitions. Suddenly he tried the guessing game.

"Hook," he called, "have you another voice?"

Now Peter could never resist a game, and he answered blithely in his own voice, "I have."

"And another name?"

"Aye, aye."

"Vegetable?" asked Hook.

"No."

"Mineral?"

"No."

"Animal?"

"Yes."

"Man?"

"No!" This answer rang out scornfully.

"Boy?"

"Yes."

"Ordinary boy?"

"No!"

"Wonderful boy?"

To Wendy's pain the answer that rang out this time was "Yes."

"Are you in England?"

"No."

"Are you here?"

"Yes."

Hook was completely puzzled. "You ask him some questions," he said to the others, wiping his damp brow.

Smee reflected. "I can't think of a thing," he said regretfully.

"Can't guess, can't guess," crowed Peter. "Do you give it up?"

Of course in his pride he was carrying the game too far, and the miscreants saw their chance.

"Yes, yes," they answered eagerly.

"Well, then," he cried, "I am Peter Pan."

Pan!

In a moment Hook was himself again, and Smee and Starkey were his faithful henchmen.

"Now we have him," Hook shouted. "Into the water, Smee. Starkey, mind the boat. Take him dead or alive."

He leaped as he spoke, and simultaneously came the gay voice of Peter.

"Are you ready, boys?"

"Aye, aye," from various parts of the lagoon.

"Then lam into the pirates."

The fight was short and sharp. First to draw blood was John, who gallantly climbed into the boat and held Starkey. There was a fierce struggle, in which the cutlass was torn from the pirate's grasp. He wriggled overboard and John leapt after him. The dinghy drifted away.

Here and there a head bobbed up in the water, and there was a flash of steel, followed by a cry or a whoop. In the confusion some struck at their own side. The corkscrew of Smee got Tootles in the fourth rib, but he was himself pinked in turn by Curly. Farther from the rock Starkey was pressing Slightly and the twins hard.

Where all this time was Peter? He was seeking bigger game.

The others were all brave boys, and they must not be blamed for backing from the pirate captain. His iron claw made a circle of dead water round him, from which they fled like affrighted fishes.

But there was one who did not fear him: there was one prepared to enter that circle.

Strangely, it was not in the water that they met. Hook rose to the rock to breathe, and at the same moment Peter scaled it on the opposite side. The rock was slippery as a ball, and they had to crawl rather than climb. Neither knew that the other was coming. Each feeling for a grip met the other's arm: in surprise they raised their heads; their faces were almost touching; so they met.

Some of the greatest heroes have confessed that just before they fell to they had a sinking. Had it been so with Peter at that moment I would admit it. After all, this was the only man that the Sea-Cook had feared. But Peter had no sinking, he had one feeling only, gladness; and he gnashed his pretty teeth with joy. Quick as thought he snatched a knife from Hook's belt and was about to drive it home, when he saw that he was higher up the rock than his foe. It would not have been fighting fair. He gave the pirate a hand to help him up.

It was then that Hook bit him.

Not the pain of this but its unfairness was what dazed Peter. It made him quite helpless. He could only stare, horrified. Every child is affected thus the first time he is treated unfairly. All he thinks he has a right to when he comes to you to be yours is fairness. After you have been unfair to him he will love you again, but he will never afterwards be quite the same boy. No one ever gets over the first unfairness; no one except Peter. He often met it, but he always forgot it. I suppose that was the real difference between him and all the rest.

So when he met it now it was like the first time; and he could just stare, helpless. Twice the iron hand clawed him.

A few minutes afterwards the other boys saw Hook in the water striking wildly for the ship; no elation on his pestilent face now, only white fear, for the crocodile was in dogged pursuit of him. On ordinary occasions the boys would have swum alongside cheering; but now they were uneasy, for they had lost both Peter and Wendy; and were scouring the lagoon for them, calling them by name. They found the dinghy and went home in it, shouting "Peter, Wendy," as they went, but no answer came save mocking laughter from the mermaids. "They must be swimming back or flying," the boys concluded. They were not very anxious, they had such faith in Peter. They chuckled, boylike, because they would be late for bed; and it was all Mother Wendy's fault!

When their voices died away there came cold silence over the lagoon, and then a feeble cry.

"Help, help!"

Two small figures were beating against the rock; the girl had fainted and lay on the boy's arm. With a last effort Peter pulled her up the rock and then lay down beside her. Even as he also fainted he saw that the water was rising. He knew that they would soon be drowned, but he could do no more.

As they lay side by side a mermaid caught Wendy by the feet, and began pulling her softly into the water. Peter, feeling her slip from him, woke with a start, and was just in time to draw her back. But he had to tell her the truth.

"We are on the rock, Wendy," he said, "but it is growing smaller. Soon the water will be over it."

She did not understand even now.

"We must go," she said almost brightly.

"Yes," he answered faintly.

"Shall we swim or fly, Peter?"

He had to tell her.

"Do you think you could swim or fly as far as the island, Wendy, without my help?"

She had to admit that she was too tired.

He moaned.

"What is it?" she asked, anxious about him at once.

"I can't help you, Wendy. Hook wounded me. I can neither fly nor swim."

"Do you mean we shall both be drowned?"

"Look how the water is rising."

They put their hands over their eyes to shut out the sight. They thought they would soon be no more. As they sat thus something brushed against Peter as light as a kiss, and stayed there, as if saying timidly, "Can I be of any use?"

It was the tail of a kite, which Michael had made some days before. It had torn itself out of his hand and floated away.

"Michael's kite," Peter said without interest, but next moment he had seized the tail, and was pulling the kite towards him.

"It lifted Michael off the ground," he cried; "why should it not carry you?"

"Both of us!"

"It can't lift two; Michael and Curly tried."

"Let us draw lots," Wendy said bravely.

"And you a lady; never." Already he had tied the tail round her. She clung to him; she refused to go without him; but with a "Good-bye, Wendy," he pushed her from the rock; and in a few minutes she was borne out of his sight. Peter was alone on the lagoon.

The rock was very small now; soon it would be submerged. Pale rays of light tiptoed across the waters; and by and by there was to be heard a sound at once the most musical and the most melancholy in the world; the mermaids calling to the moon.

Peter was not quite like other boys; but he was afraid at last. A tremor ran through him, like a shudder passing over the sea; but on the sea one shudder follows another till there are hundreds of them, and Peter felt just the one. Next moment he was standing erect on the rock again, with that smile on his face and a drum beating within him. It was saying, "To die will be an awfully big adventure."

CHAPTER NINE

THE NEVER BIRD

~

The last sounds Peter heard before he was quite alone were the mermaids retiring one by one to their bedchambers under the sea. He was too far away to hear their doors shut; but every door in the coral caves where they live rings a tiny bell when it opens or closes (as in all the nicest houses on the mainland), and he heard the bells.

Steadily the waters rose till they were nibbling at his feet; and to pass the time until they made their final gulp, he watched the only thing moving on the lagoon. He thought it was a piece of floating paper, perhaps part of the kite, and wondered idly how long it would take to drift ashore.

Presently he noticed as an odd thing that it was undoubtedly out upon the lagoon with some definite purpose, for it was fighting the tide, and sometimes winning; and when it won, Peter always sympathetic to the weaker side, could not help clapping; it was such a gallant piece of paper.

It was not really a piece of paper; it was the Never bird, making desperate efforts to reach Peter on her nest. By working her wings, in a way

299

she had learned since the nest fell into the water, she was able to some extent to guide her strange craft, but by the time Peter recognized her she was very exhausted. She had come to save him, to give him her nest, though there were eggs in it. I rather wonder at the bird, for though he had been nice to her, he had also sometimes tormented her. I can suppose only that, like Mrs Darling and the rest of them, she was melted because he had all his first teeth.

She called out to him what she had come for, and he called out to her what was she doing there; but of course neither of them understood the other's language. In fanciful stories people can talk to the birds freely, and I wish for the moment I could pretend that this was such a story, and say that Peter replied intelligently to the Never bird; but truth is best, and I want to tell only what really happened. Well, not only could they not understand each other, but they forgot their manners.

"I – want – you – to – get – into – the – nest," the bird called, speaking as slowly and distinctly as possible, "and – then – you – can – drift – ashore, but – I – am – too – tired – to – bring – it – any – nearer – so - you – must – try – to – swim – to – it."

"What are you quacking about?" Peter answered. "Why don't you let the nest drift as usual?"

"I – want – you – " the bird said, and repeated it all over.

Then Peter tried slow and distinct.

"What – are – you – quacking – about?" and so on.

The Never bird became irritated; they have very short tempers.

"You dunderheaded little jay," she screamed, "why don't you do as I tell you?"

Peter felt that she was calling him names, and at a venture he retorted hotly:

"So are you!"

Then rather curiously they both snapped out the same remark:

"Shut up!"

"Shut up!"

Nevertheless the bird was determined to save him if she could, and by one last mighty effort she propelled the nest against the rock. Then up she flew; deserting her eggs, so as to make her meaning clear.

Then at last he understood, and clutched the nest and waved his

... in a few minutes she was borne out of sight.

thanks to the bird as she fluttered overhead. It was not to receive his thanks, however, that she hung there in the sky; it was not even to watch him get into the nest; it was to see what he did with her eggs.

There were two large white eggs, and Peter lifted them up and reflected. The bird covered her face with her wings, so as not to see the last of her eggs; but she could not help peeping between the feathers.

I forget whether I have told you that there was a stave on the rock, driven into it by some buccaneers of long ago to mark the site of buried treasure. The children had discovered the glittering hoard, and when in mischievous mood used to fling showers of moidores, diamonds, pearls and pieces of eight to the gulls, who pounced upon them for food, and then flew away, raging at the scurvy trick that had been played upon them. The stave was still there, and on it Starkey had hung his hat, a deep tarpaulin, watertight, with a broad brim. Peter put the eggs into this hat and set it on the lagoon. It floated beautifully.

The Never bird saw at once what he was up to, and screamed her admiration of him; and, alas, Peter crowed his agreement with her. Then he got into the nest, reared the stave in it as a mast, and hung up his shirt for a sail. At the same moment the bird fluttered down upon the hat and once more sat snugly on her eggs. She drifted in one direction, and he was borne off in another, both cheering.

Of course when Peter landed he beached his barque in a place where the bird would easily find it; but the hat was such a great success that she abandoned the nest. It drifted about till it went to pieces, and often Starkey came to the shore of the lagoon, and with many bitter feelings, watched the bird sitting on his hat. As we shall not see her again, it may be worth mentioning here that all Never birds now build in that shape of nest, with a broad brim on which the youngsters take an airing.

Great were the rejoicings when Peter reached the home under the ground almost as soon as Wendy, who had been carried hither and thither by the kite. Every boy had adventures to tell; but perhaps the biggest adventure of all was that they were several hours late for bed. This so inflated them that they did various dodgy things to get staying up still longer, such as demanding bandages; but Wendy, though glorying in having them all home again safe and sound, was scandalized by the lateness of the hour, and cried, "To bed, to bed," in a voice that had to be obeyed.

Next day, however, she was awfully tender, and gave out bandages to every one; and they played till bedtime at limping about and carrying their arms in slings.

CHAPTER TEN

THE HAPPY HOME

~

One important result of the brush on the lagoon was that it made the redskins their friends. Peter had saved Tiger Lily from a dreadful fate, and now there was nothing she and her braves would not do for him. All night they sat above, keeping watch over the home under the ground and awaiting the big attack by the pirates which obviously could not be much longer delayed. Even by day they hung about, smoking the pipe of peace, and looking almost as if they wanted tit-bits to eat.

They called Peter the Great White Father, prostrating themselves before him; and he liked this tremendously, so that it was not really good for him.

"The Great White Father," he would say to them in a very lordly manner, as they grovelled at his feet, "is glad to see the Piccaninny warriors protecting his wigwam from the pirates."

"Me Tiger Lily," that lovely creature would reply. "Peter Pan save me, me his velly nice friend. Me not let pirates hurt him."

305

She was far too pretty to cringe in this way, but Peter thought it his due, and he would answer condescendingly, "It is good. Peter Pan has spoken."

Always when he said "Peter Pan has spoken", it meant that they must now shut up, and they accepted it humbly in that spirit; but they were by no means so respectful to the other boys, whom they looked upon as just ordinary braves. They said "How-do?" to them, and things like that; and what annoyed the boys was that Peter seemed to think this all right.

Secretly Wendy sympathized with them a little, but she was far too loyal a housewife to listen to any complaints against father. "Father knows best," she always said, whatever her private opinion might be. Her private opinion was that the redskins should not call her squaw.

We have now reached the evening that was to be known among them as the Night of Nights, because of its adventures and their upshot. The day, as if quietly gathering its forces, had been almost uneventful, and now the redskins in their blankets were at their posts above, while, below, the children were having their evening meal; all except Peter, who had gone out to get the time. The way you got the time on the island was to find the crocodile, and then stay near him till the clock struck.

This meal happened to be a make-believe tea, and they sat round the board, guzzling in their greed; and really, what with their chatter and recriminations, the noise, as Wendy said, was positively deafening. To be sure, she did not mind noise, but she simply would not have them grabbing things, and then excusing themselves by saying that Tootles had pushed their elbow. There was a fixed rule that they must never hit back at meals, but should refer the matter of dispute to Wendy by raising the right arm politely and saying, "I complain of So-and-so"; but what usually happened was that they forgot to do this or did it too much.

"Silence," cried Wendy when for the twentieth time she had told them that they were not all to speak at once. "Is your calabash empty, Slightly, darling?"

"Not quite empty, Mummy," Slightly said, after looking into an imaginary mug.

"He hasn't even begun to drink his milk," Nibs interposed.

This was telling, and Slightly seized his chance.

"I complain of Nibs," he cried promptly.

John, however, had held up his hand first.

"Well, John?"

"May I sit in Peter's chair, as he is not here?"

"Sit in father's chair, John!" Wendy was scandalized. "Certainly not."

"He is not really our father," John answered. "He didn't even know how a father does till I showed him."

This was grumbling. "We complain of John," cried the twins.

Tootles held up his hand. He was so much the humblest of them, indeed he was the only humble one, that Wendy was specially gentle with him.

"I don't suppose," Tootles said diffidently, "that I could be father."

"No, Tootles."

Once Tootles began, which was not very often, he had a silly way of going on.

"As I can't be father," he said heavily, "I don't suppose, Michael, you would let me be baby?"

"No, I won't," Michael rapped out. He was already in his basket.

"As I can't be baby," Tootles said, getting heavier and heavier, "do you think I could be a twin?"

"No, indeed," replied the twins; "it's awfully difficult to be a twin."

"As I can't be anything important," said Tootles, "would any of you like to see me do a trick?"

"No," they all replied.

Then at last he stopped. "I hadn't really any hope," he said.

The hateful telling broke out again.

"Slightly is coughing on the table."

"The twins began with mammee-apples."

"Curly is taking both tappa rolls and yams."

"Nibs is speaking with his mouth full."

"I complain of the twins."

"I complain of Curly."

"I complain of Nibs."

"Oh dear, oh dear," cried Wendy, "I'm sure I sometimes think that children are more trouble than they are worth."

She told them to clear away, and sat down to her workbasket: a heavy load of stockings and every knee with a hole in it as usual.

"Wendy," remonstrated Michael, "I'm too big for a cradle."

"I must have somebody in a cradle," she said almost tartly, "and you are the littlest. A cradle is such a nice homely thing to have about a house."

While she sewed they played around her; such a group of happy faces and dancing limbs lit up by that romantic fire. It had become a very familiar scene this in the home under the ground, but we are looking on it for the last time.

There was a step above, and Wendy, you may be sure, was the first to recognize it.

"Children, I hear your father's step. He likes you to meet him at the door."

Above, the redskins crouched before Peter.

"Watch well, braves, I have spoken."

And then, as so often before, the gay children dragged him from his tree. As so often before, but never again.

He had brought nuts for the boys as well as the correct time for Wendy.

"Peter, you just spoil them, you know," Wendy simpered.

"Aye, old lady," said Peter, hanging up his gun.

"It was me told him mothers are called old lady," Michael whispered to Curly.

"I complain of Michael," said Curly instantly.

The first twin came to Peter. "Father, we want to dance."

"Dance away, my little man," said Peter, who was in high good humour.

"But we want you to dance."

Peter was really the best dancer among them, but he pretended to be scandalized.

"Me! My old bones would rattle."

"And mummy too."

"What," cried Wendy, "the mother of such an armful, dance!"

"But on a Saturday night," Slightly insinuated.

It was not really Saturday night, at least it may have been, for they had long lost count of the days; but always if they wanted to do anything special they said this was Saturday night, and then they did it.

"Of course it is Saturday night, Peter," Wendy said, relenting.

"People of our figure, Wendy."

"But it is only among our own progeny."

"True, true."

So they were told they could dance, but they must put on their nighties first.

"Ah, old lady," Peter said aside to Wendy, warming himself by the fire and looking down at her as she sat turning a heel, "there is nothing more pleasant of an evening for you and me when the day's toil is over than to rest by the fire with the little ones near by."

"It is sweet, Peter, isn't it?" Wendy said, frightfully gratified. "Peter, I think Curly has your nose."

"Michael takes after you."

She went to him and put her hand on his shoulder.

"Dear Peter," she said, "with such a large family, of course, I have now passed my best, but you don't want to change me, do you?"

"No, Wendy."

Certainly he did not want a change, but he looked at her uncomfortably; blinking, you know, like one not sure whether he was awake or asleep.

"Peter, what is it?"

"I was just thinking," he said, a little scared. "It is only make-believe, isn't it, that I am their father?"

"Oh yes," Wendy said primly.

"You see," he continued apologetically, "it would make me seem so old to be their real father."

"But they are ours, Peter, yours and mine."

"But not really, Wendy?" he asked anxiously.

"Not if you don't wish it," she replied; and she distinctly heard his sigh of relief. "Peter," she asked, trying to speak firmly, "what are your exact feelings for me?"

"Those of a devoted son, Wendy."

"I thought so," she said, and went and sat by herself at the extreme end of the room.

"You are so queer," he said, frankly puzzled, "and Tiger Lily is just the same. There is something she wants to be to me, but she says it is not my mother."

... they pretended to be frightened at their own shadows.

"No, indeed, it is not," Wendy replied with frightful emphasis. Now we know why she was prejudiced against the redskins.

"Then, what is it?"

"It isn't for a lady to tell."

"Oh, very well," Peter said, a little nettled. "Perhaps Tinker Bell will tell me."

"Oh yes, Tinker Bell will tell you," Wendy retorted scornfully. "She is an abandoned little creature."

Here Tink, who was in her boudoir, eavesdropping, squeaked out something impudent.

"She says she glories in being abandoned," Peter interpreted.

He had a sudden idea. "Perhaps Tink wants to be my mother?"

"You silly ass!" cried Tinker Bell in a passion.

She had said it so often that Wendy needed no translation.

"I almost agree with her," Wendy snapped. Fancy Wendy snapping. But she had been much tried, and she little knew what was to happen before the night was out. If she had known she would not have snapped.

None of them knew. Perhaps it was best not to know. Their ignorance gave them one more glad hour; and as it was to be their last hour on the island, let us rejoice that there were sixty minutes in it. They sang and danced in their night-gowns. Such a deliciously creepy song it was, in which they pretended to be frightened at their own shadows; little witting that so soon shadows would close in upon them, from whom they would shrink in real fear. So uproariously gay was the dance, and how they buffeted each other on the bed and out of it! It was a pillow fight rather than a dance, and when it was finished, the pillows insisted on one bout more, like partners who know that they may never meet again. The stories they told, before it was time for Wendy's good-night story! Even Slightly tried to tell a story that night, but the beginning was so fearfully dull that it appalled even himself, and he said gloomily:

"Yes, it is a dull beginning. I say, let us pretend that it is the end."

And then at last they all got into bed for Wendy's story, the story they loved best, the story Peter hated. Usually when she began to tell this story he left the room or put his hands over his ears; and possibly if he had done either of those things this time they might all still be on the island. But tonight he remained on his stool; and we shall see what happened.

CHAPTER ELEVEN

WENDY'S STORY

~

"Listen, then," said Wendy, settling down to her story, with Michael at her feet and seven boys in the bed. "There was once a gentleman – "

"I had rather he had been a lady," Curly said.

"I wish he had been a white rat," said Nibs.

"Quiet," their mother admonished them. "There was a lady also, and – "

"O Mummy," cried the first twin, "you mean that there is a lady also, don't you? She is not dead, is she?"

"Oh, no."

"I am awfully glad she isn't dead," said Tootles. "Are you glad, John?"

"Of course I am."

"Are you glad, Nibs?"

"Rather."

"Are you glad, Twins?"

"We are just glad."

"Oh dear," sighed Wendy.

"Little less noise there," Peter called out, determined that she should have fair play, however beastly a story it might be in his opinion.

"The gentleman's name," Wendy continued, "was Mr Darling, and her name was Mrs Darling."

"I knew them," John said, to annoy the others.

"I think I knew them," said Michael rather doubtfully.

"They were married, you know," explained Wendy, "and what do you think they had?"

"White rats," cried Nibs, inspired.

"No."

"It's awfully puzzling," said Tootles, who knew the story by heart.

"Quiet, Tootles. They had three descendants."

"What is descendants?"

"Well, you are one, Twin."

"Do you hear that, John? I am a descendant."

"Descendants are only children," said John.

"Oh dear, oh dear," sighed Wendy. "Now, these three children had a faithful nurse called Nana; but Mr Darling was angry with her and chained her up in the yard; and so all the children flew away."

"It's an awfully good story," said Nibs.

"They flew away," Wendy continued, "to the Neverland, where the lost children are."

"I just thought they did," Curly broke in excitedly. "I don't know how it is, but I just thought they did."

"O Wendy," cried Tootles, "was one of the lost children called Tootles?"

"Yes, he was."

"I am in a story. Hurrah, I am in a story, Nibs."

"Hush. Now, I want you to consider the feelings of the unhappy parents with all their children flown away."

"Oo!" they all moaned, though they were not really considering the feelings of the unhappy parents one jot.

"Think of the empty beds!"

"Oo!"

"It's awfully sad," the first twin said cheerfully.

"I don't see how it can have a happy ending," said the second twin. "Do you, Nibs?"

"I'm frightfully anxious."

"If you knew how great is a mother's love," Wendy told them triumphantly, "you would have no fear." She had now come to the part that Peter hated.

"I do like a mother's love," said Tootles, hitting Nibs with a pillow. "Do you like a mother's love, Nibs?"

"I do just," said Nibs, hitting back.

"You see," Wendy said complacently, "our heroine knew that the mother would always leave the window open for her children to fly back by; so they stayed away for years and had a lovely time."

"Did they ever go back?"

"Let us now," said Wendy, bracing herself for her finest effort, "take a peep into the future;" and they all gave themselves the twist that makes peeps into the future easier. "Years have rolled by; and who is this elegant lady of uncertain age alighting at London Station?"

"O Wendy, who is she?" cried Nibs, every bit as excited as if he didn't know.

"Can it be – yes – no – it is – the fair Wendy!"

"Oh!"

"And who are the two noble portly figures accompanying her, now grown to man's estate? Can they be John and Michael? They are!"

"Oh!"

"'See, dear brothers,' says Wendy, pointing upwards, 'there is the window still standing open. Ah, now we are rewarded for our sublime faith in a mother's love.' So up they flew to their mummy and daddy; and pen cannot describe the happy scene, over which we draw a veil."

That was a story, and they were as pleased with it as the fair narrator herself. Everything just as it should be, you see. Off we skip like the most heartless things in the world, which is what children are, but so attractive; and we have an entirely selfish time; and then when we have need of special attention we nobly return for it, confident that we shall be embraced instead of smacked.

So great indeed was their faith in a mother's love that they felt they could afford to be callous for a bit longer.

But there was one there who knew better; and when Wendy finished he uttered a hollow groan.

"What is it, Peter?" she cried, running to him, thinking he was ill. She felt him solicitously, lower down than his chest. "Where is it, Peter?"

"It isn't that kind of pain," Peter replied darkly.

"Then what kind is it?"

"Wendy, you are wrong about mothers."

They all gathered round him in affright, so alarming was his agitation; and with a fine candour he told them what he had hitherto concealed.

"Long ago," he said, "I thought like you that my mother would always keep the window open for me; so I stayed away for moons and moons and moons, and then flew back; but the window was barred, for mother had forgotten all about me, and there was another little boy sleeping in my bed."

I am not sure that this was true, but Peter thought it was true; and it scared them.

"Are you sure mothers are like that?"

"Yes."

So this was the truth about mothers. The toads!

Still it is best to be careful; and no one knows so quickly as a child when he should give in. "Wendy, let us go home," cried John and Michael together.

"Yes," she said, clutching them.

"Not tonight?" asked the lost boys bewildered. They knew in what they called their hearts that one can get on quite well without a mother, and that it is only the mothers who think you can't.

"At once," Wendy replied resolutely, for the horrible thought had come to her: "Perhaps mother is in half-mourning by this time."

This dread made her forgetful of what must be Peter's feelings, and she said to him rather sharply, "Peter, will you make the necessary arrangements?"

"If you wish it," he replied as coolly as if she had asked him to pass the nuts.

Not so much as a sorry-to-lose-you between them! If she did not mind the parting, he was going to show her, was Peter, that neither did he.

But of course he cared very much; and he was so full of wrath against grown-ups, who, as usual, were spoiling everything, that as soon as he got inside his tree he breathed intentionally quick short breaths at the rate of about five to a second. He did this because there is a saying in the Neverland that every time you breathe, a grown-up dies; and Peter was killing them off vindictively as fast as possible.

Then having given the necessary instructions to the redskins he returned to the home, where an unworthy scene had been enacted in his absence. Panic-stricken at the thought of losing Wendy, the lost boys had advanced upon her threateningly.

"It will be worse than before she came," they cried.

"We shan't let her go."

"Let's keep her prisoner."

"Aye, chain her up."

In her extremity an instinct told her to which of them to turn.

"Tootles," she cried, "I appeal to you."

Was it not strange? She appealed to Tootles, quite the silliest one.

Grandly, however, did Tootles respond. For that one moment he dropped his silliness and spoke with dignity.

"I am just Tootles," he said, "and nobody minds me. But the first who does not behave to Wendy like an English gentleman I will blood him severely."

He drew his hanger; and for that instant his sun was at noon. The others held back uneasily. Then Peter returned, and they saw at once that they would get no support from him. He would keep no girl in the Neverland against her will.

"Wendy," he said, striding up and down, "I have asked the redskins to guide you through the wood, as flying tires you so."

"Thank you, Peter."

"Then," he continued in the short sharp voice of one accustomed to be obeyed, "Tinker Bell will take you across the sea. Wake her, Nibs."

Nibs had to knock twice before he got an answer, though Tink had really been sitting up in bed listening for some time.

"Who are you? How dare you? Go away," she cried.

"You are to get up, Tink," Nibs called, "and take Wendy on a journey."

Of course Tink had been delighted to hear that Wendy was going; but she was jolly well determined not to be her courier, and she said so in still more offensive language. Then she pretended to be asleep again.

"She says she won't," Nibs exclaimed, aghast at such insubordination, whereupon Peter went sternly towards the young lady's chamber.

"Tink," he rapped out, "if you don't get up and dress at once I will open the curtains, and then we shall all see you in your *négligé*."

This made her leap to the floor. "Who said I wasn't getting up?" she cried.

In the meantime the boys were gazing very forlornly at Wendy, now equipped with John and Michael for the journey. By this time they were dejected, not merely because they were about to lose her, but also because they felt that she was going off to something nice to which they had not been invited. Novelty was beckoning to them as usual.

Crediting them with a nobler feeling, Wendy melted.

"Dear ones," she said, "if you will all come with me I feel almost sure I can get my father and mother to adopt you."

The invitation was meant specially for Peter; but each of the boys was thinking exclusively of himself, and at once they jumped with joy.

"But won't they think us rather a handful?" Nibs asked in the middle of his jump.

"Oh, no," said Wendy, rapidly thinking it out, "it will only mean having a few beds in the drawing-room; they can be hidden behind screens on first Thursdays."

"Peter, can we go?" they all cried imploringly. They took it for granted that if they went he would go also, but really they scarcely cared. Thus children are ever ready, when novelty knocks, to desert their dearest ones.

"All right," Peter replied with a bitter smile; and immediately they rushed to get their things.

"And now, Peter," Wendy said, thinking she had put everything right, "I am going to give you your medicine before you go." She loved to give them medicine, and undoubtedly gave them too much. Of course it was only water, but it was out of a calabash, and she always shook the calabash and counted the drops, which gave it a certain medicinal quality.

On this occasion, however, she did not give Peter this draught, for just as she had prepared it, she saw a look on his face that made her heart sink.

"Get your things, Peter," she cried, shaking.

"No," he answered, pretending indifference, "I am not going with you, Wendy."

"Yes, Peter."

"No."

To show that her departure would leave him unmoved, he skipped up and down the room, playing gaily on his heartless pipes. She had to run about after him, though it was rather undignified.

"To find your mother," she coaxed.

Now, if Peter had ever quite had a mother, he no longer missed her. He could do very well without one. He had thought them out, and remembered only their bad points.

"No, no," he told Wendy decisively; "perhaps she would say I was old, and I just want always to be a little boy and to have fun."

"But, Peter – "

"No."

And so the others had to be told.

"Peter isn't coming."

Peter not coming! They gazed blankly at him, their sticks over their backs, and on each stick a bundle. Their first thought was that if Peter was not going he had probably changed his mind about letting them go.

But he was far too proud for that. "If you find your mothers," he said darkly, "I hope you will like them."

The awful cynicism of this made an uncomfortable impression, and most of them began to look rather doubtful. After all, their faces said, were they not noodles to want to go?

"Now then," cried Peter, "no fuss, no blubbering; goodbye, Wendy;" and he held out his hand cheerily, quite as if they must really go now, for he had something important to do.

She had to take his hand, as there was no indication that he would prefer a thimble.

"You will remember about changing your flannels, Peter?" she said, lingering over him. She was always so particular about their flannels.

"Yes."

"And you will take your medicine?"

"Yes."

That seemed to be everything; and an awkward pause followed. Peter, however, was not the kind that breaks down before people. "Are you ready, Tinker Bell?" he called out.

"Aye, aye."

"Then lead the way."

Tink darted up the nearest tree; but no one followed her, for it was at this moment that the pirates made their dreadful attack upon the redskins. Above, where all had been so still, the air was rent with shrieks and the clash of steel. Below, there was dead silence. Mouths opened and remained open. Wendy fell on her knees, but her arms were extended towards Peter. All arms were extended to him, as if suddenly blown in his direction; they were beseeching him mutely not to desert them. As for Peter, he seized his sword, the same he thought he had slain Barbecue with; and the lust of battle was in his eye.

CHAPTER TWELVE

THE CHILDREN ARE
CARRIED OFF

~

The pirate attack had been a complete surprise; a sure proof that the unscrupulous Hook had conducted it improperly, for to surprise redskins fairly is beyond the wit of the white man.

By all the unwritten laws of savage warfare it is always the redskin who attacks, and with the wiliness of his race he does it just before the dawn, at which time he knows the courage of the whites to be at its lowest ebb. The white men have in the meantime made a rude stockade on the summit of yonder undulating ground, at the foot of which a stream runs; for it is destruction to be too far from water. There they await the onslaught, the inexperienced ones clutching their revolvers and treading on twigs, but the old hands sleeping tranquilly until just before dawn. Through the long black night the savage scouts wriggle, snake-like, among the grass without stirring a blade. The brushwood closes behind them as silently as sand into which a mole has dived. Not a sound is to be heard, save when they give vent to a wonderful imitation of the lonely call of the coyote. The cry is answered by other braves; and some of them do it even better than the coyotes, who are not very good at it. So the chill hours wear on, and the long suspense is horribly trying to the paleface who has to live through it for the first time; but to the trained hand those ghastly calls and still ghastlier silences are but an intimation of how the night is marching.

That this was the usual procedure was so well known to Hook that in disregarding it he cannot be excused on the pleas of ignorance.

The Piccaninnies, on their part, trusted implicitly to his honour, and their whole action of the night stands out in marked contrast to his. They left nothing undone that was consistent with the reputation of their tribe. With that alertness of the senses which is at once the marvel and despair of civilized peoples, they knew that the pirates were on the island from the moment one of them trod on a dry stick; and in an incredibly short space of time the coyote cries began. Every foot of ground between the spot where Hook had landed his forces and the home under the trees was stealthily examined by braves wearing their moccasins with the heels in front. They found only one hillock with a stream at its base, so that Hook had no choice; here he must establish himself and wait for just before the dawn. Everything being thus mapped out with almost diabolical cunning, the main body of the redskins folded their blankets around them, and in the phlegmatic manner that is to them the pearl of manhood squatted above the children's home, awaiting the cold moment when they should deal pale death.

Here dreaming, though wide awake, of the exquisite tortures to which they were to put him at break of day, those confiding savages were found by the treacherous Hook. From the accounts afterwards supplied by such of the scouts as escaped the carnage, he does not seem even to have paused at the rising ground, though it is certain that in that grey light he must have seen it: no thought of waiting to be attacked appears from first to last to have visited his subtle mind; he would not even hold off till the night was nearly spent; on he pounded with no policy but to fall to. What could the bewildered scouts do, masters as they were of every warlike artifice save this one, but trot helplessly after him, exposing themselves fatally to view, the while they gave pathetic utterance to the coyote cry.

Around the brave Tiger Lily were a dozen of her stoutest warriors, and they suddenly saw the perfidious pirates bearing down upon them. Fell from their eyes then the film through which they had looked at victory. No more would they torture at the stake. For them the happy hunting-grounds now. They knew it; but as their fathers' sons they acquitted themselves. Even then they had time to gather in a phalanx that would have been hard to break had they risen quickly, but this they were forbidden to do by the traditions of their race. It is written that the noble savage must never express surprise in the presence of the white. Thus terrible as the sudden appearance of the pirates must have been to them, they remained stationary for a moment, not a muscle moving, as if the foe had come by invitation. Then, indeed, the tradition gallantly upheld, they seized their weapons, and the air was torn with the war-cry; but it was now too late.

It is no part of ours to describe what was a massacre rather than a fight. Thus perished many of the flower of the Piccaninny tribe. Not all unavenged did they die, for with Lean Wolf fell Alf Mason, to disturb the Spanish Main no more; and among others who bit the dust were Geo. Scourie, Chas. Turley, and the Alsatian Foggerty. Turley fell to the tomahawk of the terrible Panther, who ultimately cut a way through the pirates with Tiger Lily and a small remnant of the tribe.

To what extent Hook is to blame for his tactics on this occasion is for the historian to decide. Had he waited on the rising ground till the proper hour he and his men would probably have been butchered; and in judging him it is only fair to take this into account. What he should perhaps have done was to acquaint his opponents that he proposed to follow a new method. On the other hand this, as destroying the element of surprise, would have made his strategy of no avail, so that the whole question is beset with difficulties. One cannot at least withhold a reluctant admiration for the wit that had conceived so bold a scheme, and the fell genius with which it was carried out.

What were his own feelings about himself at that triumphant moment? Fain would his dogs have known, as breathing heavily and wiping their cutlasses, they gathered at a discreet distance from his hook, and squinted through their ferret eyes at this extraordinary man. Elation must have been in his heart, but his face did not reflect it: ever a dark and solitary enigma, he stood aloof from his followers in spirit as in substance.

The night's work was not yet over, for it was not the redskins he had come out to destroy; they were but the bees to be smoked, so that he should get at the honey. It was Pan he wanted, Pan and Wendy and their band, but chiefly Pan.

Peter was such a small boy that one tends to wonder at the man's hatred of him. True, he had flung Hook's arm to the crocodile; but even this and the increased insecurity of life to which it led, owing to the crocodile's pertinacity, hardly account for a vindictiveness so relentless and malignant. The truth is that there was a something about Peter which goaded the pirate captain to frenzy. It was not his courage, it was not his engaging appearance, it was not – There is no beating about the bush, for we know quite well what it was, and have got to tell. It was Peter's cockiness.

This had got on Hook's nerves; it made his iron claw twitch, and at night it disturbed him like an insect. While Peter lived, the tortured man felt that he was a lion in a cage into which a sparrow had come.

The question now was how to get down the trees, or how to get his dogs down. He ran his greedy eyes over them, searching for the thinnest ones. They wriggled uncomfortably, for they knew that he would not scruple to ram them down with poles.

In the meantime, what of the boys? We have seen them at the first clang of weapons, turned as it were into stone figures, open-mouthed, all appealing with outstretched arms to Peter; and we return to them as their mouths close, and their arms fall to their sides. The pandemonium above has ceased almost as suddenly as it arose, passed like a fierce gust of wind; but they know that in the passing it has determined their fate.

Which side had won?

The pirates, listening avidly at the mouths of the trees, heard the question put by every boy, and alas! they also heard Peter's answer.

"If the redskins have won," he said, "they will beat the tom-tom; it is always their sign of victory."

Now Smee had found the tom-tom, and was at that moment sitting on it. "You will never hear the tom-tom again," he muttered, but inaudibly of course, for strict silence had been enjoined. To his amazement Hook signed to him to beat the tom-tom; and slowly there came to Smee an understanding of the dreadful wickedness of the order. Never, probably, had this simple man admired Hook so much.

Twice Smee beat upon the instrument, and then stopped to listen gleefully.

"The tom-tom," the miscreants heard Peter cry; "an Indian victory!"

The doomed children answered with a cheer that was music to the black hearts above, and almost immediately they repeated their good-byes to Peter. This puzzled the pirates, but all their other feelings were swallowed by a base delight that the enemy were about to come up the trees. They smirked at each other and rubbed their hands. Rapidly and silently Hook gave his orders: one man to each tree, and the others to arrange themselves in a line two yards apart.

CHAPTER THIRTEEN

Do You Believe
In Fairies?
~

The more quickly this horror is disposed of the better. The first to emerge from his tree was Curly. He rose out of it into the arms of Cecco, who flung him to Smee, who flung him to Starkey, who flung him to Bill Jukes, who flung him to Noodler, and so he was tossed from one to another till he fell at the feet of the black pirate. All the boys were plucked from their trees in this ruthless manner; and several of them were in the air at a time, like bales of goods flung from hand to hand.

A different treatment was accorded to Wendy, who came last. With ironical politeness Hook raised his hat to her, and, offering her his arm, escorted her to the spot where the others were being gagged. He did it with such an air, he was so frightfully *distingué*, that she was too fascinated to cry out. She was only a little girl.

Perhaps it is tell-tale to divulge that for a moment Hook entranced her, and we tell on her only because her slip led to strange results. Had she haughtily unhanded him (and we should have loved to write it of her), she

327

would have been hurled through the air like the others, and then Hook would probably not have been present at the tying of the children; and had he not been at the tying he would not have discovered Slightly's secret, and without the secret he could not presently have made his foul attempt on Peter's life.

They were tied to prevent their flying away, doubled up with their knees close to their ears; and for the trussing of them the black pirate had cut a rope into nine equal pieces. All went well until Slightly's turn came, when he was found to be like those irritating parcels that use up all the string in going round and leave no tags with which to tie a knot. The pirates kicked him in their rage, just as you kick the parcel (though in fairness you should kick the string); and strange to say it was Hook who told them to belay their violence. His lip was curled with malicious triumph. While his dogs were merely sweating because every time they tried to pack the unhappy lad tight in one part he bulged out in another, Hook's master mind had gone far beneath Slightly's surface, probing not for effects but for causes; and his exultation showed that he had found them. Slightly, white to the gills, knew that Hook had surprised his secret, which was this, that no boy so blown out would use a tree wherein an average man need stick. Poor Slightly, most wretched of all the children now, for he was in a panic about Peter, bitterly regretted what he had done. Madly addicted to the drinking of water when he was hot, he had swelled in consequence to his present girth, and instead of reducing himself to fit his tree had, unknown to the others, whittled his tree to make it fit him.

Sufficient of this Hook guessed to persuade him that Peter at last lay at his mercy; but no word of the dark design that now formed in the subterranean caverns of his mind crossed his lips; he merely signed that the captives were to be conveyed to the ship, and that he would be alone.

How to convey them? Hunched up in their ropes they might indeed be rolled downhill like barrels, but most of the way lay through a morass. Again Hook's genius surmounted difficulties. He indicated that the little house must be used as a conveyance. The children were flung into it, four stout pirates raised it on their shoulders, the others fell in behind, and singing the hateful pirate chorus the strange procession set off through the wood. I don't know whether any of the children were crying; if so, the singing drowned the sound; but as the little house disappeared in the forest, a brave though tiny jet of smoke issued from its chimney as if defying Hook.

Hook saw it, and it did Peter a bad service. It dried up any trickle of pity for him that may have remained in the pirate's infuriated breast.

The first thing he did on finding himself alone in the fast-falling night was to tiptoe to Slightly's tree, and make sure that it provided him with a passage. Then for long he remained brooding; his hat of ill omen on the sward, so that a gentle breeze which had arisen might play refreshingly through his hair. Dark as were his thoughts his blue eyes were as soft as the periwinkle. Intently he listened for any sound from the nether world, but all was as silent below as above; the house under the ground seemed to be but one more empty tenement in the void. Was that boy asleep, or did he stand waiting at the foot of Slightly's tree, with his dagger in his hand?

There was no way of knowing, save by going down. Hook let his cloak slip softly to the ground, and then biting his lip till a lewd blood stood on them, he stepped into the tree. He was a brave man; but for a moment he had to stop there and wipe his brow, which was dripping like a candle. Then silently he let himself go into the unknown.

He arrived unmolested at the foot of the shaft, and stood still again, biting at his breath, which had almost left him. As his eyes became accustomed to the dim light various objects in the home under the trees took shape; but the only one on which his greedy gaze rested, long sought for and found at last, was the great bed. On the bed lay Peter fast asleep.

Unaware of the tragedy being enacted above, Peter had continued, for a little time after the children left, to play gaily on his pipes: no doubt rather a forlorn attempt to prove to himself that he did not care. Then he decided not to take his medicine, so as to grieve Wendy. Then he lay down on the bed outside the coverlet, to vex her still more; for she had always tucked them inside it, because you never know that you may not grow chilly at the turn of the night. Then he nearly cried; but it struck him how indignant she would be if he laughed instead; so he laughed a haughty laugh and fell asleep in the middle of it.

Sometimes, though not often, he had dreams, and they were more painful than the dreams of other boys. For hours he could not be separated from these dreams, though he wailed piteously in them. They had to do, I think, with the riddle of his existence. At such times it had been Wendy's custom to take him out of bed and sit with him on her lap, soothing him in dear ways of her own invention, and when he grew calmer to put him back to bed before he quite woke up, so that he should not know of the indignity to which she had subjected him. But on this occasion he had fallen at once into a dreamless sleep. One arm dropped over the edge of the bed, one leg was arched, and the unfinished part of his laugh was stranded on his mouth, which was open, showing the little pearls.

Thus defenceless, Hook found him. He stood silent at the foot of the tree looking across the chamber at his enemy. Did no feeling of compassion disturb his sombre breast? The man was not wholly evil; he loved flowers (I have been told) and sweet music (he was himself no mean performer on the harpsichord); and let it be frankly admitted, the idyllic nature of the scene stirred him profoundly. Mastered by his better self, he would have returned reluctantly up the tree but for one thing.

What stayed him was Peter's impertinent appearance as he slept. The open mouth, the drooping arm, the arched knee: they were such a personification of cockiness as, taken together, will never again, one may hope, be presented to eyes so sensitive to their offensiveness. They steeled Hook's heart. If his rage had broken him into a hundred pieces every one of them would have disregarded the incident, and leapt at the sleeper.

Though a light from the one lamp shone dimly on the bed Hook stood in darkness himself, and at the first stealthy step forward he discovered an obstacle, the door of Slightly's tree. It did not entirely fill the aperture, and he had been looking over it. Feeling for the catch, he found to his fury that it was low down, beyond his reach. To his disordered brain it seemed then that the irritating quality in Peter's face and figure visibly increased, and he rattled the door and flung himself against it. Was his enemy to escape him after all?

But what was that? The red in his eye had caught sight of Peter's medicine standing on a ledge within easy reach. He fathomed what it was straightaway, and immediately he knew that the sleeper was in his power.

Lest he should be taken alive, Hook always carried about his person a dreadful drug, blended by himself of all the death-dealing rings that had come into his possession. These he had boiled down into a yellow liquid quite unknown to science, which was probably the most virulent poison in existence.

. . . sometimes he had to give them a hiding.

Five drops of this he now added to Peter's cup. His hand shook, but it was in exultation rather than in shame. As he did it he avoided glancing at the sleeper, but not lest pity should unnerve him; merely to avoid spilling. Then one long gloating look he cast upon his victim, and turning, wormed his way with difficulty up the tree. As he emerged at the top he looked the very spirit of evil breaking from its hole. Donning his hat at its most rakish angle, he wound his cloak around him, holding one end in front as if to conceal his person from the night, of which it was the blackest part, and muttering strangely to himself stole away through the trees.

Peter slept on. The light guttered and went out, leaving the tenement in darkness; but still he slept. It must have been not less than ten o'clock by the crocodile, when he suddenly sat up in his bed, wakened by he knew not what. It was a soft cautious tapping on the door of his tree.

Soft and cautious, but in that stillness it was sinister. Peter felt for his dagger till his hand gripped it. Then he spoke.

"Who is that?"

For long there was no answer: then again the knock.

"Who are you?"

No answer.

He was thrilled, and he loved being thrilled. In two strides he reached his door. Unlike Slightly's door it filled the aperture, so that he could not see beyond it, nor could the one knocking see him.

"I won't open unless you speak," Peter cried.

Then at last the visitor spoke, in a lovely bell-like voice.

"Let me in, Peter."

It was Tink, and quickly he unbarred to her. She flew in excitedly, her face flushed and her dress stained with mud.

"What is it?"

"Oh, you could never guess," she cried, and offered him three guesses. "Out with it!" he shouted; and in one ungrammatical sentence, as long as the ribbons conjurers pull from their mouths, she told of the capture of Wendy and the boys.

Peter's heart bobbed up and down as he listened. Wendy bound, and on the pirate ship; she who loved everything to be just so!

"I'll rescue her," he cried, leaping at his weapons. As he leapt he thought of something he could do to please her. He could take his medicine.

His hand closed on the fatal draught.

"No!" shrieked Tinker Bell, who had heard Hook muttering about his deed as he sped through the forest.

"Why not?"

"It is poisoned."

"Poisoned? Who could have poisoned it?"

"Hook."

"Don't be silly. How could Hook have got down here?"

Alas! Tinker Bell could not explain this, for even she did not know the dark secret of Slightly's tree. Nevertheless Hook's words had left no room for doubt. The cup was poisoned.

"Besides," said Peter, quite believing himself, "I never fell asleep."

He raised the cup. No time for words now; time for deeds; and with one of her lightning movements Tink got between his lips and the draught, and drained it to the dregs.

"Why, Tink, how dare you drink my medicine?"

But she did not answer. Already she was reeling in the air.

"What is the matter with you?" cried Peter, suddenly afraid.

"It was poisoned, Peter," she told him softly; "and now I am going to be dead."

"O Tink, did you drink it to save me?"

"Yes."

"But why, Tink?"

Her wings would scarcely carry her now, but in reply she alighted on his shoulder and gave his chin a loving bite. She whispered in his ear, "You silly ass;" and then, tottering to her chamber, lay down on the bed.

His head almost filled the fourth wall of her little room as he knelt near her in distress. Every moment her light was growing fainter; and he knew that if it went out she would be no more. She liked his tears so much that she put out her beautiful finger and let them run over it.

Her voice was so low that at first he could not make out what she said. Then he made it out. She was saying that she thought she could get well again if children believed in fairies.

Peter flung out his arms. There were no children there, and it was night-time; but he addressed all who might be dreaming of the Neverland, and who were therefore nearer to him than you think; boys and girls in their nighties, and naked papooses in their baskets hung from trees.

"Do you believe?" he cried.

Tink sat up in bed almost briskly to listen to her fate.

She fancied she heard answers in the affirmative, and then again she wasn't sure.

"What do you think?" she asked Peter.

"If you believe," he shouted to them, "clap your hands; don't let Tink die."

Many clapped.

Some didn't.

A few little beasts hissed.

The clapping stopped suddenly, as if countless mothers had rushed to their nurseries to see what on earth was happening; but already Tink was saved. First her voice grew strong, then she popped out of bed; then she was flashing through the room more merry and impudent than ever. She never thought of thanking those who believed, but she would have liked to get at the ones who had hissed.

"And now to rescue Wendy."

The moon was riding in a cloudy heaven when Peter rose from his tree, begirt with weapons and wearing little else, to set out upon his perilous quest. It was not such a night as he would have chosen. He had hoped to fly, keeping not far from the ground, so that nothing unwonted should escape his eyes; but in that fitful light to have flown low would have meant trailing his shadow through the trees, thus disturbing the birds and acquainting a watchful foe that he was astir.

He regretted now that he had given the birds of the island such strange names that they are very wild and difficult of approach.

There was no other course but to press forward in redskin fashion, at which he was an adept. But in what direction, for he could not be sure that the children had been taken to the ship? A slight fall of snow had obliterated all footmarks; and a deathly silence pervaded the island, as if for a space Nature stood still in horror of the recent carnage. He had taught the children something of the forest lore that he had himself learned from Tiger Lily and Tinker Bell, and knew that in their dire hour they were not likely to forget it. Slightly, if he had an opportunity, would blaze the trees, for instance. Curly would drop seeds, and Wendy would leave her handkerchief at some important place. But morning was needed to search for such guidance, and he could not wait. The upper world had called him, but would give no help.

The crocodile passed him, but not another living thing, not a sound, not a movement; and yet he knew well that sudden death might be at the next tree, or stalking him from behind.

He swore this terrible oath: "Hook or me this time."

Now he crawled forward like a snake; and again, erect, he darted across a space on which the moonlight played: one finger on his lip and his dagger at the ready. He was frightfully happy.

CHAPTER FOURTEEN

THE PIRATE SHIP

~

One green light squinting over Kidd's Creek, which is near the mouth of the pirate river, marked where the brig, the *Jolly Roger*, lay, low in the water; a rakish-looking craft foul to the hull, every beam in her detestable, like ground strewn with mangled feathers. She was the cannibal of the seas, and scarce needed that watchful eye, for she floated immune in the horror of her name.

She was wrapped in the blanket of night, through which no sound from her could have reached the shore. There was little sound, and none agreeable save the whir of the ship's sewing machine at which Smee sat, ever industrious and obliging, the essence of the commonplace, pathetic Smee. I known not why he was so infinitely pathetic, unless it were because he was so pathetically unaware of it; but even strong men had to turn hastily from looking at him, and more than once on summer evenings, he had touched the fount of Hook's tears and made it flow. Of this, as of almost everything else, Smee was quite unconscious.

A few of the pirates leant over the bulwarks drinking in the miasma of the night; others sprawled by barrels over games of dice and cards; and the exhausted four who had carried the little house lay prone on the deck, where even in their sleep they rolled skilfully to this side or that out of Hook's reach, lest he should claw them mechanically in passing.

Hook trod the deck in thought. O man unfathomable. It was his hour of triumph. Peter had been removed for ever from his path, and all the other boys were on the brig, about to walk the plank. It was his grimmest deed since the days when he had brought Barbecue to heel; and knowing as we do how vain a tabernacle is man, could we be surprised had he now paced the deck unsteadily, bellied out by the winds of his success?

But there was no elation in his gait, which kept pace with the action of his sombre mind. Hook was profoundly dejected.

He was often thus when communing with himself on board ship in the quietude of the night. It was because he was so terribly alone. This inscrutable man never felt more alone than when surrounded by his dogs. They were socially so inferior to him.

Hook was not his true name. To reveal who he really was would even at this date set the country in a blaze; but as those who read between the lines must already have guessed, he had been at a famous public school; and its traditions still clung to him like garments, with which indeed they are largely concerned. Thus it was offensive to him even now to board a ship in the same dress in which he grappled her; and he still adhered in his walk to the school's distinguished slouch. But above all he retained the passion for good form.

Good form! However much he may have degenerated, he still knew that this is all that really matters.

From far within him he heard a creaking as of rusty portals, and through them came a stern tap-tap-tap, like hammering in the night when one cannot sleep. "Have you been good form today?" was their eternal question.

"Fame, fame, that glittering bauble, it is mine," he cried.

"Is it quite good form to be distinguished at anything?" the tap-tap from his school replied.

"I am the only man whom Barbecue feared," he urged; "and Flint himself feared Barbecue."

"Barbecue, Flint – what house?" came the cutting retort.

Most disquieting reflection of all, was it not bad form to think about good form.

His vitals were tortured by this problem. It was a claw within him sharper than the iron one; and as it tore him, the perspiration dripped down his sallow countenance and streaked his doublet. Oft-times he drew his sleeve across his face, but there was no damming that trickle.

Ah, envy not Hook.

There came to him a presentiment of his early dissolution. It was as if Peter's terrible oath had boarded the ship. Hook felt a gloomy desire to make his dying speech, lest presently there should be no time for it.

"Better for Hook," he cried, "if he had had less ambition." It was in his darkest hours only that he referred to himself in the third person.

"No little children love me."

Strange that he should think of this, which had never troubled him before; perhaps the sewing machine brought it to his mind. For long he muttered to himself, staring at Smee, who was hemming placidly, under the conviction that all children feared him.

Feared him! Feared Smee! There was not a child on board the brig that night who did not already love him. He had said horrid things to them and hit them with the palm of his hand, because he could not hit with his fist; but they had only clung to him the more. Michael had tried on his spectacles.

To tell poor Smee that they thought him lovable! Hook itched to do it, but it seemed too brutal. Instead, he revolved this mystery in his mind: why do they find Smee lovable? He pursued the problem like the sleuth-hound that he was. If Smee was lovable, what was it that made him so? A terrible answer suddenly presented itself: "Good form?"

Had the bo'sun good form without knowing it, which is the best form of all?

He remembered that you have to prove you don't know you have it before you are eligible for Pop.

With a cry of rage he raised his iron hand over Smee's head; but he did not tear. What arrested him was this reflection:

"To claw a man because he is good form, what would that be?"

"Bad form!"

The unhappy Hook was as impotent as he was damp, and he fell forward like a cut flower.

His dogs thinking him out of the way for a time, discipline instantly relaxed; and they broke into a bacchanalian dance, which brought him to his feet at once; all traces of human weakness gone, as if a bucket of water had passed over him.

"Quiet, you scugs," he cried, "or I'll cast anchor in you:" and at once the din was hushed. "Are all the children chained, so they cannot fly away?"

"Aye, aye."

"Then hoist them up."

The wretched prisoners were dragged from the hold, all except Wendy, and ranged in line in front of him. For a time he seemed unconscious of their presence. He lolled at his ease, humming, not unmelodiously, snatches of a rude song, and fingering a pack of cards. Ever and anon the light from his cigar gave a touch of colour to his face.

"Now then, bullies," he said briskly, "six of you walk the plank tonight, but I have room for two cabin boys. Which of you is it to be?"

"Don't irritate him unnecessarily," had been Wendy's instructions in the hold; so Tootles stepped forward politely. Tootles hated the idea of signing under such a man, but an instinct told him that it would be prudent to lay responsibility on an absent person; and though a somewhat silly boy, he knew that mothers alone are always willing to be the buffer. All children know this about mothers, and despise them for it, but make constant use of it.

So Tootles explained prudently, "You see, sir, I don't think my mother would like me to be a pirate. Would your mother like you to be a pirate, Slightly?"

He winked at Slightly, who said mournfully, "I don't think so," as if he wished things had been otherwise. "Would your mother like you to be a pirate, Twin?"

"I don't think so," said the first twin, as clever as the others. "Nibs, would – ?"

"Stow this gab," roared Hook, and the spokesmen were dragged back. "You, boy," he said, addressing John, "you look as if you had a little pluck in you. Didst never want to be a pirate, my hearty?"

Now John had sometimes experienced this hankering at maths.

prep.; and he was struck by Hook's picking him out.

"I once thought of calling myself Red-handed Jack," he said diffidently.

"And a good name too. We'll call you that here, bully, if you join."

"What do you think, Michael?" asked John.

"What would you call me if I join?" Michael demanded.

"Blackbeard Joe."

Michael was naturally impressed. "What do you think, John?" He wanted John to decide, and John wanted him to decide.

"Shall we still be respectful subjects of the King?" John inquired.

Through Hook's teeth came the answer: "You would have to swear, 'Down with the King.'"

Perhaps John had not behaved very well so far, but he shone out now.

"Then I refuse," he cried, banging the barrel in front of Hook.

"And I refuse," cried Michael.

"Rule Britannia!" squeaked Curly.

The infuriated pirates buffeted them in the mouth; and Hook roared out, "That seals your doom. Bring up their mother. Get the plank ready."

They were only boys, and they went white as they saw Jukes and Cecco preparing the fatal plank. But they tried to look brave when Wendy was brought up.

No words of mine can tell you how Wendy despised those pirates. To the boys there was at least some glamour in the pirate calling, but all that she saw was that the ship had not been scrubbed for years. There was not a port-hole on the grimy glass of which you might not have written with your finger, "Dirty pig"; and she had already written it on several. But as the boys gathered round her she had no thought, of course, save for them.

"So, my beauty," said Hook, as if he spoke in syrup, "you are to see your children walk the plank."

Fine gentleman though he was, the intensity of his communings had soiled his ruff, and suddenly he knew that she was gazing at it. With a hasty gesture he tried to hide it, but he was too late.

"Are they to die?" asked Wendy, with a look of such frightful contempt that he nearly fainted.

"They are," he snarled. "Silence all," he called gloatingly, "for a mother's last words to her children."

341

At this moment Wendy was grand. "These are my last words, dear boys," she said firmly. "I feel that I have a message to you from your real mothers, and it is this: 'We hope our sons will die like English gentlemen.'"

Even the pirates were awed; and Tootles cried out hysterically, "I am going to do what my mother hopes. What are you to do, Nibs?"

"What my mother hopes. What are you to do, Twin?"

"What my mother hopes. John, what are – ?"

But Hook had found his voice again.

"Tie her up," he shouted.

It was Smee who tied her to the mast. "See here, honey," he whispered, "I'll save you if you promise to be my mother."

But not even for Smee would she make such a promise. "I would almost rather have no children at all," she said disdainfully.

It is sad to know that not a boy was looking at her as Smee tied her to the mast; the eyes of all were on the plank; that last little walk they were about to take. They were no longer able to hope that they would walk it manfully, for the capacity to think had gone from them; they could stare and shiver only.

Hook smiled on them with his teeth closed, and took a step towards Wendy. His intention was to turn her face so that she should see the boys walking the plank one by one. But he never reached her, he never heard the cry of anguish he hoped to wring from her. He heard something else instead.

It was the terrible tick-tock of the crocodile.

They all heard it – pirates, boys, Wendy; and immediately every head was blown in one direction; not to the water whence the sound proceeded, but towards Hook. All knew that what was about to happen concerned him alone, and that from being actors they were suddenly become spectators.

Very frightful was it to see the change that came over him. It was as if he had been clipped at every joint. He fell in a little heap.

The sound came steadily nearer; and in advance of it came this ghastly thought, "The crocodile is about to board the ship."

Even the iron claw hung inactive; as if knowing that it was no intrinsic part of what the attacking force wanted. Left so fearfully alone, any other man would have lain with his eyes shut where he fell: but the gigantic brain of Hook was still working, and under its guidance he crawled on his knees along the deck as far from the sound as he could go. The pirates respectfully cleared a passage for him, and it was only when he brought up against the bulwarks that he spoke.

"Hide me," he cried hoarsely.

They gathered round him; all eyes averted from the thing that was coming aboard. They had no thought of fighting it. It was Fate.

Only when Hook was hidden from them did curiosity loosen the limbs of the boys so that they could rush to the ship's side to see the crocodile climbing it. Then they got the strangest surprise of this Night of Nights; for it was no crocodile that was coming to their aid. It was Peter.

He signed to them not to give vent to any cry of admiration that might rouse suspicion. Then he went on ticking.

CHAPTER FIFTEEN

"HOOK OR ME
THIS TIME"

~

Odd things happen to all of us on our way through life without our noticing for a time that they have happened. Thus, to take an instance, we suddenly discover that we have been deaf in one ear for we don't know how long, but, say, half an hour. Now such an experience had come that night to Peter. When last we saw him he was stealing across the island with one finger to his lips and his dagger at the ready. He had seen the crocodile pass by without noticing anything peculiar about it, but by and by he remembered that it had not been ticking. At first he thought this eerie, but soon he concluded rightly that the clock had run down.

Without giving a thought to what might be the feelings of a fellow-creature thus abruptly deprived of its closest companion, Peter at once considered how he could turn the catastrophe to his own use; and he decided to tick, so that wild beasts should believe he was the crocodile and let him pass unmolested. He ticked superbly, but with one unforeseen result. The crocodile was among those who heard the sound, and it followed him, though whether with the purpose of regaining what it had lost, or merely as a friend under the belief that it was again ticking itself, will never be certainly known, for, like all slaves to a fixed idea, it was a stupid beast.

Peter reached the shore without mishap, and went straight on; his legs encountering the water as if quite unaware that they had entered a new element. Thus many animals pass from land to water, but no other human of whom I know. As he swam he had but one thought: "Hook or me this time." He had ticked so long that he now went on ticking without knowing that he was doing it. Had he known he would have stopped, for to board the brig by the help of the tick, though an ingenious idea, had not occurred to him.

On the contrary, he thought he had scaled her side as noiseless as a mouse; and he was amazed to see the pirates cowering from him, with Hook in their midst as abject as if he had heard the crocodile.

The crocodile! No sooner did Peter remember it than he heard the ticking. At first he thought the sound did come from the crocodile, and he looked behind him swiftly. Then he realized that he was doing it himself, and in a flash he understood the situation. "How clever of me," he thought at once, and signed to the boys not to burst into applause.

It was at this moment that Ed Teynte the quartermaster emerged from the forecastle and came along the deck. Now, reader, time what happened by your watch. Peter struck true and deep. John clapped his hands on the ill-fated pirate's mouth to stifle the dying groan. He fell forward. Four boys caught him to prevent the thud. Peter gave the signal, and the carrion was cast overboard. There was a splash, and then silence. How long has it taken?

"One!" (Slightly had begun to count.)

None too soon, Peter, every inch of him on tiptoe, vanished into the cabin; for more than one pirate was screwing up his courage to look round. They could hear each other's distressed breathing now, which showed them that the more terrible sound had passed.

"It's gone, captain," Smee said, wiping his spectacles. "All's still again."

Slowly Hook let his head emerge from his ruff, and listened so intently that he could have caught the echo of the tick. There was not a sound, and he drew himself up firmly to his full height.

"Then here's to Johnny Plank," he cried brazenly, hating the boys more than ever because they had seen him unbend. He broke into the villainous ditty:

> "Yo ho, yo ho, the frisky plank,
> You walks along it so,
> Till it goes down and you goes down
> To Davy Jones below!"

To terrorize the prisoners the more, though with a certain loss of dignity, he danced along an imaginary plank, grimacing at them as he sang; and when he finished he cried, "Do you want a touch of the cat before you walk the plank?"

At that they fell on their knees. "No, no," they cried so piteously that every pirate smiled.

"Fetch the cat, Jukes," said Hook; "it's in the cabin."

The cabin! Peter was in the cabin! The children gazed at each other.

"Aye, aye," said Jukes blithely, and he strode into the cabin. They followed him with their eyes; they scarce knew that Hook had resumed his song, his dogs joining in with him:

> "Yo ho, yo ho, the scratching cat,
> Its tails are nine, you know,
> And when they're writ upon your back – "

What was the last line will never be known, for of a sudden the song was stayed by a dreadful screech from the cabin. It wailed through the ship, and died away. Then was heard a crowing sound which was well understood by the boys, but to the pirates was almost more eerie than the screech.

"What was that?" cried Hook.

"Two," said Slightly solemnly.

The Italian Cecco hesitated for a moment and then swung into the cabin. He tottered out, haggard.

"What's the matter with Bill Jukes, you dog?" hissed Hook, towering over him.

"The matter wi' him is he's dead, stabbed," replied Cecco in a hollow voice.

"Bill Jukes dead!" cried the startled pirates.

"The cabin's as black as a pit," Cecco said, almost gibbering, "but there is something terrible in there: the thing you heard crowing."

The exultation of the boys, the lowering looks of the pirates, both were seen by Hook.

"Cecco," he said in his most steely voice, "go back and fetch me out that doodle-doo."

Cecco, bravest of the brave, cowered before his captain, crying, "No, no:" but Hook was purring to his claw.

"Did you say you would go, Cecco?" he said musingly.

Cecco went, first flinging up his arms despairingly. There was no more singing, all listened now; and again came a death-screech and again a crow.

No one spoke except Slightly. "Three," he said.

Hook rallied his dogs with a gesture. "Sdeath and odds fish," he thundered, "who is to bring me that doodle-doo?"

"Wait till Cecco comes out," growled Starkey, and the others took up the cry.

"I think I heard you volunteer, Starkey," said Hook, purring again.

"No, by thunder!" Starkey cried.

"My hook thinks you did," said Hook, crossing to him. "I wonder if it would not be advisable, Starkey, to humour the hook?"

"I'll swing before I go in there," replied Starkey doggedly, and again he had the support of the crew.

"Is it mutiny?" asked Hook more pleasantly than ever. "Starkey's ring-leader."

"Captain, mercy," Starkey whimpered, all of a tremble now.

"Shake hands, Starkey," said Hook, proffering his claw.

Starkey looked round for help, but all deserted him. As he backed Hook advanced, and now the red spark was in his eye. With a despairing scream the pirate leapt upon Long Tom and precipitated himself into the sea.

"Four," said Slightly.

"And now," Hook asked courteously, "did any other gentleman say mutiny?" Seizing a lantern and raising his claw with a menacing gesture, "I'll bring out that doodle-doo myself," he said, and sped into the cabin.

"Five." How Slightly longed to say it. He wetted his lips to be ready, but Hook came staggering out, without his lantern.

"Something blew out the light," he said a little unsteadily.

"Something!" echoed Mullins.

"What of Cecco?" demanded Noodler.

"He's as dead as Jukes," said Hook shortly.

His reluctance to return to the cabin impressed them all unfavourably, and the mutinous sounds again broke forth. All pirates are superstitious; and Cookson cried, "They do say the surest sign a ship's accurst is when there's one on board more than can be accounted for."

"I've heard," muttered Mullins, "he always boards the pirate craft at last. Had he a tail, captain?"

"They say," said another, looking viciously at Hook, "that when he comes it's in the likeness of the wickedest man aboard."

"Had he a hook, captain?" asked Cookson insolently; and one after another took up the cry, "The ship's doomed." At this the children could not resist raising a cheer. Hook had wellnigh forgotten his prisoners, but as he swung round on them now his face lit up again.

"Lads," he cried to his crew, "here's a notion. Open the cabin door and drive them in. Let them fight the doodle-doo for their lives. If they kill him, we're so much the better; if he kills them we're none the worse."

For the last time his dogs admired Hook, and devotedly they did his bidding. The boys, pretending to struggle, were pushed into the cabin and the door was closed on them.

"Now, listen," cried Hook, and all listened. But not one dared to face the door. Yes, one, Wendy, who all this time had been bound to the mast. It was for neither a scream nor a crow that she was watching; it was for the reappearance of Peter.

She had not long to wait. In the cabin he had found the thing for which he had gone in search: the key that would free the children of their manacles; and now they all stole forth, armed with such weapons as they could find. First signing to them to hide, Peter cut Wendy's bonds, and then nothing could have been easier for them all to fly off together; but one thing barred the way, an oath, "Hook or me this time." So when he had freed Wendy, he whispered to her to conceal herself with the others and himself took her place by the mast, her cloak around him so that he should pass for her. Then he took a great breath and crowed.

To the pirates it was a voice crying that all the boys lay slain in the cabin; and they were panic-stricken. Hook tried to hearten them; but like the dogs he had made them they showed him their fangs, and he knew that if he took his eyes off them now they would leap at him.

"Lads," he said, ready to cajole or strike as need be, but never quailing for an instant, "I've thought it out. There's a Jonah aboard."

"Aye," they snarled, "a man wi' a hook."

"No, lads, no, it's the girl. Never was luck on a pirate ship wi' a woman on board. We'll right the ship when she's gone."

Some of them remembered that this had been a saying of Flint's. "It's worth trying," they said doubtfully.

"Fling the girl overboard," cried Hook; and they made a rush at the figure in the cloak.

"There's none can save you now, missy," Mullins hissed jeeringly.

"There's one," replied the figure.

"Who's that?"

"Peter Pan the avenger!" came the terrible answer; and as he spoke Peter flung off his cloak. Then they all knew who twas that had been undoing them in the cabin, and twice Hook essayed to speak and twice he failed. In that frightful moment I think his fierce heart broke.

At last he cried, "Cleave him to the brisket," but without conviction.

"Down, boys, and at them," Peter's voice rang out; and in another moment the clash of arms was resounding through the ship. Had the pirates kept together it is certain that they would have won; but the onset came when they were all unstrung, and they ran hither and thither, striking wildly, each thinking himself the last survivor of the crew. Man to man they were the stronger; but they fought on the defensive only, which enabled the boys to hunt in pairs and choose their quarry. Some of the miscreants leapt into the sea; others hid in dark recesses, where they were found by Slightly, who did not fight, but ran about with a lantern which he flashed in their faces, so that they were half blinded and fell an easy prey to the reeking swords of the other boys. There was little sound to be heard but the clang of weapons, an occasional screech or splash, and Slightly monotonously counting – five – six – seven – eight – nine – ten – eleven.

I think all were gone when a group of savage boys surrounded Hook, who seemed to have a charmed life, as he kept them at bay in that circle of fire. They had done for his dogs, but this man alone seemed to be a match for them all. Again and again they closed upon him, and again and again he hewed a clear space. He had lifted up one boy with his hook, and was using him as buckler, when another, who had just passed his sword through Mullins, sprang into the fray.

"Put up your swords, boys," cried the newcomer, "this man is mine."

Thus suddenly Hook found himself face to face with Peter. The others drew back and formed a ring round them.

For long the two enemies looked at one another; Hook shuddering slightly, and Peter with the strange smile upon his face.

"So, Pan," said Hook at last, "this is all your doing."

"Aye, James Hook," came the stern answer, "it is all my doing."

"Proud and insolent youth," said Hook, "prepare to meet thy doom."

"Dark and sinister man," Peter answered, "have at thee."

Without more words they fell to, and for a space there was no advantage to either blade. Peter was a superb swordsman, and parried with dazzling rapidity; ever and anon he followed up a feint with a lunge that got past his foe's defence, but his shorter reach stood him in ill stead, and he could not drive the steel home. Hook, scarcely his inferior in brilliancy, but not quite so nimble in wrist play, forced him back by the weight of his onset, hoping suddenly to end all with a favourite thrust, taught him long ago by Barbecue at Rio; but to his astonishment he found this thrust turned aside again and again. Then he sought to close and give the quietus with his iron hook, which all this time had been pawing the air; but Peter doubled under it and, lunging fiercely, pierced him in the ribs. At sight of his own blood, whose peculiar colour, you remember, was offensive to him, the sword fell from Hook's hand, and he was at Peter's mercy.

"Now!" cried all the boys; but with a magnificent gesture Peter invited his opponent to pick up his sword. Hook did so instantly, but with a tragic feeling that Peter was showing good form.

Hitherto he had thought it was some fiend fighting him, but darker suspicions assailed him now.

"Pan, who and what art thou?" he cried huskily.

"I'm youth, I'm joy," Peter answered at a venture, "I'm a little bird that has broken out of the egg."

This, of course, was nonsense; but it was proof to the unhappy Hook that Peter did not know in the least who or what he was, which is the very pinnacle of good form.

"To't again," he cried despairingly.

He fought now like a human flail, and every sweep of that terrible sword would have severed in twain any man or boy who obstructed it; but Peter fluttered round him as if the very wind it made blew him out of the danger zone. And again and again he darted in and pricked.

Hook was fighting now without hope. That passionate breast no longer asked for life; but for one boon it craved: to see Peter bad form before it was cold for ever.

Abandoning the fight he rushed into the powder magazine and fired it.

"In two minutes," he cried, "the ship will be blown to pieces."

Now, now, he thought, true form will show.

But Peter issued from the powder magazine with the shell in his hands, and calmly flung it overboard.

What sort of form was Hook himself showing? Misguided man though he was, we may be glad, without sympathizing with him, that in the end he was true to the traditions of his race. The other boys were flying around him now, flouting, scornful; and as he staggered about the deck striking up at them impotently, his mind was no longer with them; it was slouching in the playing fields of long ago, or being sent up for good, or watching the wall-game from a famous wall. And his shoes were right, and his waistcoat was right, and his tie was right, and his socks were right.

James Hook, thou not wholly unheroic figure, farewell.

For we have come to his last moment.

Seeing Peter slowly advancing upon him through the air with dagger poised, he sprang upon the bulwarks to cast himself into the sea. He did not know that the crocodile was waiting for him; for we purposely stopped the clock that this knowledge might be spared him: a little mark of respect from us at the end.

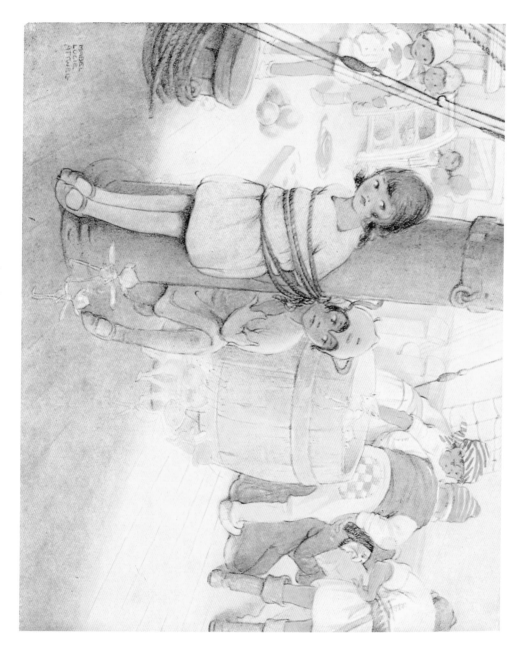

When he had freed Wendy.

When Wendy grew up.

He had one last triumph, which I think we need not grudge him. As he stood on the bulwark looking over his shoulder at Peter gliding through the air, he invited him with a gesture to use his foot. It made Peter kick instead of stab.

At last Hook got the boon for which he craved.

"Bad form," he cried jeeringly, and went content to the crocodile.

Thus perished James Hook.

"Seventeen," Slightly sang out; but he was not quite correct in his figures. Fifteen paid the penalty for their crimes that night; but two reached the shore; Starkey to be captured by the redskins, who made him nurse for all their papooses, a melancholy come-down for a pirate, and Smee, who henceforth wandered about the world in his spectacles, making a precarious living by saying he was the only man that James Hook had feared.

Wendy, of course, had stood by taking no part in the fight, though watching Peter with glistening eyes; but now that all was over she became prominent again. She praised them equally, and shuddered delightfully when Michael showed her the place where he had killed one; and then she took them into Hook's cabin and pointed to his watch which was hanging on a nail. It said, "half past one"!

The lateness of the hour was almost the biggest thing of all. She got them to bed in the pirates' bunks pretty quickly, you may be sure; all but Peter, who strutted up and down on deck, until at last he fell asleep by the side of Long Tom. He had one of his dreams that night, and cried in his sleep for a long time, and Wendy held him tight.

CHAPTER SIXTEEN

THE RETURN HOME

~

By two bells that morning they were all stirring their stumps; for there was a big sea running; and Tootles, the bo'sun, was among them, with a rope's end in his hand and chewing tobacco. They all donned pirate clothes cut off at the knee, shaved smartly, and tumbled up, with the true nautical roll and hitching their trousers.

It need not be said who was the captain. Nibs and John were first and second mate. There was a woman aboard. The rest were tars before the mast, and lived in the fo'c'sle. Peter had already lashed himself to the wheel; but he piped all hands and delivered a short address to them; said he hoped that they would do their duty like gallant hearties, but that he knew they were the scum of Rio and the Gold Coast, and if they snapped at him he would tear them. His bluff strident words struck the note sailors understand, and they cheered him lustily. Then a few sharp orders were given, and they turned the ship round, and nosed her for the mainland.

Captain Pan calculated, after consulting the ship's chart, that if this weather lasted they should strike the Azores about the 21st of June, after which it would save time to fly.

Some of them wanted it to be an honest ship and others were in favour of keeping it a pirate; but the captain treated them as dogs, and they dared not express their wishes to him even in a round robin. Instant obedience was the only safe thing. Slightly got a dozen for looking perplexed when told to take soundings. The general feeling was that Peter was honest just now to lull Wendy's suspicions, but that there might be a change when the new suit was ready, which, against her will, she was making for him out of some of Hook's wickedest garments. It was afterwards whispered among them that on the first night he wore this suit he sat long in the cabin with Hook's cigar-holder in his mouth and one hand clenched, all but the forefinger, which he bent and held threateningly aloft like a hook.

Instead of watching the ship, however, we must now return to that desolate home from which three of our characters had taken heartless flight so long ago. It seems a shame to have neglected No. 14 all this time; and yet we may be sure that Mrs Darling does not blame us. If we had returned sooner to look with sorrowful sympathy at her, she would probably have cried, "Don't be silly; what do I matter? Do go back and keep an eye on the children." So long as mothers are like this children will take advantage of them; and they may lay to that.

Even now we venture into that familiar nursery only because its lawful occupants are on their way home; we are merely hurrying on in advance of them to see that their beds are properly aired and that Mr and Mrs Darling do not go out for the evening. We are no more than servants. Why on earth should their beds be properly aired, seeing that they left them in such a thankless hurry? Would it not serve them jolly well right if they came back and found that their parents were spending the weekend in the country? It would be the moral lesson they have been in need of ever since we met them; but if we contrived things in this way Mrs Darling would never forgive us.

One thing I should like to do immensely, and that is to tell her, in the way authors have, that the children are coming back, that indeed they will be here on Thursday week. This would spoil so completely the surprise to which Wendy and John and Michael are looking forward. They have been planning it out on the ship: mother's rapture, father's shout of joy, Nana's leap through the air to embrace them first, when what they ought to be preparing for is a good hiding. How delicious to spoil it all by breaking the news in advance; so that when they enter grandly Mrs Darling may not even offer Wendy her mouth, and Mr Darling may exclaim pettishly, "Dash it all, here are those boys again." However, we should get no thanks even for this. We are beginning to know Mrs Darling by this time and may be sure that she would upbraid us for depriving the children of their little pleasure.

"But, my dear madam, it is ten days till Thursday week; so that by telling you what's what, we can save you ten days of unhappiness."

"Yes, but at what a cost! By depriving the children of ten minutes of delight."

"Oh, if you look at it in that way."

"What other way is there in which to look at it?"

You see, the woman had no proper spirit. I had meant to say extraordinary nice things about her; but I despise her, and not one of them will I say now. She does not really need to be told to have things ready, for they are ready. All the beds are aired, and she never leaves the house, and observe, the window is open. For all the use we are to her, we might go back to the ship. However, as we are here we may as well stay and look on. That is all we are, lookers-on. Nobody really wants us. So let us watch and say jaggy things, in the hope that some of them will hurt.

The only change to be seen in the night-nursery is that between nine and six the kennel is no longer there. When the children flew away, Mr Darling felt in his bones that all the blame was his for having chained Nana up, and that from first to last she had been wiser than he. Of course, as we have seen, he was quite a simple man; indeed he might have passed for a boy again if he had been able to take his baldness off; but he had also a noble sense of justice and a lion courage to do what seemed right to him; and having thought the matter out with anxious care after the flight of the children, he went down on all fours and crawled into the kennel. To all Mrs Darling's dear invitations to him to come out he replied sadly but firmly:

"No, my own one, this is the place for me."

In the bitterness of his remorse he swore that he would never leave the kennel until his children came back. Of course this was a pity; but whatever Mr Darling did he had to do in excess; otherwise he soon gave up doing it. And there never was a more humble man than the once proud George Darling, as he sat in the kennel of an evening talking with his wife of their children and all their pretty ways.

Very touching was his deference to Nana. He would not let her come into the kennel, but on all other matters he followed her wishes implicitly.

Every morning the kennel was carried with Mr Darling in it to a cab, which conveyed him to his office, and he returned home in the same way at six. Something of the strength of character of the man will be seen if we remember how sensitive he was to the opinion of neighbours: this man whose every movement now attracted surprised attention. Inwardly he must have suffered torture; but he preserved a calm exterior even when the young criticized his little home, and he always lifted his hat courteously to any lady who looked inside.

It may have been quixotic, but it was magnificent. Soon the inward meaning of it leaked out, and the great heart of the public was touched. Crowds followed the cab, cheering it lustily; charming girls scaled it to get his autograph; interviews appeared in the better class of papers, and society invited him to dinner and added, "Do come in the kennel."

On that eventful Thursday week Mrs Darling was in the night-nursery awaiting George's return home: a very sad-eyed woman. Now that we look at her closely and remember the gaiety of her in the old days, all gone now just because she has lost her babes, I find I won't be able to say nasty things about her after all. If she was too fond of her rubbishy children she couldn't help it. Look at her in her chair, where she has fallen asleep. The corner of her mouth, where one looks first, is almost withered up. Her head moves restlessly on her breast as if she had a pain there. Some like Peter best and some like Wendy best, but I like her best. Suppose, to make her happy, we whisper to her in her sleep that the brats are coming back.

They are really within two miles of the window now, and flying strong, but all we need whisper is that they are on the way. Let's.

It is a pity we did it, for she had started up, calling their names; and there is no one in the room but Nana.

"O Nana, I dreamt my dear ones had come back."

Nana had filmy eyes, but all she could do was to put her paw gently on her mistress's lap; and they were sitting together thus when the kennel

*... he swore that he would never leave the kennel until
his children came back.*

was brought back. As Mr Darling puts his head out of it to kiss his wife,
we see that his face is more worn than of yore, but has a softer expression.

He gave his hat to Liza, who took it scornfully; for she had no
imagination, and was quite incapable of understanding the motives of such
a man. Outside, the crowd who had accompanied the cab home were still
cheering, and he was naturally not unmoved.

"Listen to them," he said; "it is very gratifying."

"Lot of little boys," sneered Liza.

"There were several adults today," he assured her with a faint flush; but
when she tossed her head he had not a word of reproof for her. Social success had
not spoilt him; it had made him sweeter. For some time he sat half out of the
kennel, talking with Mrs Darling of this success, and pressing her hand
reassuringly when she said she hoped his head would not be turned by it.

"But if I had been a weak man," he said. "Good heavens, if I had been
a weak man!"

359

"And, George," she said timidly, "you are as full of remorse as ever, aren't you?"

"Full of remorse as ever, dearest! See my punishment: living in a kennel."

"But it is punishment, isn't it, George? You are sure you are not enjoying it?"

"My love!"

You may be sure she begged his pardon; and then, feeling drowsy, he curled round in the kennel.

"Won't you play me to sleep," he asked, "on the nursery piano?" and as she was crossing to the day-nursery he added thoughtlessly, "And shut that window. I feel a draught."

"O George, never ask me to do that. The window must always be left open for them, always, always."

Now it was his turn to beg her pardon; and she went into the day-nursery and played, and soon he was asleep; and while he slept, Wendy and John and Michael flew into the room.

Oh no. We have written it so, because that was the charming arrangement planned by them before we left the ship; but something must have happened since then, for it is not they who have flown in, it is Peter and Tinker Bell.

Peter's first words tell all.

"Quick, Tink," he whispered, "close the window; bar it. That's right. Now you and I must get away by the door; and when Wendy comes she will think her mother has barred her out; and she will have to go back with me."

Now I understand what had hitherto puzzled me, why when Peter had exterminated the pirates he did not return to the island and leave Tink to escort the children to the mainland. This trick had been in his head all the time.

Instead of feeling that he was behaving badly he danced with glee; then he peeped into the day-nursery to see who was playing. He whispered to Tink, "It's Wendy's mother. She is a pretty lady, but not so pretty as my mother. Her mouth is full of thimbles, but not so full as my mother's was."

Of course he knew nothing whatever about his mother; but he sometimes bragged about her.

He did not know the tune, which was "Home, Sweet Home", but he knew it was saying, "Come back, Wendy, Wendy, Wendy"; and he cried exultantly, "You will never see Wendy again, lady, for the window is barred."

He peeped in again to see why the music had stopped; and now he saw that Mrs Darling had laid her head on the box, and that two tears were sitting on her eyes.

"She wants me to unbar the window," thought Peter, "but I won't, not I."

He peeped again, and the tears were still there, or another two had taken their place.

"She's awfully fond of Wendy," he said to himself. He was angry with her now for not seeing why she could not have Wendy.

The reason was so simple: "I'm fond of her too. We can't both have her, lady."

But the lady would not make the best of it, and he was unhappy. He ceased to look at her, but even then she would not let go of him. He skipped about and made funny faces, but when he stopped it was just as if she were inside him, knocking.

"Oh, all right," he said at last, and gulped. Then he unbarred the window. "Come on, Tink," he cried, with a frightful sneer at the laws of nature; "we don't want any silly mothers;" and he flew away.

Thus Wendy and John and Michael found the window open for them after all, which of course was more than they deserved. They alighted on the floor, quite unashamed of themselves; and the youngest one had already forgotten his home.

"John," he said, looking around him doubtfully, "I think I have been here before."

"Of course you have, you silly. There is your old bed."

"So it is," Michael said, but not with much conviction.

"I say," cried John, "the kennel!" and he dashed across to look into it.

"Perhaps Nana is inside it," Wendy said.

But John whistled. "Hallo," he said, "there's a man inside it."

"It's father!" exclaimed Wendy.

"Let me see father," Michael begged eagerly, and he took a good look. "He is not so big as the pirate I killed," he said with such frank disappointment that I am glad Mr Darling was asleep; it would have been sad if those had been the first words he heard his little Michael say.

Wendy and John had been taken aback somewhat at finding their father in the kennel.

"Surely," said John, like one who has lost faith in his memory, "he used not to sleep in the kennel?"

"John," Wendy said falteringly, "perhaps we don't remember the old life as well as we thought we did."

A chill fell upon them; and serve them right.

"It is very careless of mother," said that young scoundrel John, "not to be here when we come back."

It was then that Mrs Darling began playing again.

"It's mother!" cried Wendy, peeping.

"So it is!" said John.

"Then you are not really our mother, Wendy?" asked Michael, who was surely sleepy.

"Oh dear!" exclaimed Wendy, with her first real twinge of remorse, "it is quite time we came back."

"Let us creep in," John suggested, "and put our hands over her eyes."

But Wendy, who saw that they must break the joyous news more gently, had a better plan.

"Let us all slip into our beds, and be there when she comes in, just as if we had never been away."

And so when Mrs Darling went back to the night-nursery to see if her husband was asleep, all the beds were occupied. The children waited for her cry of joy, but it did not come. She saw them, but she did not believe they were there. You see, she saw them in their beds so often in her dreams that she thought this was just the dream hanging around her still.

She sat down in the chair by the fire, where in the old days she had nursed them.

They could not understand this, and a cold fear fell upon all three of them.

"Mother!" Wendy cried.

"That's Wendy," she said, but still she was sure it was the dream.

"Mother!"

"That's John," she said.

"Mother!" cried Michael. He knew her now.

"That's Michael," she said, and she stretched out her arms for the three little selfish children they would never envelop again. Yes, they did, they went round Wendy and John and Michael, who had slipped out of bed and run to her.

"George, George," she cried when she could speak; and Mr Darling woke to share her bliss, and Nana came rushing in. There could not have been a lovelier sight; but there was none to see it except a strange boy who was staring in at the window. He had ecstasies innumerable that other children can never know; but he was looking through the window at the one joy from which he must be for ever barred.

CHAPTER SEVENTEEN

WHEN WENDY GREW UP

~

I hope you want to know what became of the other boys. They were waiting below to give Wendy time to explain about them; and when they had counted five hundred they went up. They went up by the stair, because they thought this would make a better impression. They stood in a row in front of Mrs Darling, with their hats off, and wishing they were not wearing their pirate clothes. They said nothing, but their eyes asked her to have them. They ought to have looked at Mr Darling also, but they forgot about him.

Of course Mrs Darling said at once that she would have them; but Mr Darling was curiously depressed, and they saw that he considered six a rather large number.

"I must say," he said to Wendy, "that you don't do things by halves," a grudging remark which the twins thought was pointed at them.

The first twin was the proud one, and he asked, flushing, "Do you think we should be too much of a handful, sir? Because if so we can go away."

365

"Father!" Wendy cried, shocked; but still the cloud was on him. He knew he was behaving unworthily, but he could not help it.

"We could lie doubled up," said Nibs.

"I always cut their hair," said Wendy.

"George!" Mrs Darling exclaimed, pained to see her dear one showing himself in such an unfavourable light.

Then he burst into tears, and the truth came out. He was as glad to have them as she was, he said, but he thought they should have asked his consent as well as hers, instead of treating him as a cypher in his own house.

"I don't think he is a cypher," Tootles cried instantly. "Do you think he is a cypher, Curly?"

"No, I don't. Do you think he is a cypher, Slightly?"

"Rather not. Twin, what do you think?"

It turned out that not one of them thought him a cypher; and he was absurdly gratified, and said he would find space for them all in the drawing-room if they fitted in.

"We'll fit in, sir," they assured him.

"Then follow the leader," he cried gaily. "Mind you, I am not sure that we have a drawing-room, but we pretend we have, and it's all the same. Hoop la!"

He went off dancing through the house, and they all cried "Hoop la!" and danced after him, searching for the drawing-room; and I forget whether they found it, but at any rate they found corners, and they all fitted in.

As for Peter, he saw Wendy once again before he flew away. He did not exactly come to the window, but he brushed against it in passing, so that she could open it if she liked and call to him. That was what she did.

"Hallo, Wendy, goody-bye," he said.

"Oh dear, are you going away?"

"Yes."

"You don't feel, Peter," she said falteringly, "that you would like to say anything to my parents about a very sweet subject."

"No."

"About me, Peter?"

"No."

Mrs Darling came to the window, for at present she was keeping a sharp eye on Wendy. She told Peter that she had adopted all the other boys, and would like to adopt him also.

"Would you send me to school?" he inquired craftily.

"Yes."

"And then to an office?"

"I suppose so."

"Soon I should be a man?"

"Very soon."

"I don't want to go to school and learn solemn things," he told her passionately. "I don't want to be a man. O Wendy's mother, if I was to wake up and feel there was a beard!"

"Peter!" said Wendy the comforter, "I should love you in a beard;" and Mrs Darling stretched out her arms to him, but he repulsed her.

"Keep back, lady, no one is going to catch me and make me a man."

"But where are you going to live?"

"With Tink in the house we built for Wendy. The fairies are to put it high up among the tree-tops where they sleep at nights."

"How lovely," cried Wendy so longingly that Mrs Darling tightened her grip.

"I thought all the fairies were dead," Mrs Darling said.

"There are always a lot of young ones," explained Wendy, who was now quite an authority, "because you see when a new baby laughs for the first time a new fairy is born, and as there are always new babies there are always new fairies. They live in nests on the tops of trees; and the mauve ones are boys and the white ones are girls, and the blue ones are just little sillies who are not sure what they are."

"I shall have such fun," said Peter, with one eye on Wendy.

"It will be rather lonely in the evening," she said, "sitting by the fire."

"I shall have Tink."

"Tink can't go a twentieth part of the way round," she reminded him a little tartly.

"Sneaky tell-tale!" Tink called out from somewhere round the corner.

"It doesn't matter," Peter said.

"O Peter, you know it matters."

"Well then, come with me to the little house."

"May I, Mummy?"

"Certainly not. I have got you home again, and I mean to keep you."

"But he does so need a mother."

"So do you, my love."

"Oh, all right," Peter said, as if he had asked her from politeness merely; but Mrs Darling saw his mouth twitch, and she made this handsome offer: to let Wendy go to him for a week every year to do his spring cleaning. Wendy would have preferred a more permanent arrangement; and it seemed to her that spring would be long in coming; but this promise sent Peter away quite gay again. He had no sense of time, and was so full of adventures that all I have told you about him is only a halfpenny-worth of them. I suppose it was because Wendy knew this that her last words to him were these rather plaintive ones:

"You won't forget me, Peter, will you, before spring-cleaning time comes?"

Of course Peter promised; and then he flew away. He took Mrs Darling's kiss with him. The kiss that had been for no one else Peter took quite easily. Funny. But she seemed satisfied.

Of course all the boys went to school; and most of them got into Class III but Slightly was put first into Class IV and then into Class V. Class I is the top class. Before they had attended school a week they saw what goats they had been not to remain on the island; but it was too late now, and soon they settled down to being as ordinary as you or me or Jenkins minor. It is sad to have to say that the power to fly gradually left them. At first Nana tied their feet to the bedposts so that they should not fly away in the night; and one of their diversions by day was to pretend to fall off buses; but by and by they ceased to tug at their bonds in bed, and found that they hurt themselves when they let go of the bus. In time they could not even fly after their hats. Want of practice, they called it; but what it really meant was that they no longer believed.

Michael believed longer than the other boys, though they jeered at him; so he was with Wendy when Peter came for her at the end of the first year. She flew away with Peter in the frock she had woven from leaves and berries in the Neverland, and her one fear was that he might notice how short it had become; but he never noticed, he had so much to say about himself.

They live in nests on the tops of trees. . . .

She had looked forward to thrilling talks with him about old times, but new adventures had crowded the old ones from his mind.

"Who is Captain Hook?" he asked with interest when she spoke of the arch enemy.

"Don't you remember," she asked, amazed, "how you killed him and saved all our lives?"

"I forget them after I kill them," he replied carelessly.

When she expressed a doubtful hope that Tinker Bell would be glad to see her he said, "Who is Tinker Bell?"

"O Peter," she said, shocked; but even when she explained he could not remember.

"There are such a lot of them," he said. "I expect she is no more."

I expect he was right, for fairies don't live long, but they are so little that a short time seems a good while to them.

Wendy was pained too to find that the past year was but as yesterday to Peter; it had seemed such a long year of waiting to her. But he was exactly as fascinating as ever, and they had a lovely spring cleaning in the little house on the tree-tops.

Next year he did not come to her. She waited in a new frock because the old one simply would not meet; but he never came.

"Perhaps he is ill," Michael said.

"You know he is never ill."

Michael came close to her and whispered, with a shiver, "Perhaps there is no such person, Wendy!" and then Wendy would have cried if Michael had not been crying.

Peter came next spring cleaning; and the strange thing was that he never knew he had missed a year.

That was the last time the girl Wendy ever saw him. For a little longer she tried for his sake not to have growing pains; and she felt she was untrue to him when she got a prize for general knowledge. But the years came and went without bringing the careless boy; and when they met again Wendy was a married woman, and Peter was no more to her than a little dust in the box in which she had kept her toys. Wendy was grown up. You need not be sorry for her. She was one of the kind that likes to grow up. In the end she grew up of her own free will a day quicker than other girls.

All the boys were grown up and done for by this time; so it is scarcely worth while saying anything more about them. You may see the twins and Nibs and Curly any day going to an office, each carrying a little bag and an umbrella. Michael is an engine-driver. Slightly married a lady of title, and so he became a lord. You see that judge in a wig coming out at the iron door? That used to be Tootles. The bearded man who doesn't know any story to tell his children was once John.

Wendy was married in white with a pink sash. It is strange to think that Peter did not alight in the church and forbid the bans.

Years rolled on again, and Wendy had a daughter. This ought not be written in ink but in a golden splash.

She was called Jane, and always had an odd inquiring look, as if from the moment she arrived on the mainland she wanted to ask questions. When she was old enough to ask them they were mostly about Peter Pan. She loved to hear of Peter, and Wendy told her all she could remember in the very nursery from which the famous flight had taken place. It was Jane's nursery now, for her father had bought it at the three per cents from Wendy's father, who was no longer fond of stairs. Mrs Darling was now dead and forgotten.

There were only two beds in the nursery now, Jane's and her nurse's; and there was no kennel, for Nana also had passed away. She died of old age, and at the end she had been rather difficult to get on with; being very firmly convinced that no one knew how to look after children except herself.

Once a week Jane's nurse had her evening off; and then it was Wendy's part to put Jane to bed. That was the time for stories. It was Jane's invention to raise the sheet over her mother's head and her own, thus making a tent and in the awful darkness to whisper:

"I don't think I see anything tonight," says Wendy, with a feeling that if Nana were here she would object to further conversation.

"Yes, you do," says Jane, "you see when you were a little girl."

"That is a long time ago, sweetheart," said Wendy. "Ah me, how time flies!"

"Does it fly," asks the artful child, "the way you flew when you were a little girl?"

"The way I flew! Do you know, Jane, I sometimes wonder whether I ever did really fly."

"Yes, you did."

"The dear old days when I could fly!"

"Why can't you fly now, mother?"

"Because I am grown up, dearest. When people grow up they forget the way."

"Why do they forget the way?"

"Because they are no longer gay and innocent and heartless. It is only the gay and innocent and heartless who can fly."

"What is gay and innocent and heartless? I do wish I was gay and innocent and heartless."

Or perhaps Wendy admits that she does see something. "I do believe," she says, "that it is this nursery."

"I do believe it is," says Jane. "Go on."

They are now embarked on the great adventure of the night when Peter flew in looking for his shadow.

"The foolish fellow," says Wendy, "tried to stick it on with soap, and when he could not he cried, and that woke me, and I sewed it on for him."

"You have missed a bit," interrupts Jane, who now knows the story better than her mother. "When you saw him sitting on the floor crying, what did you say?"

"I sat up in bed and I said, 'Boy, why are you crying?'"

"Yes, that was it," says Jane, with a big breath.

"And then he flew us all away to the Neverland and the fairies and the pirates and the redskins and the mermaids' lagoon, and the home under the ground, and the little house."

"Yes! Which did you like best of all?"

"I think I liked the home under the ground best of all."

"Yes, so do I. What was the last thing Peter ever said to you?"

"The last thing he ever said to me was, 'Just always be waiting for me, and then some night you will hear me crowing.'"

"Yes."

"But, alas! he forgot all about me." Wendy said it with a smile. She was as grown up as that.

"What did his crow sound like?" Jane asked one evening.

"It was like this," Wendy said, trying to imitate Peter's crow.

"No, it wasn't," Jane said gravely, "it was like this," and she did it ever so much better than her mother.

Wendy was a little startled. "My darling, how can you know?"

"I often hear it when I am sleeping," Jane said.

"Ah yes, many girls hear it when they are sleeping, but I was the only one who heard it awake."

"Lucky you," said Jane.

And then one night came the tragedy. It was the spring of the year, and the story had been told for the night, and Jane was now asleep in her bed. Wendy was sitting on the floor, very close to the fire, so as to see to darn, for there was no other light in the nursery; and while she sat darning she heard a crow. Then the window blew open as of old, and Peter dropped on the floor.

He was exactly the same as ever, and Wendy saw at once that he still had all his first teeth.

He was a little boy, and she was grown up. She huddled by the fire not daring to move, helpless and guilty, a big woman.

"Hallo, Wendy," he said, not noticing any difference, for he was thinking chiefly of himself; and in the dim light her white dress might have been the night-gown in which he had seen her first.

"Hallo, Peter," she replied faintly, squeezing herself as small as possible. Something inside her was crying, "Woman, woman, let go of me."

"Hallo, where is John?" he asked, suddenly missing the third bed.

"John is not here now," she gasped.

"Is Michael asleep?" he asked, with a careless glance at Jane.

"Yes," she answered; and now she felt that she was untrue to Jane as well as to Peter.

"That is not Michael," she said quickly, lest a judgement should fall on her.

Peter looked. "Hallo, is it a new one?"

"Yes."

"Boy or girl?"

"Girl."

Now surely he would understand; but not a bit of it.

"Peter," she said, faltering, "are you expecting me to fly away with you?"

"Of course, that is why I have come." He added a little sternly, "Have you forgotten that this is spring-cleaning time?"

She knew it was useless to say that he had let many spring-cleaning times pass.

"I can't come," she said apologetically, "I have forgotten how to fly."

"I'll soon teach you again."

"O Peter, don't waste the fairy dust on me."

She had risen; and now at last a fear assailed him. "What is it?" he cried, shrinking.

"I will turn up the light," she said, "and then you can see for yourself."

For almost the only time in his life that I know of, Peter was afraid. "Don't turn up the light," he cried.

She let her hands play in the hair of the tragic boy. She was not a little girl heart-broken about him; she was a grown woman smiling at it all, but they were wet smiles.

Then she turned up the light, and Peter saw. He gave a cry of pain; and when the tall beautiful creature stooped to lift him in her arms he drew back sharply.

"What is it?" he cried again.

"I am old, Peter. I am ever so much more than twenty. I grew up long ago."

"You promised not to!"

"I couldn't help it. I am a married woman, Peter."

"No, you're not."

"Yes, and the little girl in the bed is my baby."

"No, she's not."

But he supposed she was; and he took a step towards the sleeping child with his dagger upraised. Of course he did not strike. He sat down on the floor instead and sobbed; and Wendy did not know how to comfort him, though she could have done it so easily once. She was only a woman now, and she ran out of the room to try to think.

Peter continued to cry, and soon his sobs woke Jane. She sat up in bed and was interested at once.

"Boy," she said, "why are you crying?"

Peter rose and bowed to her, and she bowed to him from the bed.

"Hallo," he said.

"Hallo," said Jane.

"My name is Peter Pan," he told her.

"Yes, I know."

"I came back for my mother," he explained, "to take her to the Neverland."

"Yes, I know," Jane said, "I've been waiting for you."

When Wendy returned diffidently she found Peter sitting on the bedpost crowing gloriously, while Jane in her nighty was flying round the room in solemn ecstasy.

"She is my mother," Peter explained; and Jane descended and stood by his side, with the look on her face that he liked to see on ladies when they gazed at him.

"He does so need a mother," Jane said.

"Yes, I know," Wendy admitted rather forlornly; "no one knows it so well as I."

"Good-bye," said Peter to Wendy; and he rose in the air, and the shameless Jane rose with him; it was already her easiest way of moving about.

Wendy rushed to the window.

"No, no," she cried.

"It is just for spring-cleaning time," Jane said; "he wants me always to do his spring cleaning."

"If only I could go with you," Wendy sighed.

"You see you can't fly," said Jane.

Of course in the end Wendy let them fly away together. Our last glimpse of her shows her at the window, watching them receding into the sky until they were as small as stars.

As you look at Wendy you may see her hair becoming white, and her figure little again, for all this happened long ago. Jane is now a common grown-up with a daughter called Margaret; and every spring-cleaning time, except when he forgets, Peter comes for Margaret and takes her to the Neverland, where she tells him stories about himself, to which he listens eagerly. When Margaret grows up she will have a daughter, who is to be Peter's mother in turn; and thus it will go on, so long as children are gay and innocent and heartless.

Classic Library Titles

Little Women
Little Men
by Louisa May Alcott
Illustrated by Clara M. Burd

The Secret Garden
A Little Princess
by Frances Hodgson Burnett
Illustrated by Louise Hill and Jan Burridge

The Adventures of Tom Sawyer
The Adventures of Huckleberry Finn
by Mark Twain
Illustrated by David Price

The Waterbabies
by Charles Kingsley
Illustrated by Jessie Willcox Smith
Peter Pan
by J.M. Barrie
Illustrated by Mabel Lucie Attwell

Frankenstein
by Mary Shelley
Dracula
by Bram Stoker
Illustrated by Brian Lee

Black Beauty
by Anna Sewell
Rebecca of Sunnybrook Farm
by Kate Douglas Wiggin
Illustrated by Cecil Aldin and Glenn Steward

Alice's Adventures in Wonderland
Through the Looking-Glass
by Lewis Carroll
Illustrated by John Tenniel

Andersen's Fairy Tales
by Hans Christian Andersen
Grimm's Folk Tales
by the Brothers Grimm
Illustrated by A. Duncan Carse and E.H. Wehnert